Haven

Empire Rising Book 3

D. J. Holmes

https://www.facebook.com/Author.D.J.Holmes

d.j.holmess@hotmail.com

Comments welcome!

Cover art by Ivo Brankovikj

This is a work of fiction. Names, characters, places, and incidents either are the product of the author's imagination or are used fictitiously and any resemblance to any persons living or dead, business establishments, events or locales are entirely coincidental.

Contents:

Prologue

9th February, 2467 AD, Haven

Clare Edwards was a cleaner, though that term referred to something entirely different than it once did. Her job was to carry out regular sweeps of the Council Chambers for bugs or other dangerous electronic devices. That meant she had access to a lot of sensitive information, it also made her the perfect spy. An intermediary representing Councilwoman Rodriguez had approached her almost two months ago. The intermediary had offered to pay Clare a high price for any information she could smuggle out of the First Councilor's office.

As she had listened to his pitch she couldn't deny that he had done his homework. He had said all the right words; corrupt leaders, uncertain future, a need for new friends and allies. They were all thoughts that had already been going around in her head. In the end, Clare had been happy to agree and the money had been the icing on the cake.

Being on the inside of the Council Chambers had opened Clare's eyes to what went on within the Council. Especially when it came to the First Councilor. The revelations about piracy and corruption the British Captain had made hadn't surprised her in the least, but they had been the final nail in the coffin. From then on, she had decided that Haven needed to be led in a new direction.

When Councilwoman Rodriguez had contacted her, it had been the opportunity Clare had been waiting for. Since then she had been feeding the Councilwoman all the information she could get her hands on. None of it had been of great value, yet she hoped it would prove of some use. Certainly, it had given her a thrill when she had listened in to Councilwoman Rodriguez's weekly broadcasts to the populace and had heard references made to information she had slipped the councilwoman.

Today Clare knew things would be different. The First Councilor was having a private meeting with Admiral Harris and two of the most powerful Councilors on the Council. Clare was positive something was afoot and she was going to make sure Councilwoman Rodriguez heard all about it.

As she entered the First Councilor's outer offices, Clare nodded to the receptionist behind his desk. There were also two guards barring the way into the Councilor's main office but they ignored her when she looked at them.

Instead of staring she got to work. First she scanned the outer office for bugs, then she went into the adjoining bathrooms and scanned them. Once she was finished she walked confidently up to one of the two guards and handed him her identity card. He scanned the card with the portable reader he carried before stepping aside to allow her to place her hand on a DNA scanner.

As Clare reached her hand out she focused on keeping it from shaking. This was something she did every day. Yet no other day was like today. Today she was going to betray her nation's leader. Despite her outward confidence, she felt like she was about to break down. She wanted to let out a giant scream or break into a fit of giggles.

Thankfully, her hand stayed still and the DNA scanner let her enter. As she walked in she closed the doors behind her. When they shut, she let out a deep breath. She was alone, the First Councilor was not expected back for another hour and no one else would be coming in.

She got to work and carefully scanned the room for bugs. When she found nothing, she uploaded the results of the scan to the Council Chambers' main security computer. Then, very carefully, she reached into the backpack she carried her equipment in. Slowly she pulled out a bug the intermediary had given her yesterday. After examining it for a few seconds to make sure it was fully functional, she placed it under the First Councilor's desk.

The bug was impressive. She had scanned it herself with her own security equipment. With luck it would go unnoticed until she returned tomorrow to carry out the next scheduled sensor sweep. Then she could pick it up and take it home with her, leaving the First Councilor none the wiser.

Her job done, she packed up her equipment and headed out of the First Councilor's office and nodded to the receptionist again. Then she made her way to the next set of offices that needed scanning and continued her normal work day.

*

Clare sat in one of the cubicles in the public bathrooms in the Council Chambers. The receiving device the intermediary had given her was sitting on her lap. The bug had a COM unit with a very limited range to avoid detection. She had to stay near the bug to record what it picked up. With a couple of taps on the receiving device's interface she turned on the ear bud.

"Your repairs are now complete?" First Councilor Maximillian asked.

"Yes," a voice replied which Clare guessed was Admiral Harris. "*Solitude* has been restored to full functionality and both *Avenger* and *Sparrow* are ready to go."

"Ready to go where?" a female voice asked. Clare knew Councilman Farks and Councilwoman Pennington were both scheduled to meet with Maximillian and ascribed the voice to Pennington.

"That's why I invited you both here," Maximillian said. "You command the strongest following in the Council and among the populace. Together we have kept the people on board with our vision for Haven despite all the recent upsets. However, we all know that things are going to change rapidly in the coming months and years.

"Being discovered by that British Captain was one thing, but to have not just one but two alien civilizations on our back door is going to make us a target too good to give up. Unless another shift passage is discovered, the only way from Earth to the Vestarian and Kulrean homeworlds is through Haven. That means every Earth power is going to be vying for control over our system. Whatever power controls us, will control access to the aliens and will obtain a huge advantage over their rivals.

"Unless," Maximillian said and paused for effect. "Unless we act now. Admiral Harris and I have a plan; however, it is risky. That is why I have asked you both here. I thought it wise to get your approval, for if it works, we will have to make sure we cover our tracks well. And if it doesn't, then we may have a set of different problems we will need to face together."

"Just what are you suggesting?" Farks asked.

"Yes, I'm not sure I like the sound of this," Pennington said. "I overlooked your earlier actions because I think we need stability at the current time, but you are proving to be somewhat rash."

"Nonsense," Maximillian said in mock disgust. "You and I both know that everything I have done has been in the best interest of our world. I am the great grandson of our founder and I won't let it be taken over by any earthling!"

"Then what is your plan?" Pennington said. Clare could hear the concern in the Councilwoman's voice.

"You tell them," Maximillian said to Admiral Harris.

"It's simple really," Harris began. "If friendly diplomatic relations are opened between Earth and either the Vestarians or the Kulreans, then Haven is going to become the center of all the Earth nations' attention. Our plan is to stop these relations now, before they deepen any further."

"That's a grand goal, but surely one that is impossible after all that British Captain did to help the Vestarians and Kulreans," Farks said. "Their relations are hardly going to sour now."

"No, we don't think we can stop the British from becoming friends with the Vestarians and Kulreans. But we can stop the aliens from letting any other Earth powers approach their systems. And with luck, we can make it so that even the British have to tread carefully with the aliens for the next few decades."

"And just how are you going to do this?" Pennington asked.

"We are going to fake an attack on the Kulrean diplomatic envoy," Harris answered.

"What?" Pennington shouted before Harris could explain any further. "That's insane. If we attack the Kulreans we will bring the wrath of every other human power down on us. They would invade for sure and probably arrest the whole lot of us."

"We don't plan to kill the Kulreans, we only want to attack their ship and scare them off," Admiral Harris answered calmly. "A few missiles set to detonate near the Kulrean ship should be enough to send those pacifists running home. And no one will come after us if we make it look like it was another Earth power. We can intercept the Kulreans in the Alpha system and make it look like our ships are Brazilian ships. That will shift the focus of the Earth powers away from us and onto the Brazilians. More importantly, it will cool relations between Earth and the aliens. If it works, it will give us the breathing space we need to survive."

"You are talking about attacking a peaceful alien race," Pennington pleaded.
"An alien race that has done nothing against us. How can you justify this? Surly this is not who we are."

"We are survivors," Maximillian said, re-joining the conversation. "Our forefathers did everything they could to survive and make this colony feasible. We owe it to them to protect what they have built."

"But not by becoming the very thing our forefathers left Earth to avoid," Pennington said angrily. "This smacks of the very backstabbing and political maneuvering our forefathers so despised. I cannot let you do this,"

"You have very little choice," Maximillian said. "As well as being my biggest supporters and the most powerful councilors on the Council, you are the only ones who can seriously oppose me. If you don't agree to this plan, you will not be leaving this Chamber."

"Are you threatening me?" Pennington almost shouted in indignation.

Clare was shocked by what she was hearing. Instinctively she tried to up the gain on the bug to make sure she got the rest of the conversation as clearly as possible. If Councilwoman Rodriguez could leak this information she might just be able to overthrow the First Councilor.

"Hold it," Farks said before Maximillian could respond to Pennington. "My COM unit is detecting a strange signal. I have programed it to detect attempts to eavesdrop on me. When was this room last swept for bugs?"

"Shit," Clare said as she pulled the ear bud out. "Time to go." Without a moment's hesitation, she threw the receiving device the intermediary had given her into the toilet. There was no way she would be able to get out of the Council Chambers with it now. There was also no way she could just walk out the front door. If they found the bug she would be at the top of the suspect list. Thankfully, she had a backup plan in place.

Calmly, she flushed the toilet and walked out into the corridors of the Council Chambers. Without looking around, she casually walked down the nearest corridor and made a number of turns. Less than two minutes later she rounded a corner and came to a dead end.

"Hi there, Helm," Clare said to the security guard who was sitting at the end of the corridor. He was guarding an emergency exit.

"Miss Edwards," the guard said smiling. "It's good to see you. What? No coffee?" he asked when he saw her hands were empty.

"Sorry, not this time, I just came for the conversation," Clare said.

Instead of looking disappointed a pleased smile crossed Helm's face. Since she had decided to spy on the First Councilor, Clare had been working on an alternative escape route. Helm was it. He was tasked with guarding one of the emergency exits. They were to be used only in the event of an evacuation and were otherwise locked so that no one on the outside could get in. Helm did have a card key however, allowing him to override the locking mechanism in case it malfunctioned in an emergency. Clare had been visiting him regularly over the last two months, usually under the guise of bringing him a coffee from the staff canteen.

"So what's new?" Helm asked as she approached his security desk.

"Well, I've finished my scans for the day and I was wondering what I'm going to do with myself this evening," Clare said coyly. "Do you have any suggestions?"

"I dunno," Helm said as he looked down, a little taken aback. "Maybe you would like..."

He didn't get the rest of his sentence out for Clare was already racing forward and her fist made a solid cracking noise when it connected with Helm's head. Without even a groan he slumped over his desk unconscious.

Clare fished around in his jacket for his access card. She swiped it across the emergency exit's control point and its lights switched from red to green. She pushed the doors and jumped out into the open air. She heard a voice squawking over Helm's COM unit and broke into a run.

There was no doubt that a quick search of the Council Chambers' security cameras would identify her as the one who had attacked Helm. As soon as they knew who she was they would know that she had planted the bug. She needed to disappear quickly. Thankfully, the intermediary had provided her with a fake identity and some credits for just such an eventuality. She had hidden them in a rundown building less than a kilometer from the Council Chambers.

After several minutes of running at as close to a sprint as she could maintain, Clare reached her destination. There was no doubt the Council Chambers' security sensors would have been able to track her this far away from the Chamber, but with her new identity she would be able to get on the nearest maglev train without any difficulty. Then she could disappear.

As she ran to the nearest station she pulled out her COM unit and composed a message to Councilwoman Rodriguez. She wouldn't be able to give the Councilwoman any hard evidence; the politician would just have to take her word for it. Nevertheless, Clare knew Rodriguez would take her seriously, what she had to say was too important to ignore.

In the Council Chambers, Maximillian was in the main security office watching a holo recording of Clare attacking Helm. "Do we know who she is yet? Did she plant the bug?" he asked the head of security.

"Her name is Clare Edwards; she is a cleaner. Her work

records show that she scanned your offices for bugs earlier today. I think we can assume she planted the bug."

"How quickly will you have her in custody?" Maximillian asked angrily. "She is going to pay for this."

"I'm coordinating with the local defense forces. They are already closing in on her. It looks like she is heading to Hornblower station. If she tries to get on a maglev train, we'll have her in seconds. I have already alerted the local police force to apprehend her as soon as she uses her identity card to access the station."

"I'm picking up a strong COM signal coming for the fugitive's location," another security officer called from his terminal.

"Jam it, immediately!" Maximillian shouted. "She can't get her information out."

"It's too late," the officer said. "She has already finished her transmission."

"Damn it," Maximillian shouted as he punched one of the terminals.

"If they were bugging our conversation then your plans have been leaked. I'm sure this cleaner wasn't working alone. One of your opponents was behind this I'm sure," Councilwoman Pennington said from where she stood watching Maximillian. "You must publicly renounce them immediately or else they will use this against you. Worse, this information might get back to the Earth powers. You need to rescind Admiral Harris's orders."

"Arrest her," Maximillian said, "she is a coconspirator with this cleaner."

"Wait, you can't do this," Pennington said as two security guards approached her.

"I just did," Maximillian said, "lock her up," he added.

"What did the message say and where was it sent?" Farks said to show he was still on board with Maximillian's plans.

"It is encrypted," the security officer who had detected the signal said. "It will take several minutes to decode. Judging from its strength, I would say it was meant for someone in the outer system. Maybe on one of our mining operations."

"Rodriguez," Maximillian said. "That bitch. I'm going back to my office. I have a message to record for her."

*

Councilwoman Susanna Rodriguez's COM unit beeped to alert her to an incoming message. "What is it?" she asked the station manager.

"We just got a message from Haven, I think you are going to want to see it," he replied.

"I'm on my way," Susanna replied.

A couple of minutes later she stood in the command room of her family's gas mining station. "I can't believe it," she said. "I never thought Maximillian would stoop this low."

"Can we trust her?" the station manager asked.

"Yes, I believe so, all her other reports have been accurate," Suzanna said, having already asked herself the same question.

"We're getting another transmission from Haven," one of the technicians said.

"Put it on the main holo display," the station manager ordered.

"Suzanna," Maximillian said when his face appeared. "I should have known that you would be spying on me. However, I can still be reasonable. If you delete the transmission you received I will agree to meet with you for open and frank talks. On the other hand, if you leak this information, I will crush you. I will tarnish your family's name and strip you and your relatives of their wealth. The name Rodriguez will go down in infamy on Haven and you will not live to see out the year. Think carefully about what you do next councilwoman."

"Well," Suzanna said to the silence that had descended around her, "I guess that means Clare's information was legitimate. I can't see Maximillian getting so worked up about anything else." Then a thought hit her, "what are

Admiral Harris' warships doing?"

"There are a number of warships patrolling the approaches to Haven, wait, one of them has been on a heading for the last hour that will bring it very close to our station," the technician said.

"What freighter is the closest to being able to depart?" Suzanna asked.

"The *Warthog*," another technician answered.

"Order her to depart immediately and to head for the shift passage to the Gift. Tell them I will be coming on board," Suzanna said.

"You don't mean to leave us?" her station manager asked.

"I don't have any other choice," Suzanna said. "That warship is coming to arrest me. I am no longer any use to our people here. I need to get a warning out."

"Then I will help you pack," her station manager said.

"Thank you," Suzanna said as she touched his arm.

*

Twenty minutes later, Suzanna was standing on the bridge of the freighter Warthog. "How long until we reach the edge of the system's mass shadow?" she asked the Captain.

"Another twenty minutes," he answered.

"Will that warship get into weapons range before then?"

"No, we should be able to jump out before it can fire on us," the Captain answered.

"Good," Suzanna said with a smile. *Warthog* was a freighter she had purchased from one of her competitors. One that had aided Maximillian in his piracy against the Earth nations. It therefore had much more powerful engines than the rest of her freighters. *Your sins are beginning to catch up with you First Councilor,* Suzanna said to herself.

"Can you pick up Admiral Harris' flagship?" she asked the Captain.

"Yes," he answered. "*Solitude* is close to Haven, however, it looks like she is boosting towards the shift passage. There are two other ships keeping station with her.

He's still going to do it, Suzanna thought, *I have to get to James.*

Chapter 1 – Happenstance

Every war has a beginning, and the British-Indian War was no different. To understand it you must begin with the aspirations of both interstellar nations, and the actions of Haven's First Councilor. It was he who put the gears of war into motion.

-Excerpt from Empire Rising, 3002 AD

24th February, 2467 AD, HMS *Endeavour,* Chester System

Exactly one month after *Endeavour* entered the repair yard in orbit around Chester, James signed off on the readiness report for his ship. *She is whole again,* James thought with more than a hint of pride. With a large yawn, he raised his hands into the air and stretched them out wide as he felt his muscles unwind. The last month had been one of the busiest in his life.

The Chester repair yard had only been recently constructed and everything was new and untested. When things had worked, *Endeavour's* repairs had jumped forward in leaps and bounds. Yet, there were still many aspects to the new yard that were being worked out, more than one computer or human error had put a halt to the repair work during the last month.

Nevertheless, the work was now finished. *Endeavour* was

ready to detach from the repair yard and head back into space. With a grin James activated his COM unit, "Lieutenant Mallory, set us a course for Earth. Inform Rear Admiral Penn that we will be leaving Chester to return to Earth within the hour."

"Aye sir," Mallory replied over the COM channel, "it will be my pleasure."

Since his uncle had sent him to Chester to carry out repairs, James had been afraid that he would miss Pemel and the Kulrean envoy ship when it came to visit Earth. They had received word a week ago via a messenger ship from Earth that the Kulreans planned to arrive in orbit around Earth in thirty days. James had wanted to meet Pemel in the Alpha system and escort his ship into the Sol system but the timing just wasn't going to work out. If they left within the hour and made full speed back to Earth they would get to the Alpha system two days behind Pemel. Still, James was excited to see the new leader of the Kulreans again, and if he was a couple of days late, all it really meant was that he would miss the pomp and ceremony that would no doubt take up the first few days of the alien's visit. That was not such a bad thing.

James' COM beeped to inform him Lieutenant Mallory was trying to contact him. "Captain, the Rear Admiral has acknowledged our message and sent you a reply, I've transferred it to your personal datapad."

"Thank you Lieutenant," James replied and opened the message from the Rear Admiral.

Try not to get yourself into any more trouble Captain, its time you let someone else have some fun for a change. Godspeed. R.Adm. Penn.

James smiled to himself. Rear Admiral Penn wasn't the only one hoping the next few months would prove to be a lot quieter that the last few years had been.

*

James was on the bridge of *Endeavour* with Mallory watching as they approached the mass shadow of the system. "We will be able to jump into shift space in ten minutes," Sub Lieutenant Jennings said from the navigation station.

"Jump us down the shift passage as soon as you are able," James replied.

An alarm sounded at the sensor officer's station. With a couple of taps on his control terminal Sub Lieutenant Malik shut it off. "A ship has just jumped out of shift space thirty light minutes from us," he informed James. "I can't identify it from its jump signature."

"Put us into stealth mode then change our course towards this newcomer," James ordered.

Endeavour had been traveling under full power towards the shift passage that would eventually lead back to Earth and so she would be clearly visible to the newcomer. However, their sensor data would be thirty minutes old and thus by the time they realized that *Endeavour* had disappeared off their sensors James would be able to close the range to them.

On the other hand, the distance also meant that it would take thirty minutes for *Endeavour's* sensors to pick up any electromagnetic waves from the new ship as well. If the ships stayed in stealth mode it would take thirty minutes to detect it. In space warfare a lot could happen before then.

"We're in stealth mode," Mallory informed James.

"Sir," Malik called before James could issue any more orders. "The ship has lit up its main engine. It's setting a direct course for Chester."

"I guess they don't want to play hide and seek," James said.

Any ship that exerted a significant acceleration rate in space gave off gravitational waves. These waves could be tracked in real time and so it allowed ships to track each other without waiting to get a lock on their electromagnetic signals. Of course, if a ship cut its acceleration or was crusing at a steady speed like *Endeavour* had been, then the gravitational sensors wouldn't pick them up.

"What kind of reading are the gravitational sensors getting on this newcomer's acceleration profile? Does it match anything in our databanks?" James asked Malik.

"The computer is still comparing the data now," Malik answered, "wait, there is a ninety percent match. During the battle over Haven we got some readings on a number of the

Haven freighters. The computer believes the newcomer is utilizing an engine with a similar acceleration profile."

Haven? James said to himself. *How on Earth did they get here?*

Knowing he wouldn't get an answer without asking the Captain of the new ship, he ordered *Endeavour* out of stealth mode and asked Sub Lieutenant King to record a COM message to be transmitted to the ship.

"Haven vessel," James began when King told him she was ready to record, "My name is Captain Somerville of His Majesty's Ship *Endeavour.* You have entered British space, please identify yourself and prepare to be boarded for inspection."

"Message sent," King said after James stopped speaking.

"Now comes the fun part," Third Lieutenant Becket said from her position at the tactical station.

"Yes," James agreed. It would take his message just under thirty minutes to reach the Haven vessel and depending on how much of the distance *Endeavour* closed between the two ships, at least another twenty for the reply to come back. There was nothing to do but wait and watch.

Twenty-nine minutes after the message was sent, everyone on the bridge watched as the freighter rapidly decelerated and swung around towards *Endeavour.*

"I guess the Havenites are willing to play ball for once,"

Mallory said.

"Indeed," James said.

Just under twenty-four minutes after the freighter's rapid course change a message arrived from it.

"It's an audio and visual message," King informed James.

"Put it on the holo display," James said.

"Hello Captain," Susanna Rodriguez said, smiling. "I didn't expect to see you again so soon. I am very glad I found you here. I have some grave news that you need to hear. My freighter will dock with *Endeavour* and I will tell you in person. I'm afraid I need you to be my knight in shining armor again."

As all the Lieutenants on the bridge looked at him James couldn't help turning a little red at Susanna's last words. "Set an intercept course and prepare to dock with the freighter," he ordered to cover his embarrassment.

"I thought we all saved Haven in the battle with the Vestarians. Why are you her only knight in shining armor Captain?" Mallory asked a little too innocently.

"Shut up," James said, trying to sound angry.

It didn't work for both Mallory and Becket let out small chuckles and the Sub Lieutenants looked like they wanted to join them.

"I'm going to my private office," James said as he stood. "I'll meet the Councilwoman at the docking hatch once the freighter comes alongside."

"Aye sir," Mallory said somewhat more professionally.

*

James waited nervously at the docking hatch for Suzanna to appear. He had spent the majority of the time in his office wondering just how he should greet the Councilwoman. He still wanted to know how she had come to Chester and what she was doing, but he would get those answers soon enough. How to greet Suzanna had therefore seemed like the most pressing question.

As she stepped out of the docking hatch James' mind went blank and he forgot what he had decided. Instinctively, he held out his hand to her. She brushed it aside and pulled him into a hug. "I think we are a little past handshakes," she whispered into his ear.

"I guess we are," James whispered back. He pulled back from the hug and smiled at her. "Welcome aboard *Endeavour*," he said more formally for everyone else who was present.

"It is a pleasure to visit the ship that saved my world," Suzanna said in an equally formal tone as she turned and nodded to Lieutenant Mallory and the two Sub Lieutenants who were there to greet her. "This ship and crew has endeared itself to the heart of my people."

Turning back to James, Suzanna reached out and placed a hand on his arm. "Can we go somewhere to speak privately? The matter I need to talk to you about is urgent."

"Certainly," James said as he turned and placed Suzanna's hand through his elbow. "Come with me."

They walked in silence through the ship as James led the way to his office. Suzanna's mind was busy taking in the sights and smells of a state of the art warship, James was contemplating just what was going on.

When they sat down, James' steward Fox was at hand to place two cups of coffee before them. As soon as Fox left, Suzanna broke the silence. "I'll come straight to the point."

"I thought you might," James chuckled.

Suzanna smiled but when James saw that her smile didn't reach her eyes he knew something serious was going on. "Tell me, I'm listening," he said.

"I fled Haven to bring you some vital information. I had a spy within the Council Chambers, she managed to plant a bug in Maximillian's office and eavesdrop on a conversation he was having with Admiral Harris. They are planning to send three warships to the Alpha system to ambush the Kulrean envoy. They want to scare them off so that relations between Earth and the Kulreans are damaged."

"What!" James almost shouted as he struggled to take in Maximillian's foolishness.

"He is afraid that the Earth powers will try and take control of Haven for its strategic location," Suzanna tried to explain.

"I understand that," James replied. "But his actions could have serious implications for all of humanity. If the Kulreans think that humans are prepared to attack them, even if it is only a sub section of the human race, they could break off all ties with Earth. All the technological wonders the Kulreans possess would be lost to us."

"That's why I am here," Suzanna said. "I want to stop them if we can."

"When were Admiral Harris' ships to leave?" James asked with concern.

"They left the same day I did, I had to flee before they captured me. Maximillian found out I have been listening in to his plans," Suzanna answered.

"Who else have you told about this?" James asked desperately.

"No one," Suzanna said, "You are the first Earth vessel I have encountered."

"Then it is already too late," James said. "The Kulreans will be entering the Alpha system in thirty days. We can't get a warning to them in time."

"Wait," James continued as it dawned on him. "How did you get here? You must have passed through a number of Indian, French and British systems to get here. Why didn't you warn someone else?"

"This is the first Earth system I have entered since I left Haven," Suzanna said. "Maximillian blocked off the shift passage that led into the Indian colonial systems and sent a frigate ahead of my freighter to block off access to the Gift. We discovered a shift passage to Chester about eight years ago, so I came here as it was my only option."

"More discoveries we don't know about," James said shaking his head. "You Havenites have been busy out in this part of space. But that doesn't change anything. We can't get to the Alpha system in time."

"We can," Suzanna said coyly. "It's actually rather simple."

"How?" James demanded and Suzanna couldn't help but smile as she teased him.

"How do you think Captain?" she asked.

It only took a couple of seconds for it to hit him, "The Gift," James said. "You said there was a frigate defending it. That would stop your freighter, but not *Endeavour*. Can it get us to the Alpha system in time?

Suzanna's smile grew wider, "It certainly can. It looks like you are going to get your wish after all Captain. I'm going to have to tell you all my secrets."

*

Twenty minutes later James and Suzanna strode onto *Endeavour's* bridge.

"Signal the freighter's Captain and tell him we're going to detach from his ship," James ordered. "He is to take his freighter to Chester and report to Rear Admiral Penn. I have already sent the Admiral a COM message informing him of what we are up to but I think he is going to want to talk to the freighter Captain himself."

"Councilwoman Rodriguez isn't returning to the freighter then?" Mallory asked a little too innocently.

"No," James said, "she is staying on board for the present."

He didn't have time to satisfy Mallory's curiosity so he ignored the look of intrigue that had come over the First Lieutenant's face. Instead he turned to the navigation officer, "I have sent a new course to your navigation console Sub Lieutenant Jennings. Upload it to the navigation computer and take us to the first shift jump point immediately."

"Yes sir," Jennings said as she opened the datafile. "Sir," she said a few moments later, looking up from reviewing the new course. "Are these coordinates accurate?"

"Indeed they are Sub Lieutenant," James answered.

Third Lieutenant Becket let out a whistle when the new course appeared on the main holo display, showing a series of shift drive jumps that headed off into unexplored space. "It looks like we are about to go down the rabbit hole again," she said.

"I'm afraid so," James responded.

As he looked around at Mallory he couldn't help but smile at the look of confusion on the First Lieutenant's face. "Don't worry Lieutenant," he said. "All will become clear in time. Once we are in shift space I want a meeting with all our senior officers in the briefing room. Until then, you will have to live in suspense."

"Yes sir," Mallory said.

"And Becket," James added, "as a reward for your unrequested humor you can liaise with Chief Driscoll and organize for him to put a new observation chair onto the bridge. Councilwoman Rodriguez is going to need somewhere to sit.

"Aye sir," Becket acknowledged.

"For now you can sit in Mallory's command chair," James said as he turned to Suzanna.

"Thank you Captain," Suzanna answered. "And to you too First Lieutenant," she added to Mallory as he hastily jumped out of his seat.

"I'm sure our First Lieutenant doesn't mind standing until we get another chair put in place," James said.

"Not at all," Mallory replied. "It will be my pleasure to make the Councilwoman as comfortable as possible," he finished with a wink for James.

James just shook his head. Having Suzanna on board was going to be embarrassing, yet he was happy Mallory could jest with him. When Mallory had come on board *Endeavour* just over a year ago he had been a spoilt self-centered officer. Not unlike James when he had taken command of his first ship. The first battle with the Vestarians over Haven had changed Mallory and although James had missed it at first, he was developing into a good officer.

In the last two months, they had begun to get on very well. It helped that they came from very similar backgrounds and the sheer amount of work that had been involved in repairing *Endeavour's* battle damage had forced them to spend a lot of time together.

Mallory was the third First Lieutenant James had commanded and he hoped things would go better than with his last. Lieutenant Ferguson had seemed like a competent officer, but in the end he had betrayed James and tried to lead a mutiny to take over the ship and run away from battle.

James was happy with his senior officers. He and Mallory were becoming fast friends and although the First Lieutenant had a lot to learn, James knew he would make a fine Captain one day.

Trusting in Mallory's abilities, he let the Lieutenant direct *Endeavour* towards the mass shadow of the Chester system and then make the first jump into shift space. Once they were on their way, James rose from his command chair and turned to Suzanna. "Shall we retire and sort out some quarters for you to stay in during this trip?" he asked.

"Certainly Captain," she replied, "lead on."

Chapter 2 – The Gift

No one knew it at the time, but the discovery of The Gift and its first use as a strategic weapon in war would foreshadow the vital importance it would come to play in the War of Doom.

-Excerpt from Empire Rising, 3002 AD

1st March, 2467 AD, HMS *Endeavour,* unexplored space near Chester.

James sat in his office replaying the events of the last few days over in his head. As they had followed the course Suzanna had given them the trip had gone by uneventfully. After the briefing with all the senior crew a wave of excitement had swept through the ship as everyone discovered what was ahead of them. For James' part, he was more than a little concerned. Suzanna assured him that many Haven ships had used the Gift, yet that didn't make him feel any more comfortable with the idea. More than once on the trip he had wished he still had Science Officer Scott on board to reassure his worries. Sadly, the Admiralty hadn't found him a replacement Science Officer before he left Earth for Chester.

He had spent most of his time during the trip in his office as he had given Suzanna his quarters and with Fox's help he had set up a makeshift bed in his office. It wasn't the most comfortable but it would do for a couple more weeks. Suzanna spent a lot of time in her quarters reviewing her notes and the data she had brought from Haven. James had put on a special meal for her with all the senior officers the first evening after they had jumped into shift space. After that, they had shared their evening meals together in the privacy of James' quarters. James wasn't sure if they had intended it to work out that way or if it had just happened, but as he spent time with Suzanna he came to appreciate her more and more.

Most of their conversations had been about the future of Haven. She loved her people dearly and was desperate to see her planet retain its sovereignty. The suggestion James had made that Haven become a British protectorate was now the only way Suzanna saw of making that a reality, and she grilled him on the ins and outs of such an idea constantly.

In turn James had grilled Suzanna about Haven's history and the Gift. She had been much more forthcoming than the last time he had spoken to her and yet she hadn't been able to fill him in on anything but the basics. The fact of the matter was that the Havenite scientists didn't yet fully understand the Gift and Suzanna only understood half of what they did. *It doesn't matter now,* James thought to himself, *we're about to find out for ourselves.*

Almost as if his thoughts had summoned Sub Lieutenant Jennings, her voice came over James' COM unit. "We have arrived Captain."

"I'm coming now," James answered, "please inform Councilwoman Rodriguez that we have reached the Gift."

"Yes sir," Jennings replied.

As James walked onto the bridge, he was stopped dead in his tracks by what he saw. On the main holo display Mallory was projecting the feed from the gravimetric sensors. The images were like nothing he had ever seen.

Endeavour was in the middle of open space. The nearest solar system was over a light year away. Yet about thirty light minutes in front of *Endeavour* it looked like there was a gravimetric superstorm. What appeared to be a number of tight weaving balls were spitting out huge amounts of gravimetric waves that intersected and crisscrossed over one another. The closest thing James could liken the image to was when he had watched one of his science teachers completely boil off a beaker of water. The bubbles and droplets of water that vigorously shot into the air looked very similar to the waves of gravitational energy the thing in front of him was shooting into space.

"What is it?" James asked.

"We have no idea," Mallory replied. "The center of the disturbances almost look like they are miniature black holes, they are certainly producing strong gravitational forces. Yet they are nowhere near as strong as our scientists estimate a black hole should be. And there are more than eight of the disturbances. There may be more but all the gravitational waves are making it hard to know for sure."

"And which one are we supposed to fly into?" James asked.

"This one sir," Mallory said as he manipulated the display to highlight one of the tight balls that was giving off the gravitational waves. "It's right on the edge of whatever this thing is so we won't have to get too close to its center."

"This can't be safe," James said out loud as he continued to look at the image before him.

"I'm having doubts myself," Suzanna said from where she had entered the bridge. She too had paused to look at the image on the holo display. "But I assure you, it has been done before."

"I still can't believe the original Haven colonists took their colony ship through this thing. It was such a risk," Mallory said.

"Yes, but they were desperate," Suzanna said. "And they did send a probe through first. Once it returned and was able to tell the colony ship where it had gone, there was no way the colonists would simply pass this by. They had an opportunity to get more than fifty light years away from Earth in the blink of an eye. That was everything they had dreamed about."

"Well it certainly worked out for them," James said, "your people got the time they needed to set themselves up as an independent world. But now we have to use this thing to stop your leaders from shooting themselves in the foot and bringing their colony's independence to an end.

"Sub Lieutenant Jennings, as much as I don't want to, you can take us in," James ordered.

"Yes sir," Jennings said with a distinct lack of enthusiasm.

"Down to business then," James said. "Are our stealth systems working at full capacity?"

"All systems are fully operational," Mallory said.

Endeavour was equipped with the latest stealth coating and the most advanced heat sinks in the Royal Space Navy. It meant that when her reactors were powered down to their lowest operating levels and all non-essential systems were shut down, *Endeavour* became a dark hole in space. She couldn't maintain it for more than a few hours but even then she had the same technologies all RSN ships had. By incorporating heat vents into their designs, RSN ships could vent their waste electromagnetic radiation into space along specific vectors. This allowed them to remain in stealth mode for prolonged periods of time. The vents weren't nearly as effective as *Endeavour's* heat sinks, but the combination of the two put *Endeavour* in class of her own.

"Good, any sign of the Havenite frigate?" James asked.

"None yet, but we are still scanning," Mallory answered. "They are likely to have a lot of their systems powered down. If they have been stationed here for any length of time I imagine they will be trying to conserve power.

According to the data we have on the Havenite warships, they don't have our endurance for long missions,"

"Take us in slow then Jennings," James said, "no need to let the Havenite frigate pick us up on their gravitational scanners."

According to Suzanna's intel, Maximillian had stationed a frigate at the entrance to the Gift to prevent her or anyone else from Haven getting to Earth. Ordinarily James wouldn't be worried about taking on a frigate as *Endeavour* would be more than a match for such a small warship. However, entering the Gift had him nervous, he didn't want anything to go wrong. He was also worried that if they didn't deal with the frigate, it might be able to sneak up close enough to them to fire off a broadside of missiles at point blank range. *Endeavour* might be a powerful warship, but even she couldn't survive a missile salvo from point blank.

"I think I am getting something," Malik said a couple of minutes later. "There appear to be some gravitational waves coming from the edge of the Gift, yet they are not from any of the balls at the center of the structure. It might be a ship."

"It must be them," James said. "Implement plan beta."

On the journey towards the Gift the senior officers had a number of meetings where they discussed their plans for dealing with Admiral Harris and his plan to attack the Kulrean envoy ship. They had also come up with a few ideas about how to deal with the frigate that was defending the entrance to the Gift. If possible, James didn't want to cause any more deaths than necessary. Yet he wasn't going to risk his ship or his crew.

"The modified stealth drone has been launched," Sub Lieutenant King said a minute later.

"We'll be in position in five minutes Captain," Jennings reported.

When everything was in position James stood up from his command chair and walked over to Third Lieutenant Becket who was manning the tactical station. "Make sure your first shot counts."

"Don't worry Captain, I have everything under control," Becket said confidently.

James rested a hand on her shoulder and gave her a slight squeeze, "I have full confidence in you." He looked towards Sub Lieutenant King. "Send the signal to the probe."

As soon as the probe received the signal it broadcast James' pre-recorded message. It took less than ten seconds for James' voice to reach the patrolling frigate.

"Havenite frigate, this is Captain Somerville of HMS *Endeavour*, I trust you know who I am. I have reason to believe you are currently keeping station somewhere within the Gift. Reveal yourself now and surrender or I will be forced to enter the gravimetric anomaly and destroy you."

"It looks like it is working," Sub Lieutenant Malik said from the sensor station, "the frigate is altering course towards the drone."

"Good," James said, "open fire as soon as you get a firm target lock," he added for Becket's benefit.

The problem they had faced was that the gravimetric disturbances made it hard to lock onto a target within the Gift. James had toyed around with a few different ideas but in the end he had settled for the simplest one his officers had come up with. They were going to lure the Havenite frigate out.

It was risky in that they didn't know just how good the Havenite gravitational sensors were. Though so far it appeared James' guess was right. While *Endeavour's* sensors were able to penetrate into the Gift, he had estimated that the Havenite frigate would have more of a problem with all the gravimetric waves the Gift generated. The Haven colony had been out of contact with Earth for more than two hundred years. While they had astonished everyone back on Earth with the size of colony they had been able to produce in those years, they were still way behind Earth in all sorts of areas.

It seemed the ruse had worked for the captain of the Haven frigate was operating under the assumption that *Endeavour* couldn't detect him. As James watched, it was clear he was trying to maneuver to the edge of the Gift and into a position where he could open fire on the source of the transmission. By the time he found out he was stalking a drone it would be far too late

"Firing," Becket said as soon as the frigate came close enough to the edge of the Gift for her to get a lock on it. As she spoke the holo display updated to show two green plasma bolts shoot into space from one of *Endeavour's* plasma cannons.

"Hit!" Becket shouted moments later.

"I'm detecting the ship now without electromagnetic sensors, their stealth field is down. It looks like they are suffering some power fluctuations," Malik reported after several seconds.

"Transmit the second message," James ordered.

This time the message came from *Endeavour* and it took less than a second to reach the damaged Haven frigate.

"Haven Frigate, we have you in our sights, surrender now. If you make any aggressive moves we will destroy you."

"No change from the frigate Sir," Malik said after a few seconds. "There is no sign they are powering up any weapons."

"There's a message coming through now," Sub Lieutenant King reported.

"Put it on the holo display," James ordered.

"Captain Somerville," a familiar face said. "I am offering my official surrender; you have bested me. Please don't make my crew pay for my foolishness."

James tapped a few buttons on his command chair to open a COM channel to reply. "Captain Denning. I am sorry we are meeting under such circumstances. What condition is your ship in?"

"We have taken serious damage to two of our three reactors. I have had to shut both of them down. Life support and propulsion are both intact however," Denning replied.

"I'm afraid I can't spare the time to help you, can you make it back to Haven?" James asked.

Denning looked away as he consulted with one of his juniors. "Yes, I think so, it's going to take us a while with just one engine however," he replied when he looked back. "But aren't you going to relieve me of command and put a prize crew aboard?"

"Not this time," James answered. "Technically we are not at war and I have bigger fish to fry. Your government has made a grave mistake in trying to attack the Kulreans. You can return to Haven and inform Maximillian that he won't be seeing Admiral Harris or his ships again. He will have to find some other way to defend his planet."

"And Captain," Suzanna said as she walked into Denning's view. "You can tell Maximillian from me that his time in office is limited."

The surprise on Denning's face was barely hidden, "you betrayed us all," he shouted as he clenched his fists.

"If you really think that Captain, then you have already betrayed what Haven stands for," Suzanna replied. "By aiding Maximillian you are as guilty as he and Admiral Harris for attacking an unarmed friendly alien race."

James interrupted before it turned into a full-blown argument. "We don't have any more time for you Captain. I hope you make it home safely. You can think about just where you stand on Haven's future on your journey. I think the RSN will be returning to Haven in the very near future and you might want to decide just whose side you are on."

Before Denning could reply James cut the feed. Denning had proven himself a resourceful officer in the first battle of Haven and James had liked the man when he had met him in person. Yet he had aligned himself against the RSN and the British Star Kingdom and James' mercy would only go so far.

"Take us back towards the Gift," James ordered. "And open a ship wide COM."

"It's open sir," Sub Lieutenant King said.

"This is the Captain," James began, "we are going to enter the Gift in twenty minutes. Everyone who is not assigned to an essential post is to return to their quarters. We know from the Havenite data that about thirty percent of a ship's crew react badly to their first jump. If you do, don't worry, the effects will pass within the hour. Nevertheless, if you are affected I want you to inform the ship's doctor. If you are not affected, once we are through you can return to your normal duties."

When he was done James nodded to King to tell her to shut the COM channel down.

"Well here goes nothing," James said as Jennings boosted *Endeavour* towards the giant storm of gravitational waves in front of them.

Everyone on the bridge sat in silence as the ship approached their target. When they were less than a couple of light seconds out the ship was buffeted by the intense gravitational waves that washed over it.

"Ship integrity seems to be stable," Second Lieutenant Julius reported from the auxiliary bridge where she was closely monitoring the ship's status.

"Continue to take us in," James said to the bridge crew.

For the next five minutes the ship continued to be buffeted but Julius showed no signs of being concerned. Then all of a sudden everything was calm.

"We seem to be through the gravitational waves," Mallory said.

"Entering the event horizon in ten seconds," Sub Lieutenant Jennings said.

As he looked around James was pleased to see he wasn't the only one who was gripping his command chair as if his life depended on it. Even Suzanna looked more than a little scared, and she had grown up knowing about the gift.

As *Endeavour's* nose touched the event horizon time seemed to slow down for James. On the main holo display he could see his ship make contact with one of the balls of intense gravitational force. Yet on the optical feed space looked calm. Even though he was expecting it, he was still shocked to see the front end of *Endeavour* disappear. His surprise heightened as the optical feed showed more and more of his ship vanishing.

What seemed like a lifetime was actually less than two seconds and before James realized it, the bridge was engulfed in the gravitational anomaly and he blacked out.

Chapter 3 – Old Friends

It is a strange thing war. At one moment you can be fighting alongside someone you see as your closest ally, the next, you may find yourselves locked in a battle to the death.

-Excerpt from Empire Rising, 3002 AD

1st March, 2467 AD, HMS *Endeavour,* unexplored space.

James lifted his head with a start, in concern he looked around. "Glad to see you are back with us Captain," a voice said from somewhere nearby.

As he surveyed the bridge crew he saw that a few of the Sub Lieutenants were slumped over their command consoles. Becket looked fully alert and was frantically working away. As he continued to look around he saw that it was Lieutenant Mallory who was speaking to him.

"How long was I out?" he asked the Lieutenant.

"About a minute I think," Mallory answered. "I think we were all affected to some degree. I didn't black out but I do have an intense headache. A lot of our systems lost power as well but they are starting to come back on line."

"Are the sensors working?" James called to Sub Lieutenant

Malik who was stirring at the sensor console.

"Hold on sir," he answered as he looked over the information his station was giving him. "Yes, they are powering back up now."

"Confirm our position, we need to know where we are. Then scan for any nearby ships. We're supposed to be in stealth but after going through that thing we could be lighting up like a Christmas tree to anyone nearby," James ordered.

"Aye sir," Malik responded.

"Julius," James called over the COM channel to the auxiliary bridge.

"Yes Sir?" she answered back a bit groggily.

"Liaise with the doctor, give me a run down on how the crew fared when everyone reports in."

"Will do," Julius acknowledged.

"Well Malik, where are we?" James said, turning his attention back to the Sub Lieutenant.

"It seems we are right where Councilwoman Rodriguez said we would be. We're ten light years from Earth and less than two from the Alpha system. No sign of any other ships nearby," Malik answered.

"Unbelievable," Mallory said. "Almost fifty light years in the blink of an eye. It's like something out of a science fiction novel."

"More than you might think," Lieutenant Becket said. "I have been reviewing the data our sensors gathered as we entered the gravitational anomaly, my best guess is that the intense gravitational field has torn some kind of hole in the normal space time continuum, creating a pocket of subspace linking the gravitational anomaly near Chester to this one. If you look at the holo display, there is an almost identical ball of gravitational waves just off our starboard stern. I think *Endeavour* exited out of it."

"So what you're saying is that we just passed through some kind of wormhole," Mallory said.

"Well, I think that is what the news reporters are going to call it," Becket answered. "If Lieutenant Scott was here she might have a rather more long winded name."

Once again James wished Science Officer Scott was with them to have experienced this. Yet if she were here, she would have insisted they stop to take detailed sensor readings. Despite his own curiosity, James knew they had to move on. "We can all marvel at this new discovery later, for now we need to keep our minds focused on the task at hand. Sub Lieutenant Malik. Are your scans of the local dark matter consistent with Suzanna's survey data?"

"Yes sir, it looks like we can make a shift jump to within a light year of the Alpha system. We will have to fly through a dense concentration of dark matter using our impulse engines after that. If Councilwoman Rodriguez's data holds up it will take us a couple of days, then we will enter what was once a dead-end shift passage that will take us to Alpha," Malik answered.

"Very well," James said, "Jennings, lay in a course and take us to Alpha at our best possible speed. We have a job to do."

The shift drive was a wonderful invention. It allowed ships to jump into shift space and travel along a straight line at speeds that greatly exceeded the speed of light. Yet gravitational anomalies like stars, planets and the dark matter strewn between stars prevented a ship from entering shift space. This meant that ships were severely limited in where they could go by the dark matter. They could only travel down areas of space that were relatively clear of dark matter known as shift passages. In theory, *Endeavour* could use her sub light impulse drives to ignore the dark matter and go anywhere she wanted, but even traveling from the Alpha system to Earth would take decades.

That was why the Gift hadn't been discovered sooner. There was a shift passage that headed towards the Gift from the Alpha system, yet it ended in a dead end. With so many other possibilities for discovery, the shift passage had been mapped out and then forgotten about by the Earth nations. All that was about to change; the Gift was something entirely new.

If Becket was right, then they hadn't entered shift space at all as they had travelled from one end of the Gift to the other. He didn't understand the astrophysical concept of subspace very well, but he knew it was at least theoretically possible to create a tear in normal space that would link two points in space together despite the vast distances between them. It seemed that the early Havenite colonists had found humanity's first wormhole and used it to get enough distance away from Earth to start their own colony, free from being rediscovered once the shift drive had been invented. It had served them well. Yet now it would become their worst enemy. The Gift would decrease the time it took British freighters to get from Earth to Chester by over forty days, and the time it would take to get to Haven and the two alien homeworlds of Vestar and Kulthar by more than fifty.

In terms of trade, within the British Star Kingdom it would have significant ramifications, never mind how important it would become once trade with the Vestarians and Kulreans took off. James guessed the exit point from the Gift closest to Earth was too near the Alpha system for the British Star Kingdom to claim. The UN Interplanetary Committee would no doubt declare it an independent entity that no Earth power could claim control over. However, the other end of the Gift was another matter. It was very close to Chester and British territory. If Britain could claim it, they could charge transit fees for any ships that wished to use the Gift, the fees alone would be a welcome boost to the government's coffers. Never mind the increased taxes they would gain from any increase in trade in the area.

James had to suppress a grin as he thought of the implications as *Endeavour* flew towards the Alpha system. *Whatever happens at Alpha,* James thought to himself, *my uncle is going to just love me for bringing him another discovery that is going to change the balance of power in this area.*

*

8th March, 2467AD, HMS *Endeavour*, Alpha System

Seven days later, James was quietly trying to hide his frustration. They had spent the last six days cruising through the Alpha system in stealth using their passive scanners to search for Admiral Harris and his ships. So far there had been no sign of them. That didn't say very much though, for the Alpha system was the only way to get to the British, Indian, French and Canadian colonies from Earth. The system was therefore full of civilian and military ships moving through. If Admiral Harris wanted to, it wouldn't be too hard for him to hide his ships somewhere near one of the main transit lanes. All they would have to do would be to power down their main reactors and engines, and any sign of them would be lost among all the background radiation given off by all the other ships.

Due to their difficulties trying to find Admiral Harris, James and Suzanna had tried a number of different tactics. First they had sent a system wide message from Suzanna to Admiral Harris. It had been encrypted using Havenite technology and had consisted of a simple message recommending that the plan be aborted. The idea had been to allow Harris to save face by withdrawing with his cover intact. Anyone else who decrypted the message would have no clue what the plan was and so the Haven ships could have returned home whilst saving face.

When no reply had been forthcoming, James had been forced to conclude that Harris was still somewhere in the system. He had then tried taking *Endeavour* out beyond the mass shadow of the system and jumping her back in. As soon as she had reverted to normal space he had put the ship in stealth mode and launched a drone that had been altered to give off the same kind of electromagnetic signature a Kulrean ship would make. The plan had been to lure Harris into revealing his position when he opened fire on the drone. Yet, the Havenite Admiral hadn't fallen for it.

Now James had resigned himself to waiting for the Kulreans to arrive. When they did, it might show that Admiral Harris had withdrawn, but he rather suspected the Admiral would still be around to launch his attack. From his discussions with Suzanna it was clear that Maximilian saw this as his final move. If he succeeded, it would buy his world enough time to rebuild their defenses. If it failed, then Maximilian knew he was bringing the wrath of the Earth nations down on his head. James didn't think Admiral Harris had the independence to disobey a direct order from Haven's First Councilor

As James examined his own thoughts, he knew that there was a strong knot of tension forming in his neck to match the frustration he had been feeling. The Kulrean ship was due today and each minute that ticked by brought them ever closer.

The Alpha system and the Alpha colony on the third planet was an independent colony run by the UN Interplanetary Committee. As Alpha had been the first world discovered by humans from Earth using the shift drive, it had been colonized by over twenty different nations. The resultant hotchpotch of towns, cities, economies, borders and the resultant political infighting was a mess. It didn't help that as new worlds much more suited to human habitation were discovered, the main Earth powers had abandoned any claims on Alpha and sought out their own worlds. Over the decades Alpha had become a political nightmare as various factions competed with each other for the limited space and resources. In the end, the UN Interplanetary Committee had been forced to step in and take control.

The result of all this for James was that the Alpha system didn't have a dedicated defense fleet of its own and as there were no British ships passing through the system, he had no one to call on for help. If Harris were to launch his attack, James would be on his own.

Going into battle for the first time in quite a while, James also had some fears, though not about his own safety. The importance of the coming battle couldn't be overstated. If Admiral Harris managed to scare off the Kulreans it would set back human-kulrean relations for decades, if not the next century. Quite simply, it wasn't a battle they could afford to lose.

James knew he had been in similar situations before, but in each of those he had also known that if he had been killed or injured, he had a First Lieutenant who could take over and handle his ship skillfully. When it came to First Lieutenant Mallory, he had his doubts however.

I like him, a lot, James said to himself. *We have a lot in common and if we survive this I know we will likely become good friends. But is that clouding my judgment?*

Not for the first time James questioned his decision to retain Mallory as his First Lieutenant. His uncle, the First Space Lord, had offered to supply *Endeavour* with a new First Lieutenant, one with a lot more experience than Mallory. James had refused. Even though he knew that Mallory had very little command experience and had probably been promoted too quickly due to the need for more senior officers during the Void War.

His reasoning had been simple; Mallory had stood by him when his previous First Lieutenant had tried to steal control of *Endeavour*. James felt that that kind of loyalty deserved to be rewarded and so he had turned down his uncle's offer.

There's nothing for it now, James said to himself, *Mallory will just have to grow into his boots quickly, I know I did.*

Dismissing his doubts, he switched his mind to Admiral Harris and for the next two hours he played out a number of different strategies the Admiral might employ. Meanwhile, all around him the tension on the bridge continued to slowly grow.

"Picking up a ship exiting shift space," Sub Lieutenant Malik called from the sensor command console. "It's giving off a gravitational signature I've never seen before."

Every ship gave off a gravitational pulse when it exited shift space, one that could be picked up by any ship within a light hour. If *Endeavour's* computers couldn't recognize the pulse, there was only one explanation. "It must be the Kulreans, send everyone to their battlestations," he ordered.

"Plot the Kulreans' position on the main holo display," Mallory said to Malik.

A moment later a point appeared forty-five light minutes off *Endeavour's* bow. "That's within the system's mass shadow," Becket said in shock from the tactical station.

"Yes," James acknowledged. "I guess the Kulreans can jump further into a system than us. We shouldn't be surprised; they have had more than a thousand years to tinker with their shift drives."

"For them to jump so far in means their shift drives allow them to get much closer to gravitational sources than ours," Becket explained. "That would have to include dark matter. If we had their shift drive technology it might open up a whole host of shift passages that we thought were just dead ends because the dark matter closed in too tight for our ships to traverse through."

James's thoughts hadn't got there as quickly as Becket's but as he listened it hit him too. "You're right Lieutenant, their FTL technology by itself is a game changer. But this," he said, gritting his teeth in determination as he continued, "this is a battle we can't lose. Jennings, take us towards the Kulrean ship, full power."

"Aye sir," Jennings responded from the navigation console.

The Kulreans jumping further into the system than he expected had thrown off his plans. Now he would have to boost *Endeavour* to her full speed just to catch up with them. It would give away *Endeavour's* presence to Admiral Harris. James just hoped that the Kulreans' unexpected position would throw off Harris' plans as well.

"The Kulrean ship is slowing," Malik reported. "I think they have detected *Endeavour* from her acceleration. I'm sure they are more than familiar with our acceleration profile; it looks like they are waiting for us to catch them."

"Send them the prerecorded message," James said.

"Sent," Sub Lieutenant King reported a few seconds later.

James only nodded. The message contained a short greeting from him and a brief description of the situation explaining the possibility that a rogue human faction may try to attack the Kulreans in the Alpha system.

It took the message just over twenty minutes to reach the Kulrean ship but when it did James was pleased to see Pemel was taking the threat seriously. It seemed that almost immediately after the message reached the Kulrean, he ordered his ship to rendezvous with James'. Once again the speed of the Kulrean ship impressed James, the acceleration rate from Pemel's ship was almost twice that of *Endeavour's*.

As he had seen in the Kulthar System however, their top

speed didn't seem to be as impressive. His analysis of the ships they had encountered in Kulthar hadn't detected any Kulrean ships armored in valstronium armor. Whatever they used to protect their ships and crews from cosmic particles was obviously effective, just not as effective as one might expect given the Kulreans' technological advances in other fields. Seeing this, James had to let one of his last hopes of avoiding battle slip away. There was no way the Kulrean ship could maneuver away from Harris' ships. They either had to fight their way through Harris' ships or order the Kulrean ship to turn around and head home.

"The Kulreans will match our course and speed in thirty minutes," Malik reported.

As if his words had been heard by Admiral Harris, three new blips appeared on the main holo display. "New contacts," Malik shouted.

"It's Harris," James said, "get a fix on their course, then try and figure out what ships he has with him.

Damn, James said to himself, *he is still here.* If *Endeavour* just had to take on Admiral Harris's flagship *Solitude* James would have been confident of victory. *Endeavour* was an exploration cruiser but she was designed to carry out raiding operations behind enemy lines in times of war. That meant she had a full arsenal of modern weapons. Whilst *Solitude* was a larger medium cruiser, Havenite technology was at least three decades behind the RSN and *Endeavour* would be able to give a good account of herself. However, the other two ships could tip the balance firmly in Harris' favor.

"Harris' ships are on an intercept course for the Kulrean ship. If the Kulreans form up on us Harris will be able to open fire in forty minutes," Malik reported. "I can't say for sure," he continued, "but I think one of the two ships keeping station with Harris' flagship is larger than the other. From the ships we know that survived the attack on Haven I would estimate them to be a destroyer and a frigate."

"Very good Sub Lieutenant," James said. "I guess we have a fight on our hands," he added to the rest of the bridge crew. "Things never seem to be easy for us."

We have a range advantage at least, James thought as he calculated the numbers. Harris's ships would be able to fire a combined broadside of twenty Havenite missiles. *Endeavour* would only be able to respond with eight. *We'll just have to use ours wisely.*

"Becket, I think we'll have time to make a change to our first broadside, I want an additional penetrator missile loaded into the starboard missile tubes," James ordered.

"Aye sir," Becket replied.

With nothing else to do for now James sat back and watched the Kulrean ship approach, they would be within distance of two-way communication soon.

Chapter 4 – No Retreat

Space is infinite and even the largest super dreadnaught is a speck of dust compared to a solar system, never mind the entire galaxy. Some would think therefore, that getting two opposing warships together in the same area at the same time would be difficult. Yet, since its first steps into space, humanity has proven that it is the simplest of tasks.

-Excerpt from Empire Rising, 3002 AD

8th March, 2467 AD, HMS *Endeavour,* Alpha System.

"It's good to see you again Captain," Pemel said over the COM channel once his ship was close enough for two-way communication.

"And you Viceroy," James replied, addressing Pemel by the title his people had given their new leader. "I am sorry we are meeting under such circumstances."

"As am I," Pemel said. "Let me assure you though, I understand if not all of your people are pleased with our visit to your planet. Maybe better than you might believe. Despite all that you did for our world there are many factions back on Kulthar that opposed my trip. I nearly had to cancel it."

"I guess politics is the same wherever you go in the galaxy,"

James said. He had meant it as a joke but it had come out more like a depressed realization.

"Perhaps they are," Pemel said, not picking up on either connotation. "I must confess we Kulreans believed ourselves above such things but since the attack by the Overlord's fleet and our forced abandonment of our ancient traditions, we have found ourselves splintering into smaller and smaller groups. Holding things together has been growing tougher and tougher. I dread to think about what things will be like when I return."

"Regardless, it is good to see you again Pemel," James reiterated.

"Agreed," Pemel replied, "I have been looking forward to this for weeks. I'm just sorry that once again you have to put yourself between my people and danger."

"And I had been looking forward to showing you around Earth. Yet here we are," James said. "I'm afraid we don't have any more time for pleasantries, we need to get down to business. This might not be the Overlord's fleet but our opponents still outmatch us. I do not believe they will completely destroy your vessel but they will try to damage it and force you to return to Kulthar. I guess from what you have already told me that if that were to happen, support for a second visit might not be forthcoming from your people."

"That would be correct," Pemel said. "If this attack proves successful I may find myself out of a job and whoever takes over won't be so enthusiastic about opening relations with

Earth."

"Then this is a battle we have to win," James responded. "May I ask, have you equipped your ship with any kind of weapons?"

"Only defensive ones Captain," Pemel said. "We have reverse engineered the Overlord's laser technology and equipped our ships with a number of small point defense lasers. I do not believe my people will ever incorporate offensive weapons onto our ships. That is simply not who we are. However, our recent history has taught us the need to be able to defend ourselves. I believe that if these ships fire any missiles our way then we should be able to hold about a dozen of them off."

"That's perfect," James said. "I think we might need to use your defenses before this day is over. However, for now I need your ship to hang back. Let *Endeavour* engage the enemy ships and we'll see if you are needed."

"That's ok with me Captain," Pemel responded.

"Just keep your distance," James said. "I need to get back to fighting with my ship."

"Ok Captain," Pemel said, "good luck."

"Any updates?" James said as he turned his attention back to the bridge crew.

"Admiral Harris' ships haven't changed course," Mallory

reported. "However we have received their transponder signals. The three ships are all claiming to be warships registered to the Brazilian government."

"Just as my informant said they would," Suzanna said from the observation chair James had had installed beside his command chair.

"There can be no doubt then," James said. "It must be Admiral Harris who is out there. Open a COM channel, use the Havenite encryption."

"Channel open sir," Sub Lieutenant King reported.

"Admiral Harris," James began. "I know you are in command of the three warships that are approaching the Kulrean envoy ship. Stand down immediately. If you attack them, you will be forfeiting not just your own life but the freedom of your entire planet. Haven does not deserve leaders and Admirals who attack the innocent. Think about what you are doing. It is not too late to stand down."

With a motion of his hand across his throat James signaled King to cut the transmission. "The message will take thirty minutes to reach Harris' ships," she informed him once she ended the transmission.

"I know," James said. It was his last hope of ending this confrontation without conflict. Sooner or later someone would decrypt his transmission. If Admiral Harris thought that everyone else knew he was really the one who was launching this attack, James hoped he would back down. Yet

Harris was stubborn. He was as likely to keep fighting just because he couldn't see any better option.

For an hour, everyone on the bridge watched the Havenite ships get closer and closer. Suzanna had stared at the holo display in complete silence since James had sent his message to Admiral Harris. "They have had the message for over twenty minutes," she said, breaking her silence. "Why have they not turned back? Harris knows that his secret is out. Even if he destroys us, his plan won't work."

"Perhaps," James said. "I expect he is hoping that if he does destroy us and force Pemel to flee, then Maximillian will be able to deny any involvement in the attack. With *Endeavour* and her sensor logs gone there won't be any real evidence to prove that I was right about the identity of the attackers."

"But everyone will still know who was really to blame," Suzanna said in frustration.

"Likely they will, but there won't be any hard evidence," James replied. "Either way it hardly matters now. Our job is to protect the Kulreans. There's no room to be thinking about what ifs now."

"I agree," Suzanna said, after taking a moment to consider James' words. "I will stay out of your way Captain, you don't need any more distractions. I'm going to retire to my quarters."

"You're not going to stay and watch?" James asked.

"I can watch from the holo display in my quarters," Suzanna answered. "You and your crew don't need a civilian around to distract you from your duty. Besides," she said as she reached out and touched his shoulder. "I trust you, you won't let anything happen to me."

Before James could reply she had already walked past him and out of the bridge.

"She's a strange lady," Mallory commented, quickly looking at something on his command console when James looked his way.

"We'll be entering our missile range in thirty seconds," Becket said from the tactical station, bringing everyone's mind back to the battle at hand.

"Is our first broadside ready?" James asked.

"Just waiting to get into range," Becket answered.

James didn't respond, instead he waited until the range counter reached zero. "Fire!" he ordered.

Eight missiles launched out of *Endeavour's* starboard missile tubes. Missile tubes were essentially large railguns that accelerated the missiles to 0.1C. As soon as they cleared their tubes the missiles' impulse engines kicked in and they rapidly accelerated towards their targets.

"First broadside away," Becket informed James.

"Fire the second as soon as it's ready," James replied. "We need to make our range advantage count."

As the missiles approached the Havenite ships they zeroed in on Harris's flagship, *Solitude*. Even though its outer hull had been altered to make it look more like a Brazilian medium cruiser, for anyone who had seen *Solitude* in the battle over Haven she was unmistakable. As James expected, the frigate closed into a tight formation with Solitude to add her point defenses to the flagship's. The destroyer peeled out of formation to gain some distance, the position it took up would allow it to get a better angle to hit the incoming missiles with a crossfire.

James watched the numbers rapidly changing on the holo display, doing the math in his head. Despite his misspent youth, math had always been a strong point and these were exactly the kinds of situations where it came in handy. "Now," he said when he thought the timing was just right.

"Signal sent," Becket said.

James nodded as he and everyone else on the bridge watched the holo display. It would take nearly two minutes for the signal travelling at the speed of light to reach the missiles. As soon as it did they veered away from their apparent target towards the destroyer.

James had timed it perfectly; the missiles had just enough time to overcome a sufficient amount of their forward momentum to angle in on the lone destroyer. Just as it became apparent they had shifted target the two penetrator missiles switched on their powerful ECM warheads. Where the Havenite ships had been tracking eight missiles suddenly there appeared to be fifteen. All of which were homing in on the lonely destroyer.

The missiles' change of vector meant that *Solitude* and her escorting frigate could get a better shot at the missiles, yet whatever missiles survived their fire should have a good chance of overwhelming the lone destroyer's point defenses.

Everyone on the bridge missed Lieutenant Becket fire *Endeavour's* second volley as they waited to see if James's plan would work. As they watched, *Solitude* and the frigate fired their first round of anti-missile missiles. Over fifty of the smaller AM missiles swarmed out to try and intercept the British missiles. One got a hit but the others missed or flew straight through the mirage created by the penetrator missiles and the ECM from the normal missiles.

A second volley of AM missiles tried to knock out more missiles. They managed to take out two more, one of which was a penetrator. Nevertheless, the holo display showed nine missiles still targeting the destroyer, four of which were real ship killer missiles.

In desperation, the destroyer fired two volleys of its own AM missiles as soon as the British missiles entered its point defense range. Yet, it only managed to destroy three more, two ship killers and the penetrator missile. That left two ship killers to dive towards the destroyer. The destroyer tried to make a last-ditch attempt to avoid the missiles by banking hard and going into a roll. It fooled one of the missiles momentarily, which caused it to detonate its warhead before it flew by its target. The resultant explosion from the thermonuclear warhead was still close enough to burn off a large section of the destroyer's valstronium armor and cause some internal damage.

The second missile didn't lose its lock and scored a direct impact on the destroyer. On *Endeavour's* bridge everyone cheered but it cut off almost immediately. "Where's the explosion?" Malik shouted.

"It was one of the penetrator missiles that got the impact," Becket answered. "There was no warhead to explode."

"Magnify the optical scans of that destroyer," James ordered. It would take nearly two minutes for the visual data from the damaged destroyer to get to them but he still wanted to see what damage they had caused.

"Jennings, alter course," James ordered. "Put us on a new heading towards the system's gas giant."

"Aye sir," she replied.

As *Endeavour* slowly turned onto her new heading James watched the gravimetric sensors carefully. Their new heading would actually allow *Solitude* to close the range slightly quicker. However, James guessed it would force Harris' ships to use all their maneuvering thrusters to re-orientate themselves in time to gain any advantage.

"They didn't move," James said in excitement.

"Sorry Captain?" Mallory asked.

"That destroyer must have taken some serious damage. Valstronium armor is immensely strong but the momentum from a penetrator missile impact can still cause a lot of damage. If that destroyer could alter course to close the range with us it would have. Harris is keeping to his original course so that the destroyer can stay in the fight," James explained.

"Jennings, new course, keep us on the same elliptical plane but pivot us forty degrees towards the system's star," James said. His original plan had been to try and rush *Endeavour* and Pemel's ship towards the shift passage to Earth. He had hoped to hold off Harris long enough to allow Pemel to make the jump towards Earth. Now he had other options.

"We're changing course now Sir," Jennings reported.

James let a smile creep onto his face as the range slowly opened up between Harris's ships and *Endeavour*. Harris had rightly predicted that James would try and make a run for the shift passage to Earth and he had positioned his ships directly in James' way. Now that *Endeavour* was heading further into the Alpha system his ships would have to maneuver to stay with her.

"The cruiser and frigate are altering course to pursue us," Malik said excitedly, "the destroyer is staying on her original course."

"So I see," James said.

Before he could say anything more Becket interrupted him, "They are firing sir, I count twenty missiles."

"Yes," James said. Harris had fired from extreme range; his missiles would likely not have enough power left for a great deal of evasive maneuvering when they got into attack range. Though he had no other choice if he wanted the destroyer to add her missiles to Harris' first volley.

It took the Havenite missiles ten minutes to reach *Endeavour*. In the meantime, Becket's second missile salvo had reached *Solitude* and her escort. By James' estimation they had scored one proximity hit on the Havenite cruiser, yet there was little sign of any serious damage.

"Flak cannons firing," Becket announced when the Havenite missiles got into range. *Endeavour's* two flak cannons fired, when the flak rounds reached the incoming missiles they exploded, creating a wall of shrapnel the Havenite missiles had to fly through. The shrapnel took out eleven of the missiles but nine still continued. Next the point defense plasma cannons and *Endeavour's* AM missiles tried to swat the incoming Havenite missiles out of existence. It was clear they weren't going to get them all though.

"Evasive maneuvers," James shouted to Jennings at the navigation console.

Sub Lieutenant Jennings already had a preset maneuver uploaded to the computer and as soon as she hit the command button the ship fired off her maneuvering thrusters, pulling her nose up vertical to her original course and then sending the ship into a spin. All three of the remaining missiles overshot their target and exploded, two of them were too far way to do any damage to the ship but the third was close enough that a wave of electromagnetic energy washed over the ship from its thermonuclear detonation.

On the bridge, everyone was thrown about in their seats. "That was just a proximity hit," Second Lieutenant Julius called over the COM channel from the auxiliary bridge. "I'm getting minor damage reports, the most serious seems to be some damage to two of our stern starboard AM launchers."

"Understood," James said. As soon as the sensor feed stabilized he looked back to the holo display to watch *Endeavour's* third missile volley crash into the Havenite ships. It looked like they scored another proximity hit of their own, but again *Solitude* seemed to shrug it off and keep on coming.

"She's a strong ship," Mallory commented from his command chair beside James.

"I'm afraid so," James said.

For the next twenty minutes both cruisers fired missile after missile salvo at each other. *Solitude* seemed to shake off proximity hit after hit and kept advancing. *Endeavour* took two more proximity hits but in reply Becket managed to score a direct hit on the frigate accompanying *Solitude*. After the explosion had faded there had been nothing left of the smaller warship.

"Shit," Julius shouted over the COM channel, "that last proximity hit took out one of the flak cannons, I don't think I can get it repaired in time."

"Acknowledged," James said in an understanding tone. The two cruisers were now so close to each other that it was taking their missile volleys less than five minutes to close the distance.

"Incoming," Becket shouted. Despite the other flak cannon firing as fast as it could and the doubled efforts of the point defense plasma cannon operators and the AM missiles, two missiles got into attack range. Before James could order Jennings to try and dodge the missiles she had *Endeavour* diving away from them. It was to no avail, before James realized it a missile struck the forward section of his ship and exploded.

The explosive force momentarily disrupted the power flow to the bridge and as everyone was thrown about in their harnesses from the concussive force, the lights went out.

"Status report," James shouted into the dark, not sure who was still conscious or even alive to answer him.

"We're still in one piece," Julius answered over the COM channel. "But we're in a bad way. We've lost at least eighty percent of our forward point defense plasma cannons and missile tube eight isn't responding. I think that entire section of the ship has been blasted away."

"Damn," James said to himself as the lights came back on.

"Pemel is hailing us," Sub Lieutenant King called from the COM station.

"Send it to my command chair," James said. "Keep fighting the ship Mallory."

"Captain," Pemel said quickly, "you are taking a beating. You have to let us help you. We can't stand here and watch you be destroyed."

"Very well," James said reluctantly. He had been loath to let Pemel join the fight. Any kind of damage, even just from a proximity hit, could have serious repercussions for relations with the Kulreans. "I don't think we have a choice anymore, execute plan Beta."

"Very well," Pemel said, "good luck Captain."

James turned to Sub Lieutenant Jennings as soon as the COM feed ended. "Change of course Lieutenant, take us directly towards *Solitude*."

"Maneuvering now Captain," she replied.

"Sir," Malik called in concern. "The Kulrean ship isn't following us.

"I know," James replied. So far Pemel had been keeping

station with *Endeavour,* making sure his ship stayed safely behind the warship. "Pemel is going it on his own for the time being. He is joining the fight."

A small cheer erupted from the Sub Lieutenants on the bridge. They had all felt their fear growing as *Endeavour* fired broadside after broadside at the larger Haven warship with little affect.

"*Solitude* has fired again," Becket informed everyone.

"They've aimed at the Kulrean ship," Malik shouted in excitement.

"Take out as many missiles as you can as they pass us by," James ordered. "Becket switch to rapid fire on our missiles, we're close enough now that accuracy is irreverent, then power up the main plasma cannons."

"Aye sir," Becket answered.

Endeavour's main plasma cannons had a far greater range than her point defense ones. They were designed for close ship-to-ship action. Whilst the valstronium armor of warships could often brush off a direct hit from a thermonuclear explosion, a high yield plasma round was another matter. Often when ships got into plasma cannon range it spelled disaster for everyone involved.

"We took out four of the Havenite missiles, another eight are closing with the Kulrean ship," Malik reported.

James didn't respond, instead he watched the Kulrean ship, hoping their defenses would be strong enough. He wasn't disappointed. Before the Havenite missiles got close to the Kulrean ship red lasers picked off the incoming missiles. In a matter of seconds four of the eight missiles disappeared. The other four, sensing the demise of their brothers, randomly jinked about in space to throw off the Kulrean's aim. It only had limited success for although not every Kulrean shot hit its target, it only took another six seconds for the final four missiles to be destroyed.

A cheer from Sub Lieutenant Malik brought James' attention back to *Solitude*. "We got a direct hit sir," Becket informed him. "I have another salvo of missiles three minutes out."

"Well done," James said as he saw a large hole in *Solitude's* amidships that was venting
atmosphere and debris. "Hit them with the plasma cannons," he ordered. "They won't do too much damage yet but it will give Admiral Harris something to think about. *Solitude* doesn't have any plasma cannons after all."

The containment fields on the plasma bolt degraded very quickly and they were still too far away for the plasma bolts to penetrate *Solitude's* valstronium armor, yet every little would help.

Thirty seconds after the first volley of plasma bolts hit *Solitude* and caused a number of small eruptions on her armor James opened a COM link to *Solitude*. "Admiral Harris," he began. "You are beaten; you cannot destroy the Kulrean ship. Surrender now and there need not be any more loss of life. Fighting on will help no one. Surrender and I will detonate the incoming volley of missiles."

For another thirty seconds James waited for a response, the only message that came was in the form of another salvo of missiles from *Solitude*.

"Hit them again with the plasma cannons," James ordered. "Just before they open fire with their point defenses on our missile salvo."

Becket did as she was ordered and just before *Solitude* opened fire with her AM missiles four small explosions erupted on her valstronium armor. Two more plasma bolts hit *Solitude* right where the missile had blown a hole in her side and they penetrated deep into the ship, causing a number of secondary explosions. The explosions threw the ship off course and badly disrupted the targeting data of her AM missiles.

Even so, a swarm of thirty AM missiles reached out towards the incoming seven missiles from *Endeavour*. They took out five of them but two missiles pushed on through the attack and dived in towards *Solitude*. Either because there weren't enough functioning sensors to see what was happening or because there was no one left alive on *Solitude's* bridge to see the danger, the Havenite ship didn't even try to evade the incoming missiles. In the blink of an eye they both hit the warship and the twin explosions blew the entire nose section off the cruiser.

As James watched, both parts of the ship tumbled and spun

out of control. It only took a matter of seconds for a number of secondary explosions to wrack the larger section of the ship. Finally, one of *Solitude's* main reactors overloaded and a giant explosion momentarily blinded the sensors. When it cleared all that was left of *Solitude* was her tumbling nose section.

"It's over," Jennings shouted from the navigation console.

"Not yet," Mallory said. "That last broadside was aimed at us. Give them everything we have got Lieutenant Becket."

There were still ten Havenite missiles boosting towards them. "Signal Pemel," James ordered Sub Lieutenant King. "Tell him we're going to need his help."

And quickly, James thought, *we can't take another hit.*

"He says he's on his way," King reported a few seconds later.

"Firing the flak cannon," Becket reported.

James was forced to watch while others controlled *Endeavour's* various systems. The single surviving flak cannon took out three of the missiles. Then, just as the point defense plasma cannons were about to fire, more of the Havenite missiles exploded.

"Pemel is here," Mallory shouted.

"Indeed," James said in wonder at the Kulrean's impressive

technology. It only took a matter of seconds for *Endeavour's* point defense plasma cannons and Pemel's lasers to take out the remaining missiles.

"Pemel is hailing us," King reported.

"Put it on the main holo display," James said.

"I owe you my life again Captain," Pemel said with a very human like smile.

"I think it is you who has come to my rescue twice now," James replied. "Your point defenses are impressive; I think you could have held off the Havenites by yourself."

"They do work well," Pemel said. "Our analysis of the Havenite weapons technology suggests we could have held off the destroyer and the frigate on our own long enough to make the jump to Earth. The cruiser would have been too much for us though. I am very glad you were here."

"As am I," James said. "I do hope this won't impact relations between our two peoples."

"I hope it won't either," Pemel replied. "You can rest assured that at least as far as I am concerned, it won't. If things go well on Earth, then I think my people will soon forget about this."

"In that case, you better get going," James said. "It is going to take a couple of days for me to get *Endeavour* ready to enter shift space. You should head on to Earth. I wanted to escort you to my homeworld but I think it is more important that you aren't late. There is an entire world waiting for your arrival."

"If that's what you want," Pemel said, "we will make the jump to shift space now. I look forward to seeing you in person on Earth. And I hope you will pass on our thanks to your crew."

"I will," James responded. "See you in a few days," he added before he closed the COM link.

"What's the damage report?" he asked Second Lieutenant Julius who was on the auxiliary bridge.

"Sections nine and ten have taken a lot of damage sir," she replied. "Missile tube eight is also out of action. I think we will need to return to a repair yard to fix it and the flak cannon."

"And the crew?" James asked, hoping the causalities would be low.

"Nine dead I'm afraid Sir. So far the doctor has registered twelve serious injuries. Almost all of them were crewmembers stationed in the forward sections where we took the direct hit."

"Very well," James said. "I'll be down to sickbay to visit them momentarily."

"Malik," James said, turning back to face the sensor officer.

"Is there any sign of that destroyer?"

"No sir," Malik replied immediately. "I have reviewed the sensor data from the battle. I believe it changed course back towards the shift passage to the Gift. They must have been able to jump to shift space."

"Thank you Sub Lieutenant," James responded.

He tapped a few buttons on his command chair to open a COM link to the entire ship. "Crew members of *Endeavour,*" he said. "It has been an honor to fight alongside you all today. You have done your country and your ship proud. Against a superior force we showed that a strong heart and good training can still win out. You have my congratulations."

After taking a breath he continued. "We will finish our essential repairs, then I will give you all some down time to get a meal and mourn our losses, they are not to be forgotten. Each of the lives lost today were for a worthy cause. I thank you all. Captain Somerville out."

After shutting down the COM link James stood and made his way out of the bridge. "You are in charge of the repairs Lieutenant Mallory," he said. "I'm going to make sure Councilwoman Rodriguez is ok and then visit sick bay."

"Aye sir," Mallory said.

When James was out of sight he let out a breath and tried to relax. Then he refocused his attention on the problems at hand. He felt as if he had been a bystander throughout the battle, just waiting to take over in case James was injured or killed. All the tactics and moves had been of James' making, he had given little input on how the *Endeavour* fought. Secretly, he was a little ashamed and embarrassed. He knew that James' previous First Lieutenants had both contributed to James' battle plans. *I'm just going to have to get better,* Mallory promised himself. *I certainly have the best of teachers.*

*

When James walked into Suzanna's quarters she jumped up and gave him a hug. "That was magnificent," she said as she stepped back. "You saved us all again!"

"Nonsense," James said. "The crew fought bravely and the Kulrean's point defenses tipped the balance of power in our favor. We all owe you a great debt. If you hadn't warned us, Pemel and his crew might be dead now."

"I guess we can both take some of the credit," she said smiling. "What do you plan to do now?" she asked.

"I'm going to visit the wounded. Mallory is overseeing the repairs for the moment," James answered.

"Are there many wounded?" Suzanna asked in concern.

"Nine dead and at least twelve seriously hurt," James answered without trying to conceal his sadness.

"Well then I'm coming with you," she said. "They all

deserve the thanks of my people."

With that she put her arm through his, turned him around and began walking out of her quarters.

James didn't know what to do about her arm but he was deeply moved by her concern for his wounded crew so he didn't say anything. Instead he let her lead him to sickbay.

Chapter 5 – War Justification

Today the Emperor has the right to send the Navy to war whenever he pleases. Yet, even he must have a good reason to do so or he could face a rebellious senate. In the days before the Empire, each leader had to worry about what his government thought, and the other Earth nations.

-Excerpt from Empire Rising, 3002 AD

15th March, 2467 AD, HMS *Endeavour,* Sol System.

Seven days after the battle with the Havenite warships HMS *Endeavour* dropped out of shift space into the Sol System. "It's always a sight to behold," Mallory said as the main holo display updated itself with all the sensor data.

On the outer edges of the system there were a number of large blips that were the bulky inhabited asteroids that served as the mining hubs for the outer system mining operations. They were all radiating huge amounts of waste electromagnetic energy into space. Surrounding them were hundreds of smaller blips that were the independent asteroid mining operations that fed the larger asteroids with all the raw materials they needed. Going back and forth between them and the inner system were streams of freighters carrying materials towards Earth and the other industrial nodes scattered throughout the system.

Further into the system almost all the planets had large orbital installations around them and there was a swarm of ships moving back and forth going about their business. The gravitational sensors estimated that over five thousand ships had been detected moving about in the system.

Earth itself was just a glow of electromagnetic radiation on the holo display. There were so many ships and stations in orbit that it was almost impossible to make out anything at this distance.

"I never grow tired of it," James replied as he too looked at the image on the holo display.

"It's unbelievable," Suzanna said as she stood in awe of what the holo projector was showing. "I never imagined a system could be so full of life and activity. There are ships everywhere." Without realizing what she was doing she walked closer to the projector in an attempt to make out all the details it was displaying.

James wasn't surprised by Suzanna's awe. He had grown up in the Sol system and yet even he was impressed every time he came back. There were many solar travel companies that made their fortune solely by flying tourists from outer colonies to the Sol system to take this sight in. Yet, they had all grown up at least knowing what Sol looked like, Susanna had not been prepared for the sight before her.

To let her see earth better he zoomed in the holo display. "Here," James said, "have a look at your homeworld, it's hard to imagine your ancestors left here almost 200 years ago."

"It's so green," Susanna said as Earth came into focus. "I always thought Haven was pretty but this, this is something else."

"Just wait until you get to the surface," Mallory said. "The holo projector doesn't do it justice."

"It looks like Earth is even busier than normal," James said as he studied the screen.

"Aye, I imagine Pemel is drawing quite a crowd," Mallory replied.

"Take us in," James ordered the Sub Lieutenant at the navigation console.

Six hours later Suzanna was still on the bridge gazing at the Sol system, taking in every detail. James had left a few times but he too had been studying humanity's home system. He had been particularly interested in all the warships in orbit around Earth. Most of the Earth powers kept a significant proportion of their fleets around Earth but it looked like there was more than usual present. He guessed that many of the smaller Earth nations were trying to impress Pemel.

It was no surprise to see the Brazilian warships off to one side, keeping their distance from Earth. It had taken James and Mallory two days to carryout enough repairs on *Endeavour* to allow her to jump into shift space. That had been plenty of time to allow some of the freighters who had been in the Alpha system and observed the battle between Admiral Harris and *Endeavour* to jump to Sol and report the battle to the news outlets. James knew that Pemel would have assured the Earth governments that he didn't hold the Brazilians accountable for the attack, but the news reporters were unlikely to let the Brazilians off the hook so easily, especially if there were multiple freighter reports of Brazilian ships carrying out the attack. James had asked Pemel to keep the real identity of the attackers a secret and he was sure that there were a great many conspiracy theories running around Earth at the moment.

"Captain, we have just received a message from HMS *Vulcan*, you are to repair on board and report to Admiral Somerville forthwith," Sub Lieutenant King said from the COMs station.

"Acknowledge the message," James ordered, not in the least surprised. No doubt his uncle was dying to know just what had happened in the Alpha system. As soon as *Vulcan's* sensors would be able to make out *Endeavour's* battle damage he would know that whatever it was, it had been serious.

"Mallory, set course for *Vulcan*, alert me when we are thirty minutes out. I'm going to retire to my quarters," James said once King informed him that the acknowledgment had been sent.

"Aye Sir," Mallory said as James stood up and left the bridge.

*

Five minutes after *Endeavour* had docked with HMS *Vulcan* the RSN's main construction yard, James stepped into his uncle's office. Behind him Suzanna followed eagerly.

"Let me tell you boy, this is getting to be a jok..." Admiral Somerville began but when Suzanna stepped out from behind James he stopped mid-sentence. James saw a brief look of surprise cross his face before he got himself under control again.

"Councilwoman Rodriguez I presume," he said instead in a much more formal tone. "It is indeed a surprise to see you here. You are most welcome however, please take a seat."

"I'm sorry for the shock Admiral," Suzanna said, "but I needed to come to Earth urgently. Thank you for your welcome."

As James walked past his uncle to take a seat the Admiral shot him a questioning look. "We will explain everything," James assured him.

"I'm all ears then," Somerville said as he sat behind his desk. "I presume this ties in with the attack on Pemel's ship. He said you came to his rescue once again."

"Indeed we did," James said as he launched into an explanation of the events that led up to the battle in the Alpha system. He had already agreed with Suzanna that he would do the initial talking.

"So you see uncle, we really had little choice. We didn't quite know when Pemel would arrive and I thought that if we left the Alpha system to go and look for help we wouldn't be back in time to intercept Admiral Harris. In the end, it worked out, although I'm afraid *Endeavour* is going to need another stint in a repair yard. Our nose section has taken some serious damage. I wouldn't want to take her into another fight in her current condition," James finished.

"I have seen the visuals of *Endeavour* as she approached *Vulcan*, you'll be happy to know I have already put her at the top of the repair list. We have finished enough ships over the last two months that there should be a berth available for *Endeavour*. I don't plan to let you out of my sight just so quickly this time," Admiral Somerville said.

"You'll not be surprised to hear that I approve of your actions," he continued. "Though taking your ship into an unknown gravitational anomaly is going to raise a few eyebrows among the other admirals. You may have to face a disciplinary hearing for that."

James was about to protest but before he could say anything Suzanna had beaten him to it, "But Admiral, that is hardly fair, James.."

"No, it's not fair," Admiral Somerville said, breaking her off, "yet it is necessary, even if it will likely just be a formality. In light of the circumstances I think James made the right decision. He had to intercept Admiral Harris and he fought very well when he did. Nevertheless, we can't have RSN Captains running around risking their ships wily nilly so James' actions will have to be assessed by a disciplinary hearing. If only to warn other Captains that such risks will only be tolerated in the most extreme circumstances.

"What concerns me is the repercussions this will have for our plans with Haven. The King and the Prime Minister have been winning over support in the Houses of Commons and Lords for a vote on offering protectorate status to the Haven colony and its surrounding systems. Once this attack gets out I fear all support will evaporate. There will be calls for an armed intervention, not a peaceful alliance."

"That is why I am here Admiral," Suzanna said. "I want to assure you and your government that there is still a peaceful solution available for our future. First Councilor Maximillian does not represent the majority of the population of Haven. If he can be removed from power, then I think the way will be open for us to open friendly relationships. I hope to play a key role in beginning such relationships during my stay here on Earth."

"And just how do you plan to remove the First Councilor?" Admiral Somerville asked. "From what James has told me your attempts have failed to have any real impact on his power base."

"That is correct Admiral," Suzanna conceded begrudgingly. She shot James an accusing look which James returned with an apologetic shrug.

"Yet Admiral Harris' attack on Pemel's ship is the last mistake Maximillian is going to make," she continued. "If we can get the images of the attack back to Haven, the people will rise up and overthrow him. There is no way he can stay in power. As soon as the other councilors learn that he attacked a friendly alien race and that he lost almost all of Haven's surviving military ships, they will remove him from power. His actions have thrown the freedom of every colonist on Haven into jeopardy. Haven will recognize this and act swiftly. I firmly believe that if we can get the images of this attack to Haven then you will find a much friendlier government in power ready to negotiate with your leaders."

"That's as may be," Admiral Somerville said. "Yet it doesn't change things here and now. As soon as the King and Prime Minister hear that it was Haven who attacked Pemel they may decide to abandon all plans of offering a protectorate. Even if Pemel says he is ok with the attack, my government may not want to take the chance of associating with elements of humanity who have openly attacked what may well become our most important trading partner.

"However," Somerville continued. "Nothing has been decided yet and I assure you, you will get a chance to present your ideas to our leaders. In fact, even if we decide to take another approach to Haven we may well send an envoy ship to your colony to inform your populace of Maximillian's actions. Even if we don't offer you protectorate status, I imagine we would still like to remove Maximillian if we can.

"For now though we have a few other things to sort out.

First, James, Pemel has requested that you accompany him on his tour of Earth as soon as you arrive in system. We will have to arrange for you to join him.

"Second, we are going to have to find a way to explain away your involvement in the battle in the Alpha system. For now, it is best to keep the Havenite involvement in the attack a secret as well as the presence of Ms. Rodriguez. Yet we need to have a good explanation of how you came to be in the right place at the right time. And we will need to come up with some sort of story for why you weren't able to identify your attackers. I imagine we can concoct some story about how your long-range sensors were damaged."

"That won't be too hard to fake," James said, "we took quite a lot of damage in the battle. I'm sure I can get my sensor technicians to alter our battle feed to obscure the identity of the attacking ships."

"Good, well get right on that as soon as you return to *Endeavour*," Somerville said. "No doubt you'll have a lot of debriefing sessions to go through and I imagine you are going to be very busy for the next few weeks.

"As for you Councilwoman, for now, I think it is best you remain on board *Endeavour*. The less people that know about your presence here on Earth the better. You have my word that I will try and make sure we come to an agreement that will help your people, I can make no promises however. In any case, whatever will happen now, the world becoming aware of your presence will not help anyone."

"I understand Admiral, I will stay on *Endeavour* and make myself available to anyone who wants to speak to me from your government," Suzanna said.

"Very good," Somerville said pleased. "No doubt I'll be summoning you back here in a couple of hours but for now I need time to think things through and contact the Prime Minister. You can both return to your ship."

"Aye Sir," James said as he stood up and escorted Suzanna out of his uncle's office.

"Oh and one more thing," Admiral Somerville said as James was about to leave his office. "Your crew are going to be confined to their ship. I don't want even a whiff of the Gift or the fight with the Haven warships getting to the press. I'll be holding you personally responsible for your crew."

"I understand Admiral, I'll make sure everyone knows how important secrecy is," James said before he stepped out of the office.

*

21st March, 2467AD, UN Interplanetary Committee Chambers, New York.

As James dropped down into one of the Committee Chamber's seats he let out a long sigh. The last six days had been a rush of meetings. It seemed that Pemel had wanted James to accompany him everywhere he went. As the alien was meeting with almost all of Earth's leaders it meant

James was dragged all over the world. At the same time, he was expected to be present with Suzanna when she met with the King, the Prime Minister and other select Members of Parliament on a number of occasions to discuss the future of Haven. As if that hadn't been enough, he had been grilled several times by a number of senior Admirals and RSN legal aides about his actions in the Alpha system. They were all gathering evidence for James' impending disciplinary hearing and so James had been forced to go over the battle again and again. On top of all that, his uncle had been true to his word for no sooner had he left his uncles' office than the Chief Engineer of HMS *Vulcan* had contacted him. A repair berth had been cleared for *Endeavour* and his ship was currently being swarmed over by hundreds of engineers as they got to work repairing *Endeavour's* battle damage. James had been so busy he had been forced to leave most of the supervision of the work to Mallory.

The only moments of calm had been the breakfasts he had been able to share with Suzanna. As she was still staying on board *Endeavour* to help keep her presence on Earth a secret they had been able to share their mornings together before their busy schedules began. On the first morning they had mainly talked politics but on subsequent mornings their discussions had turned to more personal matters. Both of them had opened up much more about their past than they had before and as a result, James felt he knew a lot more about Suzanna's inner life. Another result had been that James had promised to show Suzanna around his family's historic home. Coming from Haven, Suzanna had grown up without all the historic buildings Earth was covered in. In her short trips off *Endeavour* she had been able to get glimpses of some things, but they had been limited. When he had offered to show her around his family's home she had been very excited.

Since the late 17th century, Badminton House had been the home of the Somerville family, being passed down from Duke to Duke. James hadn't been back to the estate since his father's suicide. His mother had died when he was still in his early childhood and all throughout his childhood and teenage years his father had made it plainly clear that his elder brother was not just the heir to the Dukedom, but also the favorite. As a result, Badminton House, despite all the history it held for his family, never really felt like home to James.

Currently, it was still being run by John Grimshaw, his father's butler. Butler was a very old fashioned word for what Grimshaw did, yet the aristocracy liked to keep their traditions. Rather than waiting on his father hand and foot Grimshaw had been in charge of overseeing the running of the estate grounds and the stately home. James remembered the elderly man as a kindly soul who had looked out for James when no one else had and so upon his father's death, he had kept Grimshaw in his position overseeing the estate.

James' thoughts of the past were interrupted when Suzanna nudged him with her knee, bringing his attention back to the present. "It's beginning," she whispered.

James smiled at the look of excitement on her face. He was glad his uncle and the Royal Space Naval Intelligence officers in charge of keeping her presence on Earth a secret had agreed to let her attend this historic meeting of the UN Interplanetary Committee. Suzanna had insisted that she needed to attend to form her own opinion on the rest of Earth's leaders. His uncle had reluctantly agreed, aware that he couldn't keep her prisoner if she really insisted on going.

RSNI had hastily made up a fake alias for Suzanna and so she was posing as a minor assistant to Admiral Somerville. As James looked around he guessed that there were over two thousand people crammed into the large Committee chambers and so there was little chance anyone would pay much attention to Suzanna. All the focus would be on Pemel after all. This was the first public speech he would be making. So far all his meetings had been private, everyone on Earth was therefore waiting with bated breath to hear what he was going to say.

Nevertheless, there was no need to risk drawing too much attention. "Calm down," James whispered back. "You are supposed to be an Admiral's aide who has been to hundreds of Committee meetings. If you look too excited someone will notice you."

"Of course," Suzanna said as she put on a bored expression. "Is this more suitable?"

James shook his head and turned his attention to the podium, squishing down into his seat to get more comfortable. As a RSN Captain James had only come before the UN Interplanetary Committee twice before, once to report his discovery of the Void and a second time to answer for his attack on an Indian mining station. Despite the significance of both occasions, a number of the Committee members had taken the opportunity to present long drawn out speeches. James suspected Pemel's address to the Committee would be no exception.

It was over an hour later when the last Committee Member stood to give his speech. Currently the Indian representative was chairing the Committee and he got the pride of place, having the honor of officially welcoming Pemel to the podium and speaking just before Pemel got up.

"Ladies and gentlemen of the Committee," Representative Pawan said to his colleagues who were sat to either side of him, "and to all those present this morning, either in our prestigious Committee chambers or watching this event from around the Sol system, and especially to you Viceroy Pemel. It is with great pleasure that I stand before you to address you all as the sitting President of the Interplanetary Committee.

"However, as many of you know a Committee member sits on this council as a representative of their nation's government and as stipulated in article fourteen point three of this Committee's constitution, the ruling head of state of any nation may take the place of their Committee representative to address the Committee. Therefore, I introduce to you Prime Minister Slaman Devgan of the Indian Star Republic."

As Pawan stood back James shot a questioning glance across the aisle to where his uncle sat. His uncle caught his glance and shrugged but from the look on his face James knew he was worried. British Prime Minister Fairfax was sitting beside his uncle and before James could glean any more information from his uncle's face, Fairfax nudged him and began to whisper into his ear.

"I bring greetings from the Indian Star Republic," Prime Minister Devgan said as he took the podium. "And along with the other speakers here this morning I offer my warmest welcome to you Viceroy Pemel. I hope that our two nations will have a long and fruitful relationship. May I say, it is a privilege to share this podium with you and to be able to speak with you."

Devgan paused to let Pemel nod his head in thanks. "However," Devgan continued, "I am afraid that I have requested this privilege for a secondary reason, one that directly impacts the future relations of our two peoples."

Here we go, James thought.

"There is a cancer within the Human Sphere, a disease that needs to be removed if we as a species are going to forge a friendly and peaceful future with our new neighbors. I am speaking of the Haven colony."

"Oh crap," James whispered only loud enough for Suzanna to hear. "He's making a move on Haven and he has got everyone in the Sol system tuned in to hear his propaganda."

Even as James spoke Devgan's words thundered around the Committee chamber and across the Sol system thanks to the live broadcast. "It has not been made public knowledge yet but I know for a fact that the Haven colony has been lying to us from the day we first made contact with them. Worse, they have been actively involved in interstellar piracy against civilian freighters in British, French and Indian colonial space. Yet this is nothing compared to their latest atrocity.

"My intelligence agents have discovered irrefutable proof that it was Haven military ships, under the orders of their First Councilor, who launched the unprovoked attack on our new friend's ship. They tried to kill Viceroy Pemel before he could get to Earth in an attempt to disrupt relations between our two nations.

"In fact, the proof of these allegations sits in this very room. For the British government, aware of these atrocities, have been actively colluding with Haven. Of this there can be no doubt for they have even gone so far as to sneak Haven Councilwoman Suzanna Rodriguez into this Committee chamber under a false name and with false papers," Devgan said as he pointed right at Suzanna.

"Oh crap," James said again as everyone turned to look at Suzanna.

A multitude of voices broke out across the committee chamber. Some shouted abuse at Devgan denying his allegations but the majority were angry comments directed in the general direction of British delegation.

In order to get a better view of Suzanna many of the

attendants nearby stood to peer over those sat beside them. This caused a ripple effect among the entire audience as everyone tried to get a glimpse of Suzanna. It also served to worsen the racket that echoed around the chamber as everyone continued to try to shout over each other.

Suzanna remained perfectly still. Her stare never moved from Devgan's face. As James gazed over to see what she was looking at he saw a small smile spread across the face of the Indian Prime Minister. With a motion of his hand he summoned Pawan back to the podium. As he was the chairman of the committee he was supposed to be keeping the proceedings under control.

"Order, order," he shouted and when that didn't work he upped the gain on his microphone and shouted the command again.

Pawan's voice was so loud the second time that many people's hands rushed to cover their ears. The noise died down and when it was quiet enough for Pawan to be heard without shouting into the microphone he continued. "Prime Minister Devgan has not finished his address yet. I am sure that at the end of this committee hearing you will all get a chance to review the information our intelligence services are releasing to corroborate all his claims."

Stepping back, Pawan turned the podium back to Devgan. "As I was saying," he began again, "there is a cancer within the Human sphere. One that has threatened the very life of my new friend Viceroy Pemel. However, I want to assure everyone gathered here in this chamber, and everyone in the

Sol system, and especially you Viceroy Pemel, the Indian Star Republic will not let this cancer threaten our future friendship.

"Even as I speak an Indian fleet is moving into the Haven system and Indian soldiers are being landed on the Haven colony itself. We will find those responsible for the attacks on our shipping and on your personal space vessel. You can rest assured that they will be brought to justice and that the people of Haven will never again be allowed to threaten your people."

James didn't have to say it this time. The look he gave Suzanna said it all. *Oh crap.*

Chapter 6 – Propaganda Wars

'All truth is relative.' Or so they once claimed. One thing has certainly remained true for centuries. The will of the people can make or break a government. Since the advent of information technology no one man has ever been able to force his will on the people.

-Excerpt from Empire Rising, 3002 AD

21st March, 2467 AD, UN Interplanetary Committee, New York.

Almost before Devgan had uttered his last sentence a renewed uproar broke out around the Committee chamber. Once again people were on their feet shouting insults towards the British delegation and Suzanna, although James was happy to see that the majority of the antagonism was being directed at Devgan.

"Order, order," Pawan's voice boomed out across the chamber, sending people's hands to their ears once again. "This is a formal meeting of the UN Interplanetary Committee. If you can't keep control of yourselves, you will be forcibly removed. This is the last warning I am going to give," he continued without even trying to turn down the gain on his microphone.

"Thank you Representative Pawan, Prime Minister Devgan

said. "Now, to close, let me make some assurances to the people of Earth. It is not the Indian Star Republic's intention to benefit from this move. We simply wish to stop the spread of this cancer. To that end, we intend to allow free traffic of all civilian ships through what was once Haven space. You have my promise that there will be no transition fees for anyone who wishes to trade with the Kulreans and the Vestarians.

As I have already said," Devgan continued as he turned to address Viceroy Pemel face to face. "It is my deepest hope that our two peoples can form a lasting friendship. And now, I look forward to hearing what you have to say to our people."

Turning back to face the chamber Devgan raised his voice and put on his best smile. "May I present to this chamber and to the people of the Sol system, Viceroy Pemel."

As Pemel stood and approached the podium James had a hard time sitting still. The Indians were already on the move. Every moment counted. If his government and the RSN were going to salvage the situation they had to act fast. Yet almost everyone who was anyone in the British government and the Admiralty was attending this meeting. They wouldn't be able to get away for hours.

Concerned, he glanced over to his uncle. The elder Somerville was already looking at James and as James caught his eye he motioned with for James to calm down. With a sigh James let out a deep breath. *How can he be so calm?* James wondered. *If the Indians get Haven they will likely dominate that entire area of space.*

Another glance at his uncle didn't provide any answers and James' attention was drawn back to the podium once Pemel began to speak.

"Men and women of the UN Interplanetary Committee and of Earth and the Sol system," Pemel began.

As he went on James' mind wandered. Pemel had discussed his speech with James at great length prior to the meeting and James had a fair idea of what was coming. Or rather, he had a fair idea of the platitudes that would be repeated a number of times. Pemel had already met privately with most of the world's leaders and this entire meeting had largely been for show. It was a chance for the people of Earth and the Sol system to see Pemel and Earth's leaders getting on.

To keep his mind off of Devgan's hijacking of the meeting and all the consequences that were soon to follow, James focused on Pemel himself. It wasn't hard, for although James had spent a few weeks with Pemel in his home system of Kulthar, the alien's appearance was still mildly shocking every time he looked at him.

From a distance, it wouldn't be surprising to find that someone could mistake Pemel for a human. Unlike the Vestarians, Pemel and his people had two legs and two arms. Whilst he stood more than half a meter above James, from a distance he held himself in a very similar way to humans. What gave him away was his blue wavy hair. The thick blue locks that fell over Pemel's shoulders as he turned his head just looked unnatural. The most unnerving thing about the Kulreans however was their three eyes. Everything else about their facial features looked somewhat human. Their eyes however, arranged in a line around their foreheads, made the Kulreans look like some monster from stories told to frighten children.

Thoughts of Pemel's appearance turned James' mind to the images of other Kulrean bodies that were still seared into his memory. After the Overlord's fleet had been defeated in the Kulthar system James had taken *Endeavour* to Kulpath, a Kulrean colony in the same system that had been bombarded from space by the Overlord's fleet.

The destruction had been almost complete, nevertheless, *Endeavour* and almost every ship the Kulreans owned had spent more than a week searching for survivors. James had watched the live images from the first shuttles as they landed near one of the large cites. What he and the rest of his crew had seen had shocked them. Hundreds and thousands of Kulrean bodies had been scattered across the landscape, every single one of them had been broken and deformed from the orbital bombardment. Even months later he often dreamt of that day.

Suddenly James's attention was drawn back to Pemel's speech. He had said something James hadn't expected. Concentrating, James tried to replay what he had heard.

"And while I respect Prime Minister Devgan greatly, I must say that on this occasion he has got his facts wrong. I was there in the Alpha system. My ship was under attack, possibly by ships from Haven. However, I also know that Captain James Somerville and HMS *Endeavour* came to our aide. If it wasn't for his ship's bravery, I may not be alive today. I also know this; Councilwoman Rodriguez was on board *Endeavour*. She risked her life just as much as the British naval officers in their fight to protect my ship.

"I want to make it plain to everyone listening. I do not hold the British government or indeed the Havenite people responsible for the attack on my ship. I know that there can be rogue elements in any society. It is not my intention to judge your people based on the actions of a few individuals.

"I do want to add this however; among my people it is customary to allow someone accused of wrongdoing to defend themselves. I therefore wish to invite Councilwoman Rodriguez to join me on the podium and address this Committee," Pemel said as he stretched out his hand, motioning for Suzanna to join him on the podium. "She too is a foreign dignitary and I believe she should be able to answer the charges laid against her."

Devgan jumped to his feet and looked like he was about to burst with indignation but before he could say anything the British representative on the Interplanetary Committee turned on his mike and addressed the chamber. "As the representative of the British Star Kingdom, I welcome Councilwoman Rodriguez to the podium to address us all here. Haven is a human colony and the Interplanetary Committee was set up to represent all of mankind. I for one look forward to hearing her speak."

Taking her cue, Suzanna stood up. Before she walked down the aisle towards the steps to the Podium she gave James a nervous smile. *Good luck,* he mouthed to her. She simply nodded as a look of determination came across her face. James knew what that meant. Suzanna would do her best to make sure her people had a safe and secure future.

As she walked the hundred meters to the podium a deathly silence descended on the chamber. No one was sure what Suzanna was going to say but they knew there would be fireworks. Prime Minister Devgan had just effectively declared an invasion on her home planet.

"Viceroy Pemel, I thank you for your kind words," Suzanna began in a loud clear voice once she got to the podium. "People of Earth, it with great pleasure that I stand before you. Over two hundred years ago my ancestors left Earth to seek their future among the stars. Since that time, we have labored to build our own world on Haven. A world where peace and justice hold sway and every citizen is free to pursue their dreams. Aspirations I am sure every single person listening to my words can empathize with. Just as importantly, we have accomplished this without any help from the major space powers. What we have built, we have built ourselves. My people are a good, hard working people who wish to be accepted back into the human community that they left two hundred years ago.

"And it is because of this, because my people are honest and hardworking, that I must be honest with you today. It is true, our current First Councilor, Harold Maximillian, ordered elements of our navy to steal British, French and

Indian freighters to acquire their technology. What's more, it is true that those same elements of our navy tried to attack Viceroy Pemel's ship to prevent him coming to Earth.

"Yet, they do not truly represent the Haven people. They have corrupted the values that my people hold so dear. That is why I am here today. I came to Earth to warn of this attack and with Captain Somerville's help I succeeded. I also came here to address the people of Earth and this Committee. The Haven people are a proud people, yet we are not too proud to know when we need help. And so, I ask for your help today. It is my desire and the desire of the people I represent, that we become a protectorate of the British Star Kingdom. That way we can keep our sovereignty and benefit from the guidance and assistance of the British Star Kingdom. With their help, Haven can join the other worlds of the Human Sphere as a productive friend and ally.

"I have come to Earth to make this request to the British government and the UN Interplanetary Committee. The British government can help remove Maximillian from power and then provide a safe environment where the people of Haven can hold a referendum on their future. I believe my people have a right to freely decide if they wish to become a protectorate of the British Star Kingdom. Or they could decide to join the Indian Star Republic. Yet that is a choice they must make themselves. No colonial power should be able to just invade our sovereign space.

"With this Committee's help, Haven can become a productive member of the Human Sphere and begin to make up for the crimes that our corrupt leaders have committed. I do not ask you for forgiveness, for I wish to see justice served to Maximillian and those who aided him. However, I do ask that you give the people of Haven a chance to prove themselves to you. Do not let us be gobbled up by a military invasion. Allow us to determine our own fate.

"This is all I ask, and it is no less than this Committee has done in the past. Former Politburo Minister Chang was declared a war criminal for his part in the recent British-Chinese war. Yet his people, the Chinese people, were not held responsible for his actions. I only ask that Haven be treated in the same way. Do not punish us all for the crimes of the few. Allow my people to determine their own future. Do not allow us to become slaves to the Indian Star Republic. Generations of Havenites have worked and sacrificed to make Haven what it is today. Allow my people to honor their memories by choosing our own future. I urge you to consider my words. Thank you."

As soon as Suzanna stepped down from the podium the British delegation rose to their feet and began to clap. As James looked around he saw that the French and American delegations had joined them. The French would be even less happy with the prospect of the Indians gaining control of Haven and the new trade routes to Vestar and Kulthar. The American's were long standing allies of the British and the French and they too would not like to see a rival gaining power. However, it was just as likely that many of the Americans were applauding Suzanna's speech for what it was. It had taken a lot of bloodshed to win back the democracy that had birthed the United States. With the rise of the American totalitarian state in the 21st century many had thought the American experiment in democracy had come to an end. Yet with the second revolution in 2270 freedom was once again the watchword of the American public. No more so than in the American colonies and so James knew Suzanna's speech would go down well there.

Just as those who supported Suzanna's speech were obvious in their approval, so too where those who disapproved. Both the Indian and the Argentinian delegations were firmly sat on their seats with stern expressions on almost every face. Both stellar powers were long standing rivals of the British Star Kingdom.

"Well," Pawan said as he returned to the podium to resume control of proceedings. "Thank you Councilwoman Rodriguez," he said without a hint of a smile. "If you are quite finished we must now get back to our scheduled speakers. It now falls to representative Muller of the German Commonwealth of Planets to take the podium.

To James' surprise Muller declined to take the podium, stating that the current events had taken precedence over what he had to say. One by one the other scheduled speakers declined to speak. The American representative, Bob Slater, was the last to speak. He didn't decline the podium but when he addressed the chamber he was obviously going off topic.

"It is my duty to bring this monumental meeting to a close. This is the first time that another species has visited Earth and we have been privileged by your presence and your words to us Viceroy Pemel. As many of the representatives have said already, we all hope our two peoples can learn to live in harmony and friendship.

"However, as you have seen today, that will not always be easy to achieve. Especially when some here on Earth are willing to use even momentous occasions such as this to manipulate events to their advantage," Slater said as he gave Prime Minister Devgan a stern glance. "I therefore suggest that this Committee reconvene in one week's time to discuss developments in the Haven colony. That should give everyone enough time to get their facts straight. I for one will be most interested to hear more about the attack on Pemel's ship and India's intentions towards the free and independent colony of Haven.

"I suggest we have an impromptu vote now by a show of hands to agree to meet in one week's time. All in favor?" Slater asked as he raised his hand.

Behind the podium where the rest of the representatives sat all hands rose into the air but those of the Indian and Argentinian representatives. "The vote has passed," Slater said, "we will reconvene in one week. I hereby declare this meeting of the UN Interplanetary Committee closed." He lifted the gavel beside the podium and banged it twice.

Immediately, everyone within the Chamber was on their feet. Someone in the British delegation must have passed on orders to protect Suzanna for no sooner had James stood up than Suzanna and he were surrounded by British aides who escorted them out of the chamber, making sure to keep the delegations from the other nations well away.

In one of the corridors James and Suzanna ran into his uncle. "Ah, there you are," Admiral Somerville said. "That was some speech lass. I can see why you were elected to your colony's council."

"Thank you Admiral, it was from the heart," Suzanna replied. "I just hope your government will be willing to intervene and grant my request. It will mean war for your Kingdom if the Indians don't back down. I fear for my people; the war may have already begun. But will your people be willing to fight again so soon after the war with China?"

"I don't know my dear," Admiral Somerville said. "But I will tell you one thing. Neither I, nor our leadership, will just sit by and let the Indians steal two colonies that they don't deserve.

"But, enough chit chat," he continued. "Our Prime Minister has already called an emergency meeting of the COBRA committee. It will begin in one hour, all three of us are expected to be there, I have a shuttle ready to take us across the Atlantic to London. Your speech has bought us some time. Not everyone will believe Devgan's propaganda, but we have to move fast, follow me."

"Aye sir," James said instinctively to an order from a superior as he stepped after his uncle with Suzanna at his side.

Chapter 7 – COBRA

I have only ever visited Earth once, but I can tell you it is a strange place. Among the tall spires of the Emperor's Palace and those of competing corporations, seemingly infinitely small and ancient buildings are preserved for school children to visit. 10 Downing Street is but one of them.

-Excerpt from Empire Rising, 3002 AD

21st March, 2467 AD, 10 Downing Street, London.

Less than an hour later James found himself sitting in the main briefing room in 10 Downing Street, the home of the British Prime Minister. Suzanna was waiting nervously with him while his uncle had already left them to talk with someone else.

"This is all rather surreal," Suzanna said. "I grew up learning about Earth, the UN and the British government and now here I am sitting in 10 Downing Street after having just addressed the UN Interplanetary Committee. And yet, I can't enjoy any of it for the future of my people hangs in the balance."

"I know," James said as he placed his hand on Suzanna's. "I can't imagine how you are feeling at the minute. At least you will get some answers soon."

"Things are moving fast, how likely do you think it is that your government will help me now?" Suzanna asked.

"People are going to be angry after the stunt Devgan pulled," James responded. "The question is, how angry? Our navy isn't close to being back to full strength after the war with China. It takes years to build new cruisers and battlecruisers and although we have quite a few under construction, the first medium cruiser isn't scheduled to be finished for another six months.

"The Indian navy isn't a push over. They have three modern battlecruisers and if they have already made a move on Haven, then they will have time to fortify their positions. Taking them on will involve a huge risk. One that my government may not think is worth the effort."

"That is what I fear," Suzanna said. "I will just have to convince them," she added as James saw the same look of determination from earlier enter her eyes.

The door to the briefing room opened and people filed in. James counted five Peers from the House of Lords. He didn't know them all but from the ones he did know he guessed they all sat on the Lords Defense Committee. Five more MP's from the House of Commons followed them, who James likewise guessed sat on the Commons Defense Committee.

Next the Prime Minister's Cabinet appeared. First came the Home Secretary, then the Defense Secretary, and then the

Foreign Secretary. After them three Admirals took their seats. James knew all of their faces but only one personally. Admiral Russell, his uncle's closest advisor, gave him a smile as he sat down. Alongside the Admirals a General from the Royal Marines had taken his seat and he was soon joined by a General from the Army. James didn't know either of them.

Last to enter was his uncle, King Edward and Prime Minister Fairfax. When Fairfax sat down the quiet conversations that had broken out around the meeting table came to an end. "Welcome everyone," Fairfax began. "You all know why I have called this emergency meeting. We need to decide what we are going to do about Haven and India's latest move. I know we have discussed this at length but things are moving fast now and if we are going to act it must be soon. As you can see, I have invited Councilwoman Rodriguez and Captain Somerville to this meeting. I believe they will both have some insights to share with us."

James felt more than a little self-conscious as everyone looked at him and Suzanna but thankfully it only lasted a few seconds as Fairfax continued. "So, where should we begin?"

James' uncle was the first to speak up. "As I see it, we have very little option. Haven's space is closer to our territory than India's. If they annex the entirety of Havenite space, they will cut off a massive area of exploration for us. Yet that doesn't even matter. The significance of the Vestarians and the Kulreans makes everything else pale into insignificance. We cannot let the Indians have a monopoly on the trade routes to Vestar and Kulthar. I don't believe for a second Prime Minister Devgan's promise to allow free trade. They will cut us out for sure."

"But can't we use our exploration ships to find new ways to Vestar and Kulthar, cutting off the need to control Haven?" The Home Secretary asked. "Thanks to the Councilwoman we already know of the Gift and an alternative route to Haven through shift space. Surely we can find a way around Haven as well?"

Admiral Russell fielded her question, "I have run a number of simulations to answer this very question. Even if we were to devote all our exploration ships to finding a way around Haven, in the best scenarios it would take at least ten years. More likely it would take between twenty and thirty. Sure, we could get lucky and find a route within a year but this is the problem of mapping out the dark matter between stars. We simply don't know what is there until we begin exploring. For all we know, there will be no way around Haven. It may be a bottle neck in that part of space."

"And what Admiral Russell's simulations didn't account for were the actions of the Indians," Admiral Somerville added. "You can bet your ass they will devote all their exploration ships to the area around Haven. They will be trying to discover any potential routes around the colony so they can claim them for themselves at the UN Interplanetary Committee.

"Yet even this question is secondary. Let's say it would just take ten years to gain access to Vestar and Kulthar. Are we willing to allow the Indians to have ten years of unrestricted access to trade and diplomatic relations with both races? The Vestarians and the Kulreans see us as close allies now, largely thanks to the efforts of my nephew. But after ten years of India's lies, we might open up trade routes to their planets only to find they do not want to trade with us. Waiting is not an option. It is my belief that we must act now. India cannot be allowed to retain control of Haven."

"I agree," King Edward said. "Our victory over the Chinese removed a huge amount of pressure from us. For the first time in a long time our future as a nation and colonial empire looks secure and healthy. Yet, if the Indians get the upper hand in Haven it could only take them a few decades to close off all our avenues of exploration. If they managed to do that, then we would be faced with choosing to become a second-rate power or a war to the death. One that we may not be able to win. If we can stop the Indians now, then I think we need to do everything we can to make it happen."

James quickly suppressed a grin. There was no love lost between the King and himself but while he despised King Edward, he knew the King had a good head on his shoulders. When he spoke everyone else listened. *There might be hope for Suzanna's people yet,* he thought.

The power of the British monarchy had risen sharply with the birth of the British Star Kingdom and although technically the British Prime Minister officially led the nation, King Edward held almost as much power.

As stated in the restoration of the Monarchy act, King

Edward had the power to veto any act the House of Commons passed into law. The Prime Minister could still try to pass a vetoed act through, but it had to get a sixty percent majority vote in both the House of Commons and the Lords. In practice this had proved very difficult for past Prime Ministers to accomplish for as well as sitting in the House of Lords themselves, the sitting King or Queen was responsible for appointing exactly half of the new Peers appointed to the Lords. This all meant that the Prime Minister and sitting Monarch had to work together.

It had caused tension in the past but James knew there were also benefits from the arrangement. The Prime Minister kept the Monarch's ambitions from trampling the wishes of the people, for if he failed he would lose the next general election. In reverse, the Monarch kept the Prime Minister from being too focused on the immediate future and the next election, as the Monarch now held ultimate responsibility for the long term good of the British Star Kingdom. The result was a fine balancing act that had threatened to topple more than once. Yet both Fairfax and Edward demonstrated how it could work at its best.

"What kind of political power can we bring to bear on the Indians?" Fairfax asked the Foreign Secretary. "Is there any chance of a peaceful resolution?"

"I'm not optimistic," Matthew Dale, the Foreign Secretary, said. "I have had brief conversations with my counterparts in America and France. The French are very keen to make sure the Indians leave Haven alone. Likewise, the Americans are not prepared to let an independent colony be conquered.

"However, according to our agents in the capitals of the other Earth powers it doesn't look so favorable. As you can imagine, the Argentinians will support anything that hurts us. I think the Japanese and some of the other powers just want the issue to go away. They are afraid that any more violence will distract from the possibilities of trade with the Kulreans.

"The Brazilians are also keen to see the Haven question answered quickly. They have taken more than a week of bad press over their supposed involvement in the attack. They want to see Haven punished and as far as they are concerned, the Indians will do a good job of that.

"In short then, I don't think we can assemble enough support to pass a UN resolution demanding India remove her troops from Haven. The best I think we will be able to manage is to release a joint statement from us, the French, the Americans and maybe the Germans. Yet, if we don't have the political will to back up our demands with force, then the Indians will ignore us.

"They know that no matter what happens the French won't move any warships away from their border with Russia. Equally, as much as the American public might baulk at an independent colony being taken over by force, their government won't want to risk American lives for a group of people no one knew existed a couple of years ago.

"The real question is, if we threaten the Indians, can we back up our threats? Or at least, can we make it appear that we are able and willing to back up them up?" Dale asked.

"Admiral, Generals, I think that is a question for you to answer," Fairfax said.

"We can certainly make it appear we are willing," Admiral Somerville said. "Admiral Cunningham has already increased the readiness of the Home Fleet and I have sent orders for elements from Britannia, Cook and New Edinburgh to make their way to Earth forthwith. My intention is to bolster our Fast Reaction Fleet based here in Sol to give us a stick we can threaten the Indians with.

"I have already liaised with Generals Hawker and Robinson and once the fleet elements are in place, I believe we can carry out a simulated ground landing on our Mars colony. Elements of the Home Fleet can play the defenders while Rooke's bolstered fast reaction fleet can play offense. It will show the Indians we mean business."

"But won't that expose our most important colonies?" the Home Secretary asked.

"For a few weeks yes," Admiral Somerville replied. "As you know, we have some new production coming on line in a few months' time. What I have kept out of the press however, is that our first three medium cruisers being built in Britannia are ahead of schedule. The first one will begin its space trials in a week and the other two a week after that. They will be able to take over from the ships I'm moving out of Britannia."

"So you plan to move the *Fearless* back to Earth?" Fairfax asked.

"Yes, we know the Indians only have four battlecruisers. One here in the Sol system and three back in their colonies," Admiral Somerville informed the gathering. "If we are going to intimidate them, then we need to match their numbers. As you know, we still have three battlecruisers under repair and another two under construction. That leaves us with five in service. Two in Home Fleet, one in our Fast Reaction Fleet and one each at Britannia and Cook. I am loath to take the *Excalibur* away from Cook, for that would open up our colonies to an attack from the Indians should war break out and some ships slip past us.

"However, if we add *Fearless* to Admiral Rooke's fleet, that should give us two battlecruisers to the Indian's three. With our tech advantage and experience, it should show the Indians we mean business. Plus, it leaves us the option of adding one or even both of our battlecruisers from home fleet to the Fast Reaction Fleet. The Indians will know that and it should make them sweat."

"And what if the Indian's call our bluff?" the Home Secretary asked. "Clearly their actions have been premeditated. Our fleet is weaker than it has been in fifty years because of the war with China. I believe we have to operate under the assumption that they may be willing to go to war. The question is, are we? And besides that, what are we going to war over? We haven't yet discussed what we will do with Haven if the Indians recall their troops or we are forced to invade ourselves."

"I can't speak to the direction we should take on Haven, though you all know my opinion." Somerville replied. "However, if the RSN is called on to retake Haven from an Indian fleet then you can rest assured we will. The Gift gives us an enormous tactical advantage. We can have ships from Earth in orbit around Haven in twenty days. It will take the Indians almost two months. As long as we can keep the Gift a secret then we can run rings around the them. My staff have already come up with a number of tactical plans to retake Haven. It will be costly, but we can do it."

"Thank you Admiral," Fairfax said. "Let's move on then. Assuming that we can intimidate the Indians, or if that fails, we can retake Haven. What should be our aims for Haven itself?"

"We would like to become a British protectorate," Suzanna said.

"But will both our peoples accept that?" Jack Cameron, the Foreign Minister, said, turning to face Suzanna. "I'm not denying that would be the ideal outcome from our perspective. We could effectively gain control over Haven and the trade routes to Vestar and Kulthar. Yet your people have committed piracy, you took in Chang, and you attacked Pemel's ship. Public opinion is going to be against simply forgiving you and taking you under our wings.

"Any move we make towards Haven will have to be ratified in both the Commons and the Lords. The Lords will pass a bill to accept Haven, yet if public opinion is against it, it is going to be very hard to pass in the Commons.

"And that pales in comparison to the difficulties we may face in convincing your population to allow the British government to take over Haven. If your people are as independent as you have said, will they really accept giving up a good portion of their sovereignty? I can't see the UN Interplanetary Committee ratifying any attempt we make to annex Haven unless the people of Haven vote for it."

"Ah, you are forgetting one thing Home Secretary," King Edward said. "The Indians have done us a favor in that department. If they really have launched an invasion, then the people of Haven will have endured months of occupation before we could possibly liberate them. I dare say they will be more susceptible to our proposals after a few months of living under Indian rule.

"Besides," Edward continued, "Fairfax and I have a plan for the governorship of Haven if they become a protectorate. One that I think will stand a good chance of encouraging the people to side with us." As he spoke Edward flashed a smile towards James which sent a shiver down his back. King Edward had a history of using people as pawns to get what he wanted when the stakes were high. *What does he think he is going to get me to do now?* James groaned to himself.

"That still doesn't solve our problem with our own populace. How do we win them over to accepting Haven?" the Foreign Minister said.

"Home Secretary," Fairfax prompted. "Can we win a vote in

the Commons?"

"It will take a lot of work, and we'll have to cash in more than a few favors, but yes. I think we can do it. The Councilwoman's speech has already helped to move the debate on from what Haven has done to how we should treat them in the future. It may take us a day or two to formulate a full plan but once we do, I think a joint press conference between you and the Councilwoman would be in order. If you both speak directly to the British people, I think you can sway public opinion in our favor. After that, we just need to make sure we have enough votes," Jillian Strider said to Fairfax.

"In that case, I want to push forward with a vote to accept Haven's request to become a protectorate," Fairfax decided. "We have already been working along these lines for the last few weeks, we just have to step up our timetable. Councilwoman Rodriguez, I'm going to schedule a debate in both Houses on the issue in four days. I want you to open the debate by formally petitioning Parliament on behalf of the Haven government to become a protectorate.

"We will hold a vote in both houses three days after that. That gives us a week people. I want everyone to call in all the favors they have. We need to pass this with a significant majority.

"Jack, I want you and the foreign office to work around the clock with the Americans and the French. We need to put together a formal declaration that we can all sign calling on the Indians to remove their troops from Haven. I want to release it the day the debate in Parliament begins."

"Yes Prime Minister," the Foreign Minister said.

"Captain Somerville," Fairfax continued, "I want you to liaise with your First Lieutenant. I'm going to give the order to *Vulcan* to make *Endeavour's* repairs a priority. When the vote passes in Parliament I'm going to dispatch you and *Endeavour* to Haven. You can sneak past the Indian defenses and broadcast our decision to the Haven people. I also want you to get in contact with whatever is left of the Haven government and get a situation update. If we are going to have to make a move on the system, both I and your uncle will be much happier if we know we can count on the Havenites to help us. Your First Lieutenant will need to make sure *Endeavour* is ready for another long space deployment."

"Yes Prime Minister, but I am sure I can oversee..."

"No you can't," Fairfax said, interrupting James. "Because you will be retiring to your family's estate. And you will be taking the Councilwoman with you. There have already been enough leaks about her to the Indians and the press for one week. I have arranged two RSN agents to smuggle her out of London to your estate. Officially you will be enjoying a few days' holiday. I don't want to see anything about you or her on the news broadcasts except what we feed them. Understood?"

"Yes sir," James said.

"In that case I think we are done for now. We will meet again this time tomorrow for an update on your progress. You all know what to do. Let's get this done," Fairfax said.

Chapter 8 – Badminton House

As I have stated elsewhere, the aristocracy of the British Star Empire played a significant role in the establishment of the Lords of the Empire. Even today there are feuds over whose titles are the oldest and who owns the most ancient feudal buildings.

-Excerpt from Empire Rising, 3002 AD

24th March, 2467 AD, Badminton House, Gloucestershire, England.

Three days after the COBRA meeting James sat on one of the rotundas outside his family home, sipping coffee from a mug one of the maids had brought him. He was thinking how surreal his life had become.

Here he was without a care in the world enjoying the morning sun as he looked out over the peaceful lake in front of him, when around him the whole world seemed to be going crazy. Just a day after the UN session Viceroy Pemel had announced that he was leaving Earth. Officially he had said it was because he did not want his presence to be a factor that caused disharmony between the different nations. Privately, he had sent James a message explaining that if his people back on Kulthar thought he was getting involved in another species' politics, they would quickly replace him. Pemel had wished James good luck and promised he would return to have more in depth trade talks once the situation with Haven had calmed down.

James had immediately sent the message to his uncle who had no doubt sent it on to the Prime Minister. If solving the Haven issue quickly hadn't already been Fairfax's highest priority, Pemel's message would have put it there. James knew his government was desperate to open up trade negotiations with the Kulreans. Their civilization was thousands of years older than Earth's and as a result, they had many technologies that humanity hadn't even dreamt of yet.

As a result of Pemel's public announcement and the rumors of war between Britain and India the tension around the world was growing rapidly. There was also an intensive propaganda war going on as both the British and Indian governments sought to gain the moral high ground.

As far as James could see, the British were winning easily in most of the neutral countries. It wasn't too hard for his government to deny any complicity in the atrocities Haven's government had committed. On the other hand, it was impossible for the Indian government to deny that they had effectively launched an invasion of an independent colony. After all, their Prime Minister had announced it to the entire Sol system live.

Yet, while all this had been going on he had spent the last three days showing Suzanna around his family's estate. They had gone horseback riding through the fields and forests of the estate, swimming in the lake and fishing for trout in the river. He had also taken her shooting and Suzanna had shot herself a deer which the cook promised would be hung and prepared for dinner in a couple of weeks. Suzanna had been amazed at all the things they had been able to enjoy. On Haven the wildlife was a lot less sophisticated and since no horses or other domesticated animals had been a part of the colony ship's inventory, they were all new to her. Her excitement and wonder had been infectious.

It seemed, for a little while at least, that James had helped her to forget everything that was happening on her world. For his part, James had found himself enjoying Suzanna's company more and more. Yet despite more than one opportunity for him to try and take their relationship further, he had found himself holding back. His memories and feelings for Christine were still just too strong.

A creak from the door behind James caused the dog that was lying at his feet to jump up and sniff the air. As Suzanna stepped out of one of the patio doors into the rotunda it bounded over to her. The dog had already learnt that it would get a lot more attention from her than James. "It's so beautiful here," Suzanna said as she came to sit beside him.

"It's truly is," James had to agree. Growing up in Badminton House had hardened him to the wonders of the estate, but seeing it through Suzanna's eyes had re-impressed on him its beauty. It wasn't hard for James to remember the look on Suzanna's face when they had come into view of the manor house. They had turned off the main road through the county into the estate's private forest. After two miles of forest, the ground vehicle had broken out of the trees into the fields that surrounded the house.

Suzanna had gasped when she saw the fields full of sheep, cows and horses and then her eyes had spotted the lake and followed it around to where it came up to the front of Badminton House. His grandfather had undertaken an expensive remodeling to return the house to its 17th century grandeur and even James had to admit that it looked impressive.

Suzanna had immediately fallen in love and she had demanded a tour of every one of the sixty-five rooms in the house. She had especially loved the sitting room and adjoining library his grandfather had decorated with 17th century furnishings. As she had walked down the main hallway where paintings of the previous Dukes of Beaufort lined the walls James had heard her whisper, "Such a legacy."

James hadn't shared his thoughts with her but he had been thinking along the same lines. This visit to his family home was the first time he had been back since he had graduated from the naval academy. Walking down the hallway with Suzanna had been the first time it had dawned on him that one day a painting of him would hang in the main hallway. Growing up he had always known that his eldest brother would inherit the Dukedom. He had been his father's favorite and it was custom to hand the title from father to eldest son. Yet when James' father had run the Dukedom into massive debt and had then killed himself, he had left the failing business and the title to James.

His brother was an irredeemable drunk who had since moved to Britannia to drink away the stipend his father had left him. James wasn't sure if being given the family estate and business had been because his father had thought he could turn things around or because his father had wanted to have one last laugh at his second son. Either way, James had been forced to make the best of it.

"I could just stay here forever," Suzanna said as she reached her arms up to stretch out on the chair beside him.

"How did you sleep?" James asked.

"Very well," Suzanna said with a smile. "That horse riding took it out of me yesterday. I slept like a baby."

"You are a natural," James said. "I was forced to take lessons as a child but it was never my thing. After a couple of days you are already more comfortable up there than me."

"I always used to love imagining what it would be like to ride a horse as a girl," Suzanna replied. "Thank you for giving me the opportunity."

"It has been my pleasure," James said. "I'm just happy I have been able to be a good host."

"Ha, that's nonsense I'm sure," Suzanna said. "I bet the Honorable James Somerville has taken plenty of women back to his father's big estate to try and impress them."

"Not as many as you might think," James said with a smile. "My family's wealth and reputation scared most of the girls off when I was younger and I was never interested in something casual. You are the first woman I have ever brought here."

"Really?" Suzanna said, genuinely surprised. "What about Empress Christine. Didn't you bring her here when she was your princess?"

"We kept our relationship a secret from our fathers when it began," James explained. "Then, after my father's death, my family's reputation was too tarnished for a member of the Royal Family to be associated with me. We kept seeing each other but we couldn't meet in public. Eventually her father found out and made sure we couldn't meet at all. That is how I ended up in my first command at the far edge of human space."

"Well I am sorry that was your experience," Suzanna said reaching over to touch James' hand. "But at the same time I am not. Was it not on *Drake* that you became the man and leader you are today?"

"I did a lot of growing up on *Drake*, if that is what you mean?" James said.

"Yes, exactly, and it was this grown-up Captain Somerville who came to the rescue of my people and I, for one, am not sorry."

"Ha," James said putting his coffee down. "I'm glad my

heartache could be of some use to you Councilwoman."

"Oh be quiet," Suzanna said as she turned her back on James in a playful manner. "You are spoiling the view."

"I'm afraid you won't have too much longer to enjoy this break from reality," James said. "I received a message from Buckingham Palace forty minutes ago. King Edward and my uncle are coming to visit us in an hour. I imagine they have a lot of things they want to talk about."

"What?" Suzanna said, whirling on him. "They will be here in an hour. Why didn't you tell me? I need to get ready!"

"I thought we could enjoy breakfast together and then you could get ready," James answered.

"You really don't have any experience with women!" Suzanna groaned as she jumped to her feet. "I'll never be ready in an hour," she added as she hurried towards the door back into the house.

"But I have ordered breakfast," James protested.

"You are eating alone this morning Captain," Suzanna called back over her shoulder. "You should have told me as soon as you heard from the palace!"

*

An hour and fifteen minutes later, James stood dressed in one of his uniforms just outside the main doors of

Badminton House. A large shuttle had just landed on one of the front lawns and James waited to greet his distinguished guests. "Send a maid to tell Suzanna that the King has arrived," James said to one of the butlers who stood waiting with him.

When the King exited the shuttle, James descended the steps to the front door and approached him. "Welcome to Badminton House your Majesty, I am at your service," James said taking the King's hand.

"Thank you Duke Somerville," King Edward said. "My, my, it certainly is in good condition," he continued as he looked at the manor house. "Someone has put a lot of care into maintaining it. It has weathered the centuries almost as well as Buckingham Palace."

"I'm sure it doesn't really compare," James said politely. "But my grandfather did take great pride in keeping the family home in good repair. It cost him a small fortune mind you."

"I'm sure, I'm sure," Edward said. "And this was your home at one time Admiral?"

"Yes, Your highness," Admiral Somerville said from beside the King. "I was born just a few years before my father, James' grandfather, began the restoration work. I still remember seeing the house without her roof on. She looked like a ruin for a couple of years before my father finally finished his work on her."

"Well it was certainly worth the expense, his work has impressed me," Edward said. "Shall we go in and get down to business?"

"If you will follow me," James said. "I have a room prepared."

It only took a few minutes to reach the room James had ready. Without having to ask, James' butler appeared with three drinks. James' coffee was just how he liked it and as neither his uncle nor the King complained about what they received, James assumed their preferences had been taken into account. *I'll have to ask him later how he already knows what the King drinks,* James thought to himself.

"Where is Ms. Rodriguez?" James' uncle asked after taking a sip of his drink.

"She should be here any minute," James answered. "I only told her about the meeting about an hour ago. She didn't take too kindly to my delay in informing her, I haven't seen her since she left to get ready."

"Ha!" Edward shouted, almost spilling his drink. "You only gave her an hour to get ready to meet the King of the British Star Kingdom. I'm surprised she didn't shoot you. Dear me my boy, you may know how to handle a warship but you have a lot to learn about women, let me tell you!"

"I think she also said something along those lines," James said.

Just then a knock sounded on the door. When James shouted, "Enter," Suzanna rushed in.

"My sincerest apologies your Majesty, Admiral, I hope I haven't kept you waiting too long?" she said as she came over to shake Edward's hand.

"Not at all Councilwoman. We have just sat down," Edward said as he stood to shake her hand.

"I am pleased then," Suzanna said as she took the remaining seat in the room. James smiled at her but in return she shot him an accusing look.

The King is right, James begrudgingly admitted, *I do have a lot to learn.*

"I don't have much time," Edward began. "So I want to get right down to business. Fairfax and I have a proposition to make to the both of you."

Uh oh, James thought. *There is no way I'm going to like this.*

"Suzanna," Edward began. "Once the bill to accept Haven as a protectorate is passed in both houses, Fairfax and I would like to appoint you as the first Governor of Haven."

"What?" Suzanna blurted out, taken completely by surprise. "But I am from Haven, I am not British. I serve on the Haven Council. I cannot be a governor. I want to represent my people," Suzanna continued without thinking as she fired out all the reasons why the King's idea was a bad one.

"We plan to abolish the Haven Council and establish a new Senate with senators elected by the Haven population after the protectorate has been set up," King Edward cut in. "We feel that you will be able to serve your people and us far more effectively as Governor rather than just a senator.

"I will confess; I have my doubts. You are still an unknown entity. Yet I am sure you will agree that even if we can remove the Indian problem. We will still face an uphill challenge in getting your people to vote to join the British Star Kingdom. If they know in advance that one of their own will be the first Governor, then I am sure that will go a long way in alleviating their fears. Don't you think?"

"I see where you are coming from," Suzanna said in a more conciliatory fashion now that she had had a few seconds to take in the King's suggestion. "If that is the wish of the King and the Prime Minister then I will have to consider it seriously. If your government can free my planet from the Indians and secure our future, then it would be an honor to serve both your people and mine."

"Excellent," Edward said. "There is just one problem however. You were right before. No non-citizen can be appointed to a position in the British government. That is why we have you both here. We have a prerequisite to you accepting the governorship. We want you both to get married."

"No way!" James almost shouted as he rose to his feet, his anger barely under control. "There is no way you are manipulating my love life again," he added as he prepared to turn and storm out of the room. The words of his uncle barely held him in place.

"Sit down Captain, now!" Admiral Somerville said. "That is an order."

James hesitated. Almost everything inside him wanted to bolt. King Edward was once again trying to ruin his life. This time it was worse. His own uncle was against him. *How can this be happening again?*

Slowly, as James stood in place, the red mist faded. Reluctantly he sat. He would obey his uncle, if only to protect his career. *It doesn't mean I am going to do what they want.*

"That's better," Admiral Somerville said. "We know this isn't something either of you have thought about. Yet it is a duty we are asking you to take on. For the sake of both our nations. James, you are a Duke of the British Star Kingdom. In fact, you are fast becoming one of the richest Dukes in the Kingdom. Your marriage is important to our country. You cannot escape that fact.

"And Suzanna, our Parliament will never fully trust you unless you have ties to us. This marriage will make you Lady Somerville. Even if it means nothing to you, many in Britain will think it will bond you to us. They will think you less likely to put yourself or Haven before the British Star Kingdom.

"What's more. You are forgetting I have read the reports of your conversation together in Haven and elsewhere. I have also been watching you both closely. Neither of you can deny that there is an attraction between you. It's not as if we are asking you to marry someone you hate or find repulsive."

James felt his face heat at his uncle's last words. He felt like protesting but he knew it would be useless. Instead he looked over to Suzanna. When he caught her eye, she looked down and her cheeks visibly reddened.

"There, you see," King Edward said at the look on both their faces. "It's not so bad. In fact, I think being married might just do both of you a bit of good."

"But what about my people?" Suzanna asked. "If they see me as part of the British nobility then they may not accept me as their Governor."

"You will just have to convince them otherwise. You forget, we have seen you speak on behalf of your people. I'm sure you can convince them," King Edward said. "Besides, it's the famous Captain Somerville you will be marrying. The hero of Haven. I'm sure your people won't hold that against you. If anything, it will serve as a constant reminder that Haven exists only because of the RSN."

"Just as you planned it I'm sure," James said bitterly.

"Listen boy," Edward said sternly. "It's time you grow up and realize this world isn't just about you. Don't you think that if I could have, I would have loved to see my daughter happily married? Get real. You have no more freedom than I do. We each have our roles to play. My daughter came to realize that and it's about time you did as well.

"If you really don't like it you can divorce after twenty years or so. That will be long enough to cement Suzanna as Governor and see her accepted among the nobility in Britain. Then you can go running off after your heart all you want. But for now, this is your duty. This is what your Prime Minister and your King are asking of you. For the good of the people of Haven, can't you set your selfish desires aside?"

James was stung. He had fallen out with the King before. Yet then the King had just dismissed him as an unworthy subordinate. Now the King was talking to him as if he was chastising a son. It hit home. If he was honest with himself he knew he liked Suzanna, quite a lot if truth be told. And he wanted to do everything he could for the people of Haven, not least because they were her people. *Yet I'm not just going to give in to the whims of the King,* James thought. *Not again.*

"I will think about it," was all he was prepared to concede.

"Good, good," Admiral Somerville said. "That is all we ask at this stage. And Ms. Rodriguez?"

"I will think about it too," Suzanna replied.

"Well, that's not the most enthusiastic start to a marriage I have ever seen," King Edward laughed. "But it will do. How is your speech coming along?" he asked.

"It is almost finished," Suzanna replied. "James has been helping me with it and I think it is what you are after."

"Good, it needs to be perfect. It will be broadcast live across Britain and our Sol colonies. If you can sway public opinion in your favor it will win us a number of votes in the Commons. That is where we are weak at the moment and so to a certain extent we will be counting on you."

"I understand," Suzanna said. "I will be giving it my best. I know what is at stake."

"Very well then," Edward said as he stood. "In that case, we will take our leave. You both have a lot to think and talk about. We will see you tomorrow in Parliament."

James walked the King and his uncle out to their shuttle. As the King walked up the ramp to the shuttle James's uncle turned back to James. "I am sorry about this James, but we need to tie her to us. And I know you like her. It's about time you got married and produced an heir. It may sound horrible now, but you will come around. And if she is half the woman she appears to be you won't regret it either."

James said nothing. He just shook his uncle's hand and then watched him ascend into the shuttle. *I knew I wouldn't like it,* he thought as he shook his head.

*

Ten hours later James was lying in his bed thinking. He hadn't stopped since the King and his uncle had left. Suzanna hadn't been in the house when he had returned from seeing them off and one of the staff said she had gone for a walk. It was just as well as James hadn't known what to say to her.

As much as he didn't like to admit it, he knew that his way of thinking about the situation was changing. He liked Suzanna, there was no point denying that. If he had examined his feelings before, then maybe deep down, he had been hoping their relationship would develop into something. Yet he had been holding himself back. Ever since he had met Christine he had dreamt of marrying her and spending the rest of his life with her. He had even promised he would marry her.

He knew that if those feelings would just go away his life would be much easier. Yet they wouldn't, and a part of him didn't want them to. He was a man of his word. He had known that his father had been a liar even before the suicide and debt scandal had hit. James' mother had died when he was young and growing up he had watched as his father had gone through woman after woman. From an early age, he had sworn to himself that he wouldn't be like his father. Giving up his promise to Christine and his feelings for her felt like a betrayal of who he was. *How can I do that, even if it is for my country?*

His thoughts were interrupted by the sound of his bedroom door opening. Instantly James was fully awake. He tensed his muscles, ready to pounce on whoever was trying to sneak into his room.

"James," Suzanna whispered. "Are you awake?"

"Yes," James whispered back as he let out a sigh of relief. "You gave me a fright. What are you doing here?"

As James had been speaking Suzanna continued towards the bed and then slipped in beside him. "Scoot over," she said.

Bewildered James obeyed. "I think we need to talk," Suzanna explained.

"Do you want the lights on?" James asked.

"No, it might be easier in the dark," Suzanna said.

"Ok," James replied. Wanting to explain about earlier he spoke first. "I'm sorry if I offended you earlier. I was upset, but it wasn't at the prospect of marrying you. King Edward has already had far more of a say in my life than I ever wanted. I got angry at him, not at the thought of having to marry you."

"So you have really wanted to marry me all along?" Suzanna asked playfully.

"No," James blurted out. "I mean; I hadn't thought about it. It was a shock, that's all."

"Well, Captain Somerville, you are going to have to think about it. I don't think it is something we can avoid now, can we?"

"What do you think?" James asked her.

"I would be lying if I said I hadn't thought about it before. The political benefits from such a marriage would help my people a lot. But it would have put me in an awkward situation. People back on Haven might say I sold them out for you," Suzanna replied.

James' heart sunk a little, *even she sees me as a political pawn,* he thought.

"But if I am honest, I also thought about what it would be like to be with you," Suzanna continued. "You may not realize it, but you are quite handsome. And you are the hero of Haven after all. What girl wouldn't want you?"

"I don't know about that," James said, embarrassed.

"Tell me, what do you know?" Suzanna asked getting more serious. "What do you think of the King's proposal?"

"I understand where they are coming from," James began. "Our marriage would solve a lot of their problems. And it would help your people in the long run. I want only what is best for them. And I would be lying if I said I didn't find you attractive. I have loved the time we have spent together on Haven, on *Endeavour* and especially here. You are more than I ever dreamed of in a wife."

"Really?" Suzanna asked coyly.

Before James could respond Suzanna leaned over and kissed him on the lips. Caught by surprise James didn't know what to do. Yet as she leaned in more, he began to return her kisses. She pressed her body against him and then she rolled on top of him and kissed him with more vigor.

Images of Christine filled James' mind.

Instinctively James broke away from Suzanna's lips and rolled her off him. "I'm sorry, I can't," he said.

Rolling onto his side away from Suzanna he stared at the rose compressed between two panes of glass that was standing on his bedside table. The moonlight coming in the overhead window illuminated it perfectly. He had to fight back the tears that threatened to run down his cheek. "I'm sorry," he said.

Suzanna looked over James' body to see what he was gazing at. "A rose, the flower of the house of Windsor?"

"Yes," James replied. "I picked it for Christine on our first date. When I gave it to her I promised to love her for the rest of my life. She sent it back to me when her father persuaded her to marry Na."

As Suzanna came to realize the depth of James' hurt she snuggled up to him. "I'm sorry," she said as she turned him around and pulled one of his arms around her. "I understand; I don't want to take her place in your heart. But I want my marriage to be real and not just a scam. Can you find room in your heart for me as well?"

"I don't know," James replied. "I would like to. You deserve to be happy, to be loved. If we have to get married, then I want to give you those things. But I can't change how I feel, I'm just confused."

"There is no rush," Suzanna said. "If we have to get married for our people then that is what I will do, and I know you, you will too. But love takes time, we just need to give it time to grow. I am prepared to wait; I know you can make me happy. And, though I don't want to boast too much, I believe I can make you fall in love with me," she finished as she gave James a playful tickle.

"I guess Councilwomen think a lot of themselves back on Haven," James said as he tickled her back.

As they struggled, Suzanna's hand brushed up James' leg. He tensed.

"I'm sorry," Suzanna said. "I don't want to rush you. Let's just talk, I don't want you to do anything you are not ready for."

"Ok," James replied as he pulled her into a tighter hug, "talking I can do."

"Do you think Haven can hold off the Indian fleet?" Suzanna asked after a couple of minutes of silence.

"I don't think so," James said, much happier to talk of

something else. "If the colony still had the defenses it had before the attack by the Overlord's fleet then maybe. The two defense stations would certainly have been a big surprise. But no, I'm afraid not.

"The Indians have three battlecruisers in their colonies. On its own, one would probably be able to destroy what is left of the Haven fleet. With all three together, Haven doesn't stand much of a chance. I'm sorry, the Indians are just too strong."

"What will they do to my people?" Suzanna asked.

"It depends," James said. "The Indians will no doubt have some ground troops with them. They maintain a far larger army than we do. Will your people try and resist a ground invasion?"

"Maximillian will, of that I am sure," Suzanna said. "I think the people will rise up too. They have all grown up hearing horror stories from Earth. Since coming to Earth I am sure they have been exaggerated over the years, but we didn't know any better."

"Then there will be fighting on the streets," James said, not wanting to hide the truth from her. "The Indians will show no mercy, at least until they have gained full control over the planet. I fear there will be a lot of deaths."

James felt a wetness on his shoulder as a few tears escaped Suzanna's eyes. "Then we have to make this marriage work," she said. "My people are counting on me. I can't protect them now, but I will be there for them in the future."

"We will both be there for them," James said, making up his mind.

Chapter 9 – Captain Denning

War is a strange thing, even in defeat and certain death mankind can find ways to claim some small victory.

-Excerpt from Empire Rising, 3002 AD

24th March, 2467 AD, *ISF Shiva*, shift space near Haven.

Admiral Kumar sat on the bridge of her Battlecruiser, *Shiva,* looking at the holo display's representation of her fleet. Alongside *Shiva's* sister ship *Vishnu,* Kumar's fleet consisted of four heavy, five medium and eight light cruisers along with twelve destroyers and twenty frigates. Her fleet counted over half of the Indian Space Force's ships among its numbers. The significance was not lost on her; her fleet was on one of the most important missions an Indian fleet had ever attempted.

In five minutes her fleet would drop out of shift space into the Haven system. Kumar didn't know exactly what to expect but she knew that there would be nothing that could stand in her way. In just a matter of days Haven would be added to India's colonial systems. After that Kumar would send ships to take the small Havenite colony in what the Havenites called the Independence System along with whatever other mining operations they had in the surrounding systems. In all, more than twenty systems would be added to Indian space. Together they would increase the number of systems under her government's control by almost twenty percent. No colonial power had seen their empire expand so quickly in over one hundred years.

"Exiting shift space in five four three..." one of the Lieutenants on the bridge announced.

Kumar braced herself for the slight wobble that went through the ship as it exited shift space. Indian intel suggested that the American and British ships didn't have such a pronounced feeling. Kumar wasn't surprised, their technology always seemed to be a step ahead of the other colonial powers. As a small amount of bile threatened to escape up her throat, she couldn't help but be jealous. *It doesn't matter,* she said to herself as she regained control, *the Havenites will find out our missiles are just as deadly as any other Earth power.*

"Fill me in on the details as our sensors update," Kumar ordered her bridge crew.

Satisfied she would be alerted if anything was out of the ordinary, she sat back in her command chair and watched her fleet form up around her. The holo display of the ships in shift space had been a projection of where the ships should be. In shift space it was impossible for ships to actually detect each other. The fleet had exited shift space slightly out of formation and those ships that needed to were maneuvering back into their allotted positions.

"I have three or four ships in the outer system. They appear to be freighters transporting raw materials to Haven," one of the Lieutenants reported. "I'm also picking up emissions from two or three warships in the inner system but I can't be sure at this range. One thing is for sure, there is a heck of a lot of activity going on in orbit. It looks like there are tens of space stations under construction."

"Move the fleet towards Haven," Kumar ordered. "Let's not give them any more time to prepare than we have to."

*

Captain Denning was taking a tour of his ship as it sat in orbit around Haven. It had taken his crew two days to repair enough of the damage *Endeavour* had caused before they could jump into shift space and return from the Gift. That had been over twenty days ago. Now they were safely back in the Haven system.

First Councilor Maximillian had been far from pleased when he heard that *Endeavour* had somehow known about the Gift. Denning wasn't sure what Admiral Harris and *Solitude* were doing in the Alpha system but he knew that whatever it was it was important. He hadn't seen Maximillian so nervous before.

Denning had requested that his ship dock with the single repair yard that had survived the Vestarian attack. However, Maximillian in his anger had refused. Denning's crew had been forced to continue the repairs in orbit. He was currently finishing an inspection of the reactor that had just been brought back online.

"Everything looks as good as new Chief," Denning said to *Dauntless'* Engineer.

"Aye Captain, I just wish we could get some specialized repair suits to send the crew out to repair the damage to the outer hull. I'm sure we look like a wreck on the outside," Chief Garcia said.

"I don't doubt it," Denning said. "But at least we are combat worthy."

Both men paused when a combat siren went off. "Captain to the bridge," Denning's First Lieutenant called over the ship's COM. "Captain to the bridge. Everyone else to battle stations. We have an incoming fleet."

"Later Chief," Denning called as he sprinted out of the reactor room towards the turbo lift to the bridge.

"Status report?" Denning demanded as he bounded onto the bridge.

"Multiple warships just lit off their impulse drives, I'm counting over thirty and the number keeps increasing as our computers get more time to analyze the data," his First Lieutenant reported.

"Any idea who they are?" Denning asked.

"They are not Vestarian, unless the Vestarians have made a major improvement in their drive technology. They must be ships from one of the Earth nations. Maybe the British sent a fleet to make sure we aren't attacked again?" the sensor officer asked hopefully.

"I doubt it," Denning said. "There is no way the British assembled a fleet this large so fast. It could only be one of the other Earth powers. India I'd guess. And if they've brought so many ships I can't see their intentions as friendly."

Two hours later, when the electromagnetic radiation from the new ships reached Haven, Denning had no doubt about the Indians' intentions. The large fleet had split off into two sections. In the front section two large warships led a host of smaller ones. Denning guessed they were both battlecruisers. Certainly, they were far larger than the Haven Defense Fleet's flagship *Solitude*. That hardly mattered for *Solitude* was a long way away from Haven at the minute.

The rear section was dominated by four ships that almost matched the battlecruisers in size. From the visuals, there was no sign of offensive weaponry and Denning guessed they were troop ships. That meant one thing. The Indians were here to stay, whether the Havenites would welcome them or not.

"I'm getting a COM message from the First Councilor, Captain," an officer on the bridge reported.

"Put it through to my office, I will take it there," Denning ordered as he stood and walked out of the bridge into his adjoining office.

"Captain Denning," First Councilor Maximillian said once Denning opened the COM channel.

"First Councilor," Denning began. "Our situation looks bleak."

"You are correct," Maximillian said. "This is what I have feared ever since we made contact with the earthlings. Yet we are still Havenites, I don't intend to make things easy for these Indian scum."

"I expected nothing less from you First Councilor." Denning said. "But I don't think there is much the Haven Defense Fleet can do to help you. This fleet is going to swat us out of existence without even having to pause for breath."

"We have the orbital missiles we have been installing for the last three months. Won't they hold the Indians off?" Maximillian asked.

"Not against such a large fleet. They may cause a dent or two, but that will be all," Denning said.

"Well, no matter," Maximillian said crossly. "I will be addressing the nation in thirty minutes. I will be calling on every able-bodied person to begin preparations for a ground resistance. If we can't stop them in space, then we will make them bleed once they land."

"Yes sir, I'm sure our people will respond to your call," Denning said. "May I suggest we set our warships onto autopilot. They can fire a single broadside to coincide with the orbital missiles. Even with the crews on board I'm not sure we could do any more than that. And having another thousand trained personnel on the ground might make a difference in the ground war."

"No you may not," Maximillian said. "You have already failed me once Denning. You should never have let *Endeavour* get past you at the Gift. You are not going to fail me again. I am placing you in charge of our space forces. You are to destroy as many of the Indian ships as possible. If you can, I want their troop ships taken out."

"But Sir," Denning protested. "*Hawk* is the larger warship, shouldn't her Captain be in charge of our forces?"

"Captain Tash was promoted from Second Lieutenant when both his seniors were killed in the battle with the Vestarians. You have far more experience. I am putting you in command. See that my orders are carried out Captain."

"Yes sir," Denning said as Maximillian cut the COM channel.

For more than half an hour Denning stared at the approaching Indian fleet on the small holo display in his office. Finally, he came up with a plan that he thought might just work. Quickly, he composed a message to every crew member on board the remaining four Haven Defense Fleet ships. They needed to know they weren't coming back from this mission. Once done he jumped up and strode into the bridge.

"You have all read the message I sent to our personnel?" he asked as he sat down in his command chair. Everyone nodded at him. "If you need to take a few minutes to compose a message to your loved ones, you have the next half an hour to do so. After that I expect everyone to be at their battle stations until the end.

"Navigation officer, take *Dauntless* along the course I have sent you. Signal the rest of our ships to take up station astern of us," Denning ordered.

As soon as *Dauntless* moved around Haven out of sight of the Indian ships the other Haven Defense Fleet ships followed. For the next three hours, *Dauntless* sped away from Haven in the opposite direction to the incoming Indian fleet. Then, as one, the Havenite ships braked, turned around and accelerated directly towards Haven.

"How are the alterations to our ship coming?" Denning asked the Chief Engineer over the COM channel.

"They are about done sir," the Chief answered. "It's not going to be perfect but if we survive it might just fool someone."

"It's the best chance we have," Denning said. "Let's just hope someone isn't paying attention in the Indian fleet."

Denning knew his plan was a long shot. Since *Endeavour* had first showed up at Haven and used a few tricks the RSN had learnt in previous interstellar wars, Admiral Harris had made it a priority for Haven spies to get as much information as possible on all the conflicts that had taken place in the Human Sphere since the Haven colony ship had left Earth. Denning knew what Admiral Harris had been up to and he had poured over the information the spies had turned up. There had been very little details about most of the battles as the various governments had classified a lot of the data. However, Denning had been able to read between the lines on a number of occasions. As he had been searching for any kind of plan on how to deal with the Indians, one encounter had popped into his memory. At the beginning of the British war with the Chinese one Captain had somehow managed to destroy a far superior foe. Denning had a fair idea of how he managed to pull off such a feat. Replicating the move was the best option he had and the damage to his ship that was not yet repaired might be the one thing that would allow them to get away with it.

After another three hours of accelerating towards Haven, Denning's four ships swung around the planet already traveling at their maximum speed. "Ignore our safety protocols, continue our maximum acceleration," Denning ordered.

"Aye sir," the navigation officer ordered.

The Valstronium armor human warships were coated in protected them from cosmic rays and particle strikes as well as from enemy fire. However, once the relativistic speeds crossed a certain threshold the armor could not protect the ships and their crew. Denning knew it hardly mattered if his crews suffered massive radiation poisoning. They would be dead long before the radiation killed them and, if by chance a stray cosmic particle destroyed one of his ships, it wouldn't decrease their chances of success. On the other hand, the faster they were going the more likely his plan was to work.

"Signal the orbital missiles to fire in thirty seconds," Denning ordered.

*

"Admiral, the Haven ships are rounding the planet, they are coming straight at us," one of *Shiva's* sensor officers called out.

"They didn't run away after all," Kumar said. "Give them a full broadside as soon as we get into range."

"That will be in ten minutes Admiral," the tactical officer called.

"Missile launch!" the sensor officer called out in alarm.

"From where?" Kumar demanded.

"From everywhere," the sensor officer blurted out. When Kumar shot him a withering look, he elaborated. "Ah, I mean, from all over the planet. They must have had missiles sitting in orbit just waiting to launch at us."

"How many?" Kumar asked, as she looked at the holo display. There were too many for her to count.

"The gravimetric sensors are picking up over one hundred and fifty," the sensor officer replied.

"Gamma formation," Kumar ordered. "Signal our lead ships to fire on the Haven warships when they enter range. The rest of the fleet is to focus on engaging those missiles. I'm not going to let those Havenites destroy one of my ships."

Damn them, she thought. *They must have been preparing for an attack for months. They are not supposed to have missiles with that kind of range.* "What are the sensors saying about those missiles?" she asked.

"They look bigger than our battlecruiser missiles," the sensor officer responded. "Their acceleration rate is not as good as ours though. They must have sacrificed payload and maneuverability for extra range."

That is more like it, Kumar thought, *they should be easy to pick off.*

*

"They are changing formation," one of Denning's officers announced.

"Good," Denning said as he watched the holo display change. "They are more worried about the missiles from Haven. After they pass us, take us in right behind them," he ordered the navigation officer.

For the next ten minutes Denning watched the missiles that had been fired from Haven catch his ships. The missiles were capable of far greater acceleration rates and had a greater top speed allowing them to quickly catchup with his small flotilla. Just as they overtook his ships, the lead ships in the Indian formation opened fire with their own missiles.

"Forty missiles inbound," his sensor officer reported.

Denning had to wait another minute before his ships could open fire, as their range was not as great as the Indians'. "Firing," the tactical officer announced as ten new dots appeared on the holo display and accelerated after the swarm of Haven missiles.

"Indian missiles entering engagement range in fifty seconds," someone on the bridge shouted.

"Signal the other ships," Denning ordered. "Wish them luck."

As the Indian missiles entered the range of the Havenite warship's point defenses tens of AM missiles reached out to take them out. Forty became thirty-five and then thirty. Yet the four Havenite warships alone and outnumbered couldn't hope to fend off so many missiles.

"It's time Chief," Denning called out over the COM channel. "Navigation, as soon as the Chief blows the charges put us into a roll along the trajectory I sent you."

This was a part of the plan Denning hadn't shared with the

other Captains. Staring death in the face had forced him to make some tough decisions. His actions would almost guarantee the other ships would be destroyed, but when they were all going to die anyway it hardly mattered.

Just seconds after giving the command Denning was thrown about in his command chair as a number of explosions rocked his small frigate. The inertial dampeners failed to adjust quickly enough to one of the largest explosions. The increased g-forces caused Denning to black out for a moment. Thankfully the navigation officer managed to stay awake just long enough to throw the ship into the roll Denning had requested.

To the sensors of the five missiles homing in on Denning's frigate it looked as if the small warship had suffered some sort of catastrophic drive failure. Their preprogrammed targeting algorithms recalculated the threat the frigate posed. Four of the five missiles retargeted themselves on the other warships. One, realizing that it couldn't re-orientate itself in time, still dove towards the stricken frigate. However, the milliseconds it had taken to make its decision and the violent roll *Dauntless* had been thrown into, caused the missile to overshoot its target. Sensing this, the missile detonated as it passed *Dauntless,* causing a wave of electromagnetic energy to wash over the ship's armor, adding to the destruction of the ship's outer hull and nudging the ship off course.

*

"All Havenite ships destroyed," the tactical officer reported to Admiral Kumar.

She only nodded as she had been watching the missile salvo's progress on the holo display. It had been the first missiles Indian ships had fired in anger in over eighty years. They had performed admirably. Now it was time to test their point defense technology.

"Order all ships to turn their ECM jammers to full," Kumar ordered. "I don't want to take any chances."

"Flak cannons firing now," her tactical officer announced.

Only *Shiva* and *Vishnu* were equipped with flak cannons. After the British had revealed the effectiveness of the technology in their war with the Chinese every other Earth power had been scrambling to design and produce their own. Kumar knew that their design wasn't yet as effective as the British one, nevertheless she was still thankful to have them.

As she watched, ten, then twenty of the one hundred and sixty missiles on the plot disappeared. Green plasma bolts filled space as the point defense plasma cannons opened up. Within seconds, hundreds of AM missiles streaked away from her ships to intercept the Havenite missiles.

The holo display became too cluttered to make anything out, as multiple explosions signaled the destruction of missile after missile. Kumar grabbed the armrests of her command chair as the navigation officer threw the large battlecruiser into an evasive roll. Without looking, she knew that one missile must have locked onto the flagship.

Before she had time to look at the holo plot to see where it was a small explosion sent a tremor through the bridge.

"Were we hit?" Kumar asked, almost shocked.

"It was a proximity detonation," an officer called out. "No damage reports coming in."

"And the rest of the fleet?" Kumar called out.

"We lost the frigate *Bhadra* and the destroyer *Ketu* took a direct hit. The Captain is reporting that they have major internal damage. His ship is no longer battle worthy."

"Damn," Kumar swore. India's small fleet meant that there was stiff competition for senior command slots. She knew the other admirals would use any ship losses she suffered against her. "Signal Ketu to fall back and join the squadron protecting the troop transports. Then fire a second missile salvo. Target anything in orbit that looks even remotely military. I don't want any more nasty surprises.

*

Denning came to with a throbbing headache. As he touched his head he saw blood on the tips of his fingers. "Are we still in one piece?" he called out.

"Mainly," his First Officer said. "We took a proximity hit which burnt off most of our valstronium armor. Parts of decks four, five and six are open to space. It also threw us slightly off course. However, both port missile tubes are still functioning, I think your plan will still work."

"No one is firing on us then?" Denning asked as he peered at the holo display. His ship had already passed the first Indian fleet and the second one was approaching them quickly.

"I think they have forgotten about us sir," the First Officer said, smiling. "Just like you said they would!"

"Do you have a firing solution set up?" Denning asked as he ignored the look of glee on his subordinate's face. There was nothing to be happy about, they would all be dead in a few minutes.

"Yes, we will reach our optimal firing point in twenty seconds," the officer answered.

"Fire when ready then," Denning ordered.

As he put his hand to his head to try and stop the throbbing, Denning sat back to watch the devastation his two missiles would cause. He was sure the troop ships were equipped with enough point defenses to take out more than two missiles. But he hoped that whoever designed the ships hadn't thought an opponent would get so close before firing. It would take the troop ship he was targeting a few vital seconds to track his missiles before they could open fire. That would hopefully be just enough time.

If only we hadn't been thrown off course, Denning thought, *then we really might have caused them some damage*. His initial plan had included ramming one of the troop ships, that was impossible now. As it was, they still had a good chance to take out one of the ships.

"Firing," the First Officer called.

Denning didn't reply, he just let a large smile play across his face. *I did it Maximillian you bastard, now it's your turn to make them bleed*!

"Sir," his sensor officer called out, "a destroyer is falling back from the main fleet. I'm detecting an energy spike. I think they are charging their plasma cannons."

I *guess we are not going to get to see if our ruse worked*, Denning thought. "It's been an hono..." he began to say but was cut off as three plasma bolts tore through the bridge, vaporizing everyone around him. Within seconds the frigate blew apart.

*

"What was that?" Kumar demanded as an explosion erupted on the holo display, dangerously close the troop transports.

"It was one of the damaged Havenite frigates," the tactical officer called out. "The *Ketu* just destroyed her. Wait! I'm detecting two missiles homing in on one of the troop transports, that frigate must have fired on it."

Kumar didn't even bother swearing, her mind had focused on the two missiles. They had crossed half the distance to the troop transport. *Come on, come on,* she thought, *open fire you fools*!

Almost as if they heard her thoughts the troop transport opened fire. A hail of plasma bolts surrounded the two missiles. Yet in their haste someone had fired too soon and they all missed. Then three AM missiles shot out. Two homed in on one of the missiles. One detonated just meters away from the missile and it disappeared in the explosion. The other missile sensed the incoming AM missile and jinked out of its way.

Before the troop transport could fire again the missile bore down on it and punched through the transport's outer armor. Kumar was about to let out a sigh of relief when nothing happened, then the sensors showed a massive explosion erupt out of the side of the transport ship. Almost a fifth of the ship's port side seemed to disappear in a fire ball.

Kumar sat back in despair. Her one command had been to get General Malhorta's troops safely to the ground. She had failed. There was no covering it up. She was going to be eaten alive when she returned to India.

I only have one hope, she said to herself as her career evaporated before her very eyes. *I need to make sure Haven is swiftly pacified, maybe then I will be allowed to keep my command.*

Ten minutes later she finally managed to get General

Malhorta on a COM channel.

"What is the damage General?" she asked nervously.

For a few seconds the General stared at her with fiery eyes. Kumar could guess what he was thinking. "Let me remind you," she said as confidently as she could. "I am still your commanding officer. If you won't follow orders I will have you replaced."

"There are almost two thousand dead," Malhorta said. "And another three thousand wounded or still missing."

"I am sorry Admiral, but we are at war." Kumar replied without thinking. The numbers had shocked her.

"Sorry!" Malhorta shouted, "Sorry? I should hope so Admiral. They are all lives that will fall on your shoulders. I haven't even landed yet and I have lost almost an eighth of my force!"

"Can you still complete your mission?" Kumar asked, trying to regain control of the conversation.

"Of course I can," Malhorta replied shortly. "I'm not going to let these backward Havenites get the best of me."

Ignoring the jibe, Kumar replied, "well then prepare to land. But remember, you must hold your fire against civilians. If and only if they open fire on you can you return fire. Don't forget, we are trying to win hearts and minds here."

"And what about any Havenite military formations?" Malhorta asked.

"You have permission to use maximum force against any military forces, I want our causalities kept to a minimum," Kumar replied.

"I would have thought that should have been a priority from the beginning of the battle," Malhorta retorted. He cut the COM channel before Kumar could reprimand him.

Chapter 10 – The Fall of Haven

It was rare for a war before the rise of the Empire to involve ground troops. The British-Indian war was one of the few exceptions.

-Excerpt from Empire Rising, 3002 AD

24th March, 2467 AD, Haven.

Twenty minutes after his heated conversation with Admiral Kumar, General Malhorta sat in one of his shuttles as it dove through Haven's atmosphere towards the landing zone he had identified near the outskirts of Liberty, Haven's capital. Already his ships in orbit had bombarded a number of military installations. From what intel he could gather, the majority of the colony's military units had entered the main cities and taken up defensive positions. They obviously planned to make him fight building to building for control of the planet.

He wasn't so naive as to think he could hold an entire planet with just thirty-five thousand men. Fighting building to building would be suicide. All he had to do was control the major industrial and political locations. He would leave the rest of the capital and the planet to the Havenites. At least until he had more intel on where the main army formations were hiding.

"We're picking up ground radar," the shuttle copilot called out. "Launching anti-radar missiles now."

"Signal the shuttles to spread out, no sense giving them easy targets," Malhorta called.

They had taken out as many anti-air installations as they could identify from orbit but he knew there would always be more too well hidden to destroy.

"SAMs are incoming," the copilot informed everyone on the shuttle. "Brace for maneuvers."

Ignoring his own safety, Malhorta watched the unfolding battle on the HUD of his combat armor. He had twenty shuttles in the first landing wave and as he watched, over fifty missiles lifted off from different parts of Haven's capital towards them. Before they even reached the shuttles, just as many missiles left the shuttles and tracked in on the launch sites.

Plasma point defenses took out most of the incoming missiles and the powerful ECM of his shuttles defeated all but one of the rest. The final one took out one of his shuttles, killing the eighty soldiers on board. When none of the launch sites returned fire Malhorta was satisfied they had been destroyed.

Before he could relax over thirty new blips appeared at the extreme edge of the HUD's field of vision. His HUD was getting updated information from the ships in orbit and as soon as the blips appeared text scrolled alongside them, informing him that they were some kind of atmospheric fighter. Clicking his COM unit to change the channel he gave an order, "Echo flight, you are free to engage."

"Acknowledged," a voice replied.

Within seconds ten new blips appeared behind the incoming fighters. Hal Tejas were the latest Indian multirole fighter. Capable of both atmospheric and space flight the Hal Tejas were designed to be able to engage shuttles trying to invade an Indian colony. They were outfitted with the latest stealth technology to allow them to wait on the edge of a planet's atmosphere and engage shuttles as they broke through the atmosphere. Malhorta had requested two squadrons of them be included in the invasion force knowing that they would come in handy in situations just like this.

The squadron of Hal Tejas swooped down behind the incoming Havenite fighters and released a spread of missiles almost before the Havenite fighters knew they were in danger. In the blink of an eye more than twenty of the Havenite fighters disappeared. The rest scattered. Four managed to launch missiles at the shuttles and Malhorta cursed when one got through, destroying another eighty of his men.

Deciding his landing forces had taken enough losses, Malhorta ordered the squadron of Hal Tejas to do a pass over the LZ. Sure enough, more than thirty ground search radars came online. Almost as soon as they came online, missiles from the Hal Tejas took them out but five ground sites managed to fire. They took out two of his fighters before the Hal Tejas accelerated back up to the edge of the atmosphere, ready to pounce on any more Havenite fighters that might show up.

Now it is our turn, Malhorta thought as the remaining eighteen shuttles approached the LZ.

A couple of anti-air installations tried to fire on them but were quickly silenced by the shuttle's fire. Then, before Malhorta realized it, the familiar bump of the shuttle touching down forced him to take his focus off his HUD. "Everyone out," one of the Lieutenants leading the soldiers in the shuttle shouted. Malhorta waited until the men were out and followed them.

"All shuttles are to take off," Malhorta ordered over the COM, "Echo flight, prepare to give us ground support if we need it."

The LZ Malhorta had chosen was in a large opening about three kilometers from the edge of Liberty city. It was surrounded on three sides by thick forest but there was an open route straight into the city. Peering around at his surroundings, Malhorta confirmed what he had already seen from space. Opening a COM channel to the Colonel in charge of the first wave of soldiers he gave out orders, "Colonel, once you set up our perimeter I want you to push a few squads into the forest on our flanks. If the Havenites try to push any forces our way, I want to have advanced warning. Then focus on our forward defenses. If I have guessed correctly, they may and try to rush us. The best way to stop an invasion is to cut off the LZ."

"Yes sir," the Colonel replied.

Malhorta left him to it, he was one of Malhorta's best officers and was well capable of handling his troops. *Now we wait,* Malhorta thought.

Malhorta wasn't disappointed. Fifteen minutes after they landed and twenty before his second wave of troops was due to arrive, he received a report of units moving in the forest around them. A number of ships in orbit were picking up heat signatures through the thick canopy of the alien trees. Then his scouts reported contact.

"Walkers," Colonel Sai called over the COM. "They have some form of large battle suits, more like mobile armor. They are able to get through the forests where tanks couldn't. Our scouts say they will be on us in a couple of minutes."

"Engage at will," Malhorta ordered. Switching his COM channel, he contacted one the destroyers in orbit and gave out fire orders. He couldn't risk calling in an orbital strike so close to his troops but he could thin out any reinforcements that were hiding in the forests. *Not yet though,* he said to himself.

For the next two minutes an eerie silence descended on the men around him. They all knew what was coming but there was nothing they could do yet. Then, just as they had been warned to expect, one, two and suddenly tens of soldiers in bulky armor appeared on the edge of the forest. As soon as they came into view of the hastily prepared Indian defenses, they opened fire.

Malhorta already knew the Havenites didn't have any plasma weapons but, as a round of whatever weapon they were using struck a soldier not twenty feet away from him, he knew the battle wouldn't be one way. Peering over the mound he was hiding behind, his suspicions were confirmed. Almost half of the enemy soldiers were hefting heavy gauss cannons. The momentum alone from rounds fired from such weapons would be enough to rip one of his men's combat armor in two. He had already seen the evidence.

"Open fire," Colonel Sai ordered his troops.

Hundreds of plasma bolts burnt through the Havenite troops. Some jumped back into cover but more than fifty were mowed down within the first few seconds. Even without targets, the Indian troops continued to pour fire into the forest, knowing that their plasma bolts would burn through leaves and branches to hit their targets.

The hail of plasma bolts kept the Havenite soldiers pinned down. Then, in ones and twos, they peeked out of their cover to return fire. A standoff developed as both sides held firm, trading pot shots at each other. Then walkers came into view.

All of a sudden the fire from the Havenites intensified. Gauss cannon fire doubled and the walkers themselves began to fire even before they cleared the tree line. The walkers held a different weapon in each hand. From one, exploding shells erupted out of what looked like a large rifle and began to cause havoc among the Indian defenses. From the other weapon, more gauss cannon rounds also peppered Malhorta's men.

Malhorta had to admit they were impressive, standing almost three times taller than he did in his combat armor and almost four times as wide, they looked like some kind of superhuman robotic construction. In addition to the walker's two handheld weapons, a large mean looking gun was mounted on the shoulders of each of the walkers. Malhorta didn't want to find out what it fired.

As soon as they cleared the trees, multiple missiles launched from the backs of each walker. "Take cover," Malhorta shouted to his men, already cursing himself for wasting so much time admiring his opponents.

Malhorta knew the AM missile units they had set up were launching counter missiles into the air. They were to take out the new ordnance. Yet he wasn't sure they would get them all. Several large explosions erupted around him suggesting they had failed.

Ignoring the damage his forces were taking, Malhorta peeked his head out from the cover he was taking. *They are still coming,* he cursed. *Surly we should have hit one by now.*

Ducking back behind his cover, Malhorta replayed the initial images of the walkers appearing on his HUD. The edge of the forest was about half a click from the front-line Colonel Sai had set up. At that range their plasma rifles should have been able to do some damage to the walkers but he saw bolt after bolt hit the walkers and appear to do no damage.

"They are armored in Valstronium," Malhorta called over the COM to Colonel Sai.

"Acknowledged," Colonel Sai responded. He switched the COM channel and issued new orders to his troops.

Malhorta switched back to watching the walkers. They had stopped firing missiles and were raining down an incredible amount of fire on the Indian positions as they advanced. Their large gauss cannons were blowing holes in the earth works his men had hastily thrown up while their rifles were firing hundreds of rounds that were exploding among his men.

More than two hundred of Malhorta's men were already down. Then the tide turned. Following Colonel Sai's orders some of his soldiers had ditched their plasma cannons and switched to shoulder mounted rockets. A number of them were hit as soon as they stood up to take aim on the walkers but enough got their shots off to take out seven walkers.

As the enemy fire withered from their losses, every soldier opened fire on the walkers and another wave of missiles reached out, taking out another four. Looking over to the other flank, Malhorta could see that the battle was going their way; there were a number of burning wrecks where walkers had been.

An explosion threw him to the ground. Warnings went off on his HUD, alerting him that his armor was dangerously close to overheating. Confused, Malhorta switched his HUD display to see through the eyes of one of his soldiers as he engaged the walkers. Instinctively, he threw his arms up to protect himself as a bright light reached out from the large cannon mounted on a walker's shoulder and vaporized the soldier whose feed he was watching. *Lasers,* Malhorta swore.

"I want those walkers taken out now!" Malhorta ordered as he picked himself up. "Concentrate all plasma fire on the nearest walker and take it down. Missiles, focus on the walkers at the back of their formation."

Malhorta poked his gun around the mound he was using as cover and added his fire to the closest walker. As tens of bolts hit it, it looked as if they were having no effect. Then, slowly, a red glow appeared on the spot where most of the bolts were hitting. The Indian soldiers focused their aim on that spot and within seconds the walker exploded. Two more exploded from missile strikes. That left only nine in the flank Malhorta was fighting on.

Satisfied that his men could handle the remaining walkers, he ducked down and looked at his HUD to get a better idea of how the whole battle was going. The other flank had been more severely hit by the walkers but they were holding their own. Thermal images from the ships in orbit indicated that there was another wave on their way. *You're too late,* Malhorta said to himself when he looked at the timer for his reinforcements. His force had been reduced from sixteen hundred fully combat ready soldiers to a little less than a thousand men. Any other force and Malhorta would be worried they might break, but Colonel Sai had trained them for just this kind of operation. He was sure they would be able to hold out for another two minutes.

"Tracked vehicles coming at us front and center," a Captain called over the COM, distracting Malhorta. He swung around to see the new threat. Whoever was in charge of the Haven ground forces was throwing everything they had at his beachhead, hoping to drive him away from the LZ. Over forty tracked vehicles were racing across the open ground between the LZ and Liberty. Behind them, there were hundreds of foot soldiers packed on transports racing to get into the action.

The tanks opened fire. The contrails from their shells allowed Malhorta to see the shells arc up and then down towards his positions. He ducked as missiles lifted off from around him and intercepted most of the shells, causing them to explode in the air above him. A few bangs and scrapes on his armor let him know pieces of shrapnel were raining down on him.

Fools, Malhorta thought as he opened his COM and gave the go ahead to the destroyers in orbit. Then he sent the go order to Echo flight.

Almost at once the fire from the two flanking attacks ceased as heavy plasma bolts rained into the forest from the destroyers. Then, within seconds, a sonic boom announced Echo flight's arrival as they sped past the LZ and dumped ordnance on the approaching tracked vehicles. A number of SAMs reached up and took out two more of the multirole fighters but it wasn't enough to stop the massive destruction the fighters wrought on the attackers. Out the open, the tanks and troop transports were sitting ducks and more than two thirds of them were taken out.

In all the commotion Malhorta's second wave of reinforcements arrived. Instead of landing in the LZ, they landed ahead of the soldiers that were already dug in. Each one of the forty shuttles had a Rohini light tank mounted on its underside which detached before the shuttle banked then landed, disgorging its eighty soldiers into the combat zone.

The tanks raced forward, firing heavy plasma bolts at the remaining Havenite vehicles. The soldiers formed up and sprinted after the tanks, taking out any soldiers that had survived the aerial bombardment.

Beside Malhorta a final shuttle hovered long enough for Malhorta's command vehicle to detach from its underside before it boosted forward to add its soldiers to the rest of the reinforcements.

"Colonels, do you understand your objectives?" Malhorta asked as soon as he entered his command vehicle and strapped himself in.

"Yes sir," the three colonels replied over the COM channel.

"Then move out, speed is our ally now."

On the holo display, Malhorta watched as the large force of tanks and marines split into four sections as they raced towards the edge of the city. The final survivors from the Havenite frontal attack having already been dealt with.

Now the fun begins, Malhorta thought as his command vehicle accelerated to join his battalion. Everything up until now had just been a ruse to lure out the Havenite defenders. Now it was time to take the city.

His analysts had identified two key energy production centers that fed most of the city. Two of the battalions entering the city would capture them and cut off power to the inhabitants. The third was targeted at the main power relay station and would secure it to prevent power being redirected from another part of the planet. Malhorta was leading the final battalion to the Haven Council Chambers.

"I'm sending you the orbital feeds," Malhorta said to the tactical officers in each of the tanks in his battalion. "There are a number of tanks lined up on our route, prepare to engage them."

Malhorta followed the progress of his battalion as it thrust into the city. The tanks slowed their progress slightly to allow the soldiers to keep up. An Indian soldier in combat armor could maintain speeds of thirty kilometers an hour until their power pack ran out and even slowed their progress was swift. Occasionally a gauss cannon would fire from the surrounding buildings. The first few bounced harmlessly off his tanks. Then they aimed at his soldiers and scored a couple of hits. None of those who opened fire survived to fire a second shot; his soldiers quickly took them out.

"The first blockade is coming up," Captain Bhat, who was commanding the advanced four squads of soldiers, reported over the COM channel. "Shall we engage?"

"Not yet," Malhorta ordered. "Wait until Alpha company meets up with you. Use their main guns to blast your way through."

"Affirmative," the Captain replied.

Malhorta's command vehicle was too far away to see the action so he switched on one of the small holo projectors to watch the visual feed from the leading tank. As he watched, it pivoted and drove straight into a nearby building. The structure was only three stories tall and the tank easily burst its way through. As it came out the other side its main gun was already tracking towards the barricade.

The Havenite defenders were momentarily caught off guard by the sudden appearance of a tank on an unexpected trajectory. As they rushed to turn their two heavy lasers on the new target, soldiers and another tank appeared down the street they had been expecting the enemy to appear from. Fire from both Indian tanks and plasma bolts from the soldiers took out both heavy lasers. A number of gauss rounds struck the Indian soldiers and then the surviving Havenites retreated into the surrounding roads and alleys of the city.

"Barricade clear Sir," Captain Bhat announced. "We're pushing forward."

Bhat and the advanced forces rolled over another three barricades that were hastily set up by the Havenites. Whoever was commanding the defenses of the city had either lost the majority of his forces at the battle for the LZ or Malhorta's quick counter attack had caught them badly off guard for they were encountering a lot less resistance than he had anticipated.

Just fifteen minutes after they had entered the city they came to a halt less than half a kilometer from their target.

"Target in sight sir," Bhat said. "There's quite a lot of open space before we get to the Council Chambers. It looks like they have it well fortified.

"Are you ready?" Malhorta asked the commander of his tanks.

"Yes Sir," Major Prata announced.

"Then go at it," Malhorta replied. "Bhat, once they knock down the main defenses I want your soldiers in there ASAP. Bring me Maximillian. I don't want to have to go door to door looking for him."

"Aye Sir," Bhat said.

"Pop smoke, and ECM to full," Prata ordered her tanks.

The long thoroughfare that led up to the Haven Council Chambers filled with smoke. Then, at her command, Prata's tanks rolled out in a standard attack formation. As soon as they came into sight of the Council Chambers, heavy lasers and rocket launchers rained fire on them. In return, the main plasma cannons on the tanks burnt swathes of the defenders out of existence.

As soon as the defenders' fire lessened enough that Malhorta thought it was safe, he gave the go order for the soldiers to join the attack. Hundreds of soldiers in combat armor charged towards the Council Chambers. The defenders who weren't able to penetrate the tanks' armor, switched their fire onto the advancing soldiers who died in fives and tens. It wasn't enough, even as two of Prata's tanks exploded from rocket hits the soldiers reached the steps to the Council Chambers.

The fighting turned to hand to hand as the soldiers hurdled the barricades the defenders had set up and got among their enemies using the immense strength of their combat armor.

"We're in," Bhat announced over the COM less than a minute later.

"Take me forward," Malhorta ordered his driver.

The driver of his command vehicle drove to the steps of the Council Chambers. When Malhorta thought he was about to stop, he accelerated instead and mounted the steps. Driving up them, he steered the vehicle straight for the main doors into the chambers. Somehow they had remained intact in all the fighting, the soldiers opting to enter the building through the holes the tanks had blown in the structure's wall.

Before Malhorta could object, the driver burst his vehicle through the wooden doors sending splinters flying everywhere. He pulled the vehicle to a stop in the main foyer, "Here you go Sir," he said.

"A bit over the top," Malhorta said, shaking his head as he got out. He couldn't help but smile.

His personal guard formed up and after locating Captain Bhat's signal on his HUD they sprinted off. It only took a couple of minutes to find the Captain. When Malhorta entered the room the captain was in, he smiled again. Bhat had captured Maximillian. The First Councilor of Haven looked like a stunned and defeated man. Just as Malhorta had planned, their counter attack from the LZ had caught the Havenites by surprise and they hadn't had time to run and hide. When he looked at the clock on his HUD he was stunned to see that it had been just over fifty minutes since he had first landed on the planet.

Walking over to the cowering Maximillian, Malhorta lowered his visor so the First Councilor could see his face. "You are defeated First Councilor. Take this," he said, thrusting a datapad towards Maximillian.

"What is this?" Maximillian asked.

"Your surrender speech. In just a moment my soldiers are

going to set up a recording device, then you are going to read it," Malhorta said.

"I will never say this," Maximillian said as he scanned the datapad.

"You will," Malhorta said confidently. "Because if you don't, I will find your family and kill them before your eyes. Then, if I have to, I will start with the outlying villages and, one by one, I will level this planet of yours. I am not here to fight a war of attrition. Your people are going to surrender. Do you understand me?"

Maximillian lowered his head and nodded slowly.

Malhorta breathed a sigh of relief. He had strict orders about how to treat civilians. His government wanted to pacify the people of Haven, not make life long enemies of them. Maximillian didn't need to know that though.

"We are ready Sir," one of Malhorta's soldiers called out.

"Begin broadcasting," Malhorta ordered as he turned to face the recording device.

"Men and women of Haven," Malhorta began. "I stand here in your Council Chambers. I have taken your First Councilor into my custody. He is charged with piracy and war crimes. If your armed forces lay down their weapons, and the civilians of Haven follow my instructions, I promise there will be no more bloodshed. The Indian Star Republic wishes to be friends with the people of Haven," Malhorta said with the best smile he could produce.

"Now, your former First Councilor wants to address his people one last time," Malhorta said as he beckoned two soldiers to lift Maximillian to his feet.

Maximillian shakily tried to stand with the support of the two soldiers and then lifted his head to face his people. "You all know me," Maximillian began. "You know I have devoted my life to protecting this colony. Well these Indians can..."

A fraction of a second too late Malhorta saw the renewed life that entered Maximillian's eyes. Before he could say something, Maximillian finished his sentence.

"...go to hell," Maximillian shouted as he pulled out the side arm of one of the soldiers holding him up. Before he could get a shot off at Malhorta one of the other marines gunned him down with two plasma bolts. One burnt a hole in his chest, the other burnt its way right through Maximillian's open mouth. For a couple of seconds Maximillian's eyes stared blankly at the recording device and then he toppled over.

"Shit," Malhorta swore. "Cut the transmission," he growled. It was too late though; Maximillian's death had just been broadcast to the entire planet. *Now there is going to be no avoiding a* guerrilla *war,* he thought as he cursed Maximillian's corpse.

Chapter 11 – No Going Back

Since the beginning of mankind weddings have formed the bedrock of many societies, none more so than the Empire's, for it was a wedding that gave birth to the Empire.

-Excerpt from Empire Rising, 3002 AD

27th March, 2467 AD, Westminster Abbey, London.

James Somerville, Duke of Beaufort and Captain of HMS *Endeavour* stood at the front of Westminster Abbey more unsure of himself than he had ever been before. In many ways, facing the entirety of the Overlord's war fleet had been less daunting than what he was about to undertake.

He had hardly seen Suzanna since their last night at his estate. After a long discussion they had come to a consensus. The marriage would go ahead for the sake of both of their nations. Yet, it was a marriage they were going to take seriously. They both wanted to be happily married and they weren't going to let their circumstances rob them of the one opportunity they might ever get. It would take time, but they were determined to be happy.

However, James was well aware that that had been three days ago. A lot had happened since then and for James at least, it felt like an eternity. He could still picture Suzanna standing before the joint gathering of the Houses of Commons and Lords. She had looked small and frail in the midst of her grand surroundings. Yet, when she had spoken out it had been with confidence and conviction.

Starting with the first day the Haven colony ship had left Earth she had recounted her people's history. At each critical point she stopped to emphasize the independent and freedom loving spirit of her people. On more than one occasion she had likened events on her planet to key experiences the British people had gone through. When she came to the end of her speech, she had turned her attention to her people's current plight. With a vigorous passion she had pleaded that all the sacrifices of her ancestors not be in vain. All her people wanted was to be an equal member of the Human race. To take their place alongside the British people who had worked and fought for their own freedom. The people of Haven were just like the people of Britain, hardworking, self-sacrificing, honorable and wanting nothing more than a bright future for their children. That was why, she had explained, she wanted to join her people to the British Star Kingdom. So that together, both peoples could prosper.

It had been at that point James had been sure of his decision from the previous night. If his marrying Suzanna could help save and protect her people, then he would do it. Her love for them was infectious and James didn't want to let her down.

The speech had made the impact the King and Prime Minister wanted. Overnight public opinion in Britain and the rest of the British colonies in the Sol system had shifted in favor of intervening on behalf of the Havenite people. Between her speech at the UN meeting and before Parliament Suzanna had become a sensation. James hadn't seen her since as she had been pulled from news broadcaster to news broadcaster doing interview after interview.

More than likely, it had been Suzanna's last announcement that had pushed the public's love for her over the edge. At the end of her speech when she had turned to thanking the RSN for all they had already done for her people, no one had expected what she was going to say next. Singling out James for specific praise, she had told of how this dashing Captain had already won the heart of her people for saving them from certain destruction. Then, to a silent audience, she had announced that he had also stolen her heart as well and that they were to get married in just three days. To finish it off, she had invited all sitting members of the Houses of Commons and Lords to their wedding in Westminster Abbey.

No one from either houses of parliament had quite known what to make of the announcement, but when Suzanna had stopped speaking there had been a large roar of applause from the visitor's gallery. It seemed that the general public approved of the match.

The global news outlets had taken up the story with a fervor. Some were calling it the love story of the century. The young dashing naval Captain who was also one of the wealthiest Dukes in the British Star Kingdom and the foreign politician he had saved from being killed or enslaved by a hostile alien race. Even James had to admit the spin Fairfax was putting on things sounded impressive.

It had worked so well in fact, that Fairfax had been forced to push back the vote on the Haven situation by two days to make sure the media attention on the wedding didn't interfere with the coverage of the vote.

James' mind was wrenched into the present and his heart skipped a beat when the organ started playing. "Here we go Sir," Mallory said from beside him.

"Aye," James said quietly as he turned around to watch the bridal procession file in. He would have loved to have Captain Gupta beside him along with Mallory, but she was commanding her own frigate in the Britannia system.

Even without Gupta, the wedding party was almost entirely a naval affair. Suzanna had become friends with Lieutenants Julius and Becket on the flight to the Alpha system and then to Earth. As Becket walked up the aisle James was stunned by how good she looked, he had never seen her dressed up before. Lieutenant Julius would be the first to admit she wasn't as pretty as Becket but even she looked amazing. Next were two of James' cousins. James hardly knew them but the King and Fairfax had insisted that the bridal procession be as big and lavish as possible and they had been drafted in to make up the numbers.

Then Suzanna appeared on the arm of James' uncle. No words came into James' mind to describe her. He was simply mesmerized. As he watched her approach, all his fears disappeared. He had known even before the marriage had been suggested that he could be falling in love. Now, seeing her like this, he had no doubts.

When she stepped up beside him she gave him a beaming smile. "No turning back now Captain," she said.

"No turning back," James agreed as he took her hands in his and they turned to face the Archbishop of Canterbury.

*

The rest of the day was a complete blur for James. After exchanging their vows, they had been whisked away with the bridal party to take images and recordings that Fairfax could use in his media campaign. Then they had spent more than three hours at the reception simply meeting and shaking the hands of the all the important officials who had been invited.

The meal had been delicious but with the speeches scheduled to happen after the cutting of the cake, James hadn't been able to enjoy the food as much as he would have liked. Mallory had shown a surprising composure in front of so many distinguished guests. James often forgot that Mallory had grown up among the nobility, and though he didn't often cut the most confident naval officer, he was at home at grand events like James' wedding. Given the fact that Mallory hadn't known James for very long his speech had also been rather good. Fairfax had ensured the entire wedding would be a propaganda opportunity and so the speeches had been recorded to be made available on Sol's datanet. Mallory had therefore been given a little help by Fairfax's staff. Though Mallory hadn't known him long, someone had obviously done their homework for there had been more than one embarrassing story about him from his time at the academy.

James too had been given a drafted speech. This was the first time the British public would hear from him. Fairfax had intentionally kept him out of the spotlight up until the wedding. He had said it would have more of an impact if James first spoke on his wedding day.

The speech itself had been what James had expected. Focusing on the aspirations and tenets of the RSN he had made a forceful argument for a British intervention on behalf of the Havenite people. Even though Suzanna had known that he hadn't written the speech he had still seen a small tear run down her cheek as he had spoken. He guessed that his passion had come across, for though they hadn't been his words, he had believed every one of them.

Despite the reception running on until past midnight, Fairfax, the King and James' uncle had insisted on accompanying them back to Badminton House. There they had discussed the strategy they had in place for the next three days until the vote. Finally, after more than an hour of discussions they had left.

Once he had seen them off James took Suzanna's hand and led her back up to the main bedroom. When they entered the room, Suzanna spun round in front of James and smiled up at him. "Here we are," she said, "it's hard to believe it was only three nights ago we talked the night away together. Now we are husband and wife."

"I don't think we have had more than a few minutes alone together since this morning. I haven't even told you how stunning you look in your dress," James said pulling her into a hug.

"You didn't have to, my husband," Suzanna said, laughing. "The look on your face when I walked into the Abbey said it all."

As she pulled out of the hug, her eyes went to the bedside table. James followed her gaze. "I put it away. I decided I didn't want it anymore," he said.

"Don't lie to me," Suzanna said in a mock scolding tone. "I know you love her. I already told you I don't want to compete with her. We are going to start something new."

With that Suzanna walked over to the bedside table and opened the top drawer. She reached in and lifted the vacuum sealed rose and placed it back on top of the bedside table. Then she pulled James into a deep kiss. "You see," she said.

"Now, I have to freshen up for a minute," she added as she walked towards the adjoining bathroom.

Shaking his head, James guessed he probably wouldn't stop being surprised by his new wife. Absentmindedly, he picked up the glass frame and examined the rose held within.

Almost everything after the wedding ceremony seemed like a daze to him. He had been pulled from talking to one person to another and another. Yet one moment stood out in his mind.

Christine, as the daughter of the King of England and Empresses of China had of course been invited to the wedding. She had intentionally avoided talking to James and for his part, he had been glad. He wasn't sure he could have trusted his own emotions. Yet, at one point during the evening he had glimpsed Suzanna pulling Christine into a secluded alcove for a private conversation. When the pair had returned to the reception James could tell Christine had been crying. He had no idea what had been said between the two women but James knew Suzanna hadn't spoken to Christine to hurt her.

The sound of Suzanna returning refocused James' mind and he quickly set the rose down. When Suzanna stepped out of the bathroom he couldn't help gaping. She had let her hair down and removed her shoes. The back of her dress had been loosened, allowing it to sink down and reveal more of her bosom.

"Would you like to help me with the rest of my dress Captain?" she asked, smiling seductively.

All thoughts of Christine gone, James stepped towards his new wife with a smile. "I think that is a mission I can accomplish."

*

30th March, 2467AD HMS *Endeavour*, Earth orbit.

Three days after the wedding, James and Suzanna were in his quarters on board *Endeavour*. James was sitting with a cup of coffee, relaxing at the small desk in his office. Around him Suzanna and his steward Fox were frantically arranging all the boxes Suzanna had brought on board. She had gone shopping for him yesterday, insisting that a naval Captain should have more uniforms and clothes to relax in when he was off duty. She had also bought a number of items to decorate his quarters and make them feel homelier.

As James watched her running around scolding Fox and rearranging everything he tried to stow away, he had to suppress a giggle. Suzanna was nervous. The combined vote in the Commons and the Lords was going on right at this minute. Poor Fox was suffering for it.

A beep on his datapad alerted him that he had a message from his uncle. Suzanna stopped what she was doing behind him. James scanned the message.

"The vote has been finished," he said. If it was anything else, he might draw out the suspense to play with Suzanna but this was too serious. "It passed, both the Commons and Lords passed it with more than eighty percent of the votes. Haven's petition has been accepted."

As James stood to smile at Suzanna she had no words. He pulled her into a hug. "We're going to help your people," James said. "My government has sent a formal request to the

UN and the Indian government demanding that all Indian ships pull back from Haven. The Prime Minister and the King have publicly issued an executive order allowing all British ships to engage any Indian warships that try to prevent Haven from holding a free democratic vote on becoming a British protectorate."

"Thank you," Suzanna said.

"I also have orders from my uncle," James added. "I am to take *Endeavour* through the Gift to Haven to assess the situation there. If possible, I am to make contact with whatever elements of your government are still functional and inform them of the situation. I am to depart within the next two hours."

"Today?" Suzanna asked.

"Yes," James replied.

"But we haven't even been married a week!"

"I know," James said, pulling her into another hug.

"Right," Suzanna said, pushing herself away from James. "Fox."

"Yes Ma'am?" Fox responded.

"Out," Suzanna said.

Before he could reply she turned on the COM link built into

James' desk. "Lieutenant Mallory," she said.

"Yes my Lady," Mallory answered.

"James has just received orders to break orbit in two hours," Suzanna said. "You are in command until he comes to the bridge. He's mine until then. I don't want us to be disturbed."

"Yes my Lady," Mallory said. James detected a hint of amusement in his voice.

"Ok Captain," Suzanna said, turning to him. "If we only have another hour or two let's make the most of them."

*

Ten hours later, James sat in his command chair watching Earth get smaller and smaller on the holo display. Never before had he been sad to leave Earth on a mission. Usually the thought of a new adventure had him full of anticipation. He had no doubts as to why this time, things were different. Nevertheless, he knew he would do his duty, for his government, but even more so, for Suzanna. Her people were now his people.

Chapter 12 – Independence

Rogue Captains have always been a problem in the Empire's Navy. With FTL communications limited to industrialized systems, most naval Captains operate outside the purview of their commanders. More than once they have taken actions the Emperor has come to regret. My research suggests this was not a problem that began with the Empire.

-Excerpt from Empire Rising, 3002 AD

21st April 2467 AD, HMS *Endeavour*, edge of the Independence System.

Twenty-one days after leaving the Sol System, James sat on the bridge of *Endeavour* surveying the Independence System. According to Suzanna, the system had been settled by Haven forty years ago. Since then, a small colony and mining outpost had been established on the system's fifth planet.

Independence was the last system *Endeavour* had to pass through before she came to Haven and James wanted to get as much intel on the system as possible. If a British fleet was going to use the Gift to attack whatever Indian forces were at Haven, they would have to pass through this system. James didn't want there to be any surprises waiting for them.

"Take us in," he ordered the Navigation Officer.

For the next eight hours *Endeavour* slowly worked her way into the inner system under stealth. Initially, there were no signs of any warships in the system, but as they neared the planet an Indian medium cruiser appeared from around the edge of the planet.

"There can be no doubt Sir," Mallory said. "If the Indians are here, then they must have taken Haven."

"Indeed," James said. "And something tells me this cruiser isn't alone. I want a spread of passive recon drones launched. Assume there are at least two or three smaller ships patrolling the approaches to the colony in stealth. Work out their likely positions if they are trying to ambush unsuspecting Haven ships and focus our drones on those areas."

"Yes Sir," Mallory said as he walked over to Sub Lieutenant Malik at the sensor console to work out James' orders.

Within ten minutes Mallory had launched the first spread of drones towards the colony. Passive recon drones were recon drones with their engines removed and more passive sensors put in instead. Being so small, they were hard to detect, yet they were expensive. Thankfully though, *Endeavour's* compliment of recon drones had been fully restocked for this mission.

Using *Endeavour's* two forward missile tubes, the drones were fired along ballistic trajectories to try and detect any ships hidden in stealth. Most warships had sophisticated stealth technologies but at close enough range, even passive sensors were able to detect the stray electromagnetic radiation that leaked from the ships or the ionized particles from a ship's impulse drive.

"I think I have got something," Malik said after another forty minutes.

"Where?" Mallory asked.

"Here," Malik said as he transferred his readings to the main holo display. "Drone three is picking up an intermittent source of gamma radiation."

"Alter course fifteen degrees above the ecliptic," James ordered. "We don't want to come close enough to them that they might detect us."

"Aye Sir," Jennings, who was at the navigation console, said.

"Track it," James ordered Sub Lieutenant Malik. "I want to know its course."

James stood and walked over to Mallory's command chair. He leant in and whispered to his First Lieutenant, "I want you to prepare a normal drone and launch it on a ballistic trajectory towards that ship. If we can get close enough to the cruiser we're going to try and take it out. If we do that however, we will need to stop this second contact from fleeing back to Haven. I don't want to show up at Haven with an Indian welcoming party already waiting for us."

"I understand Sir," Mallory said. "If we can get a recon drone close enough we can use its radar to give our missiles the targeting data they will need."

"Exactly," James said, pleased that Mallory was able to follow his thinking so quickly. "As soon as we open fire on the cruiser I want to fire a volley of missiles at this contact. We won't have very precise targeting information but once our missiles get closer we can activate the recon drone and ping the Indian ship.

"On the other hand, if it looks too risky to attack the cruiser we will pull back and send in Johnston's stealth shuttle. A landing on Independence will be a good dry run for when we get to Haven. I'm sure the locals will have some useful information to share with us."

"But an Indian medium cruiser added to *Endeavour's* kill list would be even more satisfying," Mallory whispered back.

"And be one less ship Rooke and Cunningham will have to worry about later," James agreed.

"I'll get right on it Sir," Mallory replied with a grin.

James went back to his command chair. "Send everyone to their battlestations," he ordered. *Endeavour* wouldn't get to her closest point to the Indian ship that was in stealth for another hour but he didn't want to be caught by surprise.

For a moment, James paused to consider his decision. It was

second nature now for him to launch straight into an attack. Technically his orders were to gather intel on the Indian fleet dispositions. *However,* he thought to himself, *if we can destroy the Indian ship we can talk freely with the locals, in a way this is the ideal approach to gathering intel. We are supposed to treat Indian warships as hostile after all.*

After the order went around the ship, James opened a COM channel to Major Johnston, the commander of *Endeavour's* marines.

"Major," James began, "I want you and your special forces marines to prep the stealth shuttle for launch. There is an Indian medium cruiser orbiting above the Havenite colony. We're going to try and take it out so we can contact whoever is in charge on the planet and get some intel. If it proves too dangerous to attempt to take on the cruiser, then I want you to take the shuttle down and make contact with the locals. It will have to be a quick in and out mission."

"No problem Sir," Johnston replied. "My men can be ready to go in thirty minutes."

"Get them ready then," James said. "I'll let you know if we are engaging the cruiser once we get closer to the colony," he finished as he closed the COM channel and switched his attention to the main holo display.

One of the first things Mallory had taken him to see when he had returned to *Endeavour* after his wedding had been the new stealth shuttle. It had come on board with a squad of special forces marines. Coated in the latest stealth coverings and incorporating much of the technology that went into making *Endeavour* so stealthy, it was the perfect tool for their mission to Haven. Being so new though, it wouldn't hurt if Johnston got a chance to try it out under less dangerous circumstances.

As they approached the Indian ship that was in stealth, James could feel the tension among the Sub Lieutenants on the bridge growing. There was a chance the Indian ship would be another medium or light cruiser rather than a smaller patrol craft. If it was, then a single broadside of missiles wouldn't be enough to destroy it. However, it was very unlikely. Whoever was in charge of the Indian fleet would want to keep the majority of their heavy ships at Haven. As far as the Indians knew, there was no shift passage leading from Independence back to British space and there was no need for a large fleet presence in the system. Even the one medium cruiser that was orbiting the planet seemed like overkill to James.

On the other hand, James thought, *maybe the Indians have found out about the Gift from the Havenites. That would throw a spanner in my uncle's plans.*

*

"We're approaching optimal position," Lieutenant Becket said from the tactical console twenty minutes later.

After they had successfully crept past the Indian ship in stealth James had brought *Endeavour* to rest within plasma cannon range of the medium cruiser orbiting Independence.

It would give them a chance to turn and give chase to the second Indian ship if it survived his initial attack.

"Make sure every plasma bolt counts," James said to Becket.

"Yes Sir, I understand," she reassured him.

As *Endeavour* was in stealth mode, her reactors were almost powered down. *Endeavour's* plasma cannons had their own capacitors that allowed them to fire off a single plasma bolt each in the event of an emergency. If Becket's first shots didn't work, she would have to wait at least a minute for the Chief Engineer to power up the reactors to feed her weapons more energy. A minute would be more than long enough for the Indian medium cruiser to bring her own plasma cannons to bear on *Endeavour*.

After double checking her targeting data, Becket looked up from her console at James.
James hesitated for a second. He was about to fire the first shots in another, what would likely become an interstellar, war. One his nation could ill afford to lose. His uncle hadn't given him any specific instructions about engaging targets of opportunity on this mission. He was just meant to be on a reconnaissance mission. Yet, *Endeavour* had received an updated rules of engagement from the Admiralty along with the rest of the British fleet in the Sol system before she left. Indian warships within Havenite space were now to be considered as hostiles and treated accordingly. This was too good an opportunity to miss, destroying this cruiser now could save lives in the long run.

"Fire," James ordered.

Endeavour's three twin plasma cannons fired six plasma bolts into the cold of space. Mere milliseconds later sixteen missiles erupted from their missile tubes as both *Endeavour's* starboard and port broadsides released their ordnance at their targets.

The Indian cruiser was less than three light seconds from *Endeavour.* Traveling at more than 0.8C the plasma bolts closed the distance in less than four seconds. In that time the Indian cruiser's gravitational sensors detected the launch of the eight missiles targeted at it. Just as alarms blared on the bridge of the cruiser, the plasma bolts hit. Three were aimed at each of the cruiser's plasma cannons. All three hit their targets, destroying the cruiser's ability to quickly hit back at *Endeavour.*

Two more bolts hit the cruiser amidships where RSNI intel suggested the Indian cruiser's main reactors were. One bolt managed to burn its way through the extra layers of valstronium armor the cruiser had around its reactors. Two of the cruiser's three reactors were seriously damaged. The second bolt missed the reactors, hitting one of the main crew quarters. Over forty Indian navy personnel were obliterated in their sleep.

Becket had targeted her final plasma bolt at where she judged the cruiser's bridge to be. Her guess proved correct and no sooner had the Lieutenant on watch looked at the alarms that had gone off than she was dead. The cruiser's ability to react to the incoming missiles had been crippled.

Those eight missiles had been launched from their tubes at 0.1C. As soon as they cleared the tubes their impulse engines kicked in and rapidly accelerated them towards their target. They crossed the distance between the two ships in just twenty-five seconds. Whilst the captain of the Indian cruiser had survived the first attack, he had barely made it to the auxiliary bridge when the missiles exploded around his ship.

The cruiser's automatic defenses took out two of the missiles but without a human coordinating the point defenses there was no hope for the ship. Four of the remaining missiles scored direct hits on the cruiser within less than half a second of each other. The cruiser disappeared in a massive fireball.

As soon as the fireball dissipated and James was satisfied that the cruiser was no longer a threat, he switched his attention to the second contact. It had come out of stealth as soon as it had detected the eight missiles launched in its direction. Malik had already analyzed its engine profile and there was now a line of text beside the blip on the main holo display suggesting that the contact was an Indian frigate.

"Send the signal to the recon drone to ping the target," James ordered.

Becket was already updating the second salvo of missiles with new targeting data but giving them a radar reflection from the frigate itself would make sure none of the missiles lost their target lock.

It hardly mattered at this stage, eight missiles were more than overkill for a single frigate. Maybe if it had its own flak cannon it would have a slim chance. Yet the intel James had been given on the Indian fleet suggested that only their largest warships had flak cannons.

As soon as the recon drone filled space with high intensity radar waves, the frigate re-orientated itself and tried to hit the drone with its single plasma cannon. Recon drones were tiny though and Malik had already programmed it with an evasive flight plan.

"They should be focused on the missiles," Mallory said. "The drone is the least of their worries."

"It won't matter either way," James said, already sure of the outcome.

The frigate tried desperately to take out *Endeavour's* missiles with its plasma cannon and then its point defenses once the missiles got into range. It was to no avail, six missiles broke through its defenses and the frigate was turned into an expanding ball of debris.

"Jennings, take us into orbit," James ordered the Sub Lieutenant who was manning the navigation console once the frigate was destroyed.

"Get me a COM channel with the most senior Havenite representative on the colony," he ordered Sub Lieutenant King. "And see if there are any Havenite military commanders on the colony. Put them in contact with Major Johnston. I want a full report on whatever intel we can get on the Indians."

*

Twenty minutes later, when *Endeavour* slotted into orbit around Independence, James left the bridge and walked to his private office. With a few taps on his personal COM unit the face of Independence's leader appeared.

"Greetings," James said. "May I ask whom I am speaking to?"

"You are a sight for sore eyes Captain Somerville, I have heard a lot about you of course. Though I can't say I ever expected to talk to you face to face. You are most welcome to the Independence System," the face replied.

"I am glad you are happy to see me," James replied. "You obviously know me but I'm afraid you have me at a disadvantage."

"Of course, of course. My apologies. My name is Derick Thompson. I am Independence's Councilor. I was on Independence when the Indians launched their invasion of our territory so I have been stuck here ever since," Thompson explained.

"And how are things on the ground?" James asked.

"To be honest, I can't say we have very much to complain

about," Thompson answered. "When that cruiser came into the system it blew up the unmanned satellites we had in orbit and then threatened to bombard our city if we didn't follow their instructions. Everyone was scared at first. However, the Indian's didn't land any ground troops. They seemed content to control space around our colony. Life has almost returned to normal for most of our population."

"I am glad to hear your colony is in one piece," James said. "We are here to see just what the Indians are up too. You know Councilwoman Rodriguez I presume? Well she has petitioned my government to accept Haven as a British protectorate. The British Star Kingdom has accepted and so we plan to throw the Indians out of Haven and allow your people a free vote to determine your future."

"Well that is good news," Thompson said. "At least the getting rid of the Indians part. I for one have no desire to swap one tyrant for another. I dare say Ms. Rodriguez has over stepped her authority. But then, she has always been fond of doing that."

"I would be careful what you say about the Councilwoman," James said as diplomatically as possible. "She has sacrificed a lot to try and save your people from becoming an Indian occupied territory. And she is no longer a Ms. She is now Lady Somerville."

"Lady..." Thompson said, thinking through the implications. "You mean she has married into the British aristocracy? And Somerville, you don't mean you, do you?"

"Yes," James answered. "She is now my wife and together we plan to liberate your people from the Indians. You may not have suffered too much under their rule yet, but I assure you, it would not always have been so pleasant. What's more, I'm sure things aren't going as smoothly on Haven."

"No, I don't expect they are," Thompson replied. "But I don't think that will mean the people will just run into your arms if you manage to liberate them."

"My government doesn't expect them to," James responded. "We simply want your people to have the chance to freely determine their future. When that day comes, you can rail against my wife all you want. But for now, she is the one doing everything she can to make that day a reality. That means you and I are on the same side. I need as much information as you can give me."

"The enemy of my enemy is my friend, I can see that logic," Thompson said. "I will be happy to help you. But don't think that means I will take kindly to your government when they try to sink their claws into Haven."

"Cooperation now is all I ask," James said.

"In that case let me begin," Thompson said.

For the next ten minutes James listened as Thompson described how a freighter had escaped Haven and brought news of the invasion. The Councilman was actually able to transmit some images the freighter had collected of the Indian fleet and the ground invasion before it jumped out of the Haven system. After the freighter's arrival, panic had broken out among the populace. They all knew they had no hope of holding the Indians off. News of Maximillian's death had caused many Havenites to prepare for a ground resistance. Others, knowing what such a struggle would mean, had fled the city or locked themselves in their homes in an effort to avoid any fighting.

When the cruiser had been spotted approaching the planet the panic had come to a head. Yet, when no Indian troops arrived in shuttles and no demands were made of the colonists except to get back to work and continue to mine ore, people had relaxed. The sight of the cruiser exploding in orbit had been the most exciting thing that had happened in over a week.

"Do you know the name of the Indian Admiral who commands their fleet?" James asked, interrupting Thompson.

"No, I'm afraid not," Thompson answered. "The images from the freighter I sent you have some details about the Indian fleet, but that is all I know. My analysts think there must have been more Indian ships in the attack than the freighter's sensors picked up."

"And where is the freighter now?" James queried.

"The Indians boarded it and took its crew off," Thompson answered. "They had us fill it with ore and then flew it back to Haven. I suspect it is half way to New Delhi by now."

"Most likely," James said.

Before he could ask another question, an alert on his desk display caught his attention. Malik was reporting the sensors had picked up a strange anomaly.

"Hold on," James said to Thompson just as he was about to speak.

James took another few seconds to scan through the data Malik had sent him. "One of my Lieutenants has just alerted me to a potential problem. I'm afraid I am going to have to go and attend to it. I will pass you on to another one of my officers. I need all the intel you can give me."

"I understand Captain," Thompson said. "Hopefully we can speak again before you leave for Haven. I have a few messages I would like you to take for my family there in case you get a chance to transmit them."

"I'll see what I can do," James promised. "Farewell for now Councilman."

"Farewell Captain, thank you for coming to our aid once again," Thompson said.

As soon as the COM channel closed James jumped to his feet and rushed onto the bridge. "What do you make of this signal?" he asked Mallory.

"It's strange Sir," Mallory said, "but I don't think there is any natural explanation. It must be a ship."

"Agreed," James replied.

He reviewed the data being shown on the main holo display. Malik had detected two very faint bursts of electromagnetic radiation. *Endeavour's* computers had disregarded the first burst, thinking it to be background radiation from a distant pulsar or supernova. However, the second had got Malik's attention and he had checked to see if there had been any others. As soon as he found another one he had alerted James.

As James watched the holo display a fourth dot appeared. "I'm looking back into our sensor data for more anomalies. I think the threat computer missed a few of them," Malik explained.

"Maybe it is a ship with some kind of failure in its stealth technology," Mallory said. "Because it is only giving off electromagnetic radiation at random intervals maybe no one ever noticed before. The Indians certainly have a lot of old warships in their fleet."

"Perhaps," James said.

As James watched, Malik plotted a course linking all four points where an anomaly had been detected. They formed a very uniform course around Independence and towards the shift passage to Haven.

"Take us out of orbit and put us into stealth," James ordered. "Then plot us a course directly to the shift passage to Haven.

Launch a series of stealth recon drones towards the projected course of that contact. And inform whoever is speaking with the people on Independence that they need to get whatever information they can now because we are leaving."

A chorus of, "Yes Sir," followed James' orders.

Almost as soon as *Endeavour* went into stealth the gravimetric sensor sounded an alarm as it detected a new contact. On the main holo display a new icon jumped into life right where the anomaly had been.

"Indian warship," Malik shouted. "It's accelerating hard."

As the acceleration profiles came up on the screen James quickly did the calculations in his head. It was going to be close.

"You have the bridge," James said, turning to his First Lieutenant.

"Me?" Mallory asked, momentarily surprised.

James simply nodded and turned back to the main holo display.

*

Mallory took a second to take stock of the situation and then took a deep breath and jumped to his feet. "Full military acceleration, then break out the gaseous sails. We're going to need every bit of speed we can get. Malik, what do you make of the contact?"

"Its acceleration profile looks like a Garuda destroyer," Malik answered. "They first entered service over thirty years ago. Over twenty of them are still listed as being active. It should have a broadside of five missiles."

"I don't think they are going to slow down long enough to show us their broadside," Mallory said. "What is their estimated top speed?"

"0.3C," Malik answered.

"Project our and the destroyer's course on the holo display, let's see if we are going to catch them," Mallory said.

Being just two years old, *Endeavour* was coated in the latest Valstronium armor giving her a top speed of 0.38c. The gaseous sails were a holdover from the days before Valstronium had been discovered. Before valstronium, warships pumped out ionized gasses and used electromagnetic fields to form them into large sail like structures in front of the ship to allow them to safely travel at a reasonable speed across solar systems. The dense gas clouds prevented harmful radiation or cosmic particles from damaging the ship or its crew.

With the sails deployed *Endeavour* had a top speed of 0.4c, though if she wanted to carry out any sophisticated maneuvers like trying to avoid incoming missiles she would have to slow down. *Endeavour's* electromagnetic fields could only keep the ionized gases in the required shape when the ship was going in the same direction. Any maneuvers would cause them to dissipate.

When the plot came up, Mallory saw that it was going to be very close. "We're probably only going to get two or three missile salvos at the destroyer," he said. "Becket I want you to contact Chief Driscoll, see if he can transfer a penetrator missile to the forward missile tubes, we're going to have to make each shot count."

"Aye Sir," Becket responded.

Satisfied that he couldn't do anything further, Mallory sat down in his command chair and watched his orders being carried out.

It took the destroyer fifty minutes to reach its maximum velocity of 0.3c. As *Endeavour* began her acceleration burn from a relative stand still, it took her another forty minutes to reach her full velocity. For three hours *Endeavour* slowly pulled back the distance the destroyer had opened up between the two ships.

Just forty minutes away from the system's shift limit and less than ten before *Endeavour* would enter weapons range with her bow tubes, the gravitational sensors let out a new beep. "The destroyer is accelerating again," Malik said. "It looks like they are putting caution to the wind and risking a strike from a cosmic particle."

"Damn," Mallory said as he pounded his fist into his

command chair. The plot had just updated to show that *Endeavour* would only get to fire one salvo at the destroyer.

"They have opened fire," Malik reported before Mallory could say anything else. "One missile is inbound."

"Becket, fire when ready," Mallory said, ignoring the single missile. Even though only a fraction of *Endeavour's* point defenses would be able to target the missile as it came towards the nose of the ship, they would take it out easily.

"Firing," Becket said when they entered range. As soon as she spoke two missiles erupted from *Endeavour's* forward missile tubes.

Mallory looked over to where James was sitting. The Captain appeared unperturbed by the change in events. He seemed to be confidently watching the holo plot. Mallory wished he could be so sure of himself. If Becket's missiles missed, then the destroyer would get away. Their mission would almost be over before it had begun. If the Indians knew they were coming, it might prove impossible to slip Major Johnston and his men onto Haven.

That doesn't matter now, Mallory told himself, *focus!*

"Flak cannon engaging," the Sub Lieutenant assisting Becket at the tactical console called out. *Endeavour* had two flak cannons but only one was able to target directly ahead of the warship. It did its job and the Indian missile exploded harmlessly when a piece of shrapnel penetrated its armor.

"Now it is our turn," Becket said.

On the holo plot, Mallory saw the penetrator missile activate just before the destroyer's point defenses opened up on the two British missiles. Two missiles suddenly became seven. Small plasma bolts and AM missiles filled space around the seven targets. A number of AM missiles exploded right beside some of the British missiles. When the British missiles continued on unharmed it was obvious they were just ECM ghosts. The destroyer's defenders refocused their aim and within a few seconds a real explosion announced the destruction of one of the missiles. The five fake missiles disappeared from the destroyer's sensors. *They got the penetrator missile*, Mallory thought.

It was too late; the second missile dove alongside the destroyer. Failing to get a direct hit, it exploded as close to its target as it could get. A wave of electromagnetic energy crashed into the destroyer, burning off valstronium armor, sensor blisters and point defenses emplacements. The force of the blast also buckled a number of internal struts, causing a large groan to sound throughout the destroyer as its framework bent and warped. Disregarding the damage, the destroyer's Captain hit the button to jump her ship into shift space as soon as it crossed Independence's mass shadow.

"They're gone," Malik shouted just after he reported the proximity hit.

"What?" Mallory said in concern, it didn't look like the proximity hit had caused enough damage to destroy the destroyer.

"I think they jumped out," Malik said. "There is no sign of the ship or any debris."

"Shit," Mallory said, "replay the sensor data, figure out how much damage we caused. Maybe they blew up as they tried to enter shift space."

Ten minutes later there was no doubt. The destroyer had escaped. Its Captain would get to Haven ahead of *Endeavour* and warn the Indians about *Endeavour's* presence.

"I'm sorry Sir," Mallory said, turning to James.

James ignored Mallory's comment. "Plot us a course to Haven Jennings, then jump us out as soon as we cross the mass shadow."

Standing, James walked past Mallory, "With me Lieutenant," he said.

Mallory's heart sank, he was more upset with himself for letting his Captain down than letting the Indian destroyer get away.

When they walked out of the bridge James gestured towards the door to his office. As they walked in, James called for his steward Fox to bring them both black coffee.

James smiled at Mallory and clasped him on the shoulder. "Don't look so nervous. You did a good job. If you hadn't thought to transfer that penetrator missile to the bow tubes right from the start, we would have been caught with our pants down when that destroyer exceeded their maximum velocity. As things turned out, there was nothing else you could have done."

"Thank you Sir," Mallory replied, not sure how genuine James was being.

"However, there is one thing" James continued, ignoring Mallory's tentative reply, "You need to get better control of your emotions when you are leading others into battle. Everyone on the bridge did their best today. Your reaction when the Indian ship escaped will have caused them to doubt and blame themselves. Just like you are doing now. Yet, no one is at fault, we can't win every time.

"And in the future, if you want to apologize to me, do so in private. If the crew thinks you doubt yourself, then they will doubt you for sure. If you look confident, they will trust you. You don't think I am as confident as I look all the time, do you?" James asked with a chuckle.

"Well, I thought that maybe you were..." Mallory began.

"Ha," James broke in with a laugh. "That just shows you how good an actor I am."

"Now," he went on before Mallory could say anymore. "We have to figure out the best approach to Haven. We are going to need to be a little more cautious than we originally planned. For all we know, that destroyer broke apart in shift space as soon as it jumped. However, we have to assume it didn't."

Chapter 13 – Return to Haven

Today Haven is one of the heaviest populated and most industrialized systems in the Empire. It's beginning as a small independent colony was a lot less conspicuous, yet since it was rediscovered by the Earth nations, the planet and its colonists have played a key role in human affairs.

-Excerpt from Empire Rising, 3002 AD

26th April 2467 AD, HMS *Endeavour,* edge of the Haven System.

James sat on the bridge of *Endeavour* surveying the Haven system. He had exited shift space five light hours from the system's mass shadow to avoid detection. As he expected, there was already an Indian fleet in the system. Whoever was commanding it wasn't taking any chances. There were a number of warships aggressively patrolling the three shift passages that led to the Haven system.

The gravimetric pulse a ship produced when exiting shift space could be detected by ships up to a light hour away and James was confident *Endeavour's* arrival would go unnoticed. He had planned a number of scenarios with his Lieutenants on how to approach their current mission. James had been tempted by Mallory's suggestion. The First Lieutenant wanted to launch a number of drones into the system which were programmed to give off bursts of electromagnetic radiation and strong gravitational waves at random. They would light up the patrolling warship's sensors with so many false signals that they would have no hope of finding *Endeavour.*

If the Indians had been warned about *Endeavour,* Mallory's plan would have been a real option. However, as James surveyed the Indian fleet dispositions, it looked like there were many more ships patrolling the shift passage that led to Indian space and the Sol system than that to Independence. That was where the Indian Admiral would expect any attack from the British to come from. *Of course the Indian Admiral could just be luring me into a false sense of security. There could be many more ships waiting out there in stealth,* James thought.

"We'll go with plan gamma," James said to his bridge crew, deciding he had to assume that the Indians didn't know about his attack on the cruiser at Independence yet.

The thought of the Indian Admiral chasing shadows for the next few days had made James seriously consider Mallory's plan. Yet, it would alert the Indians that something was happening in the system. Even if they couldn't find *Endeavour,* it would cause them to heighten their patrols. That would make it harder for Major Johnston to land on Haven. If the Indians didn't know they were coming, there was no sense in broadcasting their arrival.

Instead, James planned to take things slowly and make sure the Indians never even knew *Endeavour* had been in the system. At least until it was time to leave. As a result, James and the rest of *Endeavour's* crew sat silently for the next four hours as they watched the patrol patterns of the Indian ships within the system.

"I think we have enough data, Jennings, plot us a course towards Haven," James said.

"Aye Sir," Jennings answered from the navigation console. Within seconds she had two courses projected onto the main holo display. "The blue course should keep us well away from the Indian patrol ships but it is four light hours longer. The red course is shorter but it will take us close to two of the patrolling Indian ships. If either of them alters their patrol patterns it won't give us much time to alter course and avoid them."

"Let's play it safe," James said. "Take us on the blue course. Don't exceed ten percent of our maximum thrust."

"Yes Sir," Jennings said.

*

Ten hours later James returned to the bridge after taking a nap. They had successfully circumvented all the Indian patrol ships in the outer system. Now, things were about to get a lot trickier. As per his orders, *Endeavour* had come to a halt just one light hour from the colony. They were more than close enough to make out the fleet that was orbiting the planet.

"What have we got?" James asked Sub Lieutenant Malik who was manning the sensor station.

"You can see the main fleet orbiting Haven on the screen Captain," Malik began. "We have counted one battlecruiser, one heavy, three medium and four light cruisers. There are six destroyers with the main fleet as well. Around the rest of the system we have detected at least another eight destroyers and fourteen frigates."

"Any sign of the other battlecruiser the Haven freighter reported seeing?" James queried.

"None Sir," Malik answered. "Unless the Indians are keeping it permanently in stealth it's not in the system."

"Makes sense," Mallory said from his command chair. "At least it does if the Indians don't know about the Gift. They are probably keeping two of their three battlecruisers In New Delhi to block any attempt by our fleet to get to Haven."

"Perhaps," James said. "That may be the case. Or else the Indians know all about the Gift and that battlecruiser has been sent to the exit near Chester. Remember how badly our crew was effected both times we passed through? It would only take a few heavy warships to shred a much larger fleet when it came through the Gift. That second battlecruiser could be waiting to ambush Rooke's fleet."

"I hadn't thought of that," Mallory replied.

"Something we will have to investigate," James said. "What about system defenses?" he asked, moving on.

"There is no sign of any battlestations or fixed defenses being installed yet Sir," Malik answered. "But there does seem to be a lot of activity going on in orbit all across the planet. Whatever the Indians are doing, I can't make it out at this distance. We'll have to get closer and use our optical scanners to really see."

"We may have a problem Captain," Lieutenant Becket said, interrupting Malik's report. "Look at the gravimetric plot."

James saw immediately what Becket was concerned about. Just a few minutes ago there had only been two ships actively moving about at the entrance to the shift passage to Independence. Now there were five and they were moving fast. As James watched one of the new contacts changed course, then after only a few seconds it changed direction again.

James knew exactly what it was doing, Admiral Jensen had used the same tactic against the Chinese when guarding the newly discovered planet Excalibur. She had known that the Chinese had a vastly superior fleet nearby. In order to maximize her chances to get her defending fleet into an advantageous position in the event of an attack, she had worked out a signaling system with her patrol ships. The gravimetric waves given off by a ship's impulse drive when it was operating above a certain threshold were detectable in real time across an entire solar system. Admiral Jensen had assigned certain acceleration profiles that would communicate different messages. It allowed her patrolling ships to update her on what was happening in the outer system in real time.

James knew that the techs in the Admiralty were already working on a gravimetric wave generator that could be used to send signals in real time using Morse Code. From what he had read of the system's specs, it was due to be rolled out to every RSN ship in the coming months.

"One of the destroyers near the battlecruiser is accelerating out of orbit," Malik reported. "Wait, it is changing direction too."

"It's a signal for the ships in the system," James explained.

Even as he spoke a number of the ships guarding the other shift passages turned towards the shift passage to Independence and accelerated. Four frigates broke away from the main fleet in orbit around Haven and powered towards the shift passage.

"I think we can assume our friend from Independence has made it to Haven," James said.

"Maybe they had to stop to carry out some repairs," Mallory suggested.

"Maybe," James echoed. "Either way they are here now."

As the system came alive with moving ships James kept *Endeavour* powered down, a light hour away from Haven, to watch how things unfolded. Soon a pattern emerged. The four frigates that had broken orbit from Haven spread out and formed a line actively scanning in all directions as they traversed a course straight for the shift passage to Independence. Of the ships that had already been guarding the shift passage, most of them had formed up into a similar formation and were slowly making their way towards Haven. It seemed that the Indian Admiral believed *Endeavour* was already in the system. She was trying to catch his ship as he made his way to Haven.

"We're getting bombarded by radar waves from multiple sources," Becket informed James. "It's not close to the maximum our stealth coating can absorb, but there is a heck of a lot of electromagnetic radiation being thrown around out there."

James was inclined to agree. It seemed that the Indian Admiral wasn't going to take any chances, they had every one of their ships actively scanning space with their main search radars. James could hardly blame the Indian Admiral. If it hadn't already, a message from the destroyer that escaped them at Independence would be arriving telling the Admiral that one of her medium cruisers had been destroyed. *That would make anyone grumpy*! James chuckled.

"Right," James said. "We've been sitting around long enough. Keep an eye on the radiation levels Becket, let me know once they start to increase."

"Aye, Sir," Becket said.

"Jennings," James said, "plot us a course to Haven. I want to enter a high orbit and keep station on the opposite side of the planet to the Indian fleet. We're going to drop off Johnston and then beat it back to the outer system. If we stay too close to Haven we are going to get caught sooner or later.

"Mallory, I want you to take Sub Lieutenants Malik and King and work out a plan to launch a number of drones into the system. If things get hairy we may have to use your initial idea after all."

"With pleasure Sir," Mallory said as he stood and motioned for Malik and King to follow him.

*

For over an hour *Endeavour* crept closer and closer to Haven. The amount of radar rays hitting the hull continued to increase, but they still weren't near the levels that James felt he needed to get concerned about. Just when things looked like they were going to go smoothly, an update on the holo plot made James sit up in his seat.

"The destroyers are spreading out from the main Indian fleet," Malik reported. He had returned from working with Mallory twenty minutes ago.

Having already seen what was happening, orders were on the tip of James' tongue, "Project their courses."

Sure enough, the destroyers appeared to be moving out

from the main Indian fleet to take up differing orbits around Haven.

"It looks like this is going to be close," James said to the bridge. "Keep *Endeavour* on her current course. Designate the closest destroyer alpha one."

The holo display showed that one of the destroyers now moving to patrol the space immediately around Haven would get very close to *Endeavour* when she ducked in towards the planet to drop off the stealth shuttle. As James ran a few calculations on his command chair he saw there was no other choice. Any change of direction now would bring them just as close to one of the other destroyers.

"Keep us steady," he said to Sub Lieutenant Jennings when she looked to him expecting new orders.

For another ten minutes, the tension on the bridge steadily rose as *Endeavour* braked to enter Haven's orbit. James would have preferred to just fly by the planet and launch Major Johnston's shuttle. However, the stealth shuttle would have to do a prolonged burn of its own engines to slow down enough to safely enter the atmosphere. If it did that it would be detected for sure. The only way to keep it from being detected was to enter into an area where *Endeavour* was in real danger of being detected herself.

"Optical sensors are detecting an anomaly off the starboard bow. It's small but it is close," Malik said breaking into the silence. "I think it is a passive recon drone."

"Alter course to zero point seven five," James ordered. "If they have one recon drone out there, there will be others. Our best bet is to stick as close to alpha one as possible. There won't be any stealth drones close to it, they will be spread out further afield."

"Do you think that drone detected us?" Sub Lieutenant Jennings asked.

"No," James said. "If they had, those destroyers would already be gunning it straight for us." *That, or the Indian Admiral is letting us get closer to the main fleet before it pounces,* James thought.

"Radar saturation is nearing detection levels on the stealth coating," Becket warned.

"Acknowledged," James said. He opened a COM channel to Major Johnston. "How long until you can launch Major?" he asked.

"Three more minutes," Johnston said. "We'll go as soon as we get into range."

"Get ready to alter course Jennings," James said to the navigation officer. "As soon as the shuttle launches take us out of orbit."

"Sir, the destroyer we designated alpha two is altering course. It's focusing more of its radar emitters in our direction," Malik reported shrilly.

"Our stealth coating can't absorb many more radar waves," Lieutenant Becket said from the tactical station. "They may start to get returns on us."

"We're just going to have to see how good our technology really is," James said. "Lock all the plasma cannons onto alpha one and get ready to fire a volley of missiles at them. If they detect us we need to finish them off fast."

Before James realized it, Major Johnston was back on the COM, "We're launching in thirty seconds Captain, thanks for the ride. We'll contact you once we're ready to be picked up."

"Stay safe," James replied.

Opening a holo image of the secondary shuttle bay, James watched the stealth shuttle exit his ship. As soon as the shuttle doors closed he turned back to Sub Lieutenant Jennings. "Take us out of here," he ordered.

Jennings fired *Endeavour's* maneuvering thrusters to turn her nose up and away from Haven and the nearest Indian destroyer. Carefully, she engaged *Endeavour's* main impulse engines, bringing them up to three percent of their maximum thrust. Any more and the Indian ships were sure to detect them. Nothing seemed to happen for a few moments, then, slowly but surely, *Endeavour* overcame Haven's gravity and escaped into open space.

No sooner than he had given the order to turn, it seemed to James, than Malik's warning broke into his thoughts.

"Alpha one has launched a normal recon drone in our direction. It's emitting huge amounts of radar waves."

"Are we in plasma cannon range?" James asked.

"No Sir," Becket answered. "At this range we'd barely scratch their armor."

"Navigation, prepare to go to full military power," James ordered. "I want a sustained engine burn for forty minutes. We need to get some velocity. Then we're going to shut down and go back into stealth mode. Becket, fire a full broadside at that destroyer. Then switch to rapid fire. I want that destroyer hammered."

"Aye Sir," Becket said.

"Ready Captain," Becket said just a few moments later.

"Fire," James said.

As Becket gave the command to the missile crews to fire, a number of things happened at once. Both of the nearest Indian destroyers accelerated and turned towards *Endeavour*. Two recon drones that had been in a passive state switched on and beamed mega joules of radar radiation towards *Endeavour*. The combined radar waves washing over *Endeavour* from the two warships and the three recon drones overloaded her stealth coating and allowed the destroyers to get an exact location on her. It didn't matter however, for the eight missiles that shot towards alpha one shouted to the entire system that *Endeavour* was in high orbit above Haven.

"This is about to get real hairy," James said. "Mallory, keep updating the positions of those drones you let loose."

"Aye Sir," Mallory said, his attention already focused on his command console where he was directing the drones that he had fired off into various points in the system.

The first salvo of missiles dove into Haven's gravity well towards their target. The destroyer was accelerating directly towards *Endeavour* and as soon as it got a firm lock it fired a single missile from its forward missile tube.

"Alpha two is turning," Malik shouted. "It's bringing its port broadside to bear on us."

A good try, James thought, *but it's not going to work.* Whoever was commanding the two destroyers was trying to get alpha one into plasma range of *Endeavour* to cause enough critical damage to prevent her from escaping. To cover alpha one's approach, alpha two was going to pelt missiles at *Endeavour* from long range. James didn't intend to let alpha one survive long enough to get into plasma range.

"Take the safeties off the impulse engines," James said over a COM channel to Chief Driscoll. "We need everything they have got."

"Aye, Aye, Sir," Driscoll said in his thick Irish accent.

"Firing second salvo from our rear tubes," Becket

announced. "The first will enter attack range in thirty seconds."

Fools, James thought as he watched the missiles home in on alpha one. As all eight were going straight at alpha one's nose, it meant only a fraction of her point defenses were able to engage them. Just as expected, as point defense plasma bolts and AM missiles reached towards *Endeavour's* missiles it quickly became clear they weren't going to be enough.

Three missiles survived to burst through the defensive fire. A last-ditch nose dive by the Indian destroyer caused all three to fail to get direct hits, but the proximity explosions from two of the missiles were close enough to bathe the destroyer in electromagnetic energy.

"We got them Sir," Becket called excitedly. "Looks like their port amidships section has taken some serious damage. Quite a few sensor and point defense blisters have been burnt off their hull. Can't see any hull breaches though."

"Keep it up," James ordered.

He spared a couple of seconds to look at the system wide holo plot to see what the rest of the Indian ships were doing. Their reactions weren't too surprising. Three larger warships had broken away from the Indian fleet in orbit around Haven and were accelerating after *Endeavour*. At their current rates, they wouldn't be able to catch his ship on their own. They would have help though. More than two thirds of the ships that were in the outer system were now speeding towards his ship. It looked like they were forming up into a cone formation to block off any possible direction he would take. No matter where *Endeavour* went, two or even three warships would be able to bring her into missile range. The resultant engagement would likely give the pursuing cruisers a chance to catch him. *Not good,* James thought.

His attention was brought back to the immediate battle when the now familiar sound of the flak cannons opening up told him the Indian missiles were entering attack range.

"Four down," Becket called out. "I've got the rest," she added as she directed the fire of the point defenses gunners.

Within ten seconds the final three Indian missiles disappeared off the plot. No sooner had they been dispatched than another two missiles erupted from *Endeavour's* rear tubes. With her missile crews operating in rapid fire mode they were only inputing the barest of targeting information into the missiles before they were fired. The close range to alpha one meant there was no need to spend the time to work out the complicated targeting specifications a longer shot needed.

This meant that barely four minutes after the first salvo crashed into alpha one, two more missiles came crashing in. Becket cursed as the destroyer's point defenses took out one of the missiles. When the remaining missile overshot its target and exploded quite a distance away from the destroyer, she shouted, "Come on, take a hit."

"No apparent damage," Malik reported a few seconds after the explosion near the destroyer. He carefully avoided looking at Becket.

"They won't survive another salvo," Becket said crossly. Her tone suggested it was more of a promise than a prediction.

She proved true to her word for after *Endeavour* effortlessly swatted away the incoming Indian missiles, one of Becket's two missiles scored another proximity hit on alpha one.

"We're starting to pull away," Mallory said, "It looks like alpha one's maximum acceleration was only about two hundred and twenty gravities. It's starting to fade. That last hit must have caused some internal damage. We are already exceeding two eighty."

James nodded to Mallory to acknowledge the unspoken warning. *Endeavour's* impulse engines were rated for a maximum safe acceleration rate of two hundred and seventy gravities. Anything more was risking a critical failure that would leave *Endeavour* a sitting duck. Opening a COM channel to Chief Driscoll James said, "Hold our acceleration at two eighty for another ten minutes then dial it back Chief."

"A wise decision Sir, I can't guarantee what would happen if we exceed two eighty," Driscoll replied.

"Point taken Chief," James said, cutting the COM channel.

He focused on the third wave of Indian missiles. Alpha one and two were now coordinating their fire so that the five missiles from alpha two and the single one from alpha one were coming at *Endeavour* at the same time. Whilst the Indian missiles were good, with her flak cannons *Endeavour* was designed to be able to protect herself against upwards of ten incoming missiles of the latest British designs. James felt no concern as he watched the Indian missiles fail to penetrate his defensive fire.

"Got them," Becket shouted, bringing James attention back to the missiles she had fired at alpha one.

Switching to the optical feed of alpha one, he saw the destroyer veering away from her original course in a haphazard roll. As the starboard side of the ship came into view he saw a massive hole between two of her missile tubes. As he watched a series of secondary explosions rippled through the innards of the ship and her acceleration cut out.

"Good shooting," James congratulated Becket.

"Alpha two is slowing down," Malik reported. "They will be out of missile range in five minutes."

"They don't want to share the fate of their sister ship," James said. "I don't think they will go too far though. I imagine they are going to try and stay right on our heels. Becket, keep firing at them, our missiles will have to go into ballistic mode for some of their flight. The Indian captain will have to keep altering course if they want to avoid them, that should gain us a little more space."

James took a moment to check the status of the other Indian

ships in the system before he continued giving orders.

"Aim for the left edge of the enemy's formation as we face it Jennings," he said once he had formulated a plan. "They will try and move their ships to keep us in the center. I want you to match their movements."

"Yes Sir," the Navigation officer replied.

*

Forty minutes after leaving alpha two behind, *Endeavour* reached her maximum speed of 0.38c. "Cut all acceleration," James ordered. "Put us into stealth mode. Bring us to a new heading of five seven six point four."

As his bridge crew carried out his orders James watched the holo plot to see how the Indians would respond. To them it must have looked like *Endeavour* was racing to the edge of their formation to try and fight her way past the patrol ships before the larger cruisers could catch up with her. Now they would have to come to terms with the idea that James wanted to play hide and seek.

Whoever was in command of the Indian ships wasn't as slow as he had hoped, within a minute of *Endeavour* going into stealth over thirty new contacts appeared on the gravimetric plot.

"Recon drones," Malik reported. "They are all heading in our general direction."

"Map out where the Indians will be estimating we are," James ordered.

"There you go Sir," Malik said as a bubble appeared around *Endeavour* on the main holo display. The Indians would be aware of *Endeavour's* last known speed and direction. However, they had no idea what she did after she went into stealth. She could have reversed, continued on the same flight path or turned in any other direction. As the minutes went by, the bubble of space marking out where *Endeavour* could be increased exponentially.

Despite the fact that she was heading almost straight towards the approaching Indian patrol ships, it would still take the drones they had fired another hour to reach *Endeavour's* location. That meant they would be more than forty light minutes away from their motherships when they began their search. As a result, they couldn't report back their findings, nor could they receive orders, in real time. Something James had planned for.

"Mallory, wait until the first Indian drones enter Malik's bubble. Then I want you to light yours up,"

"Aye Sir," Mallory said grinning. "We'll give them more contacts than they can handle."

"Exactly. Fire off any more drones you think you need," James said.

Having already planned their route of escape before opening fire on alpha one, James had given Mallory the task of working on his part of the plan several hours ago. He now had over twenty normal and stealth recon drones nearby.

"The Drones are switching on their search radars," Malik informed everyone when the drones approached the bubble that marked out *Endeavour's* potential location.

Mallory put his plan into motion. On the holo plot a new contact appeared for a couple of seconds and then disappeared. *Endeavour's* computer estimated that the thermal bloom her sensors had picked up had been from a ship using its maneuvering thrusters to change direction.

It seemed the limited artificial intelligence on two of the nearest drones had come to the same conclusion as they altered course to investigate. As soon as they came into the general area of Mallory's drone he activated a second and then five minutes later a third.

Fifty minutes after Mallory had activated the first drone, the time it took for the drones to send their sensor data to the patrolling warships and for new orders to be sent back, ten of the drones broke off their search patterns and began a more intensive search in the area of Mallory's first drone. Then, in quick succession, a number of revisions to the drones' orders obviously came in as the drones began to move back and forth across the space around *Endeavour,* frantically trying to check out all the contacts they were picking up.

"It's working," Mallory said.

"Yes, now let's see if they take the bait," James replied.

For another forty minutes *Endeavour* moved silently into the outer system. All the while the patrol craft continued to approach the general area *Endeavour* had to be in. Then, as James watched, the formation of over sixteen patrol craft shifted as they came onto a new heading.

"Activate the rest of the drones," James ordered.

"Done," Mallory said. In response to his order six drones gave off signals that mimicked *Endeavour* in one fashion or another.

"Some of the recon drones are diverting to investigate our latest drones," Malik said. "The patrol ships are staying on their courses though.

"Perfect," James said. Mallory had carefully activated his drones in a manner that would slowly pull the Indian search towards one end of the large bubble that represented the area of space *Endeavour* could have got to in stealth mode. It had taken a while for the pattern to become recognizable, but the Indian Admiral had finally seen it. Just as James had wanted. Now the Indian Admiral was directing all their ships into the area where it looked like James had been trying to hide *Endeavour*.

In reality though, *Endeavour* was right in the middle of the area the Indian drones were searching. It had been a big risk to take. Yet, it now meant that Endeavour would pass by the outer edge of the Indian patrol ships' formation and, with luck, avoid detection by their much more powerful search radars.

For another forty minutes the Indian drones buzzed around *Endeavour* but none came close enough for their radar to overload her stealth coating. Then it came time to pass by the outer edge of the Indian formation. Everyone on the bridge watched Becket's readout of the levels of radar radiation hitting the hull slowly increase. More than one sigh of relief was heard when they passed by the Indian formation and the radar levels decreased.

"Take us into a low orbit around the gas giant," James ordered once they were well clear of the Indian ships. Haven's eighth planet had been his target all along. "I want to enter its upper atmosphere. That should hide us from any ships that might pass by looking for us. We'll lie low until we get a signal from Major Johnston. The mission rests on his shoulders now."

Chapter 14 – The Natives

At times I have thought the description 'Earth like planet' has been used far too generously. Even the most Earth like planets have required generations of toil and struggle to turn them into places where the human race can thrive.

-Excerpt from Empire Rising, 3002 AD

26th April 2467 AD, edge of Haven's atmosphere.

Major Johnston stood in the stealth shuttle, holding onto one of the ceiling rails with as firm a grip as his combat armor would allow. Every bone in his body felt like it had already been rattled into pieces as the shuttle bucked up and down. Apart from the two special forces marines in the pilot chairs, the other members of his team were bouncing up and down as they stood beside Johnston holding on for dear life. Despite his armor's heat regulating system Johnston was working up a sweat as the shuttle absorbed all the heat its plummet through Haven's atmosphere generated.

"No one told me it was going to be like standing in a furnace," he growled over the shuttle's COM.

"We did say it was going to get hot," Lieutenant Moony said.

"Yeah, hot, not boiling. How much more can the shuttle take?"

"Another thirty seconds and we will be through the upper atmosphere, we are beginning to slow now," Moony said. "If the shuttle wasn't absorbing all our heat from reentry we would be lighting up every Indian sensor in the system."

"I know, I know," Johnston said. "It doesn't mean I have to like it."

Just as Moony said, the rattling died down within thirty seconds as the shuttle stopped being buffeted about so much. As they descended, Johnston checked the external temperature reading on his combat armor. It said the temperature was falling, but he couldn't feel it yet.

When the shuttle landed and the external door opened, the cool air that hit them was like a welcome embrace. Despite the combat armor that his body was encased in, Johnston still found himself letting out a satisfied sigh along with the rest of the marines.

"I've never felt something so nice in my armor before," one of the marines said.

"And you won't ever again if I have my way," Lieutenant Moony said. "Now get your ass out of the shuttle and check the perimeter," he ordered.

By the time Johnston and Moony walked down the shuttle's ramp half of the squad's eight marines had disappeared into the forest to scout their surroundings. The other four already had one of the shuttle's side pods open and were removing the camouflage netting. The shuttle's design and stealth coating made it almost impossible to detect from orbit. However, the shuttle had set down in a small clearing in one of Haven's thick forests and from above the black shuttle stood out among the multicolored foliage.

"Get this covered ASAP," Moony said to the marines nearby. He stepped away from Johnston and opened a COM channel to the other marines and spoke to them about what they had discovered so far.

Major Johnston took a deep breath and looked around him. The Haven forests were certainly impressive. Somewhat similar to trees from Earth, they were covered in thick branches all the way down to where their trunks met the ground. Their leaves were much wider and thicker than any Johnston had seen on Earth and they sparkled with shades of pink, red and violet. They would have been beautiful if Johnston didn't know how much effort it took to trek through them.

Absentmindedly he detached the plasma lance from his armor. Thumbing the activation button brought the familiar snap hiss of the blade as it powered up. Johnston swung it round and round, watching the green glow of the lance trace out shapes in front of him. The plasma lance had belonged to Sergeant Harkin and had come in very useful the last time Johnston had been on Haven. Sadly, Harkin had been killed on Vestar. Johnston had kept the plasma lance when he had gone through Harkin's personal effects. He hoped it would come in useful again, though he couldn't use it so close to the shuttle. If he carved a path through the thick under canopy someone might stumble across it and follow it back to the shuttle.

Sighing, he thumbed the plasma lance off and brought a map of the continent they had landed on up on his HUD. Liberty, Haven's capital, was more than four hundred kilometers to the north. *Endeavour's* optical scanners had already identified a large military base a few kilometers outside the city, as well as what looked like a number of fortified outposts within the city. Any attempt to retake Haven from the Indians would need to quickly neutralize all the Indian hard points. It was his intention to scout as many of them as possible.

"Ready to move out?" Johnston asked Lieutenant Moony once he had checked their route on his HUD. By his estimate it would take more than a day to carefully cover the kilometers to Liberty and he wanted to get going. He knew *Endeavour* couldn't stay nearby forever.

"Yes Sir," Moony replied. "Samuels and McFarland have already taken point."

"Lead on then," Johnston said.

*

Five hours of tiresome hiking through the thick foliage found Johnston, Moony and the rest of the special forces marines, sat on a number of boulders taking some weight off their feet. With only a couple of spare energy packs each for their combat armor suits they were having to operate their equipment at only fifty percent of its full capacity. That meant the marines were using a significant amount of their own strength to move the heavy armor around. For normal marines such a feat would be impossible but special forces marines were a special group. Selected from the top one percent of normal marines, special forces marines then underwent a series of genetic and biomechanical alterations, the specifics of which were a tightly guarded secret. Those that survived the process had almost superhuman strength, speed and healing abilities. Even so, they were all finding it hard going in Haven's forests.

Johnston looked up when Private Samuels appeared through the foliage. She had been scouting the next section of their journey while the rest of the team rested. "I stumbled across a small village up ahead. It looks like they widened a natural clearing in the forest to build a few houses and grow some crops."

Johnston wasn't surprised. The vast majority of Haven's landmass was covered in the thick forests they had been trekking through. In a bid to produce enough food the early Haven settlers had spread out to take advantage of whatever clear ground they could find.

"We'll have to take a wide detour round it then," Moony said. "If the locals spot us and word gets out they will have the Indians breathing down their necks. That will add more time to our journey."

"You may want to investigate the village instead," Samuels said. "Or at least come and have a look for yourself. It looks abandoned. My guess is that there was a fight there a week or two ago. I think the Indians have already become a problem for whoever lived there."

"Any sign of survivors?" Johnston asked.

"No," Samuels replied. "The place looks well beat up."

"Well then, we will get some good images to send back to Earth at least," Johnston said. "Let's take a look."

Fifteen minutes later Johnston found himself standing in the middle of a primitive looking village. His guess had been right. The settlement had probably been built by the first generation of settlers. It looked like no one had bothered to improve it or expand it after it had been first set up. *Well, at least what is left of it hasn't been updated,* Johnston thought. Almost half of the buildings had been destroyed outright or had large holes blasted in them. From the look of the damage, some heavy caliber plasma cannons had ploughed their way through the village.

"Spread out," Johnston said. "Turn on your visual recording devices. The people back home will want to see just what Indian rule looks like."

"You heard him," Moony said to the other marines.

Switching on his own recording device, Johnston made for the nearest building. It had a large hole blasted in one of its sides and even with his combat armor on he was able to walk straight in. What he saw inside tugged at his heart and sent his mind back to his life before the Void War. He had walked into what looked like the living room of the settler's house, not too different from the house he had shared with his wife.

Chairs and a center table were knocked over or covered in large burn marks. Holo pictures were arrayed around what was left of the room's walls. Their images were still clearly visible as their power packs hadn't yet run out. In one corner of the room on a small seat there were a number of stuffed toys all neatly arrayed. What struck Johnston was how normal the room looked. Despite all the damage it still looked like a welcoming space where people had enjoyed a normal home life. Something Johnston hadn't experienced since he had been called back into the marines.

In another corner of the room a collection of children's toys was strewn across the floor and Johnston's mind was once again sent back to his wife. They had dreamed of starting a family together before the war. They had even started picking out a few toys that they thought their children would one day like. Johnston tried to force the memories away. He had a job to focus on. That dream could no longer be a reality, Noelle was dead. Killed by the Chinese. His anger had nearly cost him a dear friend the last time he had been on Haven. He had to move on.

Allowing himself just a few more seconds to think of his wife, Johnston turned sharply and walked out of the damaged building. When he got back into daylight

Lieutenant Moony waved him over, "We have found two survivors Sir."

Johnston picked up his pace and strode across the settlement to where Moony stood. As he got closer an older couple came into view from behind Moony's combat armor. They both looked terrified and as Johnston got close enough he could see the wife's eyes darting back and forth from Moony's armored head to his plasma rifle.

Johnston knew what the problem was. Whoever they were, the only other soldiers they had seen in combat armor had been the ones who had destroyed their village. With a flick of his thumb he disengaged his combat armor. Back sections of the armor slid up and to the sides and within a couple of seconds he was able to take a step backwards and place his feet on solid ground. He stepped around his now lifeless armor and held out his hand to the old man.

"My name is Samuel Johnston. I am a Major in the British Marines stationed on the HMS *Endeavour*," he said.

At first the man looked at him warily but as Johnston had hoped, at the mention of *Endeavour* his face changed.

"The *Endeavour*?" the man asked.

"There is only one," Johnston replied, nodding. "We have come to see what the Indians are up to."

"Oh thank goodness," the man's wife broke in. "You have come to save us. Just like you did when the Vestarians attacked."

"That is our aim," Johnston said. "We are just an advance force though. We are here to scout the Indian ground positions in preparation for an eventual attack. However, I can't make any promises about when that will be. You may have to live with the Indians for a while. How are your people bearing up under the Indian occupation? What exactly happened here?"

"I can't speak for the rest of our planet," the old man began. "And I hope you don't mind if I don't tell you my name. If you are captured, I don't want you leading the Indians back to what's left of my village."

Without waiting for a reply, he began to tell his story. "It began just over a week ago. We heard all about the Indian invasion of course. But apart from some planet wide broadcasts from the Indians we hadn't seen or heard from them. That all changed when a small band of troops showed up in our village demanding that we turn over a percentage of our crops. They said it was for the people in the cities. The problem was we had already sold our surplus before the Indians arrived.

"When we refused to just give the food over the soldiers insisted it was a legal tax they were imposing on everyone. When we still refused they left. Then the next day they returned with a shuttle full of soldiers in the same kind of armor your men are wearing. Many of the young farmers and settlers had been expecting something and they had armed themselves."

"They tried to take on soldiers in combat armor?" Moony asked in surprise.

"They tried," the old man said, nodding sadly. "One or two of the farmers had large mass driver rifles for taking down some of the bigger creatures in the forest. They managed to get one of the soldiers before they were both killed. Some of the other settlers had improvised a number of explosive devices that took out another two.

"After the initial shots, the soldiers retreated back into the forest. For a few moments we thought we had won. Then a shuttle swooped in and blasted our settlement. Just as we were picking ourselves up off the floor, the soldiers were back and moving amongst us like lightening. Almost everyone with anything resembling a weapon was killed on the spot. It was a bloodbath.

"The soldiers rounded the rest of us up and forced whoever was uninjured to help them load the shuttle up with most of our food stores. They said they were taking more than what they had initially asked for as punishment for our resistance. Then they lifted off and we haven't seen sight nor sound of them since."

"I'm very sorry," Johnston said. "Where are the rest of the settlers now?"

"They moved on," the old man answered.

"There was no food for them here and it will be another six

months before the next harvest is ready to be taken in. Most have gone to nearby settlements in the hopes of being taken in by friends or family. Others have headed for Liberty."

"Liberty?" Johnston prodded.

"Yes, there are rumors of fighting in the city," the old man said. "At least one of the Councilors is still alive and putting up a fight against the Indian soldiers. I don't know if that is true or if they are having any success, but many of the young men wanted to fight after what happened to us. They set out for Liberty to try and find whoever is still fighting."

"Thank you," Johnston said. "That is where we are heading. If there is a rebel group still fighting the Indians, we want to try and make contact with them. Are there any messages you would like us to pass on to anyone there?"

"No," the old man said looking down. "Our only son was killed in the fighting here. His wife and children have already moved back to her father's farm in a nearby settlement. May I ask," the old man continued, raising his head again. "Why are you doing all this for us?"

"Well," Johnston said. "I won't lie to you. Stopping the Indians from getting control of Haven and access to the shift passages to Vestar and Kulthar is very important to my government. But Councilwoman Rodriguez has also played a big role in sending us here."

"Rodriguez," the old man broke in. "She's a traitor. She turned tail and ran into the Indian's arms even before they arrived."

"Who told you that?" Johnston snapped. If Councilwoman's Rodriguez's name was already tarnished, using her as a political tool to win over the Havenites was going to be a lot tougher than some thought.

"It was all over the news broadcasts before the Indians arrived. Councilwoman Rodriguez fled her post and left her gas mining station for Earth. Maximillian said she had turned traitor. Putting two and two together, it's not hard to guess where she fled to. She probably saw the writing on the wall and decided to join the conquerors before the fighting even broke out."

"I wouldn't believe everything the First Councilor says," Johnston said. "Where is he anyway? Have the Indian's captured him?"

"He's dead," the old man said. "I saw the live broadcast myself. The Indians captured him and tried to make him read a statement to the planet. He made a move for one of his guard's weapons and they shot him right in front of everyone."

Really, Johnston thought, *maybe the old bastard managed to do something right after all. I'm sure that fed the fires of rebellion among the populace.*

"Then he died nobly fighting for your people," Johnston said, keeping his feelings to himself.

"And that is exactly why Councilwoman Rodriguez left when she did," Johnston tried to explain. "She did see the writing on the wall. But she didn't run to the Indians, she came to us. She has spent the last month back on Earth trying to convince my people and the rest of the Earth nations to allow Haven to democratically choose her future.

"If you remember my ship then you will remember my Captain, James Somerville? Well his full title is Duke Somerville of Beaufort. He and Councilwoman Rodriguez were married just weeks ago and so she is now Duchess Somerville. As far as I have seen, she is doing everything in her power to get the British government to send a force to liberate Haven. That is why we are here. She succeeded, and now her husband and the rest of the Royal Space Navy are on their way here to kick the Indians out."

"Well, that might just change things," the old man said. "Assuming it is true mind you."

"You mean Councilwoman Rodriguez married that naval Captain who saved us from the Vestarian's?" the old woman asked.

"Yes," Johnston said.

"How romantic," she replied.

"Oh give over," the old man said to his wife. "We are in the middle of a war. It is not the time for romance, our very future is at stake."

"Is it really true?" the old man asked as he looked back at Johnston with an earnest look in his eyes. "Is Ms. Rodriguez really coming back with a British army?"

"We're here aren't we?" Johnston asked. "We wouldn't be here unless there were more soldiers following us."

For the first time Johnston saw something other than despair in the eyes of the two old settlers. It wasn't hard to figure out what it was. Hope.

"Maybe we will pack up and go to the Fredericktown settlement," the old man said. "They will have food there and we can see our grandchildren."

"Yes," Alexandra said. "We can come back and fix up our home once all this fighting has died down. And we can tell everyone about Ms. Rodriguez."

"Just be careful who you tell about us," Johnston said. "The Indians don't know we are here yet and we would like to keep it that way. It is for your benefit too, if the Indians hear you have met us they will scoop you up for questioning."

"We understand," the old man said as he nodded.

"In that case we better get going," Major Johnston said. "Thank you for talking to us, your information will prove useful I'm sure."

"Thank you Major," the old man said. "We had lost hope for a while there. We simply don't have the technology or manpower to fight the Indians, even if our young men are willing and eager. With your help, we might yet find a measure of freedom."

"I hope so," Johnston said as he shook the old man's hand.

As they both turned and walked off back towards what must have been the remains of their house, Johnston got back into his power armor. "Ah, that feels better," he said once he powered it up.

"Time to head out Sir?" Lieutenant Moony asked.

"I think so," Johnston replied. "We have learnt all we're going to learn and the Indians might send a patrol back here at any time to check up on the settlement. It's time we got to Liberty to see what is going on with our own eyes."

"We're leaving in thirty seconds," Moony said over the COM to the rest of the marines. "Finish up what you are doing. Samuels and Fisher, you have point."

As the marines formed up and walked out of the settlement, Ferguson and Moony looked back to see the old couple standing at the door to their house waving. They both lifted their armored hands in return.

"I think that might be our cover blown," Lieutenant Moony said over a private COM channel.

"I imagine so," Johnston replied, "but at least my warning might make them hold off from telling anyone too much for a day or so. By then we will be long gone. With luck, by the time word reaches the Indians we will be ready to get off this rock."

Chapter 15 – The Councilwoman

While my expertise as a historian lies in naval warfare, the last thousand years have also seen dramatic changes in the technologies used to wage ground combat.

-Excerpt from Empire Rising, 3002 AD

27th April 2467 AD, Haven.

The next day Major Johnston stood peering through the thick foliage of the Haven forest. With a thought, he told his combat armor to inject more stimulants into his body. He and his marines had been on the move since they had disembarked from the shuttle. Several hours ago they had reached the outskirts of Liberty. They were now about four kilometers away from the city and ten from the large Indian base that had been set up in one of the few clearings in the forest near the city. Johnston guessed that the Indians had used the clearing as a LZ when they had first come to Haven. Due to the lack of space they had turned it into their main base after that.

In front of Johnston there was a small clearing in the forest that formed a path between Liberty and the Indian base. They had come across signs of fighting in the forest. Broken trees, fragmented armor pieces, exploded ordnance and a semi intact walker suggested that the Havenites were putting up a fight.

From the look of the path, it seemed it was a patrol route for Indian soldiers in power armor. Johnston had his men spread out around the path, waiting for a patrol. He wanted to lay his eyes on the Indians himself to see how good they were. If the opportunity arose, he also wanted to capture a prisoner. It would be the quickest way to find out exactly what the Indians were up to.

They had been watching the path for the last three hours and Johnston was very aware that his eyes were threatening to close over from exhaustion. *Even an enhanced special forces marine can't stay awake forever,* he reminded himself.

The next COM message sent a shot of adrenalin through his body, waking him up. "I've got movement up ahead," one of the marines reported.

Johnston checked his HUD, the marine in question was further along the path towards the Indian base. *It must be a patrol,* he thought.

"No one move," he ordered. "Let them come to us. We're only going to attack if the odds are in our favor. We need to be able to take them out quickly and get out of here fast. Samuels, double back into the forest and join the rest of us."

"Yes Sir," Samuels said. She was the marine who had spotted the incoming Indians, Johnston had sent her a klick along the path to give them an early warning of any activity.

"Here they come," Moony said as the Indians came into view around a turn in the path several minutes later.

Perfect, Johnston thought as he saw there were only ten Indian soldiers. *We can take them.*

"They look wary," Moony said and Johnston had to agree. The soldiers looked like professionals and they were panning their weapons around as if they expected an attack at any moment.

"Get ready," Johnston said. "We will wait until they get right in between us. I want the first soldier alive, Beckworth and Harte, take out his legs. The rest of us will dispatch the others."

As the marines acknowledged his orders, Johnston watched the Indians get closer. When they were a little over three hundred meters away, all hell broke loose.

An explosion erupted from right under the feet of the lead Indian soldier. It blew his power armor into the air. Even before it hit the ground, the loud thud of several gauss cannons could be heard from the forest. Two Indians took rounds right in their sternums, shattering their frontal armor and the soldier within. The gauss cannons were quickly followed by the sounds of other weapons Johnston didn't recognize. However, their results could be seen among the Indian soldiers as some form of explosive round burst against their armor.

Whilst the element of surprise allowed the Havenites to take out three of the Indian soldiers, the rest reacted quickly. Within seconds of the first explosion the remaining seven soldiers had taken cover by the edge of the path and they were mercilessly pouring fire into the side of the forest they were under attack from.

The result of their much more accurate fire was felt almost at once as the fire from the Havenites dropped off. One gauss cannon fired again, hitting an Indian soldier. The return fire from the Indian plasma rifles quickly silenced it.

Just when Johnston thought the battle was over, more than fifteen human heads popped up from the other edge of the path. Zooming in on one of them Johnston saw that the man was lifting himself out of a hole that had been covered over with soil and branches. As soon as they were on their feet they charged towards the Indian soldiers.

The Indian who had been watching their flank mowed the Havenites down. Yet too many had seemingly appeared from nowhere for him to react fast enough. In the blink of an eye five of the Havenites got close enough to attach something to their targets. As soon as they did they burst into the thick foliage and out of Johnston's sight.

Many of the Indian soldiers didn't realize what had just happened but as the Havenites ran past them they poured plasma bolts into them, cutting them down. Then, as the Indians ran out of targets, silence descended. It was short lived however; the five devices on the Indian soldiers detonated, blowing the soldiers and their combat armor into pieces.

Right on cue, the fire from the Havenites within the forest picked up again. The two remaining Indian soldiers found themselves overwhelmed and despite trying to return fire both fell to the ground injured or dead.

As soon as they hit the floor a number of unarmed humans appeared out of the forest. They picked up the plasma rifles the Indians had been carrying, and then turned and ran in the direction they came from.

Strange, Johnston thought. *I guess they are not retreating into the city.*

"What do we do now?" Moony said once the Havenites disappeared.

"We get out of here," Johnston replied. "This place is going to be crawling with Indian troops in minutes."

Johnston opened a map of the local area on his HUD. *If not the city, where would I run to?* He asked himself. *Here,* he thought, mentally tapping a valley that ran between two large mountains. I*f the Havenites want to get away from the city and the Indian base they will likely go through here.*

"Check your maps," Johnston said. "We're moving to sector six forty-five. Double time, we need to clear the area fast."

As he spoke, Johnston bounded away from the path, deeper into the forest, and the rest of the marines formed up beside him. He angled away from the area he thought the Havenites would be in. He didn't want to accidentally stumble across a group of them. Any weapons fire would attract the Indians. Then, after several kilometers, he angled back towards the valley he wanted to get to.

*

Three hours later Johnston was once again waiting patiently amongst the thick Haven forests. This time he was hoping that whoever ambushed the Indians would come across his path. Without combat armor, they were no doubt making much slower progress and he had allowed half his men to shut down their armor and take a nap nearby. The rest were silently watching for any sign of movement.

"I think they are coming up from the south-east side of the valley," Lieutenant Moony reported. "My infra-red sensors are detecting some life forms. My targeting computer suggests they may be local animals but they are moving too uniformly. I'd guess the Havenites are masking their heat signatures as well as they can."

"Wake the others," Johnston said. "I'm moving to head them off. I will confront them alone but be ready to back me up if I need you."

"Understood," Moony said.

Once Johnston got in front of the approaching group of Havenites he ducked down behind a thick tree trunk and sat perfectly still. Within minutes his armor's sensors picked up a couple of humans carefully stalking past him. *Scouts*, Johnston thought. A few minutes later the main group of Havenites came into view. There was one man in what looked almost like a small combat armor suit carrying a gauss cannon. The rest were a rag tag lot of men and women, some in torn and worn military uniforms, others just wearing civilian dress. Many didn't appear to be carrying any weapons.

When they were a stone's throw away Johnston jumped up. He held both arms in the air as a sign of peace. The Havenites jumped back in shock. The soldier with the gauss cannon raised it towards Johnston but stopped short of bringing it to bear on him.

"Who are you?" he shouted.

Johnston activated the release button on his face armor. It slid back, revealing his face. "My name is Major Johnston of the Royal Marines. I have been sent to Haven to assess the situation and make contact with any groups resisting the illegal Indian occupation. I presume I have found who I am looking for?"

"Why should we believe you?" the soldier asked. "I can just blow you away and take your weapon. I'm sure we could make better use of it than you."

"You are welcome to try," Johnston said. He was ready to dive back behind the tree he had been hiding behind at the first sign the Havenite would fire on him. The Haven soldier may have fought regular Indian soldiers before but he didn't know just what he was facing in a special forces marine.

"But then you would lose the chance to really hurt the Indians. I am here to help you and prepare the way for a British invasion. My government intends to kick the Indians out of Haven," Johnston explained.

"So what do you want with us?" the soldier asked.

"I want you to take me to whoever is in charge of this outfit. There are many things we need to discuss," Johnston said.

"And how can I trust you?" the soldier said warily.

"Because," Johnston began as he gave a hand signal to his men. In less than a second seven marines appeared all around the Havenites, plasma rifles leveled at their targets. "If I wanted to kill you I would have already. Or, if I wanted to follow you to your base and attack it instead, we'd still be in the forest watching you. As you can see, we can sneak up on you any time we want."

The Havenite soldier who was in charge looked around at the British marines for a few seconds and then lowered his gauss cannon. "Ok, I guess," he said. "You can come with us to meet Councilwoman Pennington."

"Good," Johnston said. "You may lead on."

*

For another hour the group tramped through the forest up

the valley. At some unspoken signal the Havenites turned ninety degrees to their left and climbed the side of the valley towards one of the mountains. After another hour of heavy going a large cave appeared in front of them that looked as if it went straight into the heart of the mountain. There were large trees everywhere and the cave entrance was completely invisible from above.

"You are based in here?" Johnston asked.

"For now yes," the lead soldier said. "We used to move around a lot, I'm not sure how much longer we will be here for."

Thankfully, the cave entrance was large enough for Johnston and his men to get into it with their combat armor on. However, after one hundred meters it narrowed. Seeing the problem, Johnston exited his combat armor.

"Moony, Reynolds and Harte, you are with me," Johnston ordered. "The rest of you can stay here and guard our combat armor. I want two of you on watch at all times. The rest of you can take a well-earned rest."

Twenty meters further down the passageway it widened again. Once Johnston ducked down to get through the last narrow section he looked up to see a cavern flooded with light. There were powerful lights attached all around the cavern walls, making it feel like they were all standing in daylight. The cavern itself was thronging with people, some looked military but the vast majority looked civilian. The many children that were running around suggested that this was more than just a military base.

As the rest of their group split off and went to greet people they knew, the soldier that had been their escort turned to Johnston. "Councilwoman Pennington has set up an office further up the cave. This way," he said.

Johnston saw what he meant as they approached the back of the cavern and another small tunnel appeared to go deeper into the mountain. Two soldiers, in armor similar to the leader of the attack on the Indians, stood guarding the tunnel. Both tensed as they saw Johnston and Moony approach in their British uniforms.

"They are British marines," their escort explained. "They have come to speak with Pennington. I will vouch for them."

"Very well," one of the guards said. "She has been waiting for your return."

Once past the guards, they walked down several meters of dimly lit tunnel before it too opened up into a small chamber. A desk with a woman sat behind it dominated one side of the chamber. The other side had a number of holo projectors with a number of other men and women examining them. A quick glance told Johnston most of the holo projectors were displaying maps of Liberty and the Indian army's base.

"Counselor," their escort called out. "I have some guests here who would like to meet you."

Johnston had never seen Councilwoman Pennington before but he had heard of her. As she looked up from her desk he was sure that if he had met her before, he wouldn't have recognized her now. Her blonde hair was tattered and disheveled. Under her eyes were heavy bags and fatigue oozed off her. Nevertheless, the look in her eyes showed Johnston why she was in charge. Despite everything that had happened, she still looked fierce.

"Councilwoman," Johnston said, offering his hand. "My name is Major Johnston of the Royal Space Marines. We are here to help."

A look of relief flashed across Pennington's face. "So we are not alone in this?" she asked.

"Thanks to Councilwoman Rodriguez, the British are on your side," Johnston said wishing to get Rodriguez front and center of the conversation.

"Rodriguez?" Pennington said. Before Johnston could explain she had already figured it out. "She went to the British after she fled from Maximillian. Then did she warn you about the attack on the Kulthar delegation's ship in time?"

"You know about that?" Johnston said, tensing. If Pennington was a part of the group that had been working with Maximillian, then he would have to tread carefully with her. Any help he gave her now would boost her popularity with her people and she could become a thorn in their side later on.

"Yes, Maximillian told me. Then he imprisoned me before I could do anything to stop him," Pennington said. "Now, did Rodriguez succeed?"

"Yes," Johnston answered. "She managed to get to Captain Somerville in time to allow him to stop Admiral Harris and his ships. If she hadn't, then no one would be coming to your aide. You can be sure of that."

"That is what I feared," Pennington said. "At least now we have hope. You said Somerville, is that the same Somerville that commands *Endeavour*?"

"Yes," Johnston said and plunged into the story of Suzanna's address to the UN, to the British parliament and her wedding to James.

"So your government thinks my people will just accept the idea of becoming a British protectorate do they?" Pennington said once Johnston was finished.

"That is not for me to say Ma'am." Johnston replied. "I am just a soldier. But from what I have seen so far, being a British protectorate would beat being occupied by the Indian army."

"That much is true," Pennington said. "Well, it certainly looks like Rodriguez landed on her feet. I imagine the British see her playing a key role in whatever future government they have planned for our people?"

"I can't say," Johnston said. "That's far above my pay grade. I am meant to be worrying about how to kick the Indians off your planet. That is why I am here. Whatever the future holds. I am sure you and my government can work on that together. For now, you only have to deal with me."

"Yes, I think we can come to an agreement," Pennington said. "The future will have to wait."

"Well then, can you fill me in on what has happened since the Indians entered your system?" Johnston asked.

"Yes," Pennington said as she walked towards the holo projectors. "Edward, get the reconstructions of the Indian's invasion up on the holo display. Our new friend wants to watch them."

"Right away Mam," one of the attendants said.

Johnston watched in silence as the highlights of the space battle and then the Indian army's landing were played for him. Here and there he noticed there were important segments of the battles missing but that was to be expected. Either the communications between Haven's central command and the units involved in the combat had been disrupted or, as in many cases he suspected, the units involved in the battles had been destroyed without anyone even noticing.

"They hit you hard," Johnston said once the display switched off. "Your people fought well though, I don't think they could have done much better."

"Thank you Major," Pennington said. "We have been doing our best."

"What is the situation of your military now? Johnston asked. "Are there any formations still intact?"

"No," Pennington answered. "At least not any more intact that what you have seen here. We have military personnel from over five different battalions. Yet together we don't have the numbers to even make up one. I know there are other pockets of fighters, some are holed up in the city. Others have found places to hide like we have. We have been hitting the Indians when we can. Most of the fighting is going on in the city itself. The general populace has risen up against the Indians. There are some sections of the city that the Indian soldiers simply don't enter.

"Oh they could if they wanted to," Pennington said when she saw the look of surprise on Johnston's face. "We have very few weapons that can actually penetrate their armor. However, even without such weapons, many of our people attack them with whatever they can find. I think the Indians have just found it safer to leave certain parts of the city alone.

"That is why we have started hitting their patrols around their base. It's one of the easiest ways to get to them."

"But your attacks are so costly. I must have seen more than twenty people killed in the attack on that Indian patrol," Ferguson said.

"You were nearby?" the soldier who had been their escort said in surprise.

"Barely three hundred meters away," Johnston said, smiling. "Remember how I snuck up on you?"

"Point taken," the soldier said. "Then you will also have seen that we gathered ten plasma rifles. Twenty lives for ten plasma rifles is an exchange I would make in a heartbeat. With those weapons we can easily kill another twenty Indians."

"It's hard I know Major," Pennington said in response to Johnston's look of disgust. "But that is the price we are willing to pay for our freedom. If we have to exchange one hundred Havenites for every Indian soldier, then we will. One way or another we are going to make the Indians regret ever coming to Haven."

Johnston didn't quite know what to say. The look in Pennington's eyes told him she was serious.

"How are you going to help us do that Major?" Pennington asked him.

"Well," Johnston said. "Like I explained, I am just part of the advance team. When I left Earth the plan was to send a full invasion force. If any attempt to retake Haven from the Indians is going to be successful though, whoever is leading the invasion force will need as much intel as possible. That's my job. I'm here to scout out the main Indian bases and defenses and make contact with any resistance fighters."

"You have succeeded in one of your tasks Major, now let's see how we can work together to accomplish the other shall we?" Pennington asked.

"I'm open to suggestions," Johnston said as he followed the Councilwoman back to her desk.

"Well I might have someone who can help you," Pennington replied with a smile.

Chapter 16 – Forest Guide

I have always struggled with the Sun Gates, passing them just seems so unusual. I suspect I am not alone. In fact, there is no doubt that even the best naval officers and soldiers have well-hidden fears.

-Excerpt from Empire Rising, 3002 AD

28th April 2467 AD, 10km from Liberty.

"Stop," Clare said as she held up her hand and froze in place.

"What is it?" Johnston whispered to his guide.

Instead of answering she turned her head and glared at him. Getting the point Johnston kept quiet.

About twenty seconds later Johnston heard a low buzzing sound. Off in the distance his enhanced eyesight picked out movement. If he had been in his combat armor he could have zoomed in on it. Yet Clare had made him leave it behind. As things were, he could just about make out some kind of metallic thing moving through the thick foliage. The combat fatigues he was wearing tingled in a couple of places to let him know that they were absorbing radar and laser scanning rays being directed in his direction. He prayed that the combat suit Clare was wearing was just as effective as his.

Almost as soon as it appeared, the thing disappeared. Thirty seconds later, Clare visibly relaxed and let out a deep breath.

"A drone," Johnston said, "How did you know? I didn't hear anything."

"It's not what you hear, it's what you don't hear," Clare said, turning to him smiling. "My father loved to hunt in the woods around our settlement. As soon as I was old enough he would take me with him and I know the sounds of all the birds and animals around here. If you had been listening, you would have noticed that it went quiet about a minute before the drone came by. We might not be able to sense it, but the animals around here sure can. As soon as it goes quiet, you know something is up."

"Impressive," Johnston said.

"Not really," Clare said. "This is not my first time going to the Indian base. I learnt this trick the hard way. The Indians have more than a hundred of the things patrolling the forest all around here. I have bumped into one or two before. It's the main reason we haven't tried to attack the base. They would spot us coming kilometers away."

"I'm guessing my combat armor would have the same effect on the wildlife?" Johnston asked.

"I believe so," Clare said. "I didn't want to take the chance.

Besides, even with its camouflage, your armor will draw too much attention once we get closer to the base."

Johnston wasn't too sure about that, but he didn't want to argue with his only guide. "How did you come to join the fight against the Indians? You're obviously not military," he asked as they carefully continued their journey.

"I used to work in the Council Chambers," Clare answered. "I was a cleaner, I swept the chamber for bugs and other eavesdropping devices. I had to leave over a difference of opinion just before the Indians arrived."

"So you are that Clare," Johnston said putting two and two together.

"What?" Clare asked, turning to him in alarm. "What do you mean?"

"You are Councilwoman Rodriguez's Clare," Johnston explained. "You are the one who warned her about the attack on the Kulthar delegation ship."

Clare didn't reply, prompting Johnston to add, "Well, aren't you?"

"Yes," Clare said reluctantly. "But you have to promise not to tell anyone back at the resistance base. If they find out they will lynch me. Maximillian has become a martyr to our cause. If anyone finds out I betrayed him, I will be in big trouble."

"Your secret is safe with me," Johnston assured her. "But I want to thank you for your actions. By warning Councilwoman Rodriguez, you allowed her to get to my Captain in time to stop the attack. You saved human-kulrean relations."

"Well, you are welcome," Clare said slowly. "I just did what I thought was right, just like I am now. Now, if you don't mind, let's not talk about it any further."

"Well then, what would you like to talk about?" Johnston asked.

"Nothing," Clare said, "we are here."

Peering ahead, Johnston saw that she was right. There was a break in the forest about two hundred meters ahead of them. The sunlight streaming in told him that there was open ground beyond that.

"Up we go," Clare said, pointing to one of the trees.

"After you," Johnston said, unsure of what she planned next.

Shrugging, Clare pushed past Johnston and climbed the tree she had pointed to. As Johnston watched she made quick progress. The thick foliage that began at the base of the tree provided many branches for her to use for feet and hand holds. Shrugging, still not sure of what they were doing, he began to climb anyway.

When they were about eighty meters up the tree Clare stopped and reached above her head to untie something. When her hands returned Johnston saw that she had a metallic wire in them. It stretched further up into the canopy of the trees, seemingly attached to a branch higher up.

"You are not about to do what I think you are, are you?" Johnston almost groaned.

All through marine training and then the special forces training he had endured after receiving his enhancements, Johnston had excelled at EVA missions. He was just as comfortable on the ground. Yet, he had never been able to get over his childhood fear of heights. Even when he was wearing combat armor that could easily survive a fall of over one hundred meters, he still got nervous when at height. As a result, during his first stint in the marines he had always gotten skittish on missions where he had to jump out of a shuttle, either in his power armor or with a wing suit or parachute. It had earned him a rather unsavory nickname among his peers, Johnston had been thankful to see that the name had been long forgotten by the time he re-enlisted.

"You bet, I used to love doing this with my father," Clare said to his dismay. "He built me a whole series of tree houses that I could swing to and fro from."

"And just how does this help us with our mission?" Johnston asked.

"The Indians have sophisticated movement sensors placed

around the edge of the forest. They don't want any surprise attacks catching them off guard. However, they are only on the ground. Up here we can swing to the edge of the forest and get a good look at the base. I set up all the wires we need the last time I was here."

Looking down Johnston had to physically stop his legs from twitching.

"You're not afraid of heights are you Major?" Clare asked with amusement in her voice. "If you want you can go first and I will give you a push."

"Believe it or not I am," Johnston said. "Though I am well used to having to deal with it. On you go. I'll be right behind you."

"Suit yourself," Clare said as she jumped off the branch and let the wire swing her more than twenty meters across to a nearby tree.

Once she detached herself from the wire she swung it back to Johnston. Johnston attached it to his combat suit and mimicked her jump. Not daring to look down, he focused his attention on his target. With far more ease than Clare was expecting, he landed his feet on the branch and brought himself to a complete stop.

"Like I said, I may have a fear of heights, but I know how to handle it," Johnston said to her questioning face. "Now let's keep going. I am eager to see what the Indians have built."

Four more times Clare swung from branch to branch using wires she had already set up. When they came to the final one she tied the wire up after Johnston had used it. Then, with her arms spread out for balance, she walked out along the branch they were both standing on. Johnston carefully followed, noting that the branch was getting thinner and thinner.

After six meters, Clare reached up in front of her and pulled some smaller branches out of the way. Sunlight streamed in with renewed vigor, causing Johnston to shield his eyes. When they adjusted, he was able to look out over the Indian base set up in the clearing in the forest.

"Impressive," he mumbled, mentally taking notes. The nearest side of the base was a kilometer from the edge of the forest. A large permasteel wall over ten meters high ran around its perimeter. Thanks to the fact they were over sixty meters above the forest floor, Johnston could easily see over the wall and into the base.

Right in the middle of the base there was a large flat area where five shuttles were parked. Nearby there were a number of prefab buildings. One looked like it was for servicing damaged shuttles. The others looked like offices and barracks for about a thousand troops. Near the entrance to the base that faced Liberty there was a tank depot. Ten Indian Rohini light tanks sat in formation with the access points to their turrets open. A number of mechanics were working on one of them.

The rest of the compound seemed to be equally taken up by

fixed defenses and storage crates. By Johnston's estimate, there were enough supplies in the Indian base to feed and arm ten battalions for almost half a year. It was obviously the main supply base, for it was heavily defended. At fifty meter junctions there were heavy plasma cannon emplacements along the outer wall. Each placement was backed up by four Indian soldiers in combat armor who were all milling around.

Further into the base, there were multiple rocket emplacements equipped with both SAMs and SSMs. Intriguingly, there were also two large lasers situated near the parked shuttles. Both were pointed into the sky and Johnston guessed they were for stopping any ships in orbit from bombarding the base with tungsten spears. The lasers would melt the projectiles before they hit the base. *What about plasma bolts?* Johnston thought to himself. *What am I missing?*

Conventional military wisdom said that whoever controlled a planet's orbitals controlled the planet. It was simply too easy for a ship in orbit to bombard enemy formations. Even if the Indians thought their laser could stop physical ordnance like the British tungsten spears, ten or twenty heavy plasma cannon bolts from a warship would devastate the Indian's defenses.

Yet if the Indians have gone to all the trouble to install the two large lasers to stop any physical ordnance, then they must have some plan for dealing with plasma bolts. But what? Johnston wondered.

The final pieces of equipment that caught Johnston's eye were eight large artillery guns. They looked out of place within the Indian base for everything else looked state of the art. Johnston wasn't used to seeing fixed artillery pieces alongside modern military formations. Today everything was about movement and speed. Fixed artillery pieces were a thing of the past.

What had drawn his attention to them was the frantic activity that had just begun around several of the guns. Several seconds later, five large booms reverberated around the Indian base and the surrounding forest. Caught off guard, Clare instinctively ducked when the guns erupted. Johnston barely blinked, instead, he leaned further out of the canopy to peer into the sky. With his enhanced vision, he was able to follow the five shells as they arced into the air towards Liberty.

I see, he thought.

"They have been doing that for days," Clare said. "Initially they used the plasma cannons from their ships in orbit to support their ground troops, but once the fighting broke out in the city they set those things up."

"They are howitzers," Johnston explained. "Old fashioned technology but very accurate over medium ranges. They will cause a lot less collateral damage to the city but still be more than effective enough against your people."

"From the reports I have heard I'm afraid you are right," Clare said. "As soon as a skirmish breaks out in the city those guns are lobbing explosives at our people. I imagine they have drones up all over the city just waiting to feed new targets back to those gunners."

"I'm sure they do," Johnston said. "But there are ways to avoid that kind of fire." Instead of elaborating he turned and walked back along the large branch they were both standing on.

"Right, I have seen enough," he said. "This is just a supply base. It will be useful to take it intact when the fleet comes. Or at least to destroy it. But the battle will not be won here. It's time to take me to the old Council Chambers."

*

Four hours later Johnston let out a sigh of relief. They had just broken out of the forest and were about to enter the outskirts of the city. Finally, he would be able to move freely. Pushing through the thick underbrush was distinctly unpleasant.

The sight that greeted him pulled him up short. Their stealth shuttle had come through the planet's atmosphere far to the south of the Haven capital. The last time he was on Haven he had been given a tour of the city from an aircar. He remembered a pristine city with many large, modern buildings, some forty or fifty floors in height. The sight that greeted him now was simply a mess.

Smoke rose from more than twenty different locations across

the city. Even as he stood taking in the sight, a number of loud explosions could be heard from deeper within the city. By chance they had come out of the forest not far away from the apartment buildings where Johnston had pursued Chang many months ago. A large crater was still visible where he had detonated a concussion grenade. Clearly no one had tried to clear away the destroyed building. What was more startling however, was the other buildings around it. What Johnston remembered as a series of attractive looking apartment complexes were now largely burnt out buildings. Those that weren't completely destroyed had scorch marks and holes blasted into their walls.

The damage in front of him didn't appear to be an isolated incident. Running his eye over the city's skyline suggested that at least two of the larger buildings were completely missing as well.

"Is it all like this?" Johnston asked Clare.

"Pretty much," she answered. "There are some areas that have hardly been touched. But anywhere where the populace has tried to stand against the Indians, fights have broken out. As far as we can tell, the Indians are trying to keep peaceful civilian causalities to a minimum. But when they get us in their targets they don't hold back. I think they are trying to discourage others from taking up arms."

"Knowing your people, I'm guessing that strategy isn't working too well," Johnston said.

"There were many who wanted to try and appease the

Indians," Clare said. "Yet the more of us they kill, the more those on the fence flock to our side."

"So what's the plan now?" Johnston asked.

"First we need to find some civilian clothes to help us blend in," Clare said. "There is a five PM curfew. Until then we will be free to move around the city, though of course a skirmish could break out at any time so it's not exactly safe. After that we will have to find a place to hole up for the night. We have two hours until five, we won't be able to make it to the Council Chambers by then. That sound ok?"

"Where are we going to get some civilian clothes?" Johnston asked.

"That won't be hard these days," Clare answered.

"You're in charge then," Johnston said, motioning for Clare to take the lead.

*

Half an hour later Johnston stepped out of a bedroom in one of the abandoned apartment complexes. It hadn't taken Clare long to find an apartment with plenty of clothes left behind in it. She was already dressed in a long skirt that covered the Haven military stealth suit that Pennington had given her.

"Ready to go?" she asked him.

"I think so," Johnston answered. "How do I look?"

"Like a homeless person," Clare chuckled. "You couldn't have picked something that fitted better?"

"I needed clothes baggy enough to cover my combat fatigues and side arm," Johnston said defensively.

"It will do," Clare said, shaking her head. "Most people aren't exactly looking their best these days so you will probably blend in."

"I'm glad to hear it," Johnston said.

After half an hour of carefully walking through the city Johnston decided he had to agree with Clare. There were very few people moving about on the streets and there were even fewer aircars or other signs of human activity. By Johnston's count, they had only passed three businesses that were open and each had no more than one or two customers inside. Everyone he had seen so far had kept their eyes down.

After forty more minutes of walking through the city Clare turned a corner into a small alleyway. She bent down and picked up a piece of rubble and threw it over one of the walls. A soft thud was clearly audible as the rubble hit some kind of drum that sounded like it was full of water or some other liquid.

After thirty seconds Clare stepped towards one of the doors that led into a large building and knocked out an intricate pattern on the wooden structure. Moments later the door swung open. There were no lights on within the building and the open door only revealed a black abyss.

Johnston tensed and hesitated. "Don't worry," Clare said, pushing him forward. "This is a safe house. We will be able to stay here for the night."

Reluctantly, he walked in. Once the door shut several soft lights came on, illuminating the hallway they were standing in. "Welcome," a man said from beside the closed door.

"We need a room for the night," Clare said.

"Of course," the man said. "Right this way. Do you have any information for me?" he asked as he lead them deeper into the building.

"No," Clare said. "We are on a mission for Councilwoman Pennington, that is all I can share with you."

"Very well," the man said. He didn't say anything more as he walked them down a number of twists and turns as they went deeper into the building. "Here you go," he said as he opened a door identical to many of the others they had passed. "You will not be disturbed here."

"Thank you," Clare said as he turned and left.

"This is us then?" Johnston asked.

"Yes," Clare said as she surveyed the room. There were six

beds spread out across the room. On the only table in the room there were a number of barrels of water and a pile of army rations. "We will be safe here. There are likely other fighters staying here but everyone keeps to themselves. If they are captured they don't want to know anything that could get someone else in trouble."

"A good system," Johnston said as he removed his civilian clothes and tore open one of the ration bars. "I'm guessing this will be as appetizing as one of my own military's rations?"

"I expect so," Clare said. "I try to avoid eating them as much as possible."

"So finish your story," Johnston said as Clare came over the table to get a drink. "You never told me how you ended up fighting the Indians with Pennington."

"It's not a very exciting story," Clare said, moving over to sit on one of the beds.

Johnston followed her cue and took one of the beds farthest from hers. "You can tell me anyway," he said, "maybe it will put me to sleep."

"Ha," Clare said, chuckling. "Well in that case let me make it as boring as possible."

"Please do," Johnston chuckled.

"As I said earlier," Clare began, "I had to leave the Council

Chambers in quite a hurry. I got caught recording the First Councilor's plans to attack the Kulrean delegation's ship. For more than two weeks I had to lay low, moving from hideout to hideout. Maximillian was furious with me and it seemed like he had tasked the entire Liberty security force with my capture. Thankfully, Councilwoman Rodriguez had given me enough credits and some emergency contacts that allowed me to stay hidden. It wasn't easy mind you. More than once I had to make a run for it just before they found me."

"It sounds like an exciting life," Johnston murmured.

"Hardly," Clare said. "The excitement began when the Indians arrived. As soon as they came the security forces forgot all about me. Then I watched Maximillian's death. As much as I didn't like the guy,I had to admire the way he went out. I decided there and then to do whatever I could to help the soldiers that were left fight back against the Indians. I started by helping any injured soldiers I came across hide from the Indians. After spending several weeks eluding Haven's security forces I knew where a lot of the best places to lie low were.

"After a few weeks I picked up my first weapon. I had watched soldier after soldier leave to fight the Indians and never return and I decided that it was going to take more than just soldiers to do the fighting.

"One day I joined up with a group from Pennington's forces. They had come into the city to hit an Indian outpost. After the battle, I fled with them and ended up back at one of their hideouts in the forest. They quickly realized I was at home in Haven's forests and have been using me as a scout ever since."

"Have you seen much combat before?" Clare asked Johnston when she finished her story and he didn't say anything.

When he didn't answer right away, she rolled over on her bed to look across the room at him. He was strewn out on his bed with his eyes closed. "Major?" she whispered. Johnston shifted in his sleep but didn't reply. When he didn't answer, she rolled onto her back. *I guess it was pretty boring,* she thought as she drifted off herself.

For his part Johnston tossed and turned for several hours as he dreamt of being chased by police and air cars across a broken city filled with smoking buildings and craters.

Chapter 17 - Pursuit

By today's standards the genetic and physical enhancements the Earth nations were able to apply to their best military personnel are extremely crude. Nevertheless, they were effective.

-Excerpt from Empire Rising, 3002 AD

29th April 2467 AD, Liberty.

The next day Johnston struggled to pull himself out of bed. It wasn't exactly comfortable but the last three days had been long and he had barely managed to get any sleep. Now he felt more refreshed than he had in a while. When he looked around, he saw Clare was already up and out of the room.

As he was putting on his civilian clothes she pushed the door open with her bum and swiveled around to reveal a tray in her hands. "Breakfast," she said. "I thought you might enjoy something more than rations."

"That's for sure," Johnston said eagerly. Though it wasn't the best scrambled eggs he had ever had, he didn't complain. He was just glad that Clare had managed to scrounge up some food for them.

"How far to the Council Chambers?" Johnston asked as they

finished off their food.

"At least another two hours, maybe three," Clare answered. "The Indians are always setting up new checkpoints and we'll have to avoid them. Plus, if any fighting breaks out we might have to lie low for a while. Usually they try to gather up anyone out in the streets if that happens in case any of us rebels try to slip away unnoticed."

"Then let's get going. I would like to be out of the city and on our way back to Pennington by nightfall. My men should already be on their way back by now."

"As you wish Major," Clare said as she stood and stretched.

*

Three hours later Johnston rounded a side street and came face to face with an Indian military checkpoint. Without flinching, he kept walking casually towards another street that led away from the checkpoint.

"This wasn't here a few days ago," Clare whispered.

"Just keep walking," Johnston said. Occasionally he glanced over at the checkpoint. There was a light tank blocking the street along with a heavy plasma cannon and at least ten Indians in combat armor. Beyond them he could just make out the Council Chambers in the distance. They were more than five blocks away.

"They have extended their perimeter," Johnston said as soon

as they entered another street out of sight of the checkpoint.

"It looks like it," Clare said. "Two weeks ago they evacuated everything out to three blocks away from the Council Chambers. I guess it is five blocks now."

Johnston grunted an agreement as he pulled a small holo projector out of his combat suit. Activating it he opened a map of Liberty. "I still need to get a look at the Council Chambers to see what kind of defenses they have. Where is the best place do you think?"

"Here," Clare said, pointing to the map. "We can follow the new perimeter they have set up and see how consistent it is to here. From that street you should be able to get as good a view of the Council Chambers as you are going to get.

"Let's keep moving then," Johnston said.

They passed three more Indian checkpoints blocking the roads that led to the Council Chambers on their way to Liberty Avenue. When they walked out onto the avenue they were confronted by the largest concentration of Indian forces Johnston had yet seen. Liberty Avenue led from the Council Chambers through the middle of the city to the First Councilor's residence. The central road consisted of eight lanes for ground traffic and there were wide walkways along each side of the avenue for walkers. Johnston had seen images of the avenue decorated with flowers and trees but now it looked bleak and war torn.

Right across the avenue the Indians had erected an eight-foot fence. In front of the fence there were four light tanks menacingly moving their turrets back and forth along the width of the avenue. Around the tanks there were more than fifty Indian soldiers and poking up from behind the fence Johnston could see two shuttles. They were probably loaded with more soldiers ready to take off and respond to any threat along the perimeter.

"I guess you are not going to see very much," Clare said, eyeing up the fence. Whatever defenses the Indians had in closer to the Council Chambers were obscured by the fence.

"A wasted trip I'm afraid," Johnston said. "Not your fault," he added when Clare looked momentarily hurt. "Let's just get out of here," he finished.

"That I won't complain about," Clare said.

As at the other checkpoints, they kept walking towards an alley that led away from Liberty Avenue to make it look like they were just going about their daily business. Out of the corner of his eye Johnston saw two Indian soldiers leave the group they were standing in and make their way towards Clare and him.

"Pick up the pace," Johnston whispered.

They got another ten meters towards safety when one of the soldiers got fed up chasing them and called out, "Halt you two. You have come up on our facial scanners a few too many times today. I'm taking you into custody for questioning."

Damn, Johnston thought. *I should have thought about facial scanners.* The Indians had probably picked them up at several of the checkpoints they had walked past. Someone walking the perimeter of the Council Chambers would immediately draw attention.
"Hands in the air," the other soldier called out, raising his plasma rifle when Johnston and Clare kept on walking. "My friend said halt."

"Do as he says," Johnston whispered as he came to a stop and raised his hands, his back still to the Indian soldiers. "Get ready to run."

"Turn around," one of the soldiers ordered.

Beginning a slow turn, Johnston then whipped around as fast as his enhanced reflexes would allow. He ducked onto his knees as his right hand pulled his plasma pistol from where it was concealed under his baggy clothes. In the blink of an eye he fired two bolts into the nearest soldier. The second soldier fired as soon as he saw Johnston moving aggressively but Johnston had ducked even before the soldier pulled the trigger. Momentarily astonished at the speed of his opponent the soldier didn't get a chance to fire again as two more plasma bolts burnt their way through his facial armor, killing him instantly.

Without looking at the other soldiers Johnston was already on his feet turning back to Clare. "Run," he shouted as he passed her and grabbed her by the hand. Clare didn't have time to take in what had just happened before she found herself almost pulled off her feet. Before they rounded the alley in front of them she felt an intense wave of heat pass her head as a plasma bolt narrowly missed her and burnt a large hole in the side of the building in front of her.

When they did round the alleyway, Johnston paused for a second. As Clare fought to catch her breathe he ducked back out into Liberty Avenue. He fired off a quick burst of plasma bolts, taking out the nearest Indian soldier charging after them. Then he lobed two explosive devices into the middle of the remaining soldiers. Set on a quick timer they exploded before the Indian soldiers knew what had been thrown at them, five more soldiers went down, large holes blown in their combat armor.

Before Clare could take in what he was doing he was back at her side and pulling her up the alleyway again. "We'll never be able to out run them," Johnston said. "We need to hide."

Even as he spoke he was detaching things from his combat suit and dropping them at strategic locations along the alleyway. "That might slow them down for a few seconds."

Thirty seconds after they turned another corner several loud explosions erupted from where they had just been. "Contact mines," Johnston explained. "They were charging too fast to even watch out for them. They will be more careful now."

For another two minutes, they ran flat out away from the Council Chambers. Johnston had them randomly twisting and turning down small alleyways linking the main streets that ran through Liberty.

"Stop," Clare shouted when they passed a building she recognized. "I know this place. This is one of the buildings I hid in when I was trying to avoid the security forces. We can hide here."

"Are you sure?" Johnston asked. "They are right behind us."

"I'm sure," Clare said, already making her way up the steps to the door into the building. With a kick, she opened the door and stepped inside. "Come on," she said.

Johnston dived into the building behind her. Clare pulled a flashlight from her utility belt and made her way deeper into the dark building. Johnston didn't even bother looking for a light switch. It would only draw attention to the building from anyone outside.

Walking with a purpose, Clare made her way through the maze of corridors until she found a set of stairs. "We need to get to the basement," she said as she went down them.

"If they find us, we will be trapped down there," Johnston said with concern.

"No we won't, you'll just have to trust me Major," Clare replied without turning around.

Left with little choice, Johnston continued to follow her down. After several flights of stairs, they came to the bottom of the building. It opened into a large room that seemed to cover the entire width and length of the building.

"This was a storage area," Clare explained. "When the first and second generation of settlers were building the city, space was at a premium. All the buildings were built with large storage floors to hold many of the foodstuffs and other things the residents in the buildings would need. It saved on the need to build dedicated warehouses.

"It just so happens," she continued as she walked to one end of the room, "that whoever lived in this building was into a few illicit activities." With a heave, she lifted a large piece of metal which looked like it had been abandoned where it was sitting. Underneath there were steps down into what looked like a tunnel that led away from the building. "There are more than a few buildings in Liberty with old tunnels connecting them. More than a few have been forgotten about. I found this one when I was hiding from the security forces here. It saved my neck."

"I have seen one of these before," Johnston said as he peered down the steps. "There was one in the building where Haven Intelligence were holding Chang. He tried to escape down it."

"Did he get away?" Clare asked. "We always assumed you got him; no one has seen sight nor sign of him since."

"We didn't get his body," Johnston answered. "But he didn't survive."

"Well let's hope this tunnel works out better for us," Clare said.

"Indeed," Johnston agreed.

Once they were both down the steps and in the tunnel Johnston pulled a far more powerful torch out of his combat suit and shone it down the tunnel. He wanted to see as far down as it was possible, to limit the chance of anything taking them by surprise.

"How far does it go?" he asked when he couldn't see the end.

"Almost a kilometer," Clare answered. "It comes up under another apartment complex closer to the edge of the city.

"Perfect," Johnston said. Turning around he reached up and lifted the large piece of metal back over, covering the steps down into the tunnel. Then he stepped past Clare and proceeded down the tunnel with his powerful torch lighting the way.

"Can I ask you something?" Clare said as she walked along behind him.

"Go ahead," Johnston said.

"Back at the Indian checkpoint you moved faster than I could even see. You out fought Indian soldiers in combat armor. And just now you lifted that piece of metal like it was nothing. Who exactly are you?"

"Who am I?" Johnston repeated, chuckling. "You know who

I am, Major Samuel Johnston. I think maybe the question you mean to ask is, what am I?"

"Ok then, what are you?" Clare pushed.

"A special forces marine. I was recruited out of the marines to undergo what we call enhancement. I really can't say anything more than that, its classified."

"Are you still human?" Clare asked.

"Of course," Johnston chuckling. "Or at least, I never heard my wife complaining that I wasn't."

"You have a wife," Clare said.

"Yes, or at least I did," Johnston answered in an almost whisper Clare had to strain her ears to hear. "She died in the war with the Chinese. I don't really want to talk about it."

"I understand," Clare said. "But I want you to know I am sorry to hear that. I have never lost someone close to me. But since the Indians came, I have seen many others who have. No one should have to go through something like that."

"Thank you," Johnston said.

The rest of their trip along the tunnel descended into silence as Johnston relived the memories of the day he returned to his wife after going through the enhancement process. It had taken the marine medics over a month to complete the process. Then it had taken another couple of months for him to get used to his new strength and speed. Initially, his wife had had been full of wonder and fear at what he had been able to do. It had taken him a couple of days to convince her he was the same man.

Sensing that Johnston was lost in his own thoughts, Clare remained silent, not wanting to intrude on his feelings.

"We're here," she said fifteen minutes later as she peered around Johnston's body to see the steps that were coming up. "The last time I was in this building it was inhabited, so we will have to be careful. If there are rebel fighters up there we don't want to startle them."

Climbing the stairs first, Johnston placed a hand on the metal sheet that was covering the top of the stairs. He gave it a gentle push to move it out of the way. When it wouldn't budge he raised both hands to the metal and lifted with all his strength. As it budged slightly a mound of dust and rubble streamed down on top of Johnston. He barely noticed for he was momentarily blinded by the sunlight that came streaming in.

"I think your building is gone," he said after his eyes adjusted to the light and he was able to make out what was around him. There was nothing but rubble for as far as he could see.

With a final effort, he tossed the metal sheet and the rubble that had piled up on top of it to one side. "Let's hope no one is nearby, we're going to stand out like a sore thumb," he said as he climbed the last few steps and stepped out into the middle of the rubble. Turning around, he helped Clare out of the tunnel.

"Which way?" he asked once she was out.

"This way I think," Clare said, taking several seconds to look around. "I recognize that building."

They picked their way through the rubble until they managed to get back onto one of the many alleyways that ran between Liberty's buildings. "Yes, it's this way," Clare said more confidently once they had travelled a few hundred meters.

A familiar buzzing noise caused Johnston to act quickly. Without even thinking he picked Clare up and dove behind a set of steps that jutted out into the alley way. "Shuttle," he whispered when he saw the look of bewilderment on Clare's face. "The soldiers will have recognized what I am once they analyzed our little skirmish. They will be doing everything they can to find me. I think they just called in their shuttles."

The whining from the shuttle's impulse engines grew louder and louder. Chancing a glimpse, Johnston saw that it was no more than five hundred meters in the air above them, moving in the general direction they had been traveling. Johnston could see at least three more moving back and forth over the city. One of the shuttles released a drone which hovered beside it for a second before shooting off on whatever flight path its operator had given it.

"They definitely know I am here," Johnston said. "We need

to find somewhere to hide. We'll have more of a chance to get out of the city under the cover of darkness."

"Ok," Clare said. "But where are we going to hide?"

"Right here," Johnston said, picking Clare up again just as the shuttle went out of sight. He climbed the steps they had been taking cover beside and kicked the door open at the top of them. "We can't risk moving in the open anymore while all those shuttles are monitoring every square inch of the city," he said as he put her down inside the building.

"But what if someone lives here?" she asked.

"Then they will just have to put us up for a few hours," Johnston said, closing the door behind them.

Almost before he had finished speaking a small explosion erupted from up further up the hallway. Johnston felt the displaced air hit his face from the slug that zipped past his face, barely missing him.

Johnston pushed Clare to the wall and dropped to his knees, his plasma pistol already out.

"We're not Indians," he called out when he saw the weapon that was pointed at them. It was not Indian military issue. "We just need a place to hide for a few hours."

"Go away," a woman's voice called out. "This is my home. I will defend it."

"We are not here to take your home," Clare said, emphasizing her Haven accent. "I am a Havenite like you. We are trying to escape from the Indians, we need somewhere to hide for a few hours. Then we will leave you alone."

"How can I trust you?" the voice said. "You could be Indian sympathizers looking to trap me."

"Here," Johnston said, tossing his plasma pistol down the corridor. "I am unarmed now."

"You don't sound like you are from Haven," the female voice said as a leg stretched out from where she was hiding and pulled the plasma pistol towards her.

"He is not," Clare said. "He is British. He is part of a team that has come to Haven to help fight the Indians. That is why it is vital we escape the patrols out there and stay alive. We have vital information that will help the British invasion force when they come to kick the Indians out of Haven.

"The British are coming to help us?" the young woman said, stepping out from her hiding place and into view. Johnston guessed that she couldn't be more than twenty.

"We are," he said, standing and raising his hands so that she could clearly see them. "We don't plan to leave your people to the mercy of the Indians. But if we are going to win, we need somewhere to hide for a few hours. Do you think you can help us with that?"

"I suppose," the woman said, but the weapon she had trained on Johnston didn't lower.

"My name is Major Samuel Johnston," Johnston said. "And this is Clare, ah, em, well…"

"Clare Edwards," Clare said. "I am fighting the Indians with the rebels."

"The rebels," the young woman said, finally lowering her weapon. "Maybe you have heard of my father or my brother. My name is Patricia Kimber, my father John and brother David left to fight with the rebels after my mother was killed by an Indian shell. That was four days ago. I haven't heard anything from them since," she said as she broke into a series of small sobs.

Rushing to her side, Clare took her into her arms. "I'm sorry Patricia. I haven't met a John or David Kimber, but don't worry. It is standard operational procedure to stay out of contact with loved ones. If they contacted you, the Indians could pick it up. I'm sure they are fine. They are just trying to keep you safe."

"Are you sure?" Patricia asked as she wiped her eyes.

"Yes, until you hear something for sure, there is no need for you to be so worried," Clare answered.

"I have been beside myself with fear," Patricia said. "I wish they had never left."

"They are fighting for your future," Clare said. "As are we. But that doesn't mean it is going to be easy."

"No, you are right," Patricia said. "And I should be doing my bit as well. You can both stay. I was actually about to make some stew. Would you like to have some with me?"

Just then Johnston's stomach chose to let out a loud grumble. Clare laughed, "There's your answer Patricia. Neither of us have eaten since breakfast. We would love to join you. Maybe you can tell us more about your father and brother. If we run into them then we will be able to tell them that you are ok."

"I'd love to," Patricia said as she handed Johnston back his plasma pistol. "And Major, you could tell me about Earth. I have always wanted to visit Earth."

Chapter 18 – Rumble in The Jungle

For the last thousand years, technology has progressed in leaps and bounds. Despite this, as the old saying goes, there is nothing new under the sun. Constantly, we find the old ways and technologies of war are reborn in new roles to once again wreak havoc on our enemies.

-Excerpt from Empire Rising, 3002 AD

29th April 2467 AD, Liberty.

The stew that Patricia brought out was delicious and Johnston wolfed it down. He then went to the top floor of the three-story house and, sitting well back from the window, monitored the activity in the city. Meanwhile, Clare and Patricia had a long chat in one of the other rooms.

When night fully descended, Johnston got up and went in search of Clare. "It's time to go," he said when he found her. "The Indian activity has decreased. Either they are sitting back to see if we make an appearance or they have given up finding us today. Either way, I need to get back to the rest of my team."

"Let's make a move then Major," Clare said. "And don't forget to thank Patricia," she whispered to him as she walked past.

Following her advice, Johnston then met Clare at the front of the house. Slowly, he opened the door into the dark alley. After watching for a minute to make sure there was no one lurking in the shadows, he led her out of the house, giving Patricia a final wave as they left.

For the next two hours they slowly and carefully made their way through the city. Occasionally the sound of gunfire could be heard but it was always from a distance. Once Johnston pushed Clare to the ground when his heightened hearing heard the distinctive sound of mortar shells zipping overhead. Thankfully they had continued deeper into the city and exploded a safe distance away from them.

Finally, Johnston thought to himself when the Haven forest came into sight, *safety*. Silently he chuckled to himself. After the hours he had spent traipsing thought the thick forest the day before he had been delighted to get to the city. Now he was just as happy to be leaving.

Waiting for a moment to look around, Johnston led Clare into the clearing between the last building in the city and the edge of the forest. It was forty meters wide and it would be the furthest they would be from cover all night.

They were two thirds of the way across when a voice boomed out from a nearby building, "Not so fast marine."

A large search light placed on top of the same building switched on and panned around to illuminate Johnston and Clare. "That's right, we know who you are," the voice bragged. "The Havenites don't have any plasma pistols and we know a British ship was in this system a couple of days ago. Now you have two choices, either you die here and now or you come with us. You have five seconds to decide."

Johnston thought quickly. *He called me a marine, maybe they haven't realized yet, it's our only chance.* "Brace yourself," Johnston whispered to Clare.

More loudly he called out, "You have made a critical mistake soldier. I'm not a marine."
"Stop stalling," the voice broke in. "We know that you are."

"I'm a special forces marine," Johnston finished as if he hadn't been interrupted. He waited less than a second for his words to sink in. Then he gave Clare a shove towards the forest with one hand while spinning around to face the searchlight, plasma pistol already drawn.

Before the Indian soldier even had a chance to blink, three plasma bolts blew out the searchlight and a fourth hit the soldier standing beside it in the chest. As soon as he saw the first bolt hit the light Johnston turned and raced towards the forest. Stooping as he passed Clare, he picked her off the ground where she had fallen. Behind him, the entire clearing erupted as multiple plasma bolts rained down on where they had been standing. From the sounds of the plasma rifles firing, Johnston guessed there were more than ten Indian soldiers trying to hit him.

As soon as they entered the forest Johnston turned and ran at an angle away from their entry point. Though the trees provided cover from the Indian soldier's sight, their plasma bolts could still burn right through the foliage. They weren't safe yet. Luck was on their side however, for despite the forest coming alive with plasma bolts, none hit them.

After a couple of hundred meters Johnston set Clare down. "Can you run?" he asked her quickly.

"I think so," she groaned. "Did you have to shove me to the ground so violently? I think I cracked a rib or two."

"It was that or take a plasma bolt. I didn't have time to stop and ask you," Johnston said. "You can thank me later," he added as he pulled her to her feet. "There is no time now."

As more plasma bolts burnt into the forest around them, Clare needed no convincing to start running. Desperately, she tried to keep up with the marine but after more than five minutes of full on sprinting she had to grab Johnston's arm and drag him to a stop.

"Please, I need to catch my breath. Just give me a couple of seconds," she begged.

"Ok, ok," Johnston said reluctantly. "Don't talk, just breath."

After waiting as long as he could, Johnston nevertheless had to force Clare back into a run while she was still panting heavily. He had heard the distinct sound of shuttles approaching. Less than a minute later the sound was unmistakable even for Clare and several seconds later large search lights beamed down into the forest.

Straining his ears, Johnston thought he could make out four of the damned things flying about over the forest. Their search lights would be illuminating the forest for the Indian soldiers pursuing them on foot and all of their sensors would be diligently looking for them.

Johnston had no time to worry about whether their combat suits would keep them hidden from the patrolling shuttles or not. They either would or they wouldn't. The suits were designed to absorb radar radiation and to severely limit the amount of thermal radiation they gave off. With luck they would blend in with the rest of the lifeforms in the forest. Yet they could just as easily be standing out like a sore thumb. With all the exertion they were doing their suits would be struggling to contain all the heat they were giving off.

There was nothing they could do though and for another ten minutes they ran at a slightly reduced pace so that Clare could keep up. Twice they had to break towards a new direction to avoid the flight path of one of the searching shuttles. Then Johnston heard the sound he had been dreading. Above him a faint whistling noise grew louder and louder.

"Down," he shouted.

As he and Clare dove to the ground, eight explosions erupted along a line in the forest half a kilometer from where they were.

"We're ok," Johnston said as he pulled Clare to her feet. "I don't think they know where we are yet."

Running on again the pair barely made it another hundred meters before the whistling noise returned and before they could dive for cover another eight explosions blew through the forest.

"Wait," Johnston said this time. Mentally he began to count the seconds. Right on cue eight more howitzer shells burst into the forest, this time far off to their left.

"They are trying to herd us," Johnston said.

"What do you mean?" Clare asked.

"They are using the howitzers to funnel us in one direction. They are firing incendiary shells. Look at the forest, it is ablaze. I'm guessing they have a shuttle full of soldiers waiting for us in the one direction it's safe to run," Johnston answered.

"So what do we do?" Clare said.

"We don't have a choice; we need to move through their firing line."

"Of the howitzers," Clare said in bewilderment.

"Yes," Johnston said. "Now get on my back," he added turning around. "I can't carry you for too long, but we can run faster this way. It will give us a chance."

Clare knew better than to complain. When Johnston ducked down she jumped on. Rising to his full height he turned around and gave a small jump to get used to the extra weight. Just then another eight explosions rippled through the forest, again far off to their left.

Johnston started counting under his breath, *one, two, three...*

When he reached twenty-five he charged off into the forest at right angles to where they had been originally headed. Clare was stunned by the speed that Johnston was able to reach; he had been holding back to stay with her. He could have easily escaped on his own.

Five seconds after Johnston began his sprint a wave of fire descended on the forest less than four hundred meters in front of them. Clare screamed when Johnston kept on running and the flames reached out towards them. He had timed it perfectly though for they stopped their advance just as Clare began to feel their heat on her face. Instead of incinerating them the flames pulled back in on themselves. Yet after the initial explosion cleared, a wall of fire now blocked their path as the Haven forest burnt.

Whilst the flames stopped, the shockwave from the explosions still buffeted them and Johnston stumbled and almost fell. Before Clare had time to fear they would hit the ground, he regained his balance and orientated his path towards the edge of the flames and was back to full speed in seconds.

Clare could still hear Johnston counting under his breath. He had begun at zero after the explosions in front of him. When she heard him say twenty-five she heard another series of explosions off to their left. Johnston reset his counting to zero and Clare knew this was it. They had to clear the Indian's firing line before the next round of shells came in.

As Johnston approached twenty-five Clare closed her eyes. Over the din of the shuttles and the fires now burning in the forest where the howitzers shells had landed, she heard the whistling noise of a new batch of shells falling towards their position.

It seemed to her that time must have slowed down for the whistling went on and on until it felt like the shell was right above her head. Thinking the same thing Johnston spun Clare off his back and dove to the ground, throwing her under his body for protection.

Even before they hit the ground the howitzer shells exploded, the closest one less than two hundred meters from where they were lying. A wave of fire burst out across the forest and Johnston closed his eyes as it washed over him. He tried to scream in pain as the fire licked at his face and ears. Yet as soon as he opened his mouth his cry was cut off as the flames sucked the air out of him and threatened to burn their way down his throat. Shutting his mouth, Johnston buried his face in his armpit.

No sooner had the flames arrived than they left, falling back in on themselves. As soon as she felt them leave Clare struggled to get Johnston off her, she then turned him over to look at him.

"Are you ok?" she asked frantically.

Johnston shook his head and slowly opened his eyes. His mouth felt like it was on fire but the look of concern on Clare's eyes forced him to try and speak. What he thought was a, "I'm fine," came out as a mumbled croak. The pain on his tongue and lips hampering his efforts to articulate his words.

Seeing his difficulty, Clare reached down to the water canteen attached to her combat suit and lifted it to Johnston's lips. "Take a drink," she insisted.

The first sips caused Johnston more pain but as he kept drinking it eased. "I'm ok," he croaked.

"No you're not," Clare said. "Your face is a mess!"

"It will have to do," Johnston said, all too aware of the throbbing pain coming from almost all of his face. To appease Clare and help the pain he pulled a cream from his utility belt. "Here, apply this to the burnt areas, it will quicken the healing process."

Once Clare had applied the cream she helped him to his feet. "We need to keep moving," Johnston said. "As soon as they realize they haven't caught us in their trap they will begin searching the forest beyond the burning areas. You can set the pace."

"That's ok with me," Clare said, relieved.

As she set off at a brisk jog Johnston made to follow her. A piercing pain in his right leg made him pull up short. Looking down he saw a stream of blood flowing down his leg. At its source a large splinter almost ten centimeters long jutted out of his flesh. Gritting his teeth, he reached down and yanked the splinter out. His combat suit closed over to seal the hole. Sensing his wound, it tightened around his leg to restrict the flow of blood and an antiseptic cream was released onto the area to dull the pain. Before Clare was aware of what had happened he caught up and was jogging beside her.

Two hours later they had slowed to a fast walk. Keeping up a run had proved impossible for Clare. At one point, when they had to climb a steep hill, Johnston looked out over the forest below them through a break in the trees. He clearly made out a single shuttle moving back and forth over the forest, coming in their general direction. Far off in the distance he could see three other shuttles seemingly working independently to search their own section of the forest.

"I think they have split up," Johnston said. "They may have found a few different trails to track."

"Probably old trails used by other rebel groups. Do you think that the nearest shuttle will follow us?" Clare asked.

"I think so. They are probably following the valley that leads to your base. That is how I found you guys after all."

"Then what do we do? They are gaining on us aren't they?" Clare said.

"They are," Johnston said. "We could split up. I could take them on a wild goose chase while you make it back to Pennington's base."

"But you are the one who needs to get back to your men. They need you to lead them if they are going to get our information back to your superiors. You can't take that risk when you are already injured," Clare argued. "I'm the one who should try and lead them away.

Johnston didn't answer right away. The idea of Clare trying to outrun Indian soldiers in combat armor was absurd. But he knew that in his present condition he probably wouldn't last long against them either. He needed another plan.

"Maybe we don't need to try and hide," Johnston said. "My cover is already blown. It might even prove impossible to escape Haven in our stealth shuttle. The Indians will be looking out for us."

"How does that help us?" Clare asked confused.

"It means my men can join the fight," Johnston said.

Without explaining any further, he opened his secure COM link and contacted Lieutenant Moony. The Indians would be sure to pick up trace emissions from the COM channel. It would likely draw the search party in their vicinity towards them. However, that would actually work into Johnston's plan.

*

Johnston and Clare were desperately running through the forest. The Indians had picked up Johnston's COM signal but they had been slow to triangulate it. To speed things up Johnston had put in a second unnecessary call to Lieutenant Moony to give the Indians more of an idea of his location. He was beginning to think he should have held off on the second COM message; the Indians were right behind him.

A shuttle had buzzed over their position just a couple of minutes ago. The stealth capabilities of his combat suit must have been damaged in the fire for no sooner had it flown past than they heard Indians in power armor closing on their position.

Johnston let out a breath of relief when two clicks came over the COM channel he had open to the rest of his men. They were in position. Three more clicks give him a new heading. "This way," he said to Clare as he grabbed her hand. "This is the last thing we need to do, I need you to give me everything you have," he added as he picked up the pace.

For two minutes they ran as fast as they could along Johnston's new direction. All the while the sounds of the Indian soldiers increased. All of a sudden, a string of plasma bolts flashed through the forest around them. Johnston picked up Clare and increased his pace. He grunted from the pain in his leg but the plasma bolts that continued to explode all around him kept him going.

The firing stopped. Over the COM channel Johnston heard another two clicks. With another groan he came to a halt behind a thick tree, set Clare down and fell against the tree for support.

"Are we safe?" Clare asked him.

Without the strength to answer Johnston only nodded.

*

Moments earlier Lieutenant Moony had watched his commanding officer struggle to run past the defensive line he had set up. *He looks a mess,* Moony thought before switching his mind back to the task at hand.

"Fire," he said over the COM channel to the other five special forces marines around him.

Within seconds, tens of plasma bolts reached out from their positions and cut down the first wave of Indian soldiers who had been just about to gain on Major Johnston. Then a rocket lifted off from the launcher one of his men had been aiming at the shuttle. The shuttle had been flying so close to the forest's canopy in an effort to detect Johnston that it didn't have time to dodge. The heat seeking rocket struck one of the shuttle's engines, sending it into a nose dive into the forest. The shuttle exploded as soon as it hit the ground and the fireball perfectly illuminated the second wave of Indian soldiers. Again a flurry of plasma bolts reached out from the British marines to take them out.

"Advance," Moony called out.

As one the marines stood up from the cover they had been hiding behind and charged through the forest towards the remaining Indian soldiers. Still not fully aware that the hunters had become the hunted, the Indian soldiers were overwhelmed in seconds. Equipped with the Type Two Marine Combat Armor units, the special forces marines moved far faster than anything the Indian soldiers had believed possible. The Type Twos made full use of the physical enhancements special forces marines received, allowing them to move faster than anything a normal human could withstand.

"Check the perimeter," Moony ordered his men once the last Indian in sight was gunned down. "You have sixty seconds, then we are out of here."

While the rest of his men followed his order, Moony returned to the spot Johnston had run to. "Are you ok Sir?" he asked.

"I'll survive," Johnston said. "You guys got into position just in time. Can I assume you have an Evac plan in place? If the Indians are in any way predictable there will be howitzer shells falling all around us as soon as they figure out what happened."

"I do indeed Sir," Moony said. "I borrowed your plasma lance. Samuels has it now. She is cutting us a path through the forest roughly in a south easterly direction. We're going to use it to get the hell out of here. Then we will double back to Pennington's cave."

"Well let's get on with it," Johnston said.

"All clear," Sergeant Brier said as he approached his two commanding officers. "The men are ready to move out."

"You take Clare," Johnston said to Brier. "I'll hitch a ride with Harte."

Without waiting for a reply, Johnston helped Clare to her feet. Brier turned around and knelt. Out of the back of his combat armor two hand holds and two stirrups appeared.

"I'm meant to get on the back of this thing?" Clare asked. She had caught glimpses of the metal monstrosity fighting just moments before and she thought Brier would tear her apart if he tried to move like he had done fighting the Indians.

"It's perfectly safe," Johnston said as he pushed her towards Brier. "I'm going to do it too."

Reluctantly, she reached up and grabbed the handholds to pull herself up the back of Brier's combat armor. When she got her feet into the stirrups, an elastic belt reached around her back and pulled her body tight against the cold armor.

"Don't worry Ma'am. I'll take good care of you," Brier said.

Johnston strode over to where Harte was waiting. He

jumped up into Harte's stirrups and allowed the elastic belt to extend around his body.

"Let's get out of here," he said to the waiting marines.

The marines took off towards the path in the forest Samuels had been cutting. As soon as they reached it they formed up in a single file and accelerated to their full speed of eighty kilometers an hour. For twenty minutes they kept up their relentless sprint.

Initially, Johnston watched the forest whizz past them. Within minutes his attention switched to the explosions that rang out around the forest as the Indians tried to hit whoever had attacked their men. Almost all the explosions were well behind them and Johnston quickly dismissed them. No sooner had he done so, than he fell asleep. *We made it,* were the last words on his mind.

Asleep, he missed the squad of marines meeting up with Samuels at the end of the thirty kilometer path she had cut through the thick forest underbrush. At Moony's direction, the team then made a forty-five degree turn into the forest and much more carefully and slowly, began to beat their way back towards the rebel base. Before they got there Clare had also fallen asleep, despite her initial terror at speeding through the forest on what felt like a mechanical robot, exhaustion had caught up to her too.

Chapter 19 – The Signal

It has always fascinated me how an entire fleet can waste weeks searching for a single ship which, if found, it would only take seconds to destroy. The game of cat and mouse is an old one that dates back to the water navies of Earth before the invention of the shift drive. It has hardly changed in the centuries since.

-Excerpt from Empire Rising, 3002 AD

30th April 2467 AD, Liberty.

Johnston awoke in a strange bed. His hands twitched towards his face as the burning sensation from the day before remained. He stopped them before they actually moved. Instead, his survival instincts kicked in. Cracking open his eyes he looked around him whilst pretending to be asleep. When he could see no one, he jumped to his feet. The unexpected feel of hard rock under his bare toes caused his groggy memories from the previous night to return.

He remembered being helped down from Harte's combat armor and into the cave hideout. Someone had applied some sort of cream to his face. The searing pain had momentarily woken him fully. After that, all he remembered was someone else pressing a hypo injector into his neck.

I guess we made it, he thought.

"Good to see you on your feet Major," Lieutenant Moony said as he walked into the room someone had carved out of the cave wall. "You slept like a baby all the way back from the ambush site. I'm not sure you are going to live that one down. Having to be carried out like a civilian."

"I can see I'm not going to get any sympathy," Johnston snorted as he reached for his combat suit which was lying nearby. "Let's see how you feel after escorting an unaugmented through an occupied city and more than fifteen kilometers of dense forest all the while being chased by a platoon of soldiers in combat armor with incendiary shells falling all around you."

"Oh I dunno Sir," Moony chuckled. "I think we took out that Indian platoon pretty easily. They weren't really that tough."

"Just shut up Lieutenant," Johnston said as he took a mock swing at his subordinate.

"That's unlikely Sir," Moony said. "But in all seriousness, it's a relief to see you on your feet. What do you want to do now?"

"Right now I need some food, and then I need to see someone about my face. It still stings more than I would like. After that, I need to debrief you on your missions. We need to put together a report for Captain Somerville to take back to Earth."

"The doc here says you have first and second degree burns all across your face. It will heal up in time, but until then it's going to hurt like a bitch," Moony said.

"Great," Johnston said.

"Look on the bright side, at least you will still have your looks Major, if you think that's something worth keeping mind you," Moony said as he dodged out of the way of another punch.

"Just lead me to some food," Johnston said gruffly.

*

An hour and a half later Johnston was once again in the back of the rebel's cave sitting around Councilwoman Pennington's desk. He had just heard his marines' reports. They had been sent out in pairs to scout different Indian locations within Liberty and around the city. Thankfully, none of them had got tangled up with Indian soldiers. They had all made it back to the cave in time to come to his aid.

"I think it is clear that our two main targets are the headquarters based in the old Council Chambers and the supply depot on the outskirts of the city," Johnston said after he heard the final report. "If the invasion force can take out the Indian command structure and deprive their forces the supplies they need, then the rest of the Indian soldiers will have to surrender sooner or later. I doubt the navy will be able to scrape up an invasion force large enough to take on the Indian forces toe to toe. But five to ten thousand marines should be able to retake the key sections of Liberty, then we can starve the rest of the Indians out. If they don't have access to energy cells their power armor will quickly become useless. Once that happens, the populace of Haven will eat them alive unless they surrender."

"So you think an invasion will prove successful?" Pennington asked.

"Yes," Johnston said. "If the navy can gain control of the orbitals then the Indian army can be mopped up sooner or later. The military commanders of the invasion force will have to formulate their own plans based on the information we have gathered for them, but if they follow my recommendations they will be able to take away the Indian's ability to fight a long drawn out battle."

"Then you are leaving us," Clare said from where she sat in the corner of the cave. So far she had been silent for the debriefing.

"No," Johnston said to the surprise of his men. Clare gave him a small smile. "I don't think we can. The Indians know marines are on Haven now. They will quickly put two and two together and guess that the ship they detected a few days ago dropped us here. They will be watching the orbitals very closely for any sign of us trying to leave. If we try to take off in our shuttle they could detect us and destroy us before we even got a signal off to *Endeavour*. Then Somerville will never get our info.

"I plan to use the shuttle's long range COM gear to send our info to *Endeavour,* they can bug out and get back to Earth with what we have found. We," Johnston said, looking around the room at his men, "will have to stay here until the cavalry comes."

"So you are going to fight alongside us?" Pennington asked eagerly.

"I will," Johnston answered. "But that was not a part of our mission brief. It could be at least a month or two before the fleet gets here, perhaps longer. So, no one else has to fight if they don't want. You can find a place to lie low and wait until the real fight begins," he said to his men.

"Ha," Sergeant Brier said. "Fat chance of that. We are with you Major. We got a taste for kicking some Indian ass last night and I think the rest of the men are eager for the main course."

"Well, I guess that means we are in," Johnston said to Pennington. "I will need to travel back to our shuttle to send the signal, but after that we are all yours. I'm sure there is a thing or two we can teach you about fighting a guerilla war against a superior force."

"I'll go send the message Sir," Moony said. "You need to rest. I'll take Samuels and Harte with me."

"Very well," Johnston said. "I didn't fancy another long hike through the damn forest anyway. You can have the pleasure."

*

1st May 2467 AD, HMS *Endeavour.*

James was sitting on the bridge, watching an Indian frigate run a patrol flight very close to the gas giant they were hiding in. *Endeavour* was too far down into the planet's atmosphere to detect the frigate, which hopefully meant that it couldn't detect *Endeavour.* James was watching the frigate's movements via a stealth recon drone that they had orbiting the planet.

The recon drone was able to pick up another ten ships moving around on various patrol vectors further out into the system. From what James had been able to observe, after the first day of fruitless searching, the Indian ships had shifted their focus onto Haven itself. The Indian Admiral likely suspected that *Endeavour* was in the system to make contact with someone on the planet and they were now trying to make sure no further contact was made. That was alright with James; it meant most of the Indian ships were well away from where he was hiding.

However, either by chance or design, the flight path of the frigate he was watching brought it very close to the gas giant. Having not had much to do over the last week as they waited to hear back from Major Johnston other than the usual drills, the bridge was full as many of the Sub Lieutenants came to watch the frigate's approach. Despite the risk being small, James couldn't help feel his nerves growing as the frigate approached.

"Captain, I'm detecting a laser COM link, it's coming from the planet," Sub Lieutenant King said from the COM station.

"Download the message," Mallory said eagerly. "It must be Major Johnston."

"How powerful is the laser link?" James asked, a more pressing concern weighing on him.

"It's twenty megawatts," King answered.

"Did that Indian frigate detect the laser?" James followed up.

King paused for a few seconds as she ran a few calculations. "It's possible Sir," she replied, clearly concerned. "The frigate was right on the outer edge of the laser's beam; they may have detected a faint trace of the COM link."

James didn't acknowledge King's last report. He was too busy watching the Indian frigate, if they did detect the laser it wouldn't take a genius to figure out what it meant. "Lock all starboard missiles onto that frigate," James ordered the tactical officer.

In his head he counted out five minutes. When the frigate didn't alter its course, or show any sign that it had detected the laser link, he allowed himself to relax. If the Indians thought that there was a group on Haven still in contact with *Endeavour* they would double their patrols around the planet. It would make it next to impossible for Major Johnston to escape, stealth shuttle or no stealth shuttle.

"Mallory, you have the bridge," James said. "I'm going to retire to my office to review the information Johnston just sent. Do everything you can to prepare the ship to get out of here short of taking us out of stealth mode. And keep an eye on that frigate. If it looks as if it is acting suspicious, you are to take it out."

"Understood Sir," Mallory said as James stood up and walked out.

*

ISF *Rapjut*, Haven System.

"Have you been able to decrypt that message yet?" Captain Sourav Ganguly asked his COM officer.

"No Sir," she replied. "I don't think we will be able to, not without a far more powerful computer. "

"What about the gas giant?" Ganguly said, turning to his sensor officer. "No sign of the British ship?"

"I'm not detecting anything untoward," the officer said. "If there is a British ship there, it is well hidden."

"We could maneuver closer Sir." Ganguly's First Lieutenant said. "Maybe we could launch some recon drones into the gas giant's atmosphere. That way we could be sure if there is a ship there or not."

"No!" Ganguly almost shouted. "I have already told you. The British ship is there; I am sure of it. We are not going to do anything to tip them off that we know about them. The stealth drone we have in place will be enough."

"Understood Sir," the First Lieutenant said, sounding thoroughly chastised.

"I want you to plot us a new course for when we complete this part of our patrol. I want to bring *Rapjut* past the gas giant again. Not so close that the British will suspect something, but close enough that we will be able to detect any ships that break out of the atmosphere. Understood?"

"Aye Sir," the First Lieutenant responded, happy to have the chance to do something.

"COMs," Ganguly said. "How many ships have received our message?"

"Four so far Sir," the officer answered.

"Show me on the holo display," Ganguly requested.

The COM officer altered the bridge's main holo display. It showed the Haven System centered on *Rapjut*. A sphere expanded outward from the frigate, showing the progress of his COM message. So far four other Indian ships fell within the sphere. Two timers counted down to the side of the image. One showed when the COM message Ganguly had sent out would reach the next Indian ship, the other when the message would reach the flagship.

Good, Ganguly thought to himself. *If that British Captain will just sit still long enough, we will make sure he never gets out of this system alive.*

*

In his office James quickly scanned through Major Johnston's report. When he was done he checked the sensor plot to make sure the Indian frigate wasn't showing any signs that it had detected them. Happy that they were still safe he went back to the beginning of Johnston's report and started reading again. He needed to fully understand the situation before he made any decisions. He didn't want to leave Johnston behind if there was any way they could extract him and his men.

Twenty minutes later he set the report down and turned to view some of the visuals Johnston had sent. After he had finished watching them he understood Johnston's decision. The Indians had devastated Liberty. It didn't look like the city James remembered from his brief visit to meet Maximilian. Worse, it was clear that the Indians were exacting a harsh price from the Havenites, both in terms of their wealth and more importantly, their lives. The Havenites were fighting bravely, but they stood no chance against the superior technology of the Indian military. Maybe with Johnston's help they could score some hits against the Indians, but even then, Haven faced months more of the brutal occupation.

James' heart went out to his new wife. It would cut her deep when she saw these images of her homeworld. Thinking of his wife only made his decision to leave harder. Intellectually, he knew that it would be suicide to order Johnston to try and take off from Haven in the stealth shuttle with so many Indian ships on the lookout for them. It might even be suicide to try and take *Endeavour* close enough to the planet to retrieve them. Yet, he didn't want to return to Earth having left someone behind. He also didn't want to just leave with his wife's planet in the grip of such an ordeal.

At Vestar and Kulpath he had been able to throw himself against the problems he had encountered head on. When he had seen injustice he had been able to confront it directly. Now, here in Haven, there was nothing he could do. What made it worse, was that he knew that once *Endeavour* jumped out of the system there probably wouldn't be any British ships returning for at least a couple of months. Major Johnston, his men and the Havenites would be on their own once again.

There is nothing for it, James said to himself for the fifth time. *We need to leave. Suzanna will understand.*

Pushing his doubts down, James left his office and strode back into the bridge. "Set us a course for the shift passage to Independence," he ordered once he sat down in his command chair.

"We're not going for Johnston?" Mallory asked.

"No, he and his men have decided to stay behind and join the fight against the Indians," James answered. "You can all read a synopsis of the report later. For now, all you need to know is that Johnston got the information the invasion force is going to need. It's our job to get it back to the Admiralty. I can promise you this though, we will return to Haven."

"I didn't doubt it," Becket said from the tactical station. "We may be good at sneaking around. But it isn't our style. I'm sure we'll be back to show the Indians just what *Endeavour* can do."

"Agreed," James said. "Now get to work all of you."

For another twenty minutes James watched the bridge crew get *Endeavour* ready to break out of orbit of the gas giant. Most of what they were doing could have been done as they travelled to the shift passage but James wanted to wait until the Indian frigate was well out of sensor range before he made his move.

As he watched the Indian ship it altered course. "Bring up the recorded patrol patterns of that frigate," James ordered.

On the main holo display the patrol pattern Sub Lieutenant Malik had recorded for the frigate over the last several days appeared. The Indian warship appeared to be carrying out a patrol of the space between the system's fifth and eighth planets, the seventh being the gas giant. Each time it got to roughly the point it was at now, it altered course and headed back into the system towards the fifth planet. As the Indian frigate continued to alter its current course Malik overlaid its projected course on the holo display.

“It’s making a much tighter turn that usual,” Malik said.

“Yes,” James said. “It’s new course is going to bring it almost as close to the gas giant as it was less than an hour ago.”

“That can’t be a coincidence,” Mallory said. “They must have detected Johnston’s laser signal.”

“They are trying to keep us trapped,” James said. “Whoever is captaining that frigate knows that we are unlikely to want to take the risk of breaking orbit when their ship is so near. They are passing by just close enough to make us want to stay put. Yet far enough away that it looks like they don’t know we are here.”

“They are waiting for reinforcements,” Mallory said.

“That’s what I would do,” James agreed. “It seems we are going to have to make our getaway a little sooner than we planned. Navigation, slowly move us around to the opposite side of the planet to the Indian frigate. Then bring us up out of orbit.”

“Do you think they will detect the disturbances we will make in the gas giant’s atmosphere when we exit?” Mallory asked.

“It’s likely, but they might not. With the planet’s rotation it will take three hours for our exit point to revolve around into their field of vision. If they don’t detect us right away those three hours should give us plenty of time to make a clean getaway.

Half an hour later Sub Lieutenant Jennings informed James that Endeavour was in position. In that time the Indian frigate had fully reversed its course and was approaching the gas giant again.

"Take us out," James said, seeing no other option.

Chapter 20 – Full Speed Ahead!

Today the shift drive allows us to go almost anywhere the Sun Gates cannot take us. Yet it was not always so. Before we fully understood shift space, dark matter had a far greater effect on where we could engage the shift drive. It gave rise to many interesting naval tactics.

-Excerpt from Empire Rising, 3002 AD

30th April 2467 AD, ISF *Rapjut*, Haven System.

The stealth recon drone is detecting something Captain," one of Ganguly's officers called out excitedly. "I think the British ship is making a move, it's coming out of the atmosphere on the other side of the planet."

"They will go into stealth as soon as they break out of orbit," the First Lieutenant said. "Should we alter course to intercept them?"

Ganguly didn't answer right away. Instead he looked over the holo display of the Haven system. A number of flashing green icons showed the estimated positions of four Indian warships. They had gone into stealth when they had received his message about a possible contact. Now, they were all cruising towards the gas giant. There was also a flashing blue icon much closer to the planet. It represented the *Kolkata,* a light cruiser. She had been patrolling the general area in stealth for the last four days. Ganguly wasn't exactly sure of her location, but the blue icon was his best guess.

They might be able to catch her, Ganguly thought to himself.

"Prepare to take us into stealth mode," he ordered. "We're going to fire a broadside of missiles at the British ship and then disappear. The British will have to power up their engines to deal with our missiles. As soon as they do, the rest of our ships will know they are trying to run for it."

"We're just going to fire at them and then hide?" the First Lieutenant said, trying to hide his misgivings. "Won't Admiral Kumar expect us to chase after them and bring them to action."

"No," Ganguly replied. "Kumar will expect me to look after her ship. We can stay in stealth and follow the British ship until reinforcements get into range. Don't you remember what this British ship did to our other ships. If we take it on alone we won't even slow it down. However, if *Kolkata* is as close as I believe, then we can join up with her and take down this British ship together.

"We're ready to fire Sir," a junior officer announced. "I'm using targeting data from the recon drone so the firing solution is weak, but until they come out from behind the planet this is as good as it will get."

"It will do," Ganguly said. "We only need to rattle them.

Fire."

*

"Missile launch," Malik called out in alarm. "That frigate has fired two missiles at us."

"Warm up the point defenses," Mallory ordered. "We can handle two missiles."

"They detected us," James said. "They must have had a drone orbiting the gas giant. But why fire so early, they must know they cannot cause us much harm?"

"Everyone in the system will see those two missiles on their gravimetric sensors," Becket called out. "It could be a signal."

"Yes," James said. "And if they really did detect that laser signal then they have had plenty of time to warn nearby ships about our presence. I want full military power now," he called out to Sub Lieutenant Jennings at the navigation console.

"Aye Sir," she replied. "Where to?"

"Get us out of here, head for the edge of the system's mass shadow, the closest point to us." James answered. "If my guess is right, we're going to need to jump into shift space as soon as possible. Break out the gaseous sails as well once we get to our top speed."

"I'm detecting more ships coming online," Malik called. "Four ships have just lit up their engines. They are coming straight for us."

"That frigate did get out a warning," James said. "Will they catch us?"

"It's going to be close." Malik answered. "Two of them may get close enough to fire off a single broadside before we reach the shift limit.

"One more has just appeared," Malik said. "It's close, and it's big."

"Put it on the main holo display," James ordered.

When the newest contact appeared James had to bite back a curse. From the warship's engine output, *Endeavour's* computers estimated that it was a cruiser, and it was already travelling at 0.2c. Its projected course suggested that it would get into missile range twenty minutes before *Endeavour* could jump out.

"We have a fight on our hands," he said to his bridge crew. "Becket, start working up a firing solution on that cruiser. Fire when ready."

" Aye Sir," Becket acknowledged.

For an hour *Endeavour* accelerated away from the gas giant. All that time the Indian light cruiser rapidly closed the gap between the two ships.

"Firing," Becket said when it came into range of *Endeavour's* missiles.

Two ship killers burst out of *Endeavour's* stern missile ports and ignited their engines as they boosted towards the Indian cruiser. Another two followed six minutes later.

Before the first two reached their target, the Indian cruiser responded with three missiles of its own from its forward tubes.

"That frigate is back Captain," Malik reported. "It just dropped out of stealth. It is falling into formation with the Indian cruiser."

"Understood," James said. There was nothing else he could do. The frigate would be able to add one more missile to the three the cruiser was firing at him. He just had to hope *Endeavour* could fend them off long enough to jump to safety.

For thirty minutes the three ships exchanged fire. *Endeavour's* single flak cannon that could track the incoming Indian missiles ensured that none got through. The coordinated point defenses of the two Indian ships easily dealt with the British missiles.

We're going to make it, James thought to himself. The gap between the two groups of ships was opening again. *Endeavour's* top speed was 0.06c greater than the Indian cruiser. In another fifteen minutes they would be able to jump to safety.

"The Indian ships are turning," Malik called out.

"They have realized they can't catch us," James said, seeing that the Indian Captain had come to the same conclusion he had. "They're going to try a full broadside."

Ten missiles erupted from the Indian cruiser and another two joined them from the frigate.

"Increase our speed by 0.02c," James ordered. "Inform the ship's doctor that she's going to have to issue anti-radiation drugs. It's the only way we will make it out of this."

Endeavour's valstronium armor and gaseous shields protected the crew from the cosmic radiation the ship encountered at speeds up to 0.38c. Anything over that and harmful levels of radiation would penetrate the ship. The crew would only have to endure elevated levels of radiation for another fourteen minutes. *Hopefully it won't do any lasting damage,* James thought.

Five minutes after he gave his order the ship's doctor, Gloria Anderson, appeared on the bridge. She went from officer to officer injecting them with anti-radiation drugs. When she got to James she gave him a dirty look. "I'm going to have to write up a report about this you know Captain. This is against regulations."

"I know Anderson," James said. "But this is the only way I can guarantee you will get home to submit your report."

"I hope you are right Captain," Anderson said as she left the bridge to see to the rest of the crew.

"What do the radiation levels look like?" James asked Second Lieutenant Julius, who was in the auxiliary bridge. He had given her responsibility for handling any problems that arose.

"They are climbing in the nose section," she replied over the COM channel. "I have already evacuated the forward missile tubes. "Levels are elevated elsewhere but they are not yet life threatening."

"Alert me if you have to evacuate any more sections," James said.

"Enemy missiles are increasing their acceleration rate," Malik reported.

"They won't have any power left to maneuver once they get into range of our point defenses," Becket said. "It looks like they are just hoping one of their missiles can get a proximity hit."

"It's still not going to be enough," James said as the figures on the main holo display updated. "Jump us out as soon as we cross the mass shadow Jennings. I don't want any margin of safety. Just jump us out."

"Understood Sir," she replied.

Three minutes later Jennings gave the command to the ship's shift drive. In the blink of an eye Endeavour vanished from normal space, leaving a burst of gravimetric waves behind it. Seconds later the first Indian missile exploded right where *Endeavour* had been.

The micro jump lasted less than a second and when *Endeavour* reverted to real space the bridge crew let out a cheer. "We made it," Mallory shouted to James, giving him a big smile.

"That we did," James said. "Jennings, plot us a series of jumps along the edge of the system, we're going to work our way back to towards the shift passage to Independence. Mallory, get us into stealth immediately."

"Aye Sir," Jennings and Mallory said. "The shift drive will be charged for another jump in twenty minutes," Jennings added.

"Jump us as soon as you are ready," James ordered. He sat back in his command chair and patiently watched the holo display.

Every solar system created a bubble in the dark matter that was strewn between the stars, some were bigger than others. Haven's was quite small, the bubble extended about eight light hours beyond Haven's gravity well. *Endeavour's* micro jump had taken her six light hours towards the edge of the bubble. The pursuing Indian ships wouldn't know exactly how far out she jumped, but, they only had a limited number of options from which to guess.

Just as James expected, twenty minutes after they had exited shift space alarms went off on the bridge.

"I'm detecting two ships jumping out of shift space," Malik shouted from the sensor station.

"What are they?" James demanded.

Endeavour's gravimetric sensors could detect ships exiting shift space up to a light hour away, meaning that the Indian ships were close.

"From the size of the emergence signatures I'm estimating contact bravo one is a frigate, and bravo two is a destroyer," Malik said.

"I have a lock on the destroyer," Becket said. "Shall I open fire?"

"Fire," James said.

He had wanted to make another jump as soon as the shift drive's capacitators were charged and get away from the Indians before they found him. With the two newcomers so close, they would be able to detect his next jump and follow him. They needed to be destroyed, or at least distracted.

The Indian ships had jumped in less than three light minutes from *Endeavour*. That meant it took Becket's eight missiles twelve minutes to reach their targets. The Indian ships returned fire but it had taken them a couple of crucial minutes to re-orientate themselves to present their full broadsides at *Endeavour*.

As soon as James saw his missiles explode among the two Indian ships he gave Jennings the command she had been waiting for. "Go," he shouted.

Jennings brought *Endeavour* onto a new heading and engaged the shift drive. Seconds later the ship reverted to real space to find herself alone and free from the pursuing Indian ships once again. As before, the Indian missiles that had been aimed at her had flown harmlessly through the space she had occupied moments ago.

"Plot a course to the Independence shift passage," James ordered. "We're going to stay in stealth and cruise all the way there. It will take us a couple of days but I don't want to run the risk of another Indian ship detecting us exiting shift space. If the Indian Admiral suspects that we are trying to flee to Independence she may guess there is a faster way back to Earth via Independence. We don't want that."

"I understand Sir," Mallory said.

"What about your missiles?" James asked Becket, "Did you hit anything?"

"I'm reviewing the sensor data we received just before we jumped Sir," Becket responded. "It looks like we got a proximity hit on the destroyer. We didn't see the final two missiles explode though, so we could have got another one."

"Good shooting," James said. "With luck both ships will have been too busy to detect the heading of our micro jump. I've had just about enough of this cat and mouse business."

"I couldn't agree more Sir," Mallory said. "The sooner we can come back here with the fleet and take on these Indians face to face the better."

"Agreed," James said.

For another hour he sat on the bridge watching the holo display. Finally satisfied that there were no more Indian ships following them he stood. "I think we are in the clear," he said. "You all fought well today. I'm proud of you. But now I think I need to catch up on some sleep. I'm going to order the next watch to come on an hour early, so you have another half an hour here and then you can retire too. You have the bridge Mallory."

"Aye Sir," Mallory said to James as he walked out. "We'll all appreciate an extra hour in our beds I'm sure."

*

Five hours ago, Haven.

Lieutenant Moony tried and failed to hold back a yawn.

"Long day Lieutenant? Harte asked. "If you want I can take that fancy switch and you can go back into the forest and take a nap. I am sure I can handle things."

"Not a chance," Moony said. "I didn't traipse half way across this continent just to watch you have all the fun.

It had been almost an hour since they had sent the signal from the shuttle. Even though they had used a laser link to send a signal to the gas giant *Endeavour* was hiding in, there were so many ships in orbit that it had proved impossible to get a window when no Indian ships had been in the laser's line of sight. Major Johnston had suspected that might have proved to be the case and Moony had been sent with secondary orders.

The Indian ships in orbit should have detected the laser signal right away. It was strange that they hadn't shown up yet. Just as he was beginning to wonder what they were doing Moony heard the sound he had been waiting for.

"At last," Samuels said.

"Stay down," Moony said.

The three marines were lying on the edge of a cliff several kilometers from the shuttle. From their vantage point they could see through the thick forest canopy into the clearing where the stealth shuttle was hidden.

As they watched, an Indian shuttle came into view, rocketing above the tree tops. It slowed to half its speed as it approached and flew over the clearing. It made two more passes over the clearing before it came to a complete stop the third time. Slowly it descended into the clearing.

"They are taking the bait," Harte said.

"Quiet," Moony replied.

He flipped open the protective case on the detonator he was holding. As soon as the shuttle touched down a handful of Indians in power armor jumped out the rear door. They spread out, securing the perimeter. Five of them carefully made their way towards the stealth shuttle. When the lead soldier got close enough to touch the British shuttle, Moony hit the detonator.

In the blink of an eye a small tactical nuke bathed the clearing in a giant fireball. The marines' visors automatically darkened to protect their eyes from the intense light. When the fireball cleared, there was no sign of the stealth shuttle or the marines who had been near it. The Indian shuttle was on its side, one of its wings had been blasted off and the rest of its structure was engulfed in flames. As the marines watched, the fire reached something critical and the shuttle exploded.

"There's no way anyone in combat armor could survive that," Harte said.

"No," Samuels agreed. "I think we are done."

"Done?" Moony said. "We are only just beginning. The Indians are about to face a whole new kind of hurt."

Chapter 21 – The Hornet's Nest

'Orders are there to be interpreted.' To a certain extent that has been the unofficial motto of the Imperial Navy. Of course, more than once this has been understood to mean, 'orders are there to be broken.' When that has been the case, things have not always worked out in the Empire's favor.

-Excerpt from Empire Rising, 3002 AD

31st April 2467 AD, HMS *Endeavour*, outer edge of the Haven System.

Groggily, James reached up and tapped the COM unit that was buzzing beside his bed. "What is it?" he asked reluctantly. He had been enjoying a pleasant dream about Suzanna and didn't want it to end.

"You're going to want to come see this Sir," Second Lieutenant Julius said. "New contacts have just appeared accelerating into the system."

"I'm on my way," James said.

As soon as he walked onto the bridge he looked at the main holo display. *Endeavour* had been cruising in stealth towards the shift passage to Independence for the last thirteen hours. They were now almost half way there.

"What have you got?" James asked Julius who was sitting in Mallory's command chair.

"It looks like a convoy jumped into the system about ten minutes ago. They have been slowly accelerating towards Haven," she said as she zoomed the main holo display onto a group of ships moving from the shift passage from Indian space towards Haven.

"Have you identified them yet?" James followed up.

"There are four destroyers and three frigates around the edges of the formation," Julius answered. "The rest of the ships appear to be freighters of various designs. These three ships are the ones of interest though."

When James looked at their profiles he saw what she meant. "More troop transports," he said. "Just what the people of Haven need. More Indian soldiers to contend with."

"They are moving into the system very slowly," Julius said. "It appears that some of the Indian patrol ships are moving to help escort the convoy in, but we could intercept it if we wanted."

Looking closely at the acceleration profiles of the Indian convoy James saw that Julius was right. With a slight course alteration *Endeavour* could head back into the system under stealth and get in front of the convoy. The escorts were likely to be pumping megawatts of radar waves out into space around them and *Endeavour* couldn't get too close before she was detected. But she could get close enough to fire off a couple of broadsides at the troop transports.

"Call Mallory and Becket," James said to the COMs officer on watch. "Tell them to report to the bridge."

"Aye Sir," the Sub Lieutenant said.

"You know this isn't exactly what our orders have laid out for us," James said to Julius.

"I know Sir," she said with a mischievous smile. "But you have taught us orders aren't everything. It's like the situation with the Vestarians. If we just let those troops get to Haven they will make life a lot harder for Major Johnston and the rebels fighting the Indians."

"I can't argue with that," James said. "But we have some vital information to get home to the Admiralty." *Still,* he thought to himself. *How can I walk away from such an opportunity to hurt the Indians?*

When Becket and Mallory arrived, James let Julius outline her plan. "So what do you think?" James asked his two other officers. "We'd be going right back into the hornet's nest. After we attack the convoy the Indians will be swarming all around us again."

"We have escaped from them three times now," Becket said. "I am sure we can do it again. *Endeavour's* stealth technology has proven itself better than its designers ever imagined.

"I hate to be the cautious one," Mallory said when James looked at him. "But our mission was to get as much intel as we can on the Indian invasion force. Every combat situation we have found ourselves in has been a result of trying to accomplish our mission. If we attack this convoy we will be overstepping our orders. Perhaps more importantly, we will be risking our mission. If we are destroyed, then the Admiralty won't know what is going on here."

"Then we will just have to make sure we get away," Becket said confidently. "We know we can do it."

"I don't doubt that," Mallory said. "If it was up to a vote I'd be for going after the convoy. I just think we need to know what is at stake."

"Thank you," James said. "I am well aware of our orders, but your caution is helpful."

Now what would my uncle do? James asked himself. Ever since his first command his uncle had been feeding him ancient novels about the seventeenth and eighteen century British navy. They were full of stories of daring naval captains who had won fame and glory for themselves as they had almost single handily beaten Britain's enemies. *I think he almost longs for those days. I know he has been trying to impart some of that spirit into me. I guess it has worked,* James thought.

When it came down to it there wasn't really a choice, *I'm not running away this time.* He had been faced with little choice when he had decided to leave Johnston and his men behind. There had been no way to get them off the planet safely. *But*

I'll be damned if I let another fifteen thousand troops land on my wife's planet.

"We're going after the convoy," James said.

*

Seven hours later James was still on the bridge. He was glad that he had got so much sleep before Julius had woken him up. Mallory was in the command chair beside him and Julius had moved to the auxiliary bridge, ready to take command should something happen to himself or Mallory.

The Indian convoy was moving at the speed of its slowest ship and they had ample time to line up their attack on it. James had decided to fly straight across the middle of the convoy two light minutes above their position. It would allow *Endeavour* to fire off two missile salvos before the convoy passed out of range. Traveling at her top speed of 0.38c, it also meant that none of the convoy's escorts would be able to follow her without braking and turning after *Endeavour* as she fled.

"Radiation levels are approaching maximum," Becket said from the tactical console.

"Fire as soon as they reach detection level," James said.

The four destroyers and three frigates escorting the Indian convoy had been joined by a light cruiser and another destroyer. All nine warships were filling space with radar waves and *Endeavour's* stealth coating could only absorb so much.

"Firing," Becket announced a minute later.

As soon as *Endeavour's* eight missiles erupted from her missile tubes all hell broke loose among the convoy. The escorts that could orientate their main search radars in the direction of where the missiles originated did so. Within seconds *Endeavour's* stealth coating was overwhelmed and she became visible to every ship in the convoy.

The freighters accelerated as soon as they detected the missiles. Those that had turned into *Endeavour's* path rapidly tried to reverse their course as soon as she became visible.

Whoever is commanding the convoy is good, James thought as he watched the warships' more coordinated response. As soon as it became clear that the missiles were aimed at one of the troop ships two of the destroyers accelerated closer to cover them with their point defenses. The three frigates turned onto a converging course with *Endeavour* and went to full military power.

"They are trying to get those frigates into plasma cannon range to take us out quickly," Mallory shouted as soon as he saw what was happening.

"We have the range advantage with our heavier caliber plasma cannons," James said to Mallory, "don't let them get close enough to hit us."

"Yes Sir," Mallory answered.

It only took a few more seconds to see what the commander of the convoy had ordered the rest of his ships to do. As soon as the last one had lined up its missile ports, twenty-four missiles shot out from them, all accelerating straight for *Endeavour*.

"Time to activate our decoys," James ordered.

After Mallory's stunt with the recon drones, *Endeavour's* stock of drones was almost empty. James knew the bean counters at the Admiralty would be very unhappy to find out just how many Mallory had used. Each of the drones cost over a half a million credits. Yet they would be a lot less happy about having to replace an entire exploration cruiser. With that in mind, James had launched every one of the remaining drones. They were all flying in close formation with his ship.

When Malik sent the orders, every one of them switched on their active sensors and accelerated. The added radar strength was able to burn through more of the Indian missiles' ECM, allowing Becket to more accurately target them. At the same time, the sudden explosion of new electromagnetic and gravimetric contacts confused the Indian missiles' targeting data.

As Becket focused on making sure *Endeavour's* point defenses took out as many of the incoming missiles as possible, James took a moment to watch his missiles attack the troop ship. The two destroyers that had moved to aid the troop ship had set up a cross fire on his missiles. With all the fighting *Endeavour* had been involved in, she was down to just two penetrator missiles. James had ordered one each to be used in the two broadsides. The impressive defensive fire from the destroyers and the penetrator missile canceled each other out. Two missiles got past them and dove in towards the troop ship.

Desperately, it fired off its weaker point defenses. One of the missiles exploded, taken out by a AM missile. The second one continued on. In one last effort to survive, the troop ship frantically went through a series of evasive maneuvers. The missile kept with it however and just as it turned to hit its target, the final evasive maneuver of the troop ship actually brought them both together. The missile penetrated right through the troop ship's thick valstronium armor before it exploded. The entire ship disappeared in the blast.

James punched one of his fists into the air. His reaction went unnoticed by the rest of the bridge crew as they were all frantically working to take out the incoming Indian missiles.

"The flak cannons took out twelve," Malik called over to Becket.

"Got it," Becket responded. Sweat began to fall down her forehead as she directed the fire of the point defense plasma cannon crews and picked out targets for the AM missiles.

As soon as the remaining Indian missiles came into range, space around *Endeavour* and the eight drones flying in formation with her filled with green plasma bolts. AM missiles quickly followed them as thirty were launched from the British ship. Twelve Indian missiles became eight, then six, until finally only three remained.

"They are all targeting drones," Malik called out excitedly, "we are clear."

James saw Malik was right. All three missiles broke away from *Endeavour* and homed in on two of the drones that were radiating electromagnetic energy into space. None of the missiles got direct hits, the drones were too small for their targeting computers to accurately hit, yet the resultant explosions from the thermonuclear warheads destroyed them.

"Good work," James said to Becket and the rest of the bridge crew after the last missile exploded. "We just need to beat the odds one more time! What are the frigates doing?"

"They are about a minute out from their plasma cannon range," Mallory answered. "I nailed one but the other two are still coming. They are jinking and diving, making it hard for me to hit them."

"Stay on them," James said. "They can't get a hit on us."

"They are opening fire," Malik called front the sensor station.

"They are wasting their shots," Mallory said confidently. "There, got another one!" he added.

"They are not aiming at us," Malik said after the first round of bolts flew past *Endeavour*. "They are trying to take out the drones. They can destroy them at their current range."

"Damn," James said as he saw that they had already destroyed two of the drones. As he watched, a second salvo of bolts tore into the drones and three more exploded.

"Get those drones doing some evasive maneuvers," James called out.

Malik obeyed just in time for the next round of plasma bolts washed over the drones just as the drones began to jink about. One more was destroyed.

"Second missile salvo is away," Becket called out. She had tasked the ensign assisting her at the tactical station with preparing the second salvo and as soon as *Endeavour* was clear of the Indian missiles she had given him the final targeting data.

"The remaining frigate is pulling back," Mallory said.

"It has done what it came to do," James responded. With only a couple of drones running interference he knew the next Indian missile salvo was going to be deadly. There was nothing they could do now but wait and watch.

The Indian commander had his ships well trained. Just before *Endeavour* passed out of range another twenty-four missiles were launched from the ships defending the convoy. When the missiles caught up with the remaining frigate, it turned and added two more missiles to the salvo.

There was a small cheer on the bridge as the final penetrator missile allowed Becket's second salvo to take out one more of the Indian troop transports. It was short lived however; everyone could see what was coming their way.

James felt the irony of his situation. He was the Captain of *Endeavour,* yet when she was about to face potential destruction there was nothing for him to do but watch while his crew fought the ship.

"Flak cannons engaging now," Becket announced.

On the holo display James watched the shells from the flak cannons shooting off into space. Each cannon was loaded with fifty rounds and together both cannons concentrated their fire to fill the area of space directly in front of the incoming missiles with exploding shrapnel.

"Eight missiles down," Malik called. "Eighteen remaining."

There was silence on the bridge as everyone waited for the flak cannons to be reloaded.

"Firing again," Becket said as a hundred more flak rounds shot towards the Indian missiles.

Before the final rounds exploded, the point defense plasma cannons opened up. Ten seconds later AM missiles leaped out of their launchers. As James watched, eighteen became ten and then six. A final flurry of AM missiles took out another three.

One of the Indian missiles looked like it was angling towards the remaining drone. The other two however, had a firm lock on *Endeavour*. Before he could give the order to throw *Endeavour* into a series of last ditch evasive maneuvers, Sub Lieutenant Jennings had done so. James gripped his command chair as the inertial compensators struggled to cope with the sudden changes in momentum Jennings' maneuvers were causing.

The first missile closed with *Endeavour* seconds later. When a turn from Jennings momentarily turned the ship away from the missile it detonated, sensing it wouldn't get a direct hit. The explosion from the missile's thermonuclear warhead bathed *Endeavour* in radiation, burning off armor and point defense nodes from her port amidships.

As the energy from the explosion hit his ship James was thrown around in his command chair. Before he could call out to check on the damage the second missile hit. The same maneuver that had allowed *Endeavour* to dodge the first missile allowed the second one to score a direct it on her nose section. The missile struck almost exactly the same spot as Admiral Harris' months before. It penetrated the weakened valstronium armor and punched through two bulkhead sections before it exploded.

The shockwave of the explosion rippled through *Endeavour's* superstructure. It reached the bridge only two seconds after James had been thrown about by the first explosion. The multiple sources of force pushing on the bridge momentarily overpowered the inertial dampeners. James felt an overwhelming force rip his left arm off his command chair. It was forced up into the air and back behind his shoulder before he knew what was happening. As it twisted more than his body would allow, James felt more than heard the loud pop his shoulder and elbow made together. A searing pain shot through his arm and a grunt almost escaped his lips, but before it did, the power that had wrenched his hand moved up through his shoulder and thrust his head back into its restraints with a thud. The pain in his shoulder disappeared as everything went black.

*

"Captain, Captain?" Mallory shouted from his command chair.

When James didn't respond Mallory opened a COM channel to *Endeavour's* sick bay. "Doctor Anderson, we need you on the bridge right away. The Captain is injured."

"I'm on my way," Anderson said.

Concerned about his Captain, Mallory took a second to check the read out of his vital signs from his command chair. With a sigh of relief, Mallory saw that James didn't appear to have suffered any life-threatening injuries. *He is out of the fight though,* Mallory thought. *It's time to step up.*

Opening a COM channel to Second Lieutenant Julius he asked, "How bad is it?"

"We took a direct hit to our nose section," Julius said. "We have lost communication with both forward missile tubes. I have three crew members confirmed killed, another twenty have suffered various injuries."

"And our stealth capabilities?" Mallory asked.

"I don't know yet, if we took a serious hit I'm sure we will be leaking electromagnetic radiation all over the show," Julius said.

"Ok," Mallory acknowledged. "Your priority is to reestablish communication with the forward missile tubes. Then send repair teams to get emergency armor sections put in place. We need to disappear as soon as possible."

"Yes Sir," Julius said.

The initial plan had been to reenter stealth as soon as *Endeavour* had fired her two missile salvos. The warships that were escorting the convoy were already out of missile range and it would take them almost an hour to brake and turn to pursue *Endeavour*. By then James had hoped to have disappeared and be well on the way back to the shift passage to Independence.

"Do we have any visuals from our remaining drone?" Mallory asked.

"They're coming up on the main holo display," Sub Lieutenant Malik said.

In silence the bridge crew watched the two missiles home in

on *Endeavour*. The first one appeared to do little damage. Mallory visibly flinched when the second missile hit. For a fraction of a second it appeared as if nothing had happened and then an explosion burst out of *Endeavour's* nose section. When the fireball subsided *Endeavour* was completely missing one of her forward missile tubes and over twenty meters of her port side nose section was open to space.

"That's it," Malik said. "The drone was destroyed before it could record anymore."

"That will do," Mallory said. "There is no way we can repair that damage in the next hour or two. We are not going to be stealthy enough to cut through the Indian patrols and back towards the Independence shift passage. We need a new plan. Show me the system again."

On the main holo display the plot of the system returned. All but two of the Indian destroyers that were with the convoy were braking hard and turning around in preparation for an acceleration burn after *Endeavour*. Across the rest of the system it looked like every patrol ship was likewise coming full steam towards them.

"It looks like we have kicked the hornet's nest this time," Becket said.

Mallory didn't respond. He was too busy studying the plot of the system. "Take us on this course," he said a minute later to Sub Lieutenant Jennings as he sent her a new flight path.

"This is the only direction that we can go where we will be able to keep our damaged section facing away from the Indian ships. It will take us further away from the Independence shift passage but we have no other choice. Make us as stealthy as you can Lieutenant Becket."

"Aye Sir," Becket said.

*

Twenty minutes later James' eyes shot open. Before he became aware of anything around him the shooting pain in his shoulder grabbed his attention. An involuntary grunt of pain burst from his lips.

"Hold on Captain," Doctor Anderson said. "I have a hypospray for the pain."

James felt something pressed into his neck. After a weird tingling sensation pushed into him, the pain subsided.

"You couldn't have given him that before you woke him up?" Mallory said as he looked on.

"No," Anderson said tartly. "I had to make sure he would come round first. As I already told you, I should be doing this in my sickbay."

"There is no time for that," Mallory said. "We need him awake now."

"Thank you doc," James said. "It's ok Mallory, the pain

cleared my head. What is our situation?"

Doctor Anderson answered before Mallory could. "You have dislocated your shoulder and torn your bicep tendon. I can put your shoulder in here but I will need to take you to sick bay to take care of your tendon."

"I appreciate your work doctor, but I meant with my ship," James said, motioning for Mallory to answer.

"Well as you can see we are still alive Sir," Mallory said. "Though we have taken a serious hit to our nose section. We have lost all eight crew members from forward missile tube one, that entire section has been destroyed. There have been another six deaths and more than forty injuries have been reported. The rest of us are safe for now," Mallory continued as he gestured towards the holo plot. "We are heading towards the edge of the system. Though not towards any of the shift passages. Every ship in the system is steaming for our last known location. I have put us in stealth and turned our damaged sections away from the Indian ships. Hopefully they won't pick up any stray electromagnetic radiation."

"Good work," James said as he took in the holo plot. "You acted fast. I guess we have no choice but to run to safety. Once we repair some of our damage we may be able to work our way back round to the Independence shift passage."

"What about your arm?" Doctor Anderson asked.

"You can pop my shoulder back in," James said. "I will

come see you later for the rest. It sounds like you have a lot more people to tend to."

"That I do," Anderson said. Without further warning she grabbed James' arm and lifted it, twisting at the same time. Despite the hypospray she had given him, James let out another grunt when his shoulder popped back into place.

"Open a COM channel to the ship," James said to Sub Lieutenant King once he was able to talk over the pain.

"It's open Sir," she replied a few seconds later.

"Crew of *Endeavour*. I want to thank you. You all fought well. We paid a heavy price today, I know. And we are not yet out of danger. But we destroyed two Indian troop ships. That is nearly ten thousand soldiers Major Johnston and the people of Haven won't have to contend with. Let that be how we remember those who died today."

With a nod James signaled for King to cut the transmission. "Now," James said. "It's time to figure out a way to get home."

*

Six days later, James gingerly prodded his left arm with his right hand. Doctor Anderson had put his entire arm in a cast. She said it would take another week for his tendon to fully heal after the treatment she had given it. He was once again sitting in his command chair surveying the plot of the Haven system. Since the battle with the convoy, *Endeavour's* crew had been working around the clock to repair as much of the damage as they could. Forward missile tube one was a write off, but all the sections that had been opened to space had now been closed.

For the six days they had been in the Haven system since the battle James had followed Mallory's plan. After reaching the edge of the system they had slowed *Endeavour* and turned her towards the *Independence* shift passage. Instead of heading back into the inner system however, they had angled her up and above the systems' ecliptic. Then, instead of angling back down they had pushed on towards the shift passage, flying through the dark matter clouds that surrounded the Haven system.

Just moments before *Endeavour* had finally broken out of the dark matter clouds and into the Independence shift passage. They were almost a light day up the shift passage from the edge of Haven's mass shadow and the patrolling Indian ships. No one would know where they had gone.

"Engage the shift engine," James said.

"Aye Sir," Jennings said.

With a swipe of her hand, a blinding flash announced *Endeavour's* disappearance from the Haven system.

Chapter 22 – A Not So Warm Welcome

Some argue that the British-Indian war began with the ambush of an Indian convoy. I believe it began with a court martial.

-Excerpt from Empire Rising, 3002 AD

1st June 2467 AD, HMS *Vulcan.*

"Come in," First Space Lord Admiral Somerville said as the door to his office slid open to admit his nephew.

James stepped through the office doors, glad to see his uncle. It had been a long stressful journey back from Haven. It had taken five days to sneak through the Independence system as the Indians had increased their patrols there. It had been a nerve wracking experience as at any moment the patrolling ships could have picked up a trace of electromagnetic radiation from *Endeavour's* damage.

To make matters worse, his crew had been working around the clock to repair *Endeavour* enough so that she could travel through the Gift. Even with their repairs he hadn't been entirely sure that his ship would hold together. To finally be back in the Sol system and in orbit around Earth was a huge relief.

"I have read your report of course," Somerville said as James sat down. "It has already been passed to the other Admirals and Admiral Cunningham and his officers are using it to tweak their invasion plans. But I would like to hear things in your own words."

"Certainly uncle," James said a little taken aback. Normally his uncle was a lot less formal when they met alone. *Endeavour* had docked with HMS Vulcan just a couple of hours ago. After such a long and difficult voyage, he was expecting a warmer welcome. "Where should I start?" he asked after a moment's hesitation.

"Start with Independence, walk me through your decision to attack the cruiser in orbit there," Somerville said.

Taking a deep breath, James dived into retelling the situation. For the next two hours his uncle went over his actions again and again, paying specific attention to his decision to attack the Indian convoy.

When he was done, his uncle sat back in his chair, "Reckless," he said. "After everything you have been through, I thought you would have known better by now."

"Reckless?" James repeated, shocked. "What do you mean? I thought I did exactly what you would have done in the same situation."

"That's how you came to your decision?" Admiral Somerville said, clearly disappointed.

"Yes, you go straight for the enemy and bring them to

battle," James said earnestly. "Isn't that what you have been teaching me all these years? Isn't that the motto of all the heroes in those books you have had me read?" he continued, his voice rising as the frustration of the last several weeks came boiling up. "Isn't that what you did? How you got to be where you are now?"

"I am where I am now boy," Somerville said, allowing his voice to rise to the level of his nephew's. "And don't you forget who you are talking to. I gave you those books to give you a love for the British navy, a love for our tradition. Not to turn you into a thoughtless, headstrong Captain who doesn't know how to put anyone else above his own quest for victory.

"Your past actions in the Void war and with the Vestarians and the Kulreans have shown that you excel in combat situations. Hell, you even managed to run rings around an entire Indian fleet. But did you even once stop and think about the bigger picture? About our invasion fleet sitting here in the Sol system waiting for your intel. What would have happened if *Endeavour* had been destroyed by that convoy's escorts? You were outnumbered more than three to one. You had no business attacking that convoy."

"But I did it to help Major Johnston," James pleaded. "And the people of Haven, it wasn't just about me." Even as he spoke he heard a little voice in the back of his head. *Yes, it was. You knew you could beat them. You are the hero of the Void War.*

Shaking off the voice, James pressed on, "I did it to save

lives. I stopped ten thousand more soldiers landing on Haven. Who knows how many people would have been killed."

"It's not just about the lives," Somerville cut in. "This fight is about the future of our Kingdom. About the future of our people, our way of life. Major Johnston is expendable. Hell, even you are expendable. If we lose our fleet, we lose everything. You were tasked with getting intel about the Indian fleet dispositions. Instead you attack a cruiser in orbit over an occupied world."

"But," James tried to say.

"I don't want to hear it," Somerville said over him. "You may think you have your reasons, but they were foolish. Right now, some Indian Admiral is looking over everything you did. Don't you think they will wonder why you struck at Independence first? Don't you think they will wonder if there is another route to our space via Independence? The invasion plan is counting on the fleet's advance on Haven being unopposed. You could have thrown all that into jeopardy.

"And yet that is beside the point. What would have happened if your ship had been destroyed? Let me tell you," Somerville said before James could open his mouth to answer.

"Admiral Rooke would have advanced into Indian space assuming that the main Indian fleet was still at Haven. Your scouting has identified that the majority of their fleet has left

Haven. When Rooke would have been expecting limited resistance, he could have been ambushed. Outnumbered, we could have lost almost half of our operational battlecruisers. Just what do you think that would mean for our future? Aren't the Argentinians and others just waiting for a chance to take our colonies from us? Did you think about that?"

James was reeling from his uncle's words and didn't know if he was supposed to answer.

"Well did you?" Somerville pressed.

"I thought about the importance of our intel," James insisted. "But I didn't think about what impact I could have down the line," he conceded. "I thought it was my duty to protect Haven and Major Johnston."

"And in doing so, you put not just their future, but the future of Rooke's fleet and our Kingdom in jeopardy. You see, reckless," Somerville said. He stared at his nephew until James was forced to lower his eyes.

"You have shown yourself to be a fine combat officer," Somerville continued when he felt his nephew had been sufficiently chastised. "But a great naval officer is more than someone who can charge head first at the enemy. A great naval officer knows what he needs to do to defeat his enemy. Not just how to destroy a couple of ships."

"I see," James said, trying to listen to his uncle's point fairly.

"I don't think you do," Somerville said. "But you will. Here, take these," he continued, passing a datafile over to James.

"What are they?" James asked.

"You look up to the late Admiral Jensen and I so much, I thought you should have a look at these. Maybe they will give you some perspective."

"Thank you Sir," James said.

"Now," Somerville said, lightening his tone. "Let's get you up to speed on what is happening around here. No doubt some of the other Admirals and politicians will want you to brief them on what you saw at Haven."

"Yes Sir," James said, happy for the subject to be changed. For another forty-five minutes he listened to his uncle outline all that had happened on Earth in his absence. Finally, after his uncle instructed him to keep his crew busy on *Endeavour* to keep anyone from revealing the Gift the Indians, James stood to take his leave.

"Think on what I said," Admiral Somerville said. "I have been lenient on you in the past. From here on in, your career will advance based on your merits. If you can't show the strategic awareness of when to run, then you may stay the Captain of an exploration cruiser for the rest of your career."

"Thank you uncle," James said as he turned to leave.

*

When he got out of his uncle's office and into one of *Vulcan's* many corridors, James looked down at the datapad in his hand. It was an Admiralty report. As he turned to walk back to where *Endeavour* was docked with the large construction station, he began to read.

Forty minutes later he let the datapad fall to his side with his arm. *Have I really been that self-centered?* James asked himself. His uncles' words had cut him deep, and what he had just read had rubbed salt into the fresh wound.

He knew he had been self-centered when he had stepped aboard his first command, HMS *Drake. But I thought I had grown past that.* The voice that had spoken to him in his uncle's office came back to him at that moment, *you did, you became a hero, look at all you have achieved.*

As he listened to his own pride James knew his uncle was right. There had been a part of him that had lusted to go after the Indian convoy. He had believed himself invincible. The consequences of losing the battle hadn't really registered with him, not as something that was actually going to happen. *And more than twenty of my crew members died.* The thought hit James like a ton of bricks. He had lost people before. But then he had been able to console himself with the thought that they had died doing their duty, as James had been doing his. Yet now he wasn't so sure. *How many lives are on my hands because of my pride?* he asked himself.

Looking around, he realized that he was a long way from where *Endeavour* was docked. He had lost track of what he was doing. Dismissing *Endeavour* for the moment, he continued to pace around the construction station, examining his own thoughts. He was so engrossed that an hour later he didn't notice when he eventually wandered past the docking hatch that led to his ship.

"Welcome back Sir," an Ensign supervising the hatch to *Endeavour* said, shaking James out of his thoughts. "The *Vulcan's* Chief Engineer arrived forty-five minutes ago. Mallory is showing him around our damaged sections now. Your wife is here as well. She is waiting for you in your quarters."

"Thank you Ensign," James said. "Send a message to Vulcan's Chief, let him know I will join him presently."

"Aye Sir," the Ensign said to James' back as James had already walked past him.

When he got to his quarters he found Suzanna sitting at the small desk in his bedroom, "James," she exclaimed with a large smile as she stood and almost jumped into a hug. "It's so good to have you back."

"It's good to be back," James said, drinking in Suzanna' fragrance ae he hugged her back. "I have missed you," he added before she pulled him into a deep kiss.

"Come, sit down with me," Suzanna said once they broke apart. "Tell me about your mission. I saw the damage to *Endeavour's* nose. Was it serious?"

"Ok," James said. "But I don't have long. I need to go meet with *Vulcan's* Chief Engineer. He will want to begin the repair work on *Endeavour* right away."

"I understand," Suzanna said. "You can tell me the highlights."

As James retold what had happened to him over the last several months for the second time in the space of a few hours, he couldn't help but revaluate everything in light of what his uncle had told him.

When he was finished, Suzanna moved over to sit in his lap. "I'm sorry about your crew," she said as she wrapped her arms around him. "And for my own people. They are fighting bravely for their freedom, but it is a high price they are paying."

Sensing she needed comfort as much as he did James pulled her into a deeper hug. "My uncle is working on that. With the intel we gathered Admiral Rooke should be able to begin the first part of my uncle's plan within the week."

"I know," Suzanna said. "I have been included in some of the Prime Minister's COBRA meetings."

"And just what else have you been up to?" James asked, eager to change the subject from his recent experiences.

"Well," Suzanna said. "I have made a lot of new friends among the nobility, mainly among the other countesses and duchesses. Many wanted me to join one or two of their private get togethers to discuss Haven and the potential war with India. I have also been on a few news broadcasts. I am quite the celebrity you know."

"I don't doubt it," James said. He had seen how the British public had reacted to her speeches and their wedding.

"I have also made a few enemies," Suzanna said. "Oh nothing too serious," she hastily added when the saw the look that came over James' face. "Just others among the nobility and House of Commons who oppose intervention in Haven. They like the status quo too much and they don't want to risk all that they have. They have pulled me into more than one heated conversation. But I am a politician don't forget, I know how to handle myself."

"That you do," James said proudly. "I wouldn't want to be the one to go up against you. I bet you have given one or two people a verbal lashing."

"Well, I have been trying to be on my best behavior," Suzanna answered. "But I did get carried away at a dinner I was at last week. I don't know if it was on purpose or not but I was sat at a table with a certain Lady Reynolds. She was talking to everyone about how foolish it was for British lives to be risked for a colony no one knew even existed five years ago."

"Reynolds," James said. "That name is familiar, how would I know it?"

"Her husband I expect," Suzanna said. "He is a member of

the Liberal Party; they have formed part of the opposition alongside the Moderates. Both of them are opposed to any more British military aggression. That is why they have gone into opposition together."

"I'm not totally oblivious to the mechanisms of British politics," James said, "You don't have to talk to me like I'm a complete imbecile. I know who is currently sitting in the opposition benches," he added as he tickled Suzanna's side.

"Then you should already know who Reynolds is," Suzanna said in her best school teacher voice after she fought him off. "He is the Shadow Defense Secretary; surely a military officer should know that?" she finished with a pinch back at James.

"Aahh, I guess," James said, admitting to himself that he had probably heard Reynolds' name in countless briefings, he had just never registered it as something important.

The British House of Commons operated along adversarial lines. The largest party or coalition of parties would work together to form a government to run the country. Those parties that were excluded could therefore form their own coalitions and go into opposition. They would set up a Shadow Cabinet filled with opposition MP's who made it their responsibility to set out their own parties positions on areas like defense, expansion, industry and economics. The Shadow Cabinet Ministers also sought to hold their governing counterparts accountable and, where possible, force the government to follow the opposition's plans. Now that he thought about it James had heard about Reynold's views in a number of different briefings, but he had never been someone James had worried about.

"Well, I'm sure you gave his wife a good talking to," James said as Suzanna snuggled back into his arms.

"To be honest, I actually started with her husband a few days before the dinner," Suzanna replied.

"You do like to make enemies," James chuckled. "What happened?"

"Well I was being interviewed by a news broadcaster. They asked me about my thoughts on the opposition's calls for a recension of the ultimatum Fairfax sent to India. I may have called the Shadow Defense Secretary a coward. But that was all, I don't know what all the fuss was about."

"I'm sure there was hardly any fuss at all," James said chuckling. "And someone sat you beside Reynold's wife after this?"

"I guess they were looking for fireworks," Suzanna answered.

"Did they get any?"

"A little," Suzanna said. "I simply asked Mrs. Reynolds if it was her children who were on Haven, under Indian occupation. Would she be willing to risk British lives then?"

"How did she react?" James asked.

"Well, it turns out she doesn't have any children. From what I understand, both her and her husband have a very rare genetic condition that has prevented them from having any children."

"So she took it a bit too personally then I'm guessing?"

"You could say that. She jumped up shouting profanity at me and said I had insulted her and her husband for the last time. She promised to make sure I and my people paid for it."

"It seems you have indeed made yourself an enemy then?" James said.

"Just one more to add to the list," Suzanna replied with a sign. "I hope Councilwoman Pennington isn't another one that I will have to take on when we return to Haven."

"Yes," James agreed, his countenance changing as his thoughts turned back to Haven.

"Now," Suzanna said as she sat back a bit on his lap, took his head into her hands and looked into his eyes. "Tell me what else is wrong with you. I know you well enough to know something is eating you up."

James let out a breath. He didn't really want to talk about his newly found self-loathing. But he didn't want to lie to his new wife either.

"It's something my uncle said," he began. "When I attacked that Indian convoy I put the entire fleet into danger. I put my selfish desire to win another victory over the fleet's need for intel. In the end, we were lucky to survive the attack. We could easily have been destroyed. I should never have gone near the convoy. My crew members died for no good reason. I'm not sure I'm cut out to be a Captain."

Suzanna pulled him into another hug. When she pulled back she was smiling.

"What is so funny?" James asked, hurt.

"Not funny," Suzanna said. "I'm proud of you. Don't you see? Your uncle may be partially right. You have just said so yourself. But, listen to yourself. Someone who is really self-centered, a Captain who only cared about this own fame and glory, wouldn't be talking the way you are.

"They would be trying to defend themselves. Or arguing about how wrong your uncle is. You are cut up, you do care about your crew and your country. Yes," Suzanna said as James was about to cut in. "You may have begun to believe your own press. I'm guessing I'm to blame for that in a small way. But you are not too far gone. Your concern shows that the kind of Captain your uncle wants you to be is already in there," she said as she reached over and touched James' chest. "You just have to let him grow."

"I don't know," James said, looking away. He wasn't ready to hear how wonderful he was again.

Reaching over to the datapad that James had set on the table, "Did he give you this?" Suzanna asked.

"Yes," James answered. "It's the Admiralty reports for two incidents from years ago. One involved my uncle when he commanded the *Achilles* and another involved the late Rear Admiral Jensen."

"And what are they about?" Suzanna asked.

"In both cases they retreated from the enemy when the odds were in their favor," James explained.

"So they ran away?" Suzanna said, already knowing the answer to the question.

"No, of course not," James said quickly. "They retreated because avoiding action was the best strategic option. It allowed them to fight and win a more decisive battle later on. Exactly the kind of thing I would never do. I would have just run in gung ho."

"You are too hard on yourself husband," Suzanna said sternly. "You are forgetting all you have accomplished. Tell me this, didn't your uncle almost singlehandedly thwart the Russian invasion of New France when he was commanding a heavy cruiser?"

"Yes," James said.

"And didn't he do it by being gung ho, by attacking the Russian fleet head on even though he was badly outnumbered?" Suzanna pressed.

"Yes," James said again, "but that was different."

"Different than when you stepped in to protect Haven from the Vestarian fleet, or when you protected the entire Kulrean civilization from the same fleet?"

"Well," James tried to say.

"Well nothing. You *are* too hard on yourself," Suzanna insisted, smiling. "You may still have a lot to learn. Certainly, we both know you have a lot to learn about women. But you are made of the same stuff as your uncle. You just need to learn when to jump in and when to hold back. Let me ask you this, how many perfect Captains or Admirals do you know?"

James could think of a couple. Captain Lightfoot came to mind immediately, and Rear Admiral Jensen. But after those two, the list became very sparse. He knew Captains who were good at one thing or another. But at different times he had thought each of them could be better in one area or another. Guessing Suzanna didn't want to hear any answer though, he kept quiet.

"There, you see, there is no perfect Captain," Suzanna said triumphantly. "You are setting the standard too high. Do you think you are the first Captain to make a mistake? Or the first one your uncle has had to share some harsh words with?"

"I guess not," James said.

"You see, all you need is some perspective," Suzanna continued. "By all means, learn from your mistakes, take you uncle's words to heart. But don't think that you have suddenly become the worst Captain in the navy. If you really were, your uncle would have removed you from command months ago."

"I suppose," James said, reluctantly admitting to himself that there was something to her words.

"Of course I'm right," Suzanna said smiling again. "I am your wife after all. Now get up, brush yourself off and go and see Vulcan's Chief Engineer. I will be here when you get back. Then I can tell you all about my exciting life in the British nobility. And," Suzanna added as she leaned in and kissed him again. "We can get better reacquainted."

"I think I can manage that," James said, already eager to get back.

Chapter 23 – Machiavellian Movements

History has shown that adversarial politics often work best. Whilst it may make life difficult for the ruling government, it also holds them accountable. The one downside is that governments can fall quickly, and often in times of trouble. The permanency of the Emperor and the Senate provides the perfect balance to this flaw.

-Excerpt from Empire Rising, 3002 AD

2nd June 2467 AD, Houses of Parliament, London, England.

Admiral Somerville stepped through the ornately decorated gold encrusted door into Prime Minister Fairfax's office within the Houses of Parliament. Fairfax and King Edward were already there.

"To what do I owe this summons?" Somerville asked. "The COBRA council will be meeting in several hours. What is so urgent?"

"We may have a problem," Fairfax said. "Something I think we need to discuss in private."

"What is it?" Somerville asked.

"How useful was the intel your nephew brought back from Haven?" Fairfax asked.

"Very," Somerville said, not sure where things were going. "As you will hear later. I am confident that we can move ahead with our plans immediately thanks to the information he brought back."

"Good," Fairfax said. "Then his mission was a success."

"I would describe it as such," Somerville said, now very confused.

"To get to the point then," Fairfax said. "I have information that suggests a faction within the Admiralty is pushing for an immediate court martial into your nephew's actions."

"What?" Somerville almost shouted. "I have heard of no such thing."

"Just as you were supposed to," Fairfax said. "It is being instigated by Shadow Defense Secretary Reynolds. The Liberal party is pushing to use the Indian situation to gain more power for themselves. Reynolds has been given the lead on this. He strongly opposes intervention in Haven and he is using factions loyal to him within the Admiralty to instigate this court martial.

"Your nephew attacked and destroyed several Indian warships. I believe Reynolds wishes to have him charged with actions unbefitting a naval Captain. Technically, we are not at war with the Indians, yet your nephew sought out and fought with several of their ships."

"But the executive order you released before Endeavour left for Haven called on all British warships to treat Indian warships in the Haven territories as hostile," Somerville said. "James was just following orders."

"Maybe," King Edwards said. "But the opposition doesn't see it that way. Without a formal declaration of war, they believe your nephew's actions were reckless and irresponsible. He put his ship in unnecessary danger and he engaged in open hostilities with a peaceful naval fleet."

"That's preposterous, the Indians are not peaceful," Somerville barked.

"The truth doesn't matter here Admiral," Fairfax said. "What matters is the law. Reynolds wants to make a spectacle of your nephew and by connection, you, me, and our plans to help Haven. The question is; if a court martial is convened, what do you think it will find?"

Somerville went to respond and then paused to think. His talk with his nephew from the day before still fresh in his mind. "I don't know," he conceded. "James' orders were to scout out the Haven system and get accurate information on the disposition of the Indian forces. He has been given the stealthiest warship in our navy. He should have been able to complete his mission without any combat. Yet, he did seek out the Indian warships and he fired the first shots in almost all the encounters he had. What's worse, when he had the intel he needed, instead of coming straight home, he attacked an Indian convoy.

"Heck, he did so well in evading the Indians, even though they knew he was there, they may pull more ships back to Haven to beef up the patrols there. That could actually make an invasion harder. If it's true that your executive order doesn't amount to a formal declaration of war, then a court martial may find James guilty of abandoning his orders and unlawfully engaging peaceful warships," Somerville said.

"And if that were to happen, our plans for Haven would stall," Fairfax said.

"Then what do we do?" King Edward asked. "We can't just abandon James to his fate, not now that he is married to Suzanna. And of course, he is your nephew," Edward added when he saw the look on Somerville's face.

"I won't abandon him," Somerville said. "He may be too gung ho, but he is one of the best officers I have. If James loses his command because of political maneuvering in Parliament, it will send a very bad message throughout the fleet."

"I know," Fairfax said, "but you can't get involved. It will look too much like favoritism."

"Then what do we do?" Somerville interrupted, repeating Edward's question.

"If you would let me finish," Fairfax said. "I have a plan."

"Go on then," Somerville said, "don't keep us all in suspense."

"I can't tell you all of it now," Fairfax answered. "But suffice to say. It will further our war plans. Reynolds made a mistake not keeping this quieter. He has given me a couple of days to prepare. My propaganda machine can do a lot in two days.

"What I need you to do, is to expedite the court martial. We want it to be convened as soon as the Admirals bring it up. And, I need you to speak to your nephew. We all know he can be a bit hot headed. You need to convince him that we have everything under control. I already have the best corporate lawyer picked out for his defense.

"A corporate lawyer," Somerville said. "Wouldn't a military lawyer be better suited? One who is familiar with our laws and how a court martial works."

"Not this time," Fairfax said. "This isn't just going to be a military trial. This will be a trial in front of the British public. I have just the woman for such an occasion. In fact, I have already spoken to her and we are of one mind about how to approach the trial. Your nephew will be keeping his answers simple. Here," Fairfax said as he slipped a piece of paper into Somerville's hands. "You are to give this to James."

"I wish to make no further comment. I have been advised by my counsel that my record and my actions will speak for themselves," Somerville said, reading the note out loud.

"What does this mean?" he asked Fairfax.

"It means that we have other ideas about how to defend James," Fairfax explained.

"I see," Somerville said.

"Ha," Fairfax laughed. "I don't think you do. But you will."

"Ok," Somerville said. "Then what am I to do now?"

"Just speak to James," Fairfax said. "Then, when whoever is in Reynold's pocket brings up the court martial, you are to expedite it."

"Very well," Somerville said. "The Admirals are meeting this afternoon, am I to assume that this matter will be brought up then?"

"I would expect so," Fairfax answered.

"May I take my leave," Somerville said. "I will have to speak to my nephew before the COBRA meeting."

"We will see you later," Fairfax said, shaking Somerville's hand. "If this escalates into a court martial it will be hard to keep quiet, but you and your nephew will have to be on your best behavior."

"We will," Somerville promised as he stood.

"Hold on Edward, I have a role for you in all this too," Fairfax said as King Edward stood with Somerville.

"We will speak later then Admiral," Edward said as he shook Somerville's hand.

"Aye," Somerville said before he turned and walked out.

*

"Uncle," James said as he sat down in the same seat he had been in the day before. He had received his uncle's summons barely twenty minutes ago and rushed over. Not sure what his uncle wanted, he knew he needed to get something off his chest. "I want to say you were right," he continued. "I hadn't seen it before. But I have been letting my past successes get the better of me. Attacking that convoy was a mistake. I understand now. I'm not saying I am a changed man. But you have given me perspective. If I had the situation again to do over, I wouldn't risk the intel I had gathered."

"That makes what I am about to say a lot easier," Somerville said, smiling. "I didn't say you weren't a fast learner. Just that you are too hard headed."

"Thank you uncle," James said. "I think."

"Don't thank me yet boy," Somerville said. "You still have a lot to learn. And what I am about to tell you may just be the beginning of your learning process."

"Ok," James said, even more unsure why he had been called into his uncle's office.

"There is going to be a court martial," Somerville said, getting right to the point. "Yours I'm afraid."

"I understand," James said, devastated. "I let the fleet down."

"You did boy," Somerville agreed. "But this court martial is not coming from me and it is not about letting the fleet down. There is a movement among the opposition party in the Commons to prevent the fleet intervening in Haven. They are trying to embarrass me, the Prime Minister and our plans for Haven through you. You will be charged with disobeying orders and attacking neutral shipping. They want to make it look like the Prime Minister and I have been trying to start a fight with the Indians, that the whole Haven thing is just an excuse for a war we have been trying to orchestrate.

"Here," Somerville said, slipping the piece of paper he had received from Fairfax to James, "this is your defense."

"I don't understand Sir," James said after he read the paper.

"Neither do I," Somerville answered. "But Fairfax assures me that he has everything under control."

"So I can't defend myself?" James said. "I may have risked my mission in attacking the fleet. But I didn't disobey my orders, and I engaged the Indian warships because Fairfax's executive order identified them as hostiles."

"I know you did, even if firing first was not strictly what

your orders mandated," Somerville said, reminding James of the fine line he had skirted while in Haven. "Any neutral court martial would find your actions acceptable, if just barely," he went on. "But this won't be a neutral court martial. There are enough Admirals who aren't enamored with how I run the Admiralty that Reynolds may be able to stack the deck against you."

"I see," James said.

"But look on the bright side," Somerville said in a more cheerful tone. "You have Fairfax on your side. I dare say if he was really concerned about the court martial, he would have had it quashed before it could begin. He obviously has a trick or two up his sleeve."

"And how is this to be a learning process for me?" James asked. He trusted Fairfax, but he knew the Prime Minister wasn't infallible. "My career is going to be on the line."

"I won't let it come to that," Somerville said. "And as for Fairfax. He has a plan in all this. One that is meant to help our war effort and the people of Haven. But it is one of his demands that you put the good of our plans above your own reputation. Your character, your command ability and your actions are going to be torn apart during the court martial and you are going to have to keep quiet.

"Worse, it may even be that what a lot of what they are saying is true. Yet, you are not going to be able to agree. For Fairfax's plan to work, you will need to stick to your script. I don't know what exactly he is up to, but I know that much.

Do you think you can do that?" Somerville asked.

"I'm not sure," James said. "How can I lie? I know why I chose to attack that convoy. My motives weren't pure, and people died because of it."

"No one is asking you to lie," Somerville said. "For the last three years you have led a very distinguished naval career. Do you really think one mistake means you should be thrown out of the navy?"

"I was thinking that after our conversation yesterday," James said reluctantly. "But Suzanna talked me out of it."

"Just one more way the two of you are a good match," Somerville said. "Now look at that piece of paper. Is anything on there a lie?"

"I guess not," James said. "But how will appealing to my past protect me from the charges you say are going to be brought against me?"

"To be honest, I don't know," Somerville said. "But Fairfax does, and we both need to trust him. Can you do that? Can you put your career on the line for him?"

"Yes," James replied, picking up the piece of paper and putting it into one of his pockets. "If this is what needs to be done."

"Good," Somerville said, smiling. "In that case, I will let you go tell your lovely wife the latest developments. She will need to be on her best behavior too. She has become a public figure now. She needs to make sure she doesn't turn on Reynolds or his associates. She can defend you, but if she goes on the offensive, we will lose the moral high ground."

"I see," James said. "Well I will tell her, but I can't make any promises. She doesn't do everything I say."

"And she's not supposed to," Somerville replied with a chuckle. "At least there is one positive thing that has come out of this court martial," he added becoming slightly more serious.

"What is that?" James asked.

"We now have an excuse to keep your crew confined on board *Endeavour,*" Admiral Somerville replied. "The official story will be that your crew may be called as witnesses in the court martial and so are not allowed contact with any outside news agencies. Though my real concern is that the Indians will get wind of the Gift. Our future military strategy depends on keeping it a surprise.

"You are to instruct your officers that they are to screen all outgoing communications. Your people will be allowed to send out recorded messages to their loved ones, but your officers will need to make sure there is no mention of details sensitive to the court martial or the Gift."

"My crew isn't going to be very happy," James replied carefully. "They didn't get to step off the ship even once the last time we were in Earth orbit. They are going to get very restless."

"I'll see what I can do about arranging some time on one of *Vulcan's* recreation decks," Admiral Somerville replied. "They will have to be supervised by RSNI personnel of course, but they will at least be able to stretch their legs. That is the best I can do. We are on the brink of war with the Indians. Your crew are just going to have to do their duty."

"I will make sure they understand," James replied.

"Good. Now get going. I have a COBRA meeting to attend and then the meeting of the Admiralty Board," Somerville said to dismiss his nephew.

*

When the British Navy morphed into the British Space Navy and once again became the focal point of British colonial expansion, the Admiralty Board was reinstituted to oversee the running of the Navy. Made up of Admirals who were selected by the fleet to serve as Lord Commissioners on the Board, their primary job was accept or reject the Prime Minister and King's appointment of a First Space Lord. They also held the right to dismiss said appointee with a two thirds majority vote. After a First Space Lord was appointed, the day to day running of the navy fell on him or her.

With the day to day running of the navy in the hands of the First Space Lord, the Admiralty Board played an oversight role. Ensuring that the appointee of the Prime Minister and King did not steer the navy in a direction away from the traditions and values of its Captains and Admirals.

As he sat in the Admiralty Board meeting room looking at the sixteen Lord Commissioners, Somerville couldn't help feel that maybe his last eight years as First Space Lord had been easier than he deserved. There were a number of Admirals seated around him who he knew didn't see eye to eye with everything he did. Others were rivals who he had butted heads with on more than one occasion as he had risen through the ranks of the navy. Yet, to date the Board had rarely hampered the changes he had been effecting. Something in his gut told him that was about to change.

As the last Admiral sat down Somerville rose to his feet. "Now that we are all here, I call this meeting of the Admiralty Board to session." Raising his hand Somerville brought the ornate gavel down with a bang.

"To the first order of business then," Somerville said.

For almost an hour he got lost in the drudgery of Admiralty Board meetings. Whilst he had complete control of day to day naval affairs. There were countless minor things that he had to get Board approval for in order to make long term plans. Finally, the last thing on the agenda was discussed and voted on.

"Now, is there any other business for us to discuss before I bring this meeting to a close?" Somerville asked.

"Yes," Admiral Blackwood said. "There is one more matter."

Somerville inwardly groaned, of all the Admirals who were likely to have joined their cause to Reynolds', Blackwood was the last one he wanted to see. Not many people knew, but the Blackwood and Somerville families had a long running feud that went back generations. Somerville had long ago put any past grievances aside. He wasn't interested in the ancient past. Yet he knew his brother hadn't been of the same mind. On more than one occasion he knew that his brother, James' father, had gone out of his way to make life difficult for Admiral Blackwood.

Somerville had thought that Blackwood hadn't held it against him. Certainly, he hadn't caused any problems in the past. It seemed however, that he had been biding his time. Now he had a golden opportunity to get back at the son of the man who had crossed him.

"By now all of us have had a chance to read the report Captain Somerville brought back from Haven," Blackwood continued. "I for one found it severely lacking. Worse, I believe Somerville directly disobeyed his orders when he attacked the Indian cruiser in orbit around Independence and when he attacked the Indian convoy. He was supposed to be on a reconnaissance mission, not a raiding mission. There is no state of war between India and the British Star Kingdom, and yet he attacked numerous Indian ships. All were acts of war. I believe he has been trying to provoke a war between our two nations and as such, should be court martialed for disobeying a direct order and treason against the crown."

More than one gasp escaped the lips of the gathered

Admirals. Treason was a very serious crime. Even Somerville, who had been expecting the call for a court martial, was shocked at the mention of treason. Reynolds and Blackwood were going for the jugular.

"This is an outrage," Admiral Russell said. "Captain Somerville is one of the best Captains we have. He has shown courage under fire and a willingness to risk his life in service to his country. This is no way to treat a war hero."

In desperation Russel looked to Somerville, seeking help in arguing his case. Slowly and deliberately Somerville shook his head. *This is not your fight friend,* Somerville said to himself. Russell was his closest friend and head of RSNI, the intelligence division of the RSN. He would be bitterly upset that his contacts hadn't seen this coming.

"Very well," Somerville said. "As Captain Somerville is my nephew I am forced to remove myself from the vote. Can I see a show of hands of those willing to bring these charges to a court martial?"

Somerville was depressed when he saw the hands that went up. His enemies he knew, but some of the hands belonged to friends, others he had thought were allies. He knew himself that his nephew's actions were reckless, but those who were voting against him now knew what they were doing. They weren't just voting to court martial a reckless Captain, they were trying to undermine their First Space Lord.

In the end, the vote passed by ten to six. Before Somerville could go forward with the formal procedures to ratify a court martial Admiral Blackwood spoke again, "I would like to try the case."

"This is highly unusual," Somerville said. "You are the one who brought the charges before us."

"And yet it is my right to put my name forward," Blackwood said.

"Very well," Somerville said. "Is there anyone else who wishes to put their name forward to try the case?"

He wasn't surprised when none of the ten who had voted for the court martial raised their hands. Admiral Russell made to volunteer but he stopped when Somerville shook his head again. The vote thus became a formality.

"The vote has passed," Somerville said after asking for a show of hands. "Admiral of the White Nathan Blackwood will try the court martial of Captain James Somerville on the charges of disobeying a direct order and treason.

"There is just one more thing," Somerville said. "As First Space Lord it is my right to expedite any cases that will impact upon operational matters. HMS *Endeavour* is our first exploration cruiser, she has shown herself to be invaluable over the last year and she will be needed for any future operations in Haven territory. I wish to have any ambiguity about who her commanding officer is sorted out immediately. As a result, the court martial will begin two days from now. If *Endeavour's* Captain is to be struck out of the navy, it will be done within the week."

Blackwood looked like he was about to protest but Somerville brought his gavel down hard. The boom that echoed around the meeting hall brought the gathering to an end and let everyone know just how pissed off the First Space Lord was.

Chapter 24 – The Court Martial

Despite the fact that the Empire's Navy is spread out over thousands of light years and comprises of thousands upon thousands of Captains and Admirals, if you insult one, you will quickly find all those nearby gathering around to come to his or her aid. The one exception is court martials, there, all camaraderie.

-Excerpt from Empire Rising, 3002 AD

4th June 2467 AD, Admiralty House, London.

When James sat down in his allotted chair he couldn't help but steal a glance at the assembled jury. There were seven Captains, all of them already seated in the jury box. Unsurprisingly none of them were looking at him. It was a tradition that dated back centuries. If the defendant was cleared of all charges, then the Captains who sat on the jury may very well find themselves serving with or even under the accused. No one wanted hard feelings from a court martial impacting future operations. On the other hand, if the defendant was found guilty, no one wanted to have any association with them. They were damaged goods.

To his horror, James saw that Captain Lightfoot was among the Captains who had been selected to serve on the jury. James liked Lightfoot and he didn't know what thought was worse. The thought that Lightfoot's opinion of James might be lowered because of all the accusations that would come his way, even if he was declared innocent. Or the thought that Lightfoot may end up being one of the Captains who found him guilty.

Taking a deep breath, he dismissed his concerns. He already had more than enough on his plate at the moment, worrying about how the court martial would impact his relationship with other navy Captains was something for the future.

At least it has begun, James thought. It had been two days since his meeting with his uncle. Since then his doubt and fear had been growing. It was one thing for his uncle and Fairfax to promise to protect him. It was another thing to have to wait in silence for two whole days while the entire nation seemed to have erupted over the court martial. It seemed a significant proportion of the population was horrified at the thought of another full-blown war with India, despite the popular support there had been for Fairfax's ultimatum to the Indians. At least that was how Fairfax's political opponents were making it out.

To be fair to Fairfax, his propaganda machine was working overtime. As soon as the Admiralty Board had voted to convene a court martial, Fairfax had begun a meticulous PR Campaign. James' entire naval career had been presented and analyzed across the media. Often with friendly naval officers there to sing his praises when specific battles or accomplishments were being discussed. From what he could discern, the public's initial assumption of guilt that had come from the announcement of the court martial was beginning to waver. Though James hadn't spoken to either his uncle or Fairfax since the announcement. They were both keeping their distance.

Suzanna had also played her role magnificently. After speaking to his uncle, he had gone and told Suzanna everything. She had been livid. After everything she and James had done for the British government, she couldn't believe what they were about to put her husband through. As his uncle had said, James had warned her about showing her anger in public, it would make them look defensive and entitled, rather than the injured party. He needn't have bothered. Suzanna had been interviewed on three different news broadcasters and each time her performance had been admirable. In many ways, she had simply repeated the lines Fairfax's propaganda machine was churning out, except, as a citizen of Haven, she could speak firsthand about everything he had done for her homeworld.

"Here comes the Judge," Cynthia Courland, James' legal counsel, said as she got to her feet.

Mimicking her actions, James jumped to his feet along with everyone else in the court.

"The revered Admiral of the White, Nathan Blackwood," one of the court officials called as Blackwood entered the court through one of the back doors. In silence, he ascended the steps to the bench.

"You may be seated," he said as he took his seat. "As you heard, my name is Admiral Blackwood, I have been appointed to be the Judge of this court and will be trying this case. Stand Captain Somerville."

James jumped to his feet to hear his charges.

"You have been accused of disobeying a direct order, endangering the lives of your crew, dereliction of duty leading to the loss of life and treason. You are here to be judged by a jury of your pears on these crimes against the military code of the Royal Space Navy. How do you plead?"

"Not guilty," James said as confidently as he could.

Blackwood paused from reading his script and looked at James.

"Not guilty?" he said, a gleam of delight in his eyes.

James thought desperately, trying to figure out what was going on.

"Your Honor," his counsel whispered from beside him.

"Not guilty, Your Honor," James hastily said.

"You are fined 10,000 credits dishonoring a seated Judge," Blackwood said, clearly satisfied. "This is your first and final warning. If you fail to follow the regulations of this court, I will be adding contempt of court to your offences. Is that clear?"

"Yes, Your Honor," James replied

"Sit down then," Blackwood snapped.

What was that all about?" James whispered to Cynthia.

"I don't think Blackwood is going to be the most impartial judge," she responded.

"What?" James said, struggling to keep his voice down.

"Don't worry, I have this in the bag," Cynthia replied with a grin.

"Your Honor," she said, rising to her feet. "Before this court martial begins the defense would like to submit a motion to have these proceedings closed to the public. As you can see, the public viewing galleries are already filling up. The charges against my client are of a serious nature and we would like them kept out of the public eye until a judgement has been made by the jury."

"I will consider the motion," Blackwood said. "Does the prosecution have any counter arguments?"

"We do, Your Honor," one of the opposing counselors said as he stood. "We have prepared a brief for you to look over," he added as he approached the Judge's bench and handed over a document.

"Summarize it for me," Blackwood requested.

"In short, Your Honor," the counsel began, "this trial speaks to a turning point in our nation's history. It is our belief, and we are prepared to argue for it, that Captain Somerville intentionally acted in a way so as to instigate a war between the British Star Kingdom and the Indian Star Republic. His actions do not just impact the Royal Space Navy, but the entire nation. All of our people deserve to know just what he did on his latest mission. They deserve the right to make up their own minds. An open trial therefore serves the best interest of the British people; of whom we are all here to serve."

"Do you wish to respond?" Blackwood said turning to face James' counsel.

"Only with this," Cynthia said. "While we vigorously deny any attempt to instigate a war on the part of the defendant, we agree that a fully open trial is in the best interest of the British people and we will acquiesce to the request of the prosecution."

James had to resist the urge to spin around and stare at his counsel accusingly. *What are you thinking*? James wanted to shout. He didn't understand what Cynthia and Fairfax were up to. James' one consolation was that Blackwood seemed just as taken aback.

In order for the jury to come to a proper understanding of what happened on his mission they would have to be fully briefed on all his reports. This would usually take place behind closed doors, for there were many highly classified details in his reports. To open everything to the public would give all the reporters in the public viewing gallery access to everything. Undoubtedly there were spies from the

Indians as well as other space faring nations among the reporters. They would be just jumping with anticipation at the chance to hear *Endeavour's* full mission reports.

No doubt Blackwood was thinking the same thing, for he hesitated in making a decision. James turned to follow Blackwood's stare for he appeared to be looking up at the public gallery. He turned just in time to sport Shadow Defense Secretary Reynolds give a slight nod.

"Very well," Blackwood said, pulling James' attention back to the front of the courtroom. "Motion to close these proceedings is denied, this court martial will be fully open to the public. We will hold a thirty-minute recess to allow any court reporters to leave and fetch their datapads," he finished, bringing his gavel down with a bang.

Great, James thought. Normally all electronic devices were banned in courtrooms to prevent anyone from recording the proceedings. That meant reporters typically had to use their memories to write up what happened for their broadcasts. While many of them would no doubt still observe the ban on actually making any recordings, there would be one or two unscrupulous characters who would record the whole day's events and upload them to the data net as soon as they were out of court.

Come with me," Cynthia said after Blackwood exited the court, "we have a waiting room assigned to us."

As soon as they got into the waiting room James couldn't help himself. "What is going on?" he demanded. "Why give the public full access? We will be giving away state secrets."

"Being a civilian litigator, I'm not up to speed on the rules about classified military information," Cynthia replied after she took a seat. "But as far as I understand it, your uncle has already spoken to the officer who will be giving the mission overview. He knows what he can't reveal in an open court.

"What's more, the reports have been redacted to remove anything that contains any technical secrets. For the rest, I think your uncle assumes the Indians already know it. We won't be giving too much away. And Prime Minister Fairfax thought an open court will serve our purposes a lot better."

And just what are our purposes?" James asked. "I assume you have been filled in, even if I haven't?"

"Not entirely," Cynthia said. "As I'm sure you know; Fairfax likes to keep things close to his chest. But I can tell you this much. Fairfax wants a public spectacle. His opponents think that such a spectacle will rally public support against any further intervention in Haven. There are elements of the opposition, led by Shadow Defense Sectary Reynolds, who do not want to see any open hostilities with the Indians. They are using this trial to generate the public support they need to table a bill that will accept Indian control of Haven. Fairfax disagrees, he intends to use this trial to crush the opposition and pave the way for full military intervention. I'm afraid you are caught in the middle."

"So that is why you reversed your position on having an open court?" James asked.

"Yes," Cynthia said. "If I had of argued for it, the prosecution would have suspected something and tried to stop me. This way, I had them present the arguments I wanted to make."

"Then what is going on with Admiral Blackwood? I saw him looking at Reynolds."

"We believe he is in the pocket of the opposition. He was the one who brought the charges against you at the Admiralty Board."

"And he can be the Judge in my case?" James asked, taken aback.

"Yes, I'm afraid so," Cynthia said. "But that may work out to our advantage. If he is openly hostile to you, everyone will see that. It will help us portray you as the one who is being innocently accused for political reasons."

"So he is working to see that I am found guilty?" James followed up, not at all happy with how things were shaping up. "Does he oppose war with the Indians?"

"I'm not sure about his position on intervention," Cynthia said. "But I have been told that the opposition are calling in a few favors to exert their influence over him. And, there is supposed to be some family history between the two of you. I assumed you knew that already."

"No," James said. "There is nothing that I know of. I have

met his son, Captain Blackwood, he commands a light cruiser. But I have never met Admiral Blackwood, nor am I aware of any hostile dealings my family has had with the Blackwoods outside of normal Admiralty business. I'm sure my father and Blackwood knew each other, but beyond that I never really paid much attention to what my father was up to when I was young."

"Well there must be something," Cynthia said. "Because if he does break neutrality, it will be obvious to everyone, and the rest of the fleet will know it. If he is willing to do this, he must have his reasons."

"I suppose," James said. "So what are you going to do?"

"We are going to goad him," Cynthia said. "But we have to be subtle. You can follow my lead."

"What do you mean?" James asked.

Before Cynthia could explain, the door to their waiting room opened and a military police officer stepped in, "The court is ready to reconvene," he said.

"We're right behind you," Cynthia said as she stood to follow the officer out.

*

"This court martial is back in session," Admiral Blackwood said as he banged his gavel and everyone in the courtroom sat down. "We will now turn to opening statements. The prosecution may begin."

"Thank you, Your Honor," the leading prosecution attorney said as he stood.

"Men and women of the jury. My name is Jack Rodgers, each of you have already heard the charges read out against Captain James Somerville. It is the intention of the prosecution to show that Captain Somerville directly disobeyed his orders. He was sent to Haven to observe what, if anything, the Indian military forces were up to. Instead, he bypassed Haven and went to the Havenite colony of Independence.

"Once there, he intentionally attacked and destroyed two Indian warships, one of which was a light cruiser, which resulted in the death of over nine hundred Indian naval personnel. After this, he went back to Haven to carry out his orders. Yet after landing a scouting party and surveying the defenses of the Indian fleet, he once again engaged the Indian warships in the system and went out of his way to attack an Indian convoy. In the ensuing battle, he destroyed two Indian troop ships, killing over ten thousand soldiers. He also lost twenty-four of his own crew. The prosecution will show that these actions directly disobeyed the orders Captain Somerville was given to observe the Indians, and further, that Captain Somerville willingly and intentionally disobeyed his orders so as to create a diplomatic incident that would lead to war with the Indian Star Republic. In due course, you will be shown compelling evidence that I believe will cause you to return a guilty verdict on all the charges that have been brought against Captain Somerville."

When the prosecution attorney returned to his seat, Cynthia gave James a nudge in the ribs, "I guess I'm up," she said. "Wish me luck."

James could only shake his head. *At least someone is enjoying themselves,* he thought wearily.

"Officers of the jury," Cynthia began. "My name is Cynthia Manning, I am not a military lawyer, and so I ask you to offer me some leniency if I get any military terms or ideas wrong during the course of this trial. However, I have been practicing law for over thirty years, and I know a guilty man when I see one. Captain Somerville is no such man. Whilst I may not be an expert in military matters, each of you are, and I believe that the evidence that we will present during this trial will show that James acted in a manner consistent with his orders, a manner fitting of a distinguished naval officer, a manner that reflected the heroism and patriotism that he has shown throughout all of his previous commands. And," Cynthia said, pausing for effect, "that these charges are simply the political maneuverings of Shadow Defense Sectary, Reynolds, who is trying to ruin this fine naval Captain's career in order to further his political ambitions." As she called out Reynolds she turned towards the public viewing gallery and pointed up at where he sat.

At once a wave of murmuring broke out among the public gallery, even one or two of the naval officers sat behind James who had come to observe the court martial broke into conversations with their neighbors.

"Silence," Blackwood said. "If those of you who are here to observe this court martial cannot remain quiet I will have you removed."

It took a couple of seconds, but the look on Blackwood's face said he was serious and everyone settled down.

"Your words are highly unusual Counselor," Blackwood said. "I must request that you take back your allegations against the Shadow Defense Secretary. This court martial has been convened to ascertain the truth concerning the allegations made against Captain Somerville, it does not concern the Shadow Defense Secretary."

"The truth sometimes takes us in unusual places, Your Honor," Cynthia said, her tone turning Blackwood's title into something of disgust rather than a sign of respect, allowing those who had ears to hear to discern just how far Reynold's influence reached. "I therefore cannot take back my words."

"Have it your way," Blackwood said. "You are hereby fined twenty thousand credits, and I order that your comments be stricken from the official record."

As Cynthia sat down beside James she couldn't help but give him a wink, "That's how it's done," she said.

"Didn't anyone ever tell you not to poke sleeping bears?" James whispered.

"Yes," Cynthia said, "but that only applies to bears you

don't want to attack, we want Blackwood to show his true colors."

"We will now hear the mission brief, as per regulations," Blackwood said. "I call Captain Thompson to the stand."

From behind James an officer stood and made his way to the front witness box to the left of Blackwood's bench. As he walked past the large holo projector in the middle of the room he inserted a datachip. The projector sprung to life, displaying the Independence Colony.

"You may begin," Blackwood said to Thompson once he was settled in the witness box.

"After covertly making his way to Haven territory as per his orders," Thompson began gesturing to the holo projector.

James couldn't help switching off. It was customary for court martials to begin with an independent officer walking the jury through the mission logs from the ship or ships in question. Thompson had spent the last two days memorizing all of *Endeavor's* logs from the period in question and so he was able to walk the jury through every decision James made and every action *Endeavour* took.

James had already talked through his actions with a number of Admirals over the last few days and he had replayed them over and over in his head examining his own motives. He didn't need to hear things again and so he drowned Thompson out and began to day dream.

He was pulled out of a very pleasant fantasy he had been having when he heard his name called out. Quickly he replayed the last few sentences that had been said in his mind to figure out what was happening. Blackwood had thanked Thompson for his detailed overview of events and then he had turned the trial over to the prosecution. They had called their first witness.

I guess that's me, he said to himself as he jumped to his feet and made his way to the witness box.

Chapter 25 – Silent Witness

Even today, after all the skirmishes we have had with the Antari, there are many who campaign to cut our military spending and recall the fleets. They so easily forget that our history has shown that those who let down their guard quickly disappear into the history books.

-Excerpt from Empire Rising, 3002 AD

4th June 2467 AD, Admiralty House, London.

As James sat down in the witness box he stole a glance at the jury. As one the Captains averted their gaze, everyone except Captain Lightfoot. He gave James a small, almost imperceptible nod, then he too looked away. James took it as a positive sign. Lightfoot would be one to make up his own mind and if he was willing to meet James' eye, it meant that the official report they had listened to justified James' actions. *At least to Lightfoot.* His confidence disappeared when another thought hit him. *If the opposition has Admiral Blackwood in their pocket, might they not have some of the jurors as well?*

The voice of the prosecution attorney prevented James dwelling on his latest concern. "Now Captain Somerville," Rodgers said as he approached the witness box. "It seems you have a lot of explaining to do. Let's begin with the obvious, why did you attack the Indian cruiser?"

James cleared his throat and spoke his well-rehearsed line, "I have been advised by my counsel that my record and my actions will speak for themselves."

"Really?" the prosecution attorney said. "That is surprising. So, you are not going to answer any of my questions?"

"I have been advised by my counsel that my record and my actions will speak for themselves," James said again.

"So you have already said," Rodgers said. "But maybe that record needs a little explaining. Let's begin with your actions in the Haven system. Did you intentionally allow *Endeavour* to be detected as you approached Haven to drop off Major Johnston?"

"My record and actions speak for themselves," James said, his anger growing.

"I think you did, in fact, I think it was your plan all along. What's more, I think you attacked the cruiser in Independence so that word would get back to Haven that you were operating in the area. What do you think of that?" Rodgers asked.

"My record and actions speak for themselves," James struggled to say.

"Maybe that is why you let the Indian frigate escape from Independence, so that it could return to Haven and warn the Indian fleet there. That way when you came back to the system, you would be able to engage any ships that tried to stop you completing your mission.

"What, no response?" the prosecution attorney asked.

When James glanced at Cynthia she gave him a nod. Forcing himself, James said the words everyone was expecting, "My record and my actions speak for themselves."

"So they do Captain. Let's consider them for a moment," Rodgers continued. "Let's go back to your first mission with *Endeavour*. You were sent to the Chester system to map out the unexplored space in that sector. How did you come to attack an Indian mining station, more than thirty light years away from your assigned station?"

Now James got really angry, the prosecution had been made fully aware of the details of his previous mission. He had been sent into Indian space to hunt down Chang. Yet it wasn't public knowledge. The hearing he had attended at the UN Interplanetary Committee more than six months ago had made it clear that he had been searching for Chang, but unless anyone was to go back and look up the transcript of the hearing, they wouldn't know what he was really doing in Indian space, and the prosecution attorney knew that.

"Cat got your tongue Captain? Then I will continue," Rodgers said. "I believe you went there intentionally seeking out a confrontation with the Indians. It has been your desire all along to try to start a war with them. Your latest actions are only the tip of the iceberg. Weren't you the one who started the war with the Chinese in the Void?"

Now James' anger really began to boil, that was a blatant lie. Still, knowing that this was what his uncle wanted, he tried to reply as calmly as he could. "My record and actions speak for themselves."

"And after you fought with the Vestarian fleet that had come to Haven, didn't you take your ship to Vestar? There you openly fought and overthrew the ruling government of the planet. All without supervision or orders from the Admiralty. And then, as if that wasn't enough. You went to Kulthar and fought two more battles with alien ships that were not your enemy. Admit it Captain, you are a bloodthirsty killer. You go out of your way to seek out wars and battles because you enjoy killing and crave the attention it gets you. You put your own ambitions and desires above those of your country and your fellow naval officers. Go on, deny it if it is not true," Rodgers said, a smile on his face as he knew what James was going to say.

"My record and actions speak for themselves," James said, head bowed in shame and anger, giving the prosecution exactly what they wanted.

"You see," the prosecution attorney said, turning to face the jury, "Captain Somerville's actions do speak for themselves. They speak of a bloodthirsty traitor who will ignore his orders whenever he pleases to satisfy his bloodlust."

"Objection," Cynthia shouted out playing her role. "The prosecution is testifying."

"Abstained," Blackwood said slowly. "The jury will ignore those last remarks."

Despite being reprimanded, when he turned back to James, Rodgers had a confident smile on his face. He knew the jury would remember what he said and so he obviously thought he had won this round. Stealing a glance at the jury, James wasn't sure why. More than one of the Captains looked visibly angry at the attorney's behavior and accusations, Lightfoot looked furious. *Maybe Fairfax and Cynthia are on to something after all,* James said to his anger, allowing it to lessen.

"But his record is secondary to this court martial, it is his actions in and around Haven that we wish to focus on," Rodgers continued. "Captain, let's turn to the attack you made on the Indian convoy. Your direct orders were to scout out the Indian fleet positions and to deliver a marine recon team to the planet's surface. At the time, you detected the convoy, had you completed your mission?"

This was the most difficult part for James, the rest of the charges he could easily dismiss as the opposition seeking to discredit him and his uncle. But his attack on the convoy had been rash. It had put the fleet in danger. Yet, for the sake of that same fleet he couldn't speak up now, either to confess or to defend himself.

"My record and actions speak for themselves," James simply said.

"That does not answer the question Captain," Rodgers

responded. "It is a simple yes or no, had you already completed your mission?"

"My record and actions speak for themselves," James repeated, sure his words were condemning him.

"Your Honor," the attorney said, tuning to face the bench. "I request that you compel Captain Somerville to answer my line of questioning. This is the turning point of the court martial. If Somerville had completed his order and if he knew that, then the attack on the Indian convoy was in direct disobedience to his orders and was an act of treason against the crown."

"The prosecution is right," Admiral Blackwood said, "Captain Somerville, I command you to answer these questions."

James wasn't sure what to do, he couldn't just ignore a fleet Admiral's command could he? That would itself be disobeying a direct order. He looked to Cynthia for advice. She had already picked up the piece of paper he had left on the table. She held it in her hand and nodded to him.

Stealing himself for Blackwood's response, he once again said what the paper said, "My record and actions speak for themselves."

This time Blackwood seemed unable to control his anger. "You insubordinate bastard," he shouted. "You cannot hide behind your record; your record shows that you have been a glory hunter all of your career. Now answer the damn question or I will have you thrown out of this court."

"As I have said," James replied slowly, "my record and my actions speak for themselves, I do not think I requested the independent Judge of this court martial to interpret them for me," James couldn't help adding.

For a second a fierce look of anger flooded Blackwood's face. James thought he was about to fulfil his earlier promise and add a charge of insubordination to his crimes. All of a sudden though, the Admiral seemed to regain control and calmed down.

Maybe he realizes he overstepped his authority, James thought, he certainly hoped everyone else would come to that conclusion.

"Are you finished with your line of questioning?" Blackwood asked the prosecution attorney.

"If this is all Captain Somerville is going to say, then yes, Your Honor," Rodgers answered.

"And I assume you have no questions for Captain Somerville?" Blackwood asked, turning to Cynthia. "Seeing as he is not going to answer them anyway."

"That is correct your honor, we believe his record and actions will speak for themselves," Cynthia said with a smile as she emphasized 'themselves.'

For another second, Blackwood's anger appeared to swell

before it dissipated. "Very well then, this court is adjourned for today, we will reconvene at 10am tomorrow."

As they walked out of the court James couldn't help asking, "Is this how the plan is meant to be going?"

Pulling him into a quiet alcove Cynthia peered up into James' face with a look of compassion. "I know it is hard to just sit there Captain, especially when so many lies are flying about. You have to trust me. Think it through for yourself. The Captains on the jury are experienced Captains, they will be able to see through the prosecution's lies. It is the public's opinion you need to worry about. Fairfax has his own reporters in the public gallery. Within an hour, full visuals of the entire proceedings will be on the data net. The public will be wondering just what it is about your past that makes you so confident that you can rely on your record to defend you. And let me assure you, Fairfax plans to show them. You should go home Captain, relax, you have done your part. The rest is up to me. Tomorrow may be difficult for you. But by the end of the day, you will be vindicated. And if my plan comes to fruition, we may well have a little fun along the way."

"I don't think I will be able to relax, but I will take your advice, I don't want to stay in the capital another second. The place is swarming with reporters."

"I will see you tomorrow then Captain," Cynthia said. "I have a lot of work to do, so you will have to excuse me."

"Until tomorrow then," James said, Cynthia simply nodded

and turned and strode off down the corridor. James was left wondering just how close she was to Fairfax, she seemed to know a great deal about what he was up to.

Still, that's out of my hands for now, James thought, *at least I can go and see Suzanna.*

*

Three hours later James was sitting, stroking his wife's hair in one of Badminton House's sitting rooms. A large fire was crackling in the fireplace. James didn't remember the last time a fire had been lit in the summer, but Suzanna had insisted. The trees back on Haven gave off poisonous fumes when they were burnt and so she had never experienced a log fire before. Now she was basking in the heat as she snuggled up to her husband. They had already discussed the day's proceedings. Suzanna was fully up to speed on the details, she had watched the highlights from the court martial before he had arrived home. She had been more concerned about how James was handling it.

"Let's see what the news reports are making of everything," Suzanna said, reaching over to power up the room's holo projector.

"Do we have to?" James asked, already tired of thinking about it.

"Yes," Suzanna said. "If Fairfax really does have a plan, we need to know if it is working."

"If you insist," James said reluctantly.

With James' approval, Suzanna switched the holo projector on to show the broadcast from one of the British Broadcasting Cooperation's main news channels.

"Look, it's Admiral Cunningham," Suzanna said.

"What is he doing on there?" James wondered. "He's the commander of the Home Fleet, not a political commentator.

"I don't know," Suzanna said, "but this should be interesting, let's listen,"

"Welcome to the show," the presenter said to Cunningham.

"Thank you for the invitation," Cunningham said.

"Now for those of you who don't know, do you mind telling us a bit about yourself?" the presenter asked.

"Certainly," Cunningham responded. "I am Admiral Keith Cunningham, Commander of the British Home Fleet."

"And you were posted to the Home Fleet after your victory over the Chinese fleet in the Void War weren't you Admiral?"

"Yes," Cunningham said.

"Captain Somerville served under you during the war?" the presenter followed up.

"He served under the late Rear Admiral Jensen first, and then both officers came under my command when my fleet was sent into the Void," Cunningham explained.

"What can you tell us about this young Captain. Did his actions while under your command lead you to believe that he is a bloodthirsty warmonger as the court martial material released today would suggest?" the presenter asked eagerly.

"I can't speak for his most recent actions, they are currently the focus of this court martial after all," Cunningham began. "But I can say this. While under my command Captain Somerville showed himself to be a fine officer. He fought bravely and with skill, so much so that he was promoted from commanding an exploration frigate to a destroyer in the middle of the Void War.

"His actions since then have only confirmed to me that he is one of the navy's rising stars. His intervention in Haven saved the colony from certain destruction. To prevent another attack, he took his single ship into the depths of unknown space. He confronted the leader of a ruthless government set on genocide. Removed the leader, bringing freedom to his subjects, and then, to top it all off, he went on to defeat the fleet that the leader had sent to wipe out another civilization.

"In one mission Captain Somerville won the safety of two worlds, the freedom of another, and earned the respect and thanks of two alien races. He may be young and brash, but he has always acted in the best interests of his crew and his nation. I believe this whole court martial is just a political farce. As James said himself, his record speaks for itself. You only have to listen to the praise he has received from the leaders of the Vestarians and Kulreans to see for yourselves. I for one cannot fathom why this court martial has been convened. Certainly, it is not because of any military concerns with James' actions."

"So you think there are other motivations at play, political ones?" the presenter asked.

"Yes, there must be. I can see no other reason to ruin a fine young officer's career and put our relationship with the Kulreans and Vestarians in jeopardy," Cunningham answered.

"You think our relationship with the aliens will be threatened by this court martial?" the presenter followed up.

"Yes," Cunningham said. "If you look at what both leaders of those civilizations have said about Captain Somerville, it is clear they hold him in very high regard. If we punish the very person who helped them, they will see it as a policy statement. It will look like our government and our people regret what James did for them. They will surely take that as some form of insult."

"I see," the presenter said. "Well, it just so happens, we have excerpts of the words the alien leaders have spoken about Captain Somerville available for us to play. We were saving them for a later news segment, but I think it would be appropriate to show them to our viewers now if that is ok

Admiral?"

"By all means," Cunningham said.

"I can't believe they have Cunningham on a news broadcast," James said. "He must be hating every minute of this. The last time I saw him he wasn't too impressed with me. In fact, it was just after I had ignored a direct order from both him and Rear Admiral Jensen. I'm glad the prosecution in my trial doesn't know about that."

"That is probably a good thing," Suzanna agreed. "But you know Cunningham approved of your actions after the battle, it stopped that Chinese Admiral from getting home and continuing the war."

"I know," James said, once again amazed by how quickly Suzanna was picking up all the intricacies of government and naval politics, "but I still don't get what he is doing being interviewed."

"Don't you understand?" Suzanna asked, the tone of her voice rising. "Even Admirals have to make sacrifices for the greater good. I bet Fairfax put him up to this, it has to be part of the Prime Minister's plan."

"A plan I would love to be filled in on," James said.

"James," Suzanna said sternly, "has no one ever taught you to read between the lines? Fairfax wants to portray you as the young innocent Captain whose naval career is being railroaded by the political elites to further their selfish causes."

"But why am I so important?" James protested.

"What is this?" Suzanna said instead of answering while she motioned for James to be quiet and let her listen.

"There is one more thing we wish to show you," the presenter was saying. "This is a press release from the Swedish military, if you all remember, we mentioned earlier in our show that Captain Somerville received the Swedish Medal of the Sword in thanks for a battle he fought against a Chinese destroyer that was attacking a defenseless Swedish colony ship."

"Oh great," James said as the presenter read the press release. "Do you know I wanted to run away when those Chinese destroyers appeared? I very nearly did. Half of the things they are saying about me aren't true."

"Nonsense," Suzanna said after the press release was read. "But even if you are right, if only half of them are true, then you are still a remarkable man. And you are shaping up to be a pretty good husband," she added with a smirk.

"One that gets far more political and news attention than he would like. You are supposed to be the politician," James complained.

"And I am, that is why I understand what is going on," Suzanna said. "Every good politician needs someone who can rally support for his cause. Fairfax can't be the one to lead the people to war. In their eyes, he is a paper pusher. But you, you are a hero, and by the time Fairfax is done everyone on Earth is going to know it. He is using you to rally the support he needs. Who better than the innocent Captain who is wrongfully accused of treason by those who wish to leave a colony in the grip of hostile invaders? You are just going to have to put up with it, for the good of your nation and my people."

"Hmmph," James sighed. "You are sounding too much like my uncle,"

"He must be a wise man then," Suzanna said with a chuckle. "You know, come to think of it, I think I already knew that. He did force us together after all," she added as she reached up to pull James' lips to hers.

"Let's forget about the trial for tonight," Suzanna said after their lips parted. "Take me for a walk around the estate, then we can make the most of your time here. You will be back on board *Endeavour* and heading towards Haven before you know it."

Whatever happens, at least I can face it with Suzanna supporting me, James thought, knowing that her suggestions were just what he needed. "Your wish is my command my Duchess," he said as he stood and pulled Suzanna to her feet.

"Lead on then good Sir," Suzanna said as she hooked her arm around his elbow.

Chapter 26 – Betrayal

Growing up we are all taught to give the Emperor our utmost loyalty. After joining the Navy, I was taught to be loyal to my crewmates and my fellow officers. Even so, I always knew that every person's loyalty had a breaking point, it just depended on how many credits it would take.

-Excerpt from Empire Rising, 3002 AD

4th June 2467 AD, Admiralty House, London.

When James pushed through the large wooden double doors into the court martial chamber, he was relieved to see the proceedings hadn't started. He had been late leaving Badminton house.

"I'm glad you decided to join us," Cynthia said when he sat down beside her.

"I don't think I can afford another one of Blackwood's fines," James said with a chuckle.

"Someone is in a better mood," Cynthia replied with a raised eyebrow.

"After all the press about me last night, how could I not be bouncing off the walls?" James said sarcastically. "But yes,

Suzanna has given me a bit more perspective. I'm just eager to see this thing through to the end now."

"Good," Cynthia said. "The prosecution will be calling a number of witnesses from *Endeavour,* so I imagine things will get worse before they get better, but just hang in there. This should be over by the end of the day. All you have to do is sit there and look innocent."

"I'm not sure how to do that," James replied, "but I'm happy to leave everything else up to you."

"Then let's begin," Cynthia said as she stood to acknowledge Blackwood's entrance into the courtroom.

"You may be seated," Blackwood said as he took his own seat behind the bench. "I believe the prosecution has more witnesses to call."

James couldn't help noticing the bags under Blackwood's eyes. *They weren't there yesterday,* he thought, *maybe he watched the news broadcasts too.* James smiled at the idea.

"Yes, Your Honor," the main prosecution attorney said.

Where Blackwood looked tired, Rodgers looked determined. *On the other hand,* James thought to himself, *if they both watched the news, then they will be doubly determined to make me look bad today.*

"We would like to begin by calling Ensign Jackson," Rodgers said.

For the next two hours the prosecution called minor witness after minor witness. In each case, the prosecution attorney sought to turn the witnesses against James. He asked questions about the crew members view of their Captain, about friends and colleagues who they had lost under James' command. About the fear they had endured while on the mission to Haven and about any doubts they had concerning James' abilities as a Captain and his fitness to lead. Rarely did he actually turn to the events that directly spoke to the charges James was facing. It was clear to everyone in the court what the attorney was doing. He was playing things up for the public at home. Making it look like James was not the hero Captain Fairfax was trying to portray to the public. From the glances James stole at the jurors, it was clear that more than one of them was getting irritated at Rodger's tactics.

To a man, as each of the witness walked out of the witness stand and past James they mouthed an apology. James graciously accepted them. It was natural for crew members to complain about their Captain and have doubts from time to time. No one expected to be brought up in front of a court martial and forced to reveal their inner thoughts. He already knew from their time in Haven that when push came to shove, each of them would back him and willingly follow him into battle.

Cynthia was quick to pick up on that and she asked a few penetrating questions to show that each witness' opinion didn't matter a great deal, for their junior position on *Endeavour* meant they had little knowledge of the key events in question. She ended each cross examination with a simple question.

"Now Sub Lieutenant West," Cynthia said to the latest witness, "if you were to have your time on *Endeavour* over again. Would you willingly follow Captain Somerville into battle?"

"Yes," West answered with relief. As with the other witnesses, his sense of letting his Captain down had been growing as the prosecution attorney had been asking question after question. "Yes, I most definitely would," he added, jumping at the chance to articulate his support for his Captain.

"Thank you Sub Lieutenant, that was my last question," Cynthia said.

James couldn't help smiling at the look on Blackwood's face. So far all five of his crew members who had been questioned had responded the same way.

"The prosecution calls Petty Officer Dick Warren," Cynthia's opposite number said after West left the witness stand.

Murmurs ran through the public gallery as Petty Officer Warren hobbled his way to the stand. James' heart went out to the Petty Officer. He had been one of the few survivors from the missile strike on *Endeavour's* nose section. He had lost a leg and an arm and his face was covered in hideous burn scars. *Endeavour's* doctor had done her best to stabilize Warren, but the ship's medical facilities were limited. She couldn't grow the skin or limbs Warren needed. His limbs, and skin for the skin grafts, were being grown in the naval hospital in London, for now though, he was obviously still waiting on them. In an age where people weren't used to the sight of sickness and death, Warren was a shocking display of what warfare was really like.

"In your own words Petty Officer Warren," Rodgers said after Warren was sworn in. "Can you tell us what happened to you when you received these injuries?"

"Yes," Warren answered. "My battlestation was in *Endeavour's* forward port nose section. I was in charge of overseeing the battery of point defense plasma cannons in that section. It was my job to carryout repairs and override any technical malfunctions that might occur in battle. From my display, I was able to watch the Indian missiles that the point defenses were tracking."

"And how many missiles did you see homing in on *Endeavour*?" the prosecution attorney asked.

"I'm not sure," Warren said. "There were too many for me to count."

"The sensor readings from the bridge says there were exactly twenty-six in the final missile salvo the Indian escorts fired at *Endeavour*," Rodgers supplied.

"That sounds about right," Warren said.

"And how many missiles is *Endeavour's* point defenses rated to be able to defend against?" Rodgers asked.

"From between ten and fourteen," Warren said. "Of course the exact number depends on the technological capabilities of the missiles' ECM and seeker heads, as well as the circumstances of the battle. Things like closing speed make a big difference to the effectiveness of point defense fire."

"That may be," Rodgers said, "but isn't it true that Captain Somerville knew how many Indian ships were escorting the convoy he attacked?"

"I'm sure he did," Warren said. "The Indian ships weren't hiding."

"Didn't he know that it was possible upwards of twenty or even thirty missiles could be fired at his ship?"

"Yes, I'm sure Captain Somerville was able to do the math," Warren answered.

"Captain Somerville knew that Endeavour would be facing far more missiles than she was rated to be able to handle. Wouldn't that make Captain Somerville responsible for the twenty-four lives that were lost in that battle? Wouldn't it make him responsible for the injuries that we see you have today?" Rodgers asked.

"Yes it would," Warren said. "But it would also make him responsible for destroying two Indian troop ships and preventing them from landing on Haven."

"Exactly," Rodgers said, "Something that was an act of war and an act of treason. You are right Petty Officer; Captain Somerville is responsible for that."

Warren looked like he wanted to protest but before he could say anything the prosecution attorney beat him to it. "No further questions, Your Honor," he said.

"Your witness," Blackwood said to Cynthia.

"Should I ask him if he would still follow you if he had it to do again?" she asked, leaning over to whisper to James.

James took a moment to think. He had spoken to Warren a number of times after his injuries on the way back from Haven, he thought they had got on well. Yet he wasn't sure how the officer would respond.

"Yes," James said, deciding that he wanted to know the truth, whether it would hurt him or not.

"I would like to begin by thanking you for your service Petty Officer," Cynthia said as she stood and approached the witness box.

"Thank you Ma'am," Warren said.

"I don't want to make this any more difficult that it has already been," Cynthia continued. "I have just two questions for you. Your record says you have served on *Endeavour* since she was launched. That means you served under Captain Somerville during *Endeavour's* first cruise. Let me ask you this Petty Officer, do you remember how many missiles the former Vestarian Overlord's fleet fired at *Endeavour* in its attack on Haven or in its attack on the Kulrean home system?"

"I don't remember the exact figures off hand," Warren answered.

"Can you give me a rough estimate?" Cynthia asked.

"There were more than a hundred, maybe as many as one fifty," Warren answered.

"So twenty-six wasn't a surprisingly large number in reality," Cynthia said, "You might say it is within the risks a navy ship must face in times of war."

James knew that that wasn't strictly true, facing twenty-six missiles had been a big risk. The Captains on the jury would know that full well, but he guessed Cynthia was betting that the public wouldn't.

"It wasn't large compared to some of the scrapes our Captain got us out of before, no Ma'am," Warren answered. "I'm sure he knew the risks involved."

"Then let me ask you my second question," Cynthia said. "Despite everything that has happened to you, if you had your time under Captain Somerville again to do over, would you request a transfer away from his command?"

"No Ma'am," Warren answered passionately. "I knew the

risks when I signed up to the navy. I also knew what the navy stands for. I wanted to be in a position to help the defenseless. That is what we were doing in the Haven system. I am proud of my injuries."

"Thank you Petty Officer," Cynthia said. "I hope you make a speedy recovery."

"Thank you Ma'am," Warren said as he stood to vacate the witness stand.

When the prosecution attorney got back to his feet he shot Cynthia a dirty look, she smiled sweetly in return. "He hasn't vetted his witnesses as well as he thought," Cynthia whispered to James. "Your uncle's insistence that this be an expedited court martial has thrown them off."

"Your Honor, the prosecution now calls Naval Engineer Cadet Julie Hanson," Rodgers said.

"This one is likely to be trouble," Cynthia whispered to James.

"Why?" he asked, he didn't know Hanson personally and he had no idea why she would be a concern.

"Because I have done my homework," Cynthia said cryptically.

"Julie," Rodgers asked as soon as Julie was sworn in. "Can you tell us all where you were stationed during the raid on the Indian convoy?"

"My post was the forward port damage control station," Julie responded.

"Not the nose section itself?" Rodgers followed up.

"No," Julie answered, as she reached a hand up to wipe her eyes. "The damage control team stationed there were killed."

"Ok, Julie," Rodgers said, "I'm sorry you have to re-live all this, but can you tell us in your own words what you saw when you went to the forward sections after the missile strike?"

"Yes," Julie said. "It was horrible. I was the first one on the scene, there was no one else left alive who was able to come and help me. Almost a third of the forward port bulkhead was gone, and the rest had been twisted into a grotesque shape. I hardly noticed though. The emergency stasis fields had kicked in within seconds of the explosion, sealing parts of the nose section off from the vacuum of space."

"What did you see?" Rodgers prompted.

"It was horrible," Julie said again, "I can hardly describe it, there were body parts everywhere. The explosion caused a burst of metal shards to blow through the damage control station. The entire damage control team was on the ground cut to ribbons. There was blood splattered all over the walls."

"I believe you captured an image of the scene?" Rodgers asked.

"Yes," Julie responded. "All damage repair crew carry visual recorders with them so that the officers can receive live updates on any damage the ship takes."

"I would like to submit these images into evidence," Rodgers said as he walked over to the large holo projector in the middle of the court and slipped a datachip into it.

A number of gasps broke out from the observation gallery when the first image appeared. The scene was exactly as Julia had described. Bodies were everywhere, many of them torn into pieces. As the still images progressed, faces came into view, dead faces filled with the frozen looks of pain that had been their owner's last experiences.

It took all of James' self-control not to jump out of his seat and rip the data chip out of the holo projector. Each one of those faces belonged to crew members who had parents, husbands, wives and children. Family members who James had written to, to tell them of their loss. Now they were going to see their loved ones' broken bodies flashed across every news broadcast in the nation.

"So," Rodgers said, turning to face the jury when the visuals came to an end, "we have already seen what damage Captain Somerville's treasonous actions caused to Petty Officer Warren, now we are beginning to see how much his actions cost other men and women who placed their trust in him.

"And he would have our entire nation go to war with the Indians," he said, as he shook his head. "This is not a Captain who should be commanding anything, never mind a warship."

Turning back to Julia, Rodgers continued, "I have just one final question for you Cadet, a question the defense is fond of. Would you follow James into battle again?"

"No," Julia said with a strong hint of disgust. "He is reckless and he throws the lives of his crew away like they are nothing. I could not serve under such an officer."

"I have no further questions for this witness," Rodgers said, returning to his seat.

This is outrageous, James thought to himself. *Every Captain on the jury has lost crew members in battle. They all know the cost of warfare; Julia's testimony won't sway them one bit. This is all for whoever Reynolds has recording this court martial!*

"Defenses' witness," Blackwood said.

"Thank you Your Honor," Cynthia said as she approached the witness box.

"Julia," she began as she handed a document to the Cadet, "Can you tell me what this is?"

"It looks like one of my latest financial reports from my accountant," Julia answered hesitantly.

"You are correct," Cynthia said. "And can you tell me what these two lines say here."

"It's an explanation from my accountant detailing what happened to one of my investment accounts," Julia said.

"And just what does it say?" Cynthia pushed.

"It is hardly relevant to this court martial," Julia said.

"It is if you came back from your mission to Haven to find yourself over twenty thousand credits in debt," Cynthia said.

"I have a visual of my own I would like to submit into evidence," she continued as she walked over to the holo projector and slipped in a datachip.

"Who is this?" Cynthia said when an image of a woman standing on what looked like a London street appeared.

"I believe it is me," Julia said.

"And who are you meeting with?" Cynthia asked as the visual began to play.

Within seconds a man appeared and approached Julia as she stood looking around. He appeared to talk to her. Then, less than thirty seconds later he turned and walked off.

"I don't know," Julia said. "That happened just yesterday. I remember it clearly. I had never met that man before. He approached me, tried to ask me out and when I rebuffed him, he went away. I admit, I was very taken aback by the whole thing. But like my finances, I'm not sure what this has to do with anything."

"And neither do I," Blackwood said, cutting in.

"I think this will illuminate things," Cynthia said. With a push of a button the visual rewound to a point where the man's face was just about visible. Then it zoomed in. At the same time another image appeared on the holo display. It was a personnel file with the official Houses of Parliament badge on the document.

"This is Alex Norwood," Cynthia said. "He is a minor aide who works for Shadow Defense Sectary Reynolds. And this," Cynthia said as she touched another button, causing the image of Norwood and Julia to pan down to waist height where a small package could be seen being passed between them, "is Norwood handing something over to Julia. Just yesterday I might add.

"So tell me this," Cynthia said, turning to Julia again. "Just what did Norwood give you for your testimony here today?"

"That is enough," Blackwood almost shouted as he came to Julia's rescue. "This witness is not on trial in this court martial. If you have any questions regarding her testimony and her actions during the events in question, you may ask them. If you want to make allegations of corruption or whatever you are insinuating, you can bring charges against Julia on your own time."

"I see," Cynthia said. "So we are to accept the trustworthiness of this witness on your say so?"

"That is not what I said," Blackwood responded, his anger threatening to bubble over. "You are walking very close to a charge of contempt of court. What I said was that unless you have any direct evidence of corruption. Keep your questions limited to the matter at hand."

"Very well," Cynthia said. "If I cannot ask Cadet Hanson about her finances and the possible ramification for her trustworthiness, then I have no further questions for her."

"Then we will recess for lunch," Blackwood said bringing down his gravel. "When we return the prosecution will call their final witnesses."

"Come with me," Cynthia said as James got to his feet, "I have food being sent to our waiting room."

James reluctantly turned to look at Cynthia. He had almost gone off after Julia, *she must have known the prosecution would use her images. She betrayed the families of the very people she was supposedly so concerned about.* And all for money!

"You have to control your emotions," Cynthia added when she saw the look on his face. "We must look like the ones who are being persecuted unfairly."

"I'm trying," James said as they walked out of the courtroom.

"So how do you think this morning went?" James asked once they got to the privacy of their waiting room.

"That depends," Cynthia said. "I don't think the prosecution scored any points with the jury. There was nothing in those testimonies that suggested any actual wrongdoing on your part. However, with the public it depends."

"On what?" James pushed.

"On whether the public just looks at the visuals that will come out of the trial," Cynthia answered. "And you can be sure Reynolds will make sure they come out. Or if they will also look at what was actually said in the trial. Warren would clearly follow you anywhere. And I think we threw enough dirt at Julia to call her testimony into question. Heck, Blackwood's intervention on her behalf should scream to anyone who is really listening that he is dead set against you. It really just depends on where the public looks."

"Do you really think she took money from Reynolds?" James asked.

"She took something," Cynthia replied. "That much is clear. If it was money, we have made sure she can't use it anytime soon. The navy will be watching her closely now. If she just happens to show a very healthy bank balance in the near future, she is going to have some questions to answer."

"How did you know she would be bribed?" James asked.

"We didn't," Cynthia answered. "But since Fairfax learnt of Reynolds' plan to convene a court martial against you, we have been watching all of your crew, just in case Reynolds tried to get to them. If was a good thing we did don't you think?"

"I guess," James conceded, though the wasn't entirely pleased to hear his whole crew was under suspicion. "What happens now?" he asked.

"Everything up until now has just been a skirmish," Cynthia explained. "Yes the prosecution is on the back foot, but now they are going to go for broke. The only ones who can really confirm the charges against you are your immediate subordinates. They are the ones who were fully aware of the situation. The prosecution needs to use them against you. No doubt they have a plan and this is the problem with an expedited court martial, we have not had time to go through all the evidence they have included in their brief. So the question is Captain, what are they going to say?"

James didn't know how to respond. He knew that if they were called as witnesses, Becket, Julius and Mallory would do whatever they could to back him up. But they would be under oath, and he remembered full well what his attitude had been when he had ordered the attack on the convoy.

Chapter 27 – Subordinates

The Imperial Navy reflects the amalgamation of the Royal Navy and the American Starfleet. As their fleets made up the bulk of the new Imperial navy, and the structure of their naval ranks were very similar, it made the most sense.

-Excerpt from Empire Rising, 3002 AD

4th June 2467 AD, Admiralty House, London.

"The prosecution calls Second Lieutenant Anne Julius of HMS *Endeavour* to the stand," Rodgers said as soon as the court martial reconvened.

As Julius walked past James she gave him an apologetic look. James nodded to her to let her know he was ok.

"Now Lieutenant," Rodgers said. "I want to focus in on the attack on the Indian convoy. That is where the heart of the charges against Captain Somerville lie. You were the first to spot the convoy, were you not?"

"Yes," Julius answered. "I was the officer of the watch when we detected the Indian convoy."

"What did you do then?"

"I woke up the Captain and called him to the bridge, when he got there, I updated him on the Indian convoy," Julius said.

"And what did Captain Somerville want to do?" Rodgers asked.

"Well, it was actually me who suggested we go after the convoy." Julius explained. "I had already worked out the trajectories and from our position at the time, we had the opportunity to alter course and intercept the convoy before they reached the inner system and the protection of the main Indian fleet."

"How did Captain Somerville respond to your idea?" the prosecution attorney followed up.

"I believe he took it under consideration," Julius said. "After I spoke with him he called for Lieutenants Becket and Mallory, at the time I believed it was because he wanted to discuss the possibilities for an attack with all of his senior officers."

"That is not what I meant," Rodgers said. "I want to know exactly what Captain Somerville said in response to your idea to attack the convoy."

"Well," Julius said with some hesitation. "I'm not entirely sure. I don't remember word for word what the Captain said."

"Luckily you don't have to," Rodgers said. "I have another

piece of evidence I would like to submit for the jury's consideration. This is a recording of a part of the conversation between Captain Somerville and Lieutenant Julius."

"Objection," Cynthia shouted before Rodgers could play the recording. "This recording is not part of the evidence brief the prosecution submitted at the start of this court martial."

"On the contrary," Rodgers said with a victorious smile. "This recording has always been a part of our evidence. It is officially labelled as the COM message from the COM officer of the watch to Lieutenants Becket and Mallory calling them to the bridge just moments after Captain Somerville arrived to hear Julius' report about the convoy.

"What you must have overlooked counsellor, is that the recording also picked up James and Julius' conversation in the background. The gain had to be significantly improved, but we can clearly hear what is being said.

"Objection overturned, play the recording," Blackwood said when Cynthia looked at him for a ruling.

"You know this isn't exactly what our orders have laid out for us," James' voice said before the recording was paused.

"Now Lieutenant," Rodgers began again. "Does that jog your memory? Can you tell us what Captain Somerville was saying this in response to?"

"I believe I had just suggested we attack the convoy," Julius said, a look of defeat on her face.

"Then let's hear how the conversation continued," Rodgers said, resuming the recording.

"I know Sir," Julius' voices said. "But you have taught us orders aren't everything. It's like the situation with the Vestarians. If we just let those troops get to Haven they will make life harder for Major Johnston and the rebels fighting the Indians."

"I can't argue with that," James said. "But we have some vital information to get home to the Admiralty."

"There you have it," Rodgers said triumphantly. "Is that not Captain Somerville saying that it was against his orders to attack the convoy?"

"I guess so," Julius mumbled.

"And what was this vital information that Captain Somerville said he had to get back to the Admiralty?" Rodgers asked. "Wasn't it the Indian fleet dispositions, the very thing he had been sent to Haven to acquire?"

"Yes," Julius said, her voice barely above a whisper.

"And after this conversation, didn't Captain Somerville go on to attack the convoy, despite everything we just heard him say?" Rodgers pressed.

Julius glanced up at James, a deep look of shame on her face.

When James gave a slight nod, she nodded her head as well.

"What's wrong, has the cat got your tongue Lieutenant?" Rodgers snapped. "I need more than a nod; we need a verbal assent for the record."

"Yes," Julius admitted.

"There it is ladies and gentlemen of the jury," Rodgers announced. "The facts are beyond dispute. Captain Somerville knowingly attacked the Indian convoy against orders and he intentionally tried to start a war for his own purposes and benefit.

"Now Lieutenant," Rodgers said, returning his gaze to Julius. "I have one last line of questioning for you. "In the recording, you said the attack on the convoy was like the situation with the Vestarians, can you explain what you mean by that?"

"I meant that we were faced with a situation our orders didn't account for," Julius tried to explain. "In Vestar we didn't have orders about first contact situations, we had to make do. Likewise, we had no orders one way or another about Indian convoys. Yet, we had been told to treat all Indian ships in the Haven system as hostile. The convoy's appearance presented us with a chance to act, to try and stop it before any more troops got to Haven. We had already seen the devastation the first wave of soldiers caused."

"I don't think so Lieutenant. I think there was more to your words. In fact, I think your words are evidence that you yourself have been corrupted by Captain Somerville's example of disobeying orders and putting his own desires above his orders.

"Let me elaborate. When *Endeavour* was first sent out to survey the space around Chester, did Captain Somerville disobey orders by taking his ship into Indian territory?"

"No, because we received subsequent orders to head into Indian space to search for former politburo member Chang, to bring him to justice," Julius said.

"Ok then," Rodgers said. "And I presume that those orders included a command to attack, disable and board an Indian mining station within Indian sovereign territory?"

Julius stole a nervous glance towards James, not sure how to answer.

"Don't look to Somerville for help Lieutenant," Rodgers said. "He is on trial for treason, you don't want to be seen collaborating with him. Now answer the question. Did Captain Somerville have orders to attack an Indian mining station?"

"No," Julius said, "but we had strong reason to believe..."

"Thank you Lieutenant," Rodgers cut in, "That answers my question. Now, what about after the attack on Haven, did Captain Somerville receive orders to take his ship towards Vestar?"

"No," Julius said.

Again, before she could elaborate Rodgers went on. "And when you got there, did Captain Somerville have any orders that would have permitted him to interfere in another civilization's affairs, and effectively start a civil war?"

"No," Julius was forced to answer.

"And when he was sent to Haven, did Captain Somerville have any direct orders to launch attacks against Indian warships?" Rodgers asked.

"The Prime Minister released an executive order stating that all Indian warships in the Haven system were to be treated as hostiles," Julius said.

"Yes," Rodgers acknowledged, "and the legality of that order may be a matter for another hearing. But the question still stands. Did Captain Somerville's orders or Prime Minister Fairfax's executive order specifically contain orders to seek out and attack Indian ships?"

"No," Julius said once again in defeat, tears ran down her face as the pressure became too much for her.

"Thank you Lieutenant, your testimony has proven very illuminating," Rodgers said. "I hand over the witness to the defense."

Cynthia got on her feet and approached Julius, pulling out a tissue from her pocket as she walked. "I have just one question for you Lieutenant," she said stepping back. "You were there, you experienced the pressure of the situation. Do you think Captain Somerville made the right decision, or do you think he disobeyed his orders and committed treason by attacking the Indians in a rage of bloodlust as the prosecution seems to think?"

"He made the right decision," Julius said, regaining her composure. "I know Captain Somerville, he loves the navy and he loves his country. He would never do anything to hurt either. I believe he has also come to see the Haven people as his own. He wasn't acting out of bloodlust, he was acting to try and help a people who have been conquered and occupied by a hostile force. That is something our nation has stood against for centuries. I believe Captain Somerville did us all proud that day, he did what any naval officer would have done."

"If you really believe that, then you are just as much of a fool as your Captain," Blackwood broke in, unable to hold his tongue. "I have over fifty years of command experience, I know what should have been done, and yet you think you can sit here and tell me Captain Somerville did what any naval Captain would do. You are just a Second Lieutenant."

Julius looked shocked at Blackwood's intervention and for a second it looked like her tears would return.

"I believe the witness is mine to question," Cynthia said, coming to her aid. "I thought your fifty years of experience were to be used to try this court martial, were they not, Your Honor?"

"I will not have junior Lieutenants parading their opinions around here like they are facts," Blackwood said.

"Then it is the responsibility of the prosecution to show they are not facts, it is not yours," Cynthia retorted. Before Blackwood could say anymore she turned back to Julius, "Thank you Lieutenant. I believe you are speaking for more than yourself with those words. You may retire from the witness box."

"The defense calls *Endeavour's* First Lieutenant to the witness stand now," Rodgers announced once Julius returned to her seat at the back of the courtroom.

Mallory who was in the seat beside her, squeezed Julius' hand to reassure she had done ok, then he stood and made his way to the witness box.

"Thank you for agreeing to testify today," Rodgers said once Mallory was sworn in.

"I am happy to speak on behalf of my Captain," Mallory answered.

"Very good," Rodgers said. "We have already established what occurred after the Indian convoy was spotted. What I want to know from you Lieutenant, is what advice did you give Captain Somerville when he outlined the possibility of attacking the convoy?"

James had been expecting the question. The prosecution

seemed to have an inside track on the discussions that went on that day. As soon as the recording of him and Julius had been played, he knew her testimony would hurt him. Mallory's however, had always been the one that he had feared would cause him the biggest problems. Julius's plan had been to attack the convoy from the start, Mallory on the other hand, had seen the potential problem right away.

Mallory too had been anticipating this question, yet he hadn't been able to come up with an answer that would protect his Captain. "I warned Captain Somerville about the dangers of attacking the convoy," Mallory began. "I reminded him that our mission was to get back the intel we had gathered. I said that should be our priority. There was a real possibility that *Endeavour* could have been destroyed. If that had of happened, our intel would have been lost and the Admiralty would have been operating in the dark."

"So Captain Somerville knew the risks, and yet he still chose to attack the Indian convoy?" Rodgers asked.

"Yes," Mallory answered. "He weighed the risks, and came to a decision that the risk of losing the intel was worth the chance to try and stop more Indian troops from landing on Haven."

"But was it really worth the risk?" Rodgers asked. "Surely the Indians could be landing thousands or even hundreds of thousands of troops in Haven right now. Why was one convoy so important?"

"The Indians don't have hundreds of thousands of ground

troops in their colonies," Mallory answered. "Yes, they could be landing more troops now. But they don't have unlimited numbers. The troops we stopped bought the Havenites more time to fight back against the Indians and free their world."

"But you recognized that the risk wasn't worth it, did you not?" Rodgers pressed.

"I wasn't sure," Mallory answered. "I felt it was my duty as Captain Somerville's second in command to make the risks known, that is all."

"What about now," Rodgers asked. "You have had weeks to think about it. What do you think now?"

For the first time Mallory paused. *You're under oath,* he told himself, *there is nothing you can do.*

"I believe it was a mistake," Mallory said. "The risk was too great. The intel we had was more important."

"Thank you Lieutenant, that is all the questions I have for you," Rodgers said.

"I'm afraid I'm going to have to break him," Cynthia said. "His testimony is the only one that can really hurt us."

"No," James said sharply, catching her arm in a vice like grip. "You won't."

"I have to, it doesn't mean I am going to like it," Cynthia

whispered back as she tried to pull her arm free.

"What he said was true," James whispered back. "If I had to do it again, I wouldn't attack the convoy. It was reckless, maybe not court martial level reckless, but then maybe it was. That is for the jury to decide. But if you tear Mallory apart for saying what he thinks is right, you will ruin him. He will never have the confidence to become a real naval officer. I won't let you do that."

"You have no choice in the matter, this is bigger than you," Cynthia said.

"I am all too aware of that," James replied. "But if you do this, then I will stand up for him, I will tell everyone that Mallory was right, that I did make a mistake. I agreed to keep quiet for the sake of Fairfax's plan, but I did not agree to throw my First Lieutenant under the aircar. I have already watched Julius be torn apart, I couldn't stop that, but I can this, I will not watch it happen again. Those are my terms."

"Fine," Cynthia said. "But if I didn't already have another plan in motion I would still be doing this."

When James let her arm go, she rubbed the spot he had been gripping.

"The defense has no questions for this witness," she said.

Blackwood's eyebrows raised in surprise but only for a moment. Then he turned to Mallory and told him to leave.

"The prosecution rests for now Your Honor," Rodgers said

"You may call your first witness counselor," Blackwood said to Cynthia, giving her permission to start her main defense.

"Thank you Your Honor," Cynthia said, "the defense calls Admiral of the White Nathan Blackwood to the stand."

An uproar reverberated around the court as surprise broke out among the observers. Cynthia simply stood in place, a feral smile on her face as she gazed at Blackwood.

Chapter 28 – Political Drama

The Emperor is the Head and Supreme Commander of the Navy; this tradition goes back to the British Monarchy.

-Excerpt from Empire Rising, 3002 AD

4th June 2467 AD, Admiralty House, London.

"Order, order," Blackwood shouted as he beat his gavel on its wooden block. "This is a court martial hearing, not a London side street market. I will have silence!"

The noise quickly quieted, yet there was still a ripple of murmurs passing back and forth across those in the courtroom.

"That is an outrageous proposal," Rodgers said, rising to his feet. "You cannot call the seated judge of a court martial to be a witness in that very same court martial."

"I think I just did, didn't I?" Cynthia said. "And I think I can, if the sitting judge has information that is vital to the attestation of guilt, I must be able to question him."

"But this is against the regulations, section eighty-five point four of the naval code of law states that no judge can take any role in favor of either party in a court martial," Rodgers said.

"And yet Admiral Blackwood has seen fit to interfere with my cross examination and contradict a witness statement in favor of the prosecution not once, but twice. Just moments ago, Your Honor," Cynthia said turning to Blackwood, "you said to Second Lieutenant Julius regarding James' actions, and I quote, 'I have over fifty years of command experience, I know what should have been done.' I simply want to question you on your experience, experience you have already volunteered to this court.

"Moreover," Cynthia said, "section seventy-eight point one of the naval code says that a court martial may compel any witness who carries a military rank to testify in a court martial, provided the sitting judge agrees that their testimony will benefit the hearing. Unless you are going to remove your previous statements from the official record, I believe you have already declared that your opinions are beneficial to this hearing, are they not?"

James had to put a considerable effort into not smiling. He had been confused before when Cynthia hadn't objected to Blackwood's obvious attempts to interfere with witnesses who gave testimony in his favor. Now he knew what she was up to, and so did Blackwood. The look on his face was priceless.

For a moment Blackwood looked into the observation gallery but his look of indecision didn't fade. Turning around James saw why, there was no sign of the Shadow Defense Secretary.

"Are you going to answer my questions?" Cynthia pushed. "Maybe if I tell you my questions, you can decide for yourself?" Before Blackwood had a chance to answer she hurried on. "I would ask you about your relationship with the Shadow Defense Secretary and his opposition to any war with India, and I would ask if you were the one who brought the charges against Captain Somerville in the first place. And I would ask that in light of the fact that you did indeed bring these charges, if you are fit to judge this trial impartially? Those are my questions for you Admiral Blackwood."

Before she had finished her last sentence, a commotion broke out in the courtroom. James wasn't surprised, if Cynthia's allegations were even half true, and he knew that they were, then the entire court martial was a complete farce, and the public were about to see that. No wonder Fairfax had been happy to let the whole thing go ahead. He had enough information to bring it down anytime he wanted.

Blackwood looked shell shocked, he was probably stunned that anyone would talk to him in such a manner. It took him a few seconds but he quickly realized he had to do something. "Order, order," he shouted again. "I said order," he boomed at the top of his lungs.

"This proposal is ludicrous," he continued once it was quiet. "I have been appointed to be the impartial judge of this court martial by the Admiralty board. Everything has been done in accordance with military law. Furthermore, I will not be answering any questions, I am the sitting judge of this court martial. If you utter one more word about me or make any further allegations, I will hold you in contempt of court counselor. This is my final warning. I will have you thrown into jail, do I make myself clear?"

"Crystal, Your Honor," Cynthia said with as much venom as she could muster.

"Well, in that case, call your next witness or return to your seat," Blackwood spat.

"Fine," Cynthia said, "The defense calls Edward the sixth, King of the British Star Kingdom, Head of the Commonwealth and Lord Protector of the Bradford colony to the witness box."

Despite her best efforts to speak up, Edwards' honorifics were completely lost in the uproar that once again broke out in the courtroom.

"Objection," Rodgers said as soon as Blackwood brought order to the court. "This is highly inappropriate, what could the King possibly have to say that relates to this court?"

"In case you are forgetting," Cynthia responded. "The King is the head of the military, including the Royal Space Navy. I would think he might have a lot to say about the conduct of one of his officers."

Blackwood looked like he was about to make a ruling, doubtless to deny Cynthia's witness request. However, he never got that far, for the back doors to the courtroom burst open. Ten security personnel quickly filed in followed by King Edward.

"I hear I have been called as a witness?" Edward said as he walked up to the front of the room.

"You were Your Highness," Blackwood said. "I was just about to make a ruling on such an unorthodox situation."

"You are not going to send me home now are you?" Edward said. "I have come all this way."

"I..." Blackwood began, but then he hesitated. It was clear that everyone in the court was eager to see what King Edward was doing there. The sight of everyone watching made him lose his nerve. "I was just about to welcome you to my court Your Majesty. You may enter the witness box and then we can proceed."

"Thank you," King Edward said as he moved towards the box.

"On behalf of the defense I would like to thank you for agreeing to be a witness in this court martial," Cynthia began.

"It is my pleasure dear," Edward said. "I am the head of the Royal Space Navy after all, so I do have a thing or two to say about this situation."

"Can you elaborate on that Your Highness?" Cynthia said.

"Certainly," Edward began. "This entire court martial has been convened upon the assumption that Captain Somerville attacked the Indian ships in the Haven territories against orders, and that those actions were carried out in direct contradiction to his actual orders.

"I must say, if that was the case, then I would be in full agreement with the prosecution. Captain Somerville should be charged with treason. I'm afraid however, they have got their facts wrong. First, as you all know, I co-signed the executive order Prime Minister Fairfax released calling for the RSN to treat Indian warships in the Haven territories as hostile. I can tell you clearly, the intention of that document was to give legal power to RSN ships to engage any Indian ships they encountered in the Haven territories. James' actions cannot be painted as treasonous, in fact, they were in perfect accord with the will of his government.

"Second, as you all know, Captain Somerville has been intimately involved in the entire Haven affair. He discovered the Haven colony, he is married to one of Haven's leading political figures. Both he and his wife have been involved in the discussions and planning our government has gone through as they have decided how to respond to the illegal actions of the Indian Star Republic. Captain Somerville therefore had additional verbal orders from me as the head of the military, orders that both the First Space Lord and the Prime Minister were aware of."

"And what were these orders?" Cynthia asked.

"Captain Somerville was ordered to do whatever it took to ensure the long-term safety of the Haven people and to protect British interests in the area," Edward replied. "He knew full well that meant that he had free range to engage Indian warships if the situation called for it."

James shifted in his seat uncomfortably. Technically, the King was speaking the truth. But he had said those words to James when they had been discussing his marriage with Suzanna, they hardly applied to his mission to Haven. *I guess all the information I took away from the discussions I had with Edward, Fairfax and my uncle tainted my decision in Haven. If I hadn't of known their thinking, and their desire to actively help Haven, maybe I mightn't have confronted the Indian ships in the way I did. Still, the King is walking a fine line,* James thought. *Just another person who is having to put their neck on the line because of my actions.*

"So, the charge of disobeying a direct order does not apply in this situation?" Cynthia asked.

"Certainly not, Captain Somerville was acting in full accordance with my verbal orders," Edward replied. "I have been King of this nation for more than thirty years. In all that time, we as a British people, despite the fact that we are spread across many planets and systems, have stood up to tyranny and fought for the right everyone has to determine their own future. We cannot just stand by and watch an entire colony fall into occupation and under the rule of a foreign hostile power. That is not who we are."

James could tell Edward and Cynthia were playing off a

script, but it was a good script. He could just imagine this playing out on the national news broadcasts.

"What do you make of this court martial Your Highness?" Cynthia continued. "If James' actions were not just legal, but actually in accord with your orders, why are we all here?"

"I think we all know why we are here," King Edward said, "and it is an outrage. This entire court martial is a political charade orchestrated by the Liberal party. Just because they oppose any intervention in Haven, they think they can destroy the career of a fine young naval officer in order to further their political ambitions. What's worse, this court martial has released into the public record details about our fleet and our marine forces that may very well put British lives at risk. This is unacceptable."

"Those are strong allegations," Cynthia said. "Do you have any proof Your Highness?"

"My word should be proof enough," Edward said. "But if that isn't enough, there is someone here who can confirm what I have said. Admiral Blackwood," Edward said, turning to face the bench. "Did you not swear an oath to obey your King when you entered the navy?"

"Yes, Your Highness, I did," Blackwood said nervously.

"Then I order you to answer the questions the counselor put to you earlier today," Edward said sternly. "Did you and Shadow Defense Minister Reynolds discuss bringing charges against Captain Somerville? And were you the one who brought these charges against the Captain at the latest Admiralty Board?"

"I refuse to answer any such questions," Blackwood responded.

"This is not a request for you to refuse Admiral. As your King, I am ordering you to answer," Edward said.

"This is still a court martial," Blackwood answered. "I am therefore exercising my right under article ninety-five of the military code, I refuse to answer on the grounds that my answer may incriminate me."

Once again an uproar broke out in the courtroom. Everyone knew what Blackwood's words meant. For more than two minutes the commotion continued, Blackwood made no effort to stop it.

As the noise died down to a level where Cynthia could make herself heard she shouted, "I move that the charges against my client be immediately dismissed."

"I cannot do that," Blackwood said in response.

"Then the defense rests its case. We are ready for the jury to vote on these charges," Cynthia said.

"Does the prosecution have any questions for King Edward?" Blackwood said, visibly shaking from the tension he was feeling.

"No, Your Honor," Rodgers answered. He was already packing up his things, he looked like he wanted to get as far away from the court martial as possible.

"Then the jury may vote on the charges that have been laid against Captain Somerville," Blackwood said.

"I suggest you bring this court to order before you hold the vote," Edward advised, disgusted that Blackwood was willing to let the vote be missed in the all commotion. "I insist on it in fact," he added when Blackwood made no move to bring silence.

"Order," his voice boomed out. "The jury will now vote."

James felt a moment of nausea as his nerves spiked. His career was on the line. As he looked over the jury though his nerves quickly faded. As each Captain electronically voted from their seat, they looked towards James and gave him a nod or a smile.

"The votes are in," a court aid announced moments later. "On the charge of treason, the jury finds Captain Somerville, not guilty. On the charge of dereliction of duty and disobeying a direct order, the jury finds Captain Somerville not guilty. All charges against Captain Somerville have therefore been dropped."

As the chorus of voices rose again, Blackwood rose from his seat and stormed out of the room without officially bringing the court martial to a close.

"I guess that is our cue to leave," Cynthia said.

"Come with me," King Edward said a few moments later when he came to their side. "The day's festivities aren't over with yet. Fairfax wants you both at the Houses of Parliament."

*

The next several hours were a whirlwind for James. By the time they finally made their way out the front entrance of Admiralty House there were hundreds of reporters blocking their path. King Edward refused to answer all the questions that were thrown at them bar one. One reporter had asked where they were going now.

'Prime Minister Fairfax has called an emergency meeting of both Houses of Parliament this evening. We are going there now to prepare for that,' Edward had answered.

Now James found himself sitting in the observation platform that overlooked the main chamber of the House of Commons. Both the observation platform and the main chamber was cramped, as along with all the MP's, each sitting member of the House of Lords was crammed into the room. Initially, a lot of the interest from the more than one thousand people crammed into the observation platform had been on him and Suzanna, who was now at his side. When Fairfax had entered the Chamber followed by King Edward, that attention had shifted to them.

"Members of the Commons and the Lords, I have gathered

you all here today to call for an emergency vote on the Haven situation," Fairfax said as he stood to address the large gathering. "Eight weeks ago we voted to send an ultimatum to the Indian Star Republic demanding that they remove their troops from the Haven colony. After that vote, one of our brave naval officers was sent to Haven to ascertain what was going on there. You have all seen the disturbing images he brought back. The Indians haven't just invaded Haven, they are tearing it apart. And they are doing it without any legal or moral precedence.

"What's worse, so far we, along with every other Earth nation, have stood still. We have warned the Indians, but we have not been prepared to do anything more. Well, we have here with us today someone who was prepared to do something more," Fairfax said as he pointed to James.

"Captain Somerville was prepared to risk his life to help the Haven people. Despite this, the opposition tried to use him as a political pawn. They were prepared to ruin his career for their own gains. Well, I will not allow that. Rather than ruin Captain Somerville's career, I believe we should all look to it for inspiration. Our nation must rise up as he did to defend those who cannot defend themselves.

"That is why I am submitting a bill for immediate consideration before both houses, to be voted on tonight. This bill will declare a state of war to exist between the British Star Kingdom and the Indian Star Republic until such time as their troops and warships are removed from the Haven territories. We will vote in one hour."

As Fairfax sat down many of the MP's and Lords rose to their feet and applauded the Prime Minister. Fairfax stood again and gestured that he appreciated the recognition, then he turned and raised his hands to applaud James. Many of those around James in the observation platform also stood and clapped in his direction.

Suzanna leaned over and whispered in his ear, "And that is how heroes are born."

The clapping lasted for several minutes and then it died down as MP's and Lords discussed the upcoming bill. They only had an hour and things needed to move fast.

With so many people thronging about the Houses of Parliament James didn't think they would be able to get far so he and Suzanna remained in their seats to await the outcome of the vote.

"Does he have the votes to win?" James asked his wife.

"You still aren't learning are you?" Suzanna said with a smirk. "He wouldn't have gone through all this fanfare if he hadn't."

"Then we are going to war," James said. "Your people will be liberated."

"Yes," Suzanna said as a tear ran down her cheek. "Thank you my love," she whispered in his ear over the din of the parliament chamber.

Chapter 29 – Captain Somerville

As with many of the events that led to the formation of the Empire, the then Captain Somerville was to play a major role in the British-Indian war of 2467-2468.

-Excerpt from Empire Rising, 3002 AD

9th June 2467 AD, HMS *Endeavour,* Earth orbit.

Five days after the combined vote, James strode onto the bridge of his ship with Suzanna at his side. He had been away for more than a week.

Lieutenants Mallory, Julius and Becket, along with almost all the Sub Lieutenants were crowded into the bridge to welcome back their Captain. As soon as James walked through they began clapping.

"Stop that," James said as he waved their clapping silent. "I don't deserve that."

As silence descended on the bridge an air of tension quickly rose. "Let me begin by saying that nothing has changed between us. Those of you who had to testify at my trial, by now we all know what the prosecution was trying to do. You all told the truth and for that I am happy. I don't intend to hold anything against anyone, we were put into a very difficult position," as James spoke he intentionally caught both Mallory's and Julius' eyes.

"Let me also say this," James continued. "Whilst I was cleared in the court martial, I did make mistakes on our last voyage. I should have listened to Lieutenant Mallory, the information we were carrying was vital to the war with India. His testimony in my court martial was the truth, he could say nothing else. I should have left the convoy alone and come straight home with our intel. My uncle told me the very same thing the day we returned, before any of this court martial business began.

"I hope to learn from my mistake, and I hope you all will too. Now, let's get back to work before this turns into a sob story," James finished, waving for everyone to turn back to their stations.

Mallory let out a sigh of relief. He had been fearing James' return for the last five days. Everything had worked out alright in the end, but he knew his testimony had been damaging. There had been a lot of tension in the air, the rest of *Endeavour's* officers felt Mallory had let their Captain down. Hopefully, James' words would go a long way in calming things down.

To further aid that Mallory spoke up, stopping everyone from turning back to their work. "On behalf of the crew," he began, catching everyone's attention. "I just want to say how happy we are to have you back Captain. There is no one else we would rather serve under. If we are going to war with the Indians, you are the man we want to follow."

"Thank you," James said. "I hope I can live up to your trust, now back to work."

"It's good to see you again Duchess Somerville," Mallory said with a genuine smile once everyone turned back to their tasks. He jumped to his feet and took her hand to his lips. "Our last trip was a lot less exciting without your presence."

"I find that hard to believe," Suzanna said. "From what I understand, my husband always finds ways to keep things interesting for his crew."

"I can't deny that," Mallory said.

James was relieved Mallory was so forthcoming; he had been worried his relationship with his First Lieutenant had been damaged. "No welcome for me?" he asked, feigning disappointment.

"When you look as good as the Duchess, I will welcome you with the same level of enthusiasm," Mallory said as he held out his hand. "While you have been off rubbing shoulders with the high and mighty the rest of us have been busy getting *Endeavour* ready for another long deployment. You can't blame us if we didn't arrange a party for when you finally decided to return."

"Ha," James said, laughing. "If that is how you feel then you can be the one who goes through a court martial the next time we return to Earth. Then maybe my uncle will want you to go before the King and the defense committee to give a full update on the situation at Haven."

"Well, eh, I'm sure you did a fine job Sir," Mallory said, backtracking fast.

"That's what I thought," James said. "But if you want to be a Captain someday, you're going to have to mingle with the high and mighty eventually. Besides," James continued taking his wife's hand. "Suzanna and I had to take a proper honeymoon."

"I don't begrudge that," Mallory said. "After everything the Shadow Defense Secretary and Admiral Blackwood put you through, you deserved a break. And it's hard to make a relationship work in the navy."

"Are you speaking from experience?" Suzanna asked.

"Yes, I had a fiancée before I joined *Endeavour*," Mallory answered, rather than meeting James or Suzanna's eyes he kept his firmly locked on the deck. "She was from another noble family. Our families had suggested the match when we were younger and we had been trying to see if a marriage would work. Initially things went well, but when I was away from Earth for such long periods, she decided it wasn't what she wanted. She has already married someone else. The Earl of Durham I think."

"I'm sorry to hear that," Suzanna said, reaching out and placing her hand on Mallory's arm. "But on the bright side, it means you are available. *Endeavour's* First Lieutenant would be quite a catch on Haven. Especially after you have beaten the Indians. The women would be lining up for you. And you know, I'm sure one of the richer families on Haven would love to marry into the British nobility. If James and I had to get married for political reasons, there is no reason why you shouldn't too.

"What type of women do you like?" Suzanna followed up. "I'm sure I can think of a few of my friends who would be perfect for you."

"I, eh, ah, I'm not sure," Mallory stumbled.

"Don't be silly," Suzanna said. "I'm sure you know full well what you like. Maybe it is Haven that doesn't tickle your fancy? You know, as the latest Duchess to join the British nobility I have been mingling with a lot of young noblewomen, maybe I could set you up with someone here on Earth?"

"That's enough of that," James said, rescuing his First Lieutenant from his wife. He could see by the look in Suzanna's eyes that she was having too much fun tormenting Mallory. "I came to see how the re-provisioning is going."

"It will be done within the hour Sir," Mallory responded, relieved to be talking about something else.

"Good," James said. "We already have our orders. We will be rendezvousing with Rear Admiral Rooke's Fast Reaction Fleet in orbit over Mars. After that we will be heading into Indian space."

"We're not taking the Gift to Haven?" Mallory asked.

"Not right away," James said. "That is all I'm permitted to reveal at the moment."

"I think I understand Sir," Mallory said as he thought about what Rooke's mission might be.

"Suzanna and I will be dining in my dining room in two hours, I was going to invite all the senior officers to join us. After that we will be departing for Mars," James explained.

"Very good Sir," Mallory said. "I'll pass the word along."

"We will retire until then," James responded. "I'm sure you can finish overseeing the final provisions."

"Aye Sir," Mallory replied.

When they got to James' quarters his steward, Fox, already had two cups of coffee waiting for them. "So," Suzanna said. "Tell me about your final meeting with your uncle. How are his plans progressing?"

"Everything is in place," James said. "The ships my uncle sent for from our colonies arrived just before *Endeavour* got back. They have been drilling with Blackwood's fleet since then. I suspect Blackwood will be departing for Indian space within the next couple of days. After that it is up to him. He will have complete operational freedom to harass the Indians as he sees fit."

"Do you think your uncle's plan will work?" Suzanna asked.

"It should," James said. "The Indians have already removed some of their ships from Haven after the invasion. Blackwood has enough ships to take Haven if we went straight there through the Gift. He wouldn't be able to hold it though. That's where my uncle's plan will come in. If Blackwood can draw the Indian fleet to the edge of their territory, we can run back to the Alpha system and be in orbit for a couple of weeks before they could hope to come and engage us. With reinforcements from the home fleet, the Indians might realize they have been beat and give up. Though such level headedness is unlikely.

"Will *Endeavour* be in the thick of the fighting?" Suzanna asked, changing the subject to the real question on her mind.

"I imagine so," James answered, not wanting to lie to his wife. "She is a raiding cruiser after all. She was designed to operate behind enemy lines. I suspect Rooke will want to use her to disrupt Indian shipping around their colonies."

"Well, you will just have to promise to stay safe," Suzanna said as she came over and sat on his lap. "You will break a lot of hearts back on Haven if you don't make it there in one piece to liberate everyone from the Indians."

"Just on Haven?" James asked coyly.

"Well maybe one or two here as well," Suzanna said as she leaned in to kiss him.

*

"Do you think she will work out for us?" Fairfax asked the two other men in Admiral Somerville's office. They were all standing by the observation window watching *Endeavour* detach from *Vulcan* and boost out of orbit. On the observation deck, just above where *Endeavour* had been docked, Duchess Somerville was plainly visible as she stood and watched her husband's ship depart.

"She has a genuine desire to help her people," King Edward said. "I'm not saying she is above seeking after her own political power. But she will use that power for their good. As long as we don't seek to take advantage of the people of Haven, I think she will be on our side. She knows we are the best chance they have."

"For now we are," Fairfax said. "But after British lives have been spent to buy their freedom, how long will she or her people continue to think that? They are going to have to get used to the idea that we are coming to stay. We will have paid a price in blood for the privilege."

"She knows that we have long term plans for her people and her planet. She didn't get into bed with us blindly," Admiral Somerville said. "It sounds more like this Pennington could be a problem. If she continues to successfully lead the resistance against the Indian military she will have a lot of political capital to spend once order is restored. She could become a real thorn in our side."

"That is why we need Duchess Somerville," King Edward said. "She will be our counterweight to any Havenite popular support for total independence. She has joined herself to us and look how well she has done out of it. She is a Duchess now, and a rich one to boot."

"We will need to make sure James is at the forefront of the liberation effort all the same," Fairfax said. "We need the people of Haven to know who saved them."

"Don't worry," Somerville said. "Admiral Cunningham knows what he is about. When his fleet makes its move, James will be front and center."

"Good," Fairfax said.

"How are the public taking to the latest visuals James brought back from Haven?" Somerville asked to change the subject. He had grown fond of his nephew's wife and had entertained her at his own residence more than once in the weeks *Endeavour* had been away. She was fast becoming one of the family. He didn't like talking about her as a political pawn any more than he did his nephew.

"Very well," Fairfax said. "There has been outrage at what the Indians have done to a peaceful planet. We are running the latest images alongside the visuals of what Liberty looked like the first time Captain Somerville visited the planet. After the court martial and the emergency declaration of war, support for intervention is almost as high as it was after the Duchess' speech to parliament."

"Then you will be announcing the decision to send in the Fast Reaction Fleet soon?" Somerville said.

"Yes," Fairfax said. "If Rear Admiral Rooke is ready to depart, then I will announce our plans later today. You can draft your final orders for him and send them once we are done here. He can depart as soon as I go public."

"I just received his final readiness report," Admiral Somerville said. "As soon as *Endeavour* rendezvous with Rooke's fleet they will be ready to break orbit."

"Good," King Edward said. "The sooner this begins the better. We won't have popular support for this war forever. Especially if the initial stages of your plan work out as expected. You do insist on going forward with it?" Edward asked, not for the first time.

"I think it is the best chance we have," Somerville said. "If we want this war to end quickly then we need to present the Indians with a situation they can't win. That is only going to work if they give us enough time around Haven to fortify it. And that is only going to happen if we can draw their fleet away from Haven and give them a victory."

"And you think you can hold public opinion in our favor even if we lose the first round of the war?" Edward asked Fairfax.

"Yes," Fairfax said. "For a while at least. That is all we will need. Even if support for intervention wavers after Blackwood returns, it will be to late. By then Cunningham will be on the move."

"Very well," Edward said. "Then we go forward. If this works, we will be the undisputed power of our area of space. We may even come to rival the Americans in time."

"I am sure they will love that," Somerville said, chuckling.

Epilogue

Prime Minister's Residence, New Delhi, India.

"I have just received word from our ships stationed at Mars, the British fleet has broken orbit," Admiral Kapoor said as he walked into the Indian Prime Minister's office.

"Then it has begun," Prime Minister Slaman Devgan said. "I hoped it wouldn't come to this."

"As did we all," Kapoor said. "That damn woman riled the British up. There was no way we could have factored her presence into our plans."

"I know that," Devgan said. "But that won't matter if the British manage to beat us. Parliament will have me impeached within a week if that happens."

"That's a long way off yet," Kapoor responded. "Admiral Khan should be able to stop the British from getting to Haven. It will likely be a costly battle, but it is one we can win."

"Can we?" Devgan asked. "The British have proven they can do the impossible. I still haven't heard a reasonable explanation of how they got images of our invasion of Haven back to Earth so quickly. We just heard from the invasion force yesterday."

"The visuals the British have are troubling I agree," Kapoor said. "It is likely the British had a ship hiding in the Haven system when Admiral Kumar attacked it. She must have missed the British ship, just like she let Captain Somerville's ship slip past her."

"And lost us some vital warships to boot," Devgan jumped in. "You said we could take Haven without any losses."

"I predicted we would take Haven without any losses if their defenses were as our scouts indicated," Kapoor corrected. "*If* was the critical word. Clearly the Havenites had a trick or two up their sleeves Kapoor hadn't counted on. However, the losses she suffered to that damned British ship are inexcusable.

"If it wasn't so difficult to send out a replacement commander, and her latest report wasn't so positive, she would already be removed from duty. At least now she largely has the planet under her control."

"Largely," Devgan said. "And just what does that mean? Her report was a touch vaguer than I would have liked."

Kapoor bit back a curse. He had been hoping Devgan hadn't picked up on Kumar's careful choice of words. He had already sent a messenger freighter back to Haven demanding a clarification on how the occupation was going. He didn't want to give his Prime Minister any bad news before he had too.

"You may be right Sir," Kapoor said. "Hopefully Kumar's next update will go into more detail."

"And you predict that Admiral Khan can stop the British?" Devgan said. "Just what ifs are in that statement?"

"Nothing is certain in war Prime Minister," Kapoor answered. "I have told you as much before. I laid out all the risks to you before we set off down this path. We always knew that if the British chose to openly oppose our move on Haven, then the outcome would not be certain."

"I know, I know," Devgan said. "But now that it is happening I can't help second guessing myself. This will make or break our colonial ambitions. Either we defeat the British and put a curb on their expansion. Or they beat us and box us in, leaving us nowhere to go. We have been a second rate power for too long. The philosophies of our past have hampered us for centuries. Our people may not see if fully yet, but if we are going to ensure the Indian Star Republic endures for many more centuries, we need to be able to be aggressive when the opportunity presents itself. Yet, if we cannot beat the British now, when they are in such a weak state, we never will."

"We will just have to beat them," Kapoor said. "Our people may not see the need for territorial expansion, but my Captains do. They all know the importance of Haven and what it means for our future. I know they can beat the British if we give them the chance.

"Well we are about to find out," Devgan replied. "Have you

sent a warning to Khan that the British are on their way?"

"Yes," Kapoor answered. "A messenger freighter is already on its way to our colonies. It should give Khan at least a couple of days to prepare for the British. I have ordered him to meet them in the Aror system. I don't want the British ships slipping past him into our colonies."

"Good," Devgan said. "We can't afford to rebuild our infrastructure in the colonies. We have spent too much of our recent budget expanding your fleet.

"Speaking of which," Devgan continued. "I have been reviewing Home Fleet. Surely there are more ships you could send to reinforce Khan's fleet?"

"I am working on it," Kapoor said. "I have already sent Khan all the ships I can. Many of the ships in Home Fleet haven't been out of the system in over a decade. We are scrambling to get them ready to depart. The main hold up is our final battlecruiser, *Centaur*. She needed her shift drive replaced. As soon as the repair work is finished, I will be dispatching her to New Delhi. She may be too late for the first battle with the British, but if we lose that, she can meet up with the survivors and reinforce Admiral Kumar. With two fully functional battlecruisers she should be able to beat back the British, even if they beat Khan."

"When she is ready I want you to take command of Home Fleet," Devgan said.

"Me?" Kapoor asked in shock. "But my place is here."

"Your place is where I send you," Devgan said raising his voice. "My neck is on the line here. It is time you risked something as well. Besides," Devgan said, calming down. "You know how important this is. If we lose the first battle we cannot afford to lose any others. It will be your job to ensure the British do not defeat us, for if they do, your life will be on the line just as much as mine."

"And what if Admiral Khan has defeated the British before I get there?" Kapoor asked.

"Then go on the offensive, attack the British colonies. You aren't to take any risks, but if you can hurt them, then the British are much more likely to come to the peace table ready to accept our claims on Haven."

"I understand," Kapoor said. "If you don't mind, I will retire. If I am going to take command of Home Fleet I have a lot of arrangements to make."

"You may go," Devgan said. "Just make sure you don't fail me."

The End

You can follow James, Gupta and all the others in the next book in the Empire Rising series where the dispute over Haven will break out into full scale war – coming early 2017.

If you enjoyed the book don't forget to leave a review with some stars. As this is my first self-published series every review helps to get my work noticed.

https://www.facebook.com/Author.D.J.Holmes

d.j.holmess@hotmail.com

Comments welcome!

Made in United States
North Haven, CT
24 June 2023